Foreword

I HOPE the reader will forgive me for beginning celebration. By its completion I celebrate my fortieth birthday, my ninth book, my sixteenth year in the writing game, and a new departure. "Hearts of Three" is a new departure. I have certainly never done anything like it before; I am pretty certain never to do anything like it again. And I haven't the least bit of reticence in proclaiming my pride in having done it. And now, for the reader who likes action, I advise him to skip the rest of this brag and foreword, and plunge into the narrative, and tell me if it just doesn't read along.

For the more curious let me explain a bit further. With the rise of moving pictures into the overwhelmingly most popular form of amusement in the entire world, the stock of plots and stories in the world's fiction fund began rapidly to be exhausted. In a year a single producing company, with a score of directors, is capable of filming the entire literary output of the entire lives of Shakespeare, Balzac, Dickens, Scott, Zola, Tolstoy, and of dozens of less voluminous writers. And since there are hundreds of moving pictures producing companies, it can be readily grasped how quickly they found themselves face to face with a shortage of the raw material of which moving pictures are fashioned.

The film rights in all novels, short stories, and plays that were still covered by copyright, were bought or contracted for, while all similar raw material on which copyright had expired was being screened as swiftly as sailors on a placer beach would pick up nuggets. Thousands of scenario writers literally tens of thousands, for no man, nor woman, nor child was too mean not to write scenarios tens of thousands of scenario writers pirated through all literature (copyright or otherwise), and snatched the magazines hot from the press to steal any new scene or plot or story hit upon by their writing brethren.

In passing, it is only fair to point out that, though only the other day, it was in the days ere scenario writers became respectable, in the days when they worked overtime for rough-neck directors for fifteen and twenty a week or freelanced their wares for from ten to twenty dollars per scenario and half the time were beaten out of the due payment, or had their stolen goods stolen from them by their equally graceless and shameless fellows who slaved by the week. But to-day, which is only a day since the other day, I know scenario writers who keep their three. machines, their two chauffeurs, send their children to the most exclusive prep schools, and maintain an unwavering solvency.

It was largely because of the shortage in raw material that scenario writers appreciated in value and esteem. They found themselves in demand, treated with respect, better remunerated, and, in return, expected to deliver a higher grade of commodity. One phase of this new quest for material was the attempt to enlist Jmown authors in the work. But because a man had written a score of novels was no guarantee that he could write a good scenario. Quite to the contrary, it was quickly discovered that the surest guarantee of failure was a previous record of success in novelwriting.

But the moving pictures producers were not to be denied. Division of labor was the thing. Allying themselves with powerful newspaper organisations, or, in the case of "Hearts of Three," the very reverse, they had highly-skilled writers of scenario (who couldn't write novels to save themselves) make scenarios, which, in turn, were translated into novels by novel-writers (who couldn't, to save themselves, write scenarios).

Comes now Mr. Charles Goddard to one, Jack London, saying: "The time, the place, and the men are met; the moving pictures producers, the newspapers, and the capital, are ready: let us get together." And we got. Eesult: "Hearts of Three." When I state that Mr. Goddard has been responsible for "The Perils of Pauline," "The Exploits of Elaine," "The Goddess," the "Get Rich Quick Wallingford "series, etc., no question of his skilled fitness can be raised. Also, the name of the present heroine, Leoncia, is of his own devising.

On the ranch, in the Valley of the Moon, he wrote his first several episodes. But he wrote faster than I, and was done with his fifteen episodes weeks ahead of me. Do not be misled by the word "episode." The first episode covers three thousand feet of film. The succeeding fourteen episodes cover each two thousand feet of film. And each episode contains about ninety scenes, which makes a total of some thirteen hundred scenes. Nevertheless, we worked simultaneously at our respective tasks. I could not build for what was going to happen next or a dozen chapters away, because I did not know. Neither did Mr. Goddard know. The inevitable result was that "Hearts of Three" may not be very vertebrate, although it is certainly consecutive.

Imagine my surprise, down here in Hawaii and toiling at the novelization of the tenth episode, to receive by mail from Mr. Goddard in New York the scenario of the fourteenth episode, and glancing therein, to find my hero married to the wrong woman! and with only one more episode in which to get rid of the wrong woman and duly tie my hero up with the right and only woman. For all of wilich please see last chapter of fifteenth episode. Trust Mr. Goddard to show me how.

For Mr. Goddard is the master of action and lord of speed. Action doesn't bother him at all.

1

"Register," he calmly says in a film direction to the moving picture actor. Evidently the actor registers, for Mr. Goddard goes right on with more action. "Register grief," he commands, or "sorrow," or "anger," or "melting sympathy," or "homicidal intent," or "suicidal tendency." That's all. It has to be all, or how else would he ever accomplish the whole thirteen hundred scenes?

But imagine the poor devil of a me, who can't utter the talismanic "register" but who must describe, and at some length inevitably, these moods and modes so airily created in passing by Mr. Goddard! Why, Dickens thought nothing of consuming a thousand w r ords or so in describing and subtly characterizing the particular grief of a particular person. But Mr. Goddard says, "Register," and the slaves of the camera obey.

And action! I have written some novels of adventure in my time, but never, in all of the many of them, have I perpetrated a totality of action equal to what is contained in "Hearts of Three."

But I know, now, why moving pictures are popular. I know, now, why Messrs. "Barnes of New York" and "Potter of Texas" sold by the millions of copies. I know, now, why one stump speech of high-falutin' is a more efficient vote-getter than a finest and highest act or thought of statesmanship. It has been an interesting experience, this novelization by me of Mr. Goddard's scenario; and it has been instructive. It has given me high lights, foundation lines, cross-bearings, and illumination on my anciently founded sociological generalizations. I have come, by this adventure in writing, to understand the mass mind of the people more thoroughly than I thought I had understood it before, and to realize, more fully than ever, the graphic entertainment delivered by the demagogue who wins the vote of the mass out of his mastery of its mind. I should be surprised if this book does not have a large sale. ("Register surprise," Mr. Goddard would say; or "Register large sale").

If this adventure of "Hearts of Three "be collaboration, I am transported by it. But alack! I fear me Mr. Goddard must then be the one collaborator in a million. We have never had a word, an argument, nor a discussion. But then, I must be a jewel of a collaborator myself. Have I not, without whisper or whimper of complaint, let him "register" through fifteen episodes of scenario, through thirteen hundred scenes and thirty-one thousand feet of film, through one hundred and eleven thousand words of novelization? Just the same, having completed the task, I wish I'd never written it for the reason that I'd like to read it myself to see if it reads along. I am curious to know. I am curious to know.

JACK LONDON.
Waikiki, Hawaii,
March 23, 1916.

Back to Back Against the Mainmast
Do ye seek for fun and fortune?
Listen, rovers, now to me!
Look ye for them on the ocean:
Ye shall find them on the sea.
CHORUS:
Roaring wind and deep blue water!
We're the jolly devils who,
Back to back against the mainmast,
Held at bay the entire crew.
Bring the dagger, bring the pistols!
We will have our own to-day!
Let the cannon smash the bulwarks!
Let the cutlass clear the way!
CHORUS:
Bearing wind and deep blue water!
We're the jolly devils who,
Back to back against the mainmast,
Held at bay the entire crew.
Here's to rum and here's to plunder!
Here's to all the gales that blow!
Let the seamen cry for mercy!
Let the blood of captains flow!
CHORUS:
Roaring wind and deep blue water!
We're the jolly devils who,
Back to back against the mainmast,

Held at bay the entire crew.
Here's to ships that we have taken!
They have seen which men were best.
We have lifted maids and cargo,
And the sharks have had the rest.
CHORUS:
Roaring wind and deep blue water!
We're the jolly devils who,
Back to back against the mainmast,
Held at bay the entire crew.
—George Sterling

Chapter 1

EVENTS happened very rapidly with Francis Morgan that late spring morning. If ever a man leaped across time into the raw, red drama and tragedy of the primitive and the medieval melodrama of sentiment and passion of the New World Latin, Francis Morgan was destined to be that man, and Destiny was very immediate upon him.

Yet he was lazily unaware that aught in the world was stirring, and was scarcely astir himself. A late night at bridge had necessitated a late rising. A late breakfast of fruit and cereal had occurred along the route to the library the austerely elegant room from which his father, toward the last, had directed vast and manifold affairs.

"Parker," he said to the valet who had been his father's before him, "did you ever notice any signs of fat on E.H.M. in his last days?"

"'Oh, no, sir," was the answer, uttered with all the due humility of the trained servant, but accompanied by an involuntarily measuring glance that scanned the young man's splendid proportions. "Your father, sir, never lost his leanness. His figure was always the same, broad-shouldered, deep in the chest, big-boned, but lean, always lean, sir, in the middle. When he was laid out, sir, and bathed, his body would have shamed most of the young men about town. He always took good care of himself ; it was those exercises in bed, sir. Half an hour every morning. Nothing prevented. He called it religion."

"Yes, he was a fine figure of a man," the young man responded idly, glancing to the stock-ticker and the several telephones his father had installed.

"He was that," Parker agreed eagerly. "He was lean and aristocratic in spite of his shoulders and bone and chest. And you've inherited it, sir, only on more generous lines."

Young Francis Morgan, inheritor of many millions as well as brawn, lolled back luxuriously in a huge leather chair, stretched his legs after the manner of a full-vigored menagerie lion that is over-spilling with vigor, and glanced at a headline of the morning paper which informed him of a fresh slide in the Culebra Cut at Panama.

"If I didn't know we Morgans didn't run that way," he yawned, "I'd be fat already from this existence... Eh, Parker?"

The elderly valet, who Had neglected prompt reply, startled at the abrupt interrogative interruption of the pause.

"Oh, yes, sir," he said hastily. "I mean, no, sir. You are in the pink of condition."

"Not on your life," the young man assured him. "I may not be getting fat, but I am certainly growing soft... Eh, Parker?"

"Yes, sir. No, sir; no, I mean no, sir. You're just the same as when you came home from college three years ago."

"And took up loafing as a vocation," Francis laughed. "Parker!"

Parker was alert attention. His master debated with himself ponderously, as if the problem were of profound importance, rubbing the while the bristly thatch of the small toothbrush moustache he had recently begun to sport on his upper lip.

"Parker, I'm going fishing."

"Yes, sir!"

"I ordered some rods sent up. Please joint them and let me give them the once over. The idea drifts through my mind that two weeks in the woods is what I need. If I don't, I'll surely^ start laying on flesh and disgrace the whole family tree. You remember Sir Henry? the old original Sir Henry, the buccaneer old swashbuckler?" "Yes, sir; I've read of him, sir."

Parker had paused in the doorway until such time as the ebbing of his young master's volubility would permit him to depart on the errand.

3

"Nothing to be proud of, the old pirate."

"Oh, no, sir," Parker protested. "He was Governor of Jamaica. He died respected."

"It was a mercy he didn't die hanged," Francis laughed. "As it was, he's the only disgrace in the family that he founded. But what I was going to say is that I've looked him up very carefully. He kept his figure and he died lean in the middle, thank God. It's a good inheritance he passed down. We Morgans never found his treasure; but beyond rubies is the lean-in-the-middle legacy he bequeathed us. It's what is called a fixed character in the breed that's what the profs taught me in the biology course."

Parker faded out of the room in the ensuing silence, during which Francis Morgan buried himself in the Panama column and learned that the canal was not expected to be open for traffic for three weeks to come.

A telephone buzzed, and, through the electric nerves of a consummate civilization, Destiny made the first out-reach of its tentacles and contacted with Francis Morgan in the library of the mansion his father had builded on Riverside Drive.

"But my dear Mrs. Carruthers," was his protest into the transmitter. "Whatever it is, it is a mere local flurry. Tampico Petroleum is all right. It is not a gambling proposition. It is legitimate investment. Stay with. Tie to it ... Some Minnesota farmer's come to town and is trying to buy a block or two because it looks as solid as it really is... What if it is up two points? Don't sell. Tampico Petroleum is not a lottery or a roulette proposition. It's bona fide industry. I wish it hadn't been so almighty big or I'd have financed it all myself... Listen, please, it's not a flyer. Our present contracts for tanks is over a million. Our railroad and our three pipe-lines are costing more than five millions. Why, we've a hundred millions in producing wells right now, and our problem is to get it down country to the oil-steamers. This is the sober investment time. A year from now, or two years, and your shares will make government bonds look like something the cat brought in...

"Yes, yes, please. Never mind how the market goes. Also, please, I didn't advise you to go in in the first place. I never advised a friend to that. But now that they are in, stick. It's as solid as the Bank of England... Yes, Dicky and I divided the spoils last night. Lovely party, though Dicky's got too much temperament for bridge... Yes, bull luck... Ha! ha! My temperament? Ha! Ha!... Yes?... Tell Harry I'm off and away for a couple of weeks... Fishing, troutlets, you know, the springtime and the streams, the rise of sap, the budding and the blossoming and all the rest... Yes, good-bye, and hold on to Tampico Petroleum. If it goes down, after that Minnesota farmer's bulled it, buy a little more. I'm going to. It's finding money... Yes... Yes, surely... It's too good to dare sell on a flyer now, because it mayn't ever again go down... Of course I know what I'm talking about. I've just had eight hours' sleep, and haven't had a drink... Yes, yes... Good-bye."

He pulled the ticker tape into the comfort of his chair and languidly ran over it, noting with mildly growing interest the message it conveyed.

Parker returned with several slender rods, each a glittering gem of artisanship and art. Francis was out of his chair, ticker flung aside and forgotten as with the exultant joy of a boy he examined the toys and, one after another, began trying them, switching them through the air till they made shrill whip-like noises, moving them gently with prudence and precision under the lofty ceiling as he made believe to cast across the floor into some unseen pool of trout-lurking mystery.

A telephone buzzed. Irritation was swift on his face.

"For heaven's sake answer it, Parker, he commanded. "If it is some silly stock-gambling female, tell her I'm dead, or drunk, or down with typhoid, or getting married, or anything calamitous."

After a moment's dialogue, conducted on Parker's part, in the discreet and modulated tones that befitted absolutely the cool, chaste, noble dignity of the room, with a "One moment, sir," into the transmitter, he muffled the transmitter with his hand and said:

"It's Mr. Bascom, sir. He wants you."

"Tell Mr. Bascom to go to hell," said Francis, simulating so long a cast, that, had it been in verity a cast, and had it pursued the course his fascinated gaze indicated, it would have gone through the window and most likely startled the gardener outside kneeling over the rose bush he was planting.

"Mr. Bascom says it's about the market, sir, and that he'd like to talk with you only a moment," Parker urged, but so delicately and subduedly as to seem to be merely repeating an immaterial and unnecessary message.

"All right." Francis carefully leaned the rod against a table and went to the 'phone.

"Hello," he said into the telephone. "Yes, this is I, Morgan. Sboot? What is it?"

He listened for a minute, then interrupted irritably: "Sell hell. Nothing of the sort... Of course, I'm glad to know. Even if it goes up ten points, which it won't, hold on to everything. It may be a legitimate rise, and it mayn't ever come down. It's solid. It's worth far more than it's listed. I know, if the public doesn't. A year from now it'll list at two hundred... that is, if Mexico can cut the revolution stuff...

4

Whenever it drops you'll have buying orders from me... Nonsense. Who wants control? It's purely sporadic ... eh? I beg your pardon. I mean it's merely temporary. Now I'm going off fishing for a fortnight. If it goes down five points, buy. Buy all that's offered. Say, when a fellow's got a real bona fide property, being bulled is almost as bad as having the bears after one... yes... Sure... yes. Good-bye."

And while Francis returned delightedly to his fishing-rods, Destiny, in Thomas Regan's down-town private office, was working overtime. Having arranged with his various brokers to buy, and, through his divers channels of secret publicity having let slip the cryptic tip that something was wrong with Tampico Petroleum's concessions from the Mexican government, Thomas Regan studied a report of his own oil-expert emissary who had spent two months on the spot spying out what Tampico Petroleum really had in sight and prospect.

A clerk brought in a card with the information that the visitor was importunate and foreign. Regan listened, glanced at the card, and said:

"Tell this Mister Senor Alvarez Torres of Ciodad de Colon that I can't see him."

Five minutes later the clerk was back, this time with a message pencilled on the card. Regan grinned as he read it:

"Dear Mr. Regan,

"Honoured Sir:

"I have the honour to inform you that I have a tip on the location of the treasure Sir Henry Morgan buried in old pirate days.

"Alvarez Torres."

Regan shook his head, and the clerk was nearly out of the room when his employer suddenly recalled him.

"Show him in at once."

In the interval of being alone, Regan chuckled to himself as he rolled the new idea over in his mind. "The unlicked cub!" he muttered through the smoke of the cigar he was lighting. "Thinks he can play the lion part old E.H.M. played. A trimming is what he needs, and old Grayhead Thomas B. will see that he gets it."

Senor Alvarez Torres' English was as correct as his modish spring suit, and though the bleached yellow of his skin advertised his Latin-American origin, and though his black eyes were eloquent of the mixed lustres of Spanish and Indian long compounded, nevertheless he was as thoroughly New Yorkish as Thomas Regan could have wished.

"By great effort, and years of research, I have finally won to the clue to the buccaneer gold of Sir Henry Morgan," he preambled. "Of course it's on the Mosquito Coast. I'll tell you now that it's not a thousand miles from the Chiriqui Lagoon, and that Bocas del Toro, within reason, may be described as the nearest town. I was born there educated in Paris, however and I know the neighbourhood like a book. A small schooner the outlay is cheap, most very cheap but the returns, the reward the treasure!"

Senor Torres paused in eloquent inability to describe more definitely, and Thomas Regan, hard man used to dealing with hard- men, proceeded to bore into him and his data like a cross-examining criminal lawyer.

"Yes," Senor Torres quickly admitted, "I am somewhat embarrassed how shall I say? for immediate funds."

"You need the money," the stock operator assured him brutally, and he bowed pained acquiescence.

Much more he admitted under the rapid-fire interrogation. It was true, he had but recently left Bocas del Toro, but he hoped never again to go back. And yet he would go back if possibly some arrangement...

But Regan shut him off with the abrupt way of the masterman dealing with lesser fellow-creatures. He wrote a check, in the name of Alvarez Torres, and when that gentleman glanced at it he read the figures of a thousand dollars.

"Now here's the idea," said Regan. "I put no belief whatsoever in your story. But I have a young friend my heart is bound up in the boy but he is too much about town, the white lights and the white-lighted ladies, and the rest you understand?" And Senor Alvarez Torres bowed as one man of the world to another. "Now, for the good of his health, as well as his wealth and the saving of his soul, the best thing that could happen to him is a trip after treasure, adventure, exercise, and... you readily understand, I am sure."

Again Alvarez Torres bowed.

"You need the money," Regan continued. "Strive to interest him. That thousand is for your effort. Succeed io interesting him so that he departs after old Morgan's gold, and two thousand more is yours. So thoroughly succeed in interesting him that he remains away three months, two thousand more six months, five thousand. Oh, believe me, I knew his father. We were comrades, partners, I might say, almost brothers. I would sacrifice any sum to win his son to manhood's wholesome path. What do you say? The thousand is yours to begin with. Well?"

With trembling fingers Senor Alvarez Torres folded and unfolded the check.

"I... I accept," he stammered and faltered in his eagerness. "I... I... How shall I say? ... I am yours to command."

Five minutes later, as he arose to go, fully instructed in the part he was to play and with his story of Morgan's treasure revised to convincingness by the brass-tack business acumen of the stock-gambler, he blurted out, almost facetiously, yet even more pathetically:

"And the funniest thing about it, Mr. Regan, is that it is true. Your advised changes in my narrative make it sound more true, but true it is under it all. I need the money. You are most munificent, and I shall do my best... I... I pride myself that I am an artist. But the real and solemn truth is that the clue to Morgan's buried loot is genuine. I have had access to records inaccessible to the public, which is neither here nor there, for the men of my own family they are family records have had similar access, and have wasted their lives before me in the futile search. Yet were they on the right clue except that their wits made them miss the spot by twenty miles. It was there in the records. They missed it, because it was, I think, a deliberate trick, a conundrum, a puzzle, a disguisement, a maze, which I, and I alone, have penetrated and solved. The early navigators all played such tricks on the charts they drew. My Spanish race so hid the Hawaiian Islands by five degrees of longitude."

All of which was in turn Greek to Thomas Regan, who smiled his acceptance of listening and with the same smile conveyed his busy business-man's tolerant unbelief.

Scarcely was Senor Torres gone, when Francis Morgan was shown in.

"Just thought I'd drop around for a bit of counsel," he said, greetings over. "And to whom but you should I apply, who so closely played the game with my father? You and he were partners, I understand, on some of the biggest deals. He always told me to trust your judgment. And, well, here I am, and I want to go fishing. What's up with Tampico Petroleum?"

"What is up?" Regan countered, with fine simulation of ignorance of the very thing of moment he was responsible for precipitating. "Tampico Petroleum?"

Francis nodded, dropped into a chair, and lighted a cigarette, while Regan consulted the ticker.

"Tampico Petroleum is up two points you should worry," he opined.

"That's what I say," Francis concurred. "I should worry. But just the same, do you think some bunch, onto the inside value of it and it's big I speak under the rose, you know, I mean in absolute confidence?" Regan nodded. "It is big. It is right. It is the real thing. It is legitimate. Now this activity would you think that somebody, or some bunch, is trying to get control?"

His father's associate, with the reverend gray of hair thatching his roof of crooked brain, shook the thatch.

"Why," he amplified, "it may be just a flurry, or it may be a hunch on the stock public that it's really good. What do you say?"

"Of course it's good," was Francis' warm response. "I've got reports, Regan, so good they'd make your hair stand up. As I tell all my friends, this is the real legitimate. It's a damned shame I had to let the public in on it. It was so big, I just had to. Even all the money my father left me, couldn't swing it I mean, free money, not the stuff tied up money to work with."

"Are you short?" the older man queried.

"Oh, I've got a tidy bit to operate with," was the airy reply of youth.

"You mean... ?"

"Sure. Just that. If she drops, I'll buy. It's finding money."

"Just about how far would you buy?" was the next searching interrogation, masked by an expression of mingled good humor and approbation.

"All I've got," came Francis Morgan's prompt answer. "I tell you, Regan, it's immense."

"I haven't looked into it to amount to anything, Francis; but I will say from the little I know that it listens good."

"Listens! I tell you, Regan, it's the Simon-pure, straight legitimate, and it's a shame to have it listed at all. I don't have to wreck anybody or anything to pull it across. The world will be better for my shooting into it I am afraid to say how many hundreds of millions of barrels of real oil say, I've got one well alone, in ths Huasteca field, that's gushed 27,000 barrels a day for seven months. And it's still doing it. That's the drop in the bucket we've got piped to market now. And it's twenty -two gravity, and carries less than two-tenths of one per cent, of sediment. And there's one gusher sixty miles of pipe to build to it, and pinched down to the limit of safety, that's pouring cut all over the landscape just about seventy thousand barrels a day. Of course, all in confidence, you know. We're doing nicely, and I don't want Tampico Petroleum to skyrocket."

"Don't you worry about that, my lad. You've got to get your oil piped, and the Mexican revolution straightened out before ever Tampico Petroleum soars. You go fishing and forget it." Regan paused, with finely simulated sudden recollection, and picked up Alvarez Torres' card with the pencilled note. "Look, who's just been to see me." Apparently struck with an idea, Regan retained the card a moment. "Why go fishing for mere trout? After all, it's only recreation. Here's a thing to go fishing after that there's real recreation in, full-size man's recreation, and not the Persianpalace recreation of an Adirondack camp, with ice and servants and electric push-buttons. Your father always was more than a mite proud of that old family pirate. He claimed to look like him, and you certainly look like your dad."

"Sir Henry," Francis smiled, reaching for the card. "So am I a mite proud of the old scoundrel."

He looked up questioningly from the reading of the card.

"He's a plausible cuss," Regan explained. "Claims 'to have been born right down there on the Mosquito Coast, and to have got the tip from private papers in his family. Not that I believe a word of it. I haven't time or interest to get started believing in stuff outside my own field."

"Just the same, Sir Henry died practically a poor man," Francis asserted, the lines of the Morgan stubbornness knitting themselves for a flash on his brows. "And they never did find any of his buried treasure."

"Good fishing," Regan girded good-humoredly.

"I'd like to meet this Alvarez Torres just the same," the young man responded.

"Fool's gold," Regan continued. "Though I must admit that the cuss is most exasperatingly plausible. Why, if I were younger but oh, the devil, my work's cut out for me here."

"Do you know where I can find him?" Francis was asking the next moment, all unwittingly putting his neck into the net of tentacles that Destiny, in the visible incarnation of Thomas Regan, was casting out to snare him.

The next morning the meeting took place in Regan's office. Senor Alvarez Torres startled and controlled himself at first sight of Francis' face. This was not missed by Regan, who grinningly demanded:

"Looks like the old pirate himself, eh?"

"Yes, the resemblance is most striking," Torres lied, or half-lied, for he did recognize the resemblance to the portraits he had seen of Sir Henry Morgan; although at the same time under his eyelids he saw the vision of another and living man who, no less than Francis and Sir Henry, looked as much like both of them as either looked like the other.

Francis was youth that was not to be denied. Modern maps and ancient charts were pored over, as well as old documents, handwritten in faded ink on time-yellowed paper, and at the end of half an hour he announced that the next fish he caught would be on either the Bull or the Calf the two islets off the Lagoon of Chiriqui, on one or the other of which Torres averred the treasure lay.

"I'll catch to-night's train for New Orleans," Francis announced. "That will just make connection with one of the United Fruit Company's boats for Colon oh, I had it all looked up before I slept last night."

"But don't charter a schooner at Colon," Torres advised. "Take the overland trip by horseback to Belen. There's the place to charter, with unsophisticated native sailors and everything else unsophisticated."

"Listens good!" Francis agreed. "I always wanted to see that country down there. You'll be ready to catch to-night's train, Senor Torres? … Of course, you understand, under the circumstances, I'll be the treasurer and foot the expenses."

But at a privy glance from Regan, Alvarez Torres lied with swift efficientness.

"I must join you later, I regret, Mr. Morgan. Some little business that presses how shall I say? an insignificant little lawsuit that must be settled first. Not that the sum at issue is important. But it is a family matter, and therefore gravely important. We Torres have our pride, which is a silly thing, I acknowledge, in this country, but which with us is very serious."

"He can join afterward, and straighten you out if you've missed the scent," Regan assured Francis. "And, before it slips your mind, it might be just as well to arrange with Senor Torres some division of the loot … if you ever find it."

"What would you say?" Francis asked.

"Equal division, fifty-fifty," Regan answered, magnificently arranging the apportionment between the two men of something he was certain did not exist.

"And you will follow after as soon as you can?" Francis asked the Latin American. "Regan, take hold of his little law affair yourself and expedite it, won't you?"

"Sure, boy," was the answer. "And, if it's needed, shall I advance cash to Senor Alvarez?"

"Fine!" Francis shook their hands in both of his. "It will save me bother. And I've got to rush to pack and break engagements and catch that train. So long, Regan. Good-bye, Senor Torres, until we meet somewhere around Bocas del Toro, or in a little hole in the ground on the Bull or the Calf you say you think it's the Calf? Well, until then adios!"

And Senor Alvarez Torres remained with Regan some time longer, receiving explicit instructions for the part he was to play, beginning with retardation and delay of Francis' expedition, and culminating in similar retardation and delay always to be continued.

"In short," Regan concluded, "I don't almost care if he never comes back if you can keep him down there for the good of his health that long and longer."

Chapter 2

MONEY, like youth, will not be denied, and Francis Morgan, who was the man-legal and nature-certain representative of both youth and money, found himself one afternoon, three weeks after he had said good-bye to Regan, becalmed close under the land on board his schooner, the Angelique. The water was glassy, the smooth roll scarcely perceptible, and, in sheer ennui and overplus of energy that likewise declined to be denied, he asked the captain, a breed, half Jamaica negro and half Indian, to order a small skiff over the side.

"Looks like I might shoot a parrot or a monkey or something," he explained, searching the jungle-clad shore, half a mile away, through a twelve-power Zeiss glass.

"Most problematic, sir, that you are bitten by a labarri, which is deadly viper in these parts," grinned the breed skipper and owner of the Angelique, who, from his Jamaica father had inherited the gift of tongues.

But Francis was not to be deterred; for at the moment, through his glass, he had picked out, first, in the middle ground, a white hacienda, and second, on the beach, a white-clad woman's form, and further, had seen that she was scrutinising him and the schooner through a pair of binoculars.

"Put the skiff over, skipper," he ordered. "Who lives around here? white folks?"

"The Enrico Solano family, sir," was the answer. "My word, they are important gentlefolk, old Spanish, and they own the entire general landscape from the sea to the Cordilleras and half of the Chiriqui Lagoon as well. They are very poor, most powerful rich ... in landscape and they are prideful and fiery as cayenne pepper."

As Francis, in the tiny skiff, rowed shoreward, the skipper's alert eye noted that he had neglected to take along either rifle or shotgun for the contemplated parrot or monkey. And, next, the skipper's eye picked up the whiteclad woman's figure against the dark edge of the jungle.

Straight to the white beach of coral sand Francis rowed, not trusting himself to look over his shoulder to see if the woman remained or had vanished. In his mind was merely a young man's healthy idea of encountering a bucolic young lady, or a half-wild white woman for that matter, or at the best a very provincial one, with whom he could fool and fun away a few minutes of the calm that fettered the Ang clique to immobility. When the skifl grounded, he stepped out, and with one sturdy arm lifted its nose high enough up the sand to fasten it by its own weight. Then he turned around. The beach to the jungle was bare. He strode forward confidently. Any traveller, on so strange a shore, had a right to seek inhabitants for information on his way was the idea he was acting out.

And he, who had anticipated a few moments of diversion merely, was diverted beyond his fondest expectations. Like a jack-in-the-box, the woman, who, in the flash of vision vouchsafed him demonstrated that she was a girl-woman, ripely mature and yet mostly girl, sprang out of the green wall of jungle and with both hands seized his arm. The hearty weight of grip in the seizure surprised him. He fumbled his hat off with his free hand and bowed to the strange woman with the imperturbableness of a Morgan, New York trained and disciplined to be surprised at nothing, and received another surprise, or several surprises compounded. Not alone was it her semi-brunette beauty that impacted upon him with the weight of a blow, but it was her gaze, driven into him, that was all of sternness. Almost it seemed to him that he must know her. Strangers, in his experience, never so looked at one another.

The double grip on his arm became a draw, as she muttered tensely:

"Quick! Follow me!"

A moment he resisted. She shook him in the fervor of her desire, and strove to pull him toward her and after her. With the feeling that it was some unusual game, such as one might meet up with on the coast of Central America, he yielded, smilingly, scarcely knowing whether he followed voluntarily or was being dragged into the jungle by her impetuosity.

"Do as I do," she shot back at him over her shoulder, by this time leading him with one hand of hers in his.

He smiled and obeyed, crouching when she crouched, doubling over when she doubled, while

8

memories of John Smith and Pocahontas glimmered up in his fancy.

Abruptly she checked him and sat down, her hand directing him to sit beside her ere she released him, and pressed it to her heart while she panted:

"Thank God! Oh, merciful Virgin!"

In imitation, such having been her will of him, and such seeming to be the cue of the game, he smilingly pressed his own hand to his heart, although he called neither on God nor the Virgin.

"Won't you ever be serious?" she flashed at him, noting his action.

And Francis was immediately and profoundly, as well as naturally, serious.

"My dear lady… " he began.

But an abrupt gesture checked him; and, with growing wonder, he watched her bend and listen, and heard the movement of bodies paddling down some runway several yards away.

With a soft warm palm pressed commandingly to his to be silent, she left him with the abruptness that he had already come to consider as customary with her, and slipped away down the runway. Almost he whistled with astonishment. He might have whistled it, had he not heard her voice, not distant, in Spanish, sharply interrogate men whose Spanish voices, half-humbly, half-insistently and half-rebelliously, answered her.

He heard them move on, still talking, and, after five minutes of dead silence, heard her call for him peremptorily to come out.

"Gee! I wonder what Regan would do under such circumstances!" he smiled to himself as he obeyed.

He followed her, no longer hand in hand, through the jungle to the beach. When she paused, he came beside her and faced her, still under the impress of the fantasy which possessed him that it was a game.

"Tag!" he laughed, touching her on the shoulder. "Tag!" he reiterated. "You're It!"

The anger of her blazing dark eyes scorched him.

"You fool!" she cried, lifting her finger with what he considered, undue intimacy to his toothbrush moustache. "As if that could disguise you!"

"But my dear lady … " he began to protest his certain unacquaintance with her.

Her retort, which broke off his speech, was as unreal and bizarre as everything else which had gone before. So quick was it, that he failed to see whence the tiny silver revolver had been drawn, the muzzle of which was not presented merely toward his abdomen, but pressed closely against it.

"My dear lady… " he tried again.

"I won't talk with you," she shut him off. "Go back to your schooner, and go away… " He guessed the inaudible sob of the pause, ere she concluded, "Forever."

This time his mouth opened to speech that was aborted on his lips by the stiff thrust of the muzzle of the weapon into his abdomen.

"If you ever come back the Madonna forgive me I shall shoot myself."

"Guess I'd better go, then," he uttered airily, as he turned to the skiff, toward which he walked in stately embarrassment, half-filled with laughter for himself and for the ridiculous and incomprehensible figure he was cutting.

Endeavoring to retain a last shred of dignity, he took no notice that she had followed him. As he lifted the skiff's nose from the sand, he was aware that a faint wind was rustling the palm fronds. A long breeze was darkening the water close at hand, while, far out across the mirrored water the outlying keys of Chiriqui Lagoon shimmered like a mirage above the dark-crisping water.

A sob compelled him to desist from stepping into the skiff, and to turn his head. The strange young woman, revolver dropped to her side, was crying. His step back to her was instant, and the touch of his hand on her arm was sympathetic and inquiring. She shuddered at his touch, drew away from him, and gazed at him reproachfully through her tears. With a shrug of shoulders to her many moods and of surrender to the incomprehensibleness of the situation, he was about to turn to the boat, when she stopped him.

"At least you… " she began, then faltered and swallowed, "you might kiss me good-bye."

She advanced impulsively, with outstretched arms, the revolver dangling incongruously from her right hand. Francis hesitated a puzzled moment, then gathered her in to receive an astounding passionate kiss on his lips ere she dropped her head on his shoulder in a breakdown of tears. Despite his amazement he was aware of the revolver pressing flat-wise against his back between the shoulders. She lifted her tear-wet face and kissed him again and again, and he wondered to himself if he were a cad for meeting her kisses with almost equal and fully as mysterious impulsiveness.

With a feeling that he did not in the least care how long the tender episode might last, he was startled by her quick drawing away from him, as anger and contempt blazed back in her face, and as she

9

menacingly directed him with the revolver to get into the boat.

He shrugged his shoulders as if to say that he could not say no to a lovely lady, and obeyed, sitting to the oars and facing her as he began rowing- away.

"The Virgin save me from my wayward heart," she cried, with her free hand tearing a locket from her bosom, and, in a shower of golden beads, flinging the ornament into the waterway midway between them.

From the edge of the jungle he saw three men, armed with rifles, run toward her where she had sunk down in the sand. In the midst of lifting her up, they caught sight of Francis, who had begun rowing a strong stroke. Over his shoulder he glimpsed the Angelique, close hauled and slightly heeling, cutting through the water toward him. The next moment, one of the trio on the beach, a bearded elderly man, was directing the girl's binoculars on him. And the moment after, dropping the glasses, he was taking aim with his rifle.

The bullet spat on the water within a yard of the skiff's side, and Francis saw the girl spring to her feet, knock up the rifle with her arm, and spoil the second shot. Next, pulling lustily, he saw the men separate from her to sight their rifles, and saw her threatening them with the revolver into lowering their weapons.

The Angelique, thrown up into the wind to stop way, foamed alongside, and with an agile leap Francis was aboard, while already, the skipper putting the wheel up, the schooner was paying off and filling. With boyish zest, Francis wafted a kiss of farewell to the girl, who was staring toward him, and saw her collapse on the shoulders of the bearded elderly man.

"Cayenne pepper, eh those damned, horrible, crazyproud Solanos," the breed skipper flashed at Francis with white teeth of laughter.

"Just bugs clean crazy, nobody at home," Francis laughed back, as he sprang to the rail to waft further kisses to the strange damsel.

Before the land wind, the Ang clique made the outer rim of Chiriqui Lagoon and the Bull and Calf, some fifty miles farther along on the rim, by midnight, when the skipper hove to to wait for daylight. After breakfast, rowed by a Jamaica negro sailor in the skiff, Francis landed to reconnoiter on the Bull, which was the larger island and which the skipper had told him ho might find occupied at that season of the year by turtle-catching Indians from the mainland.

And Francis very immediately found that he had traversed not merely thirty degrees of latitude from New York but thirty hundred years, or centuries for that matter, from the last word of civilisation to almost the first word of the primeval. Naked, except for breech-clouts of gunnysacking, armed with cruelly heavy hacking blades of machetes, the turtle-catchers were swift in proving themselves arrant beggars and dangerous man-killers. The Bull belonged to them, they told him through the medium of his Jamaican sailor's interpreting; but the Calf, which used to belong to them for the turtle season now was possessed by a madly impossible Gringo, whose reckless, dominating ways had won from them the respect of fear for a twolegged human creature who was more fearful than themselves.

While Francis, for a silver dollar, dispatched one of them with a message to the mysterious Gringo that he desired to call on him, the rest of them clustered about Francis' skiff, whining for money, glowering upon him, and even impudently stealing his pipe, yet warm from his lips, which he had laid beside him in the sternsheets. Promptly he had laid a blow on the ear of the thief, and the next thief who seized it, and recovered the pipe. Machetes out and sun-glistening their clean-slicing menace, Francis covered and controlled the gang with an automatic pistol; and, while they drew apart in a group and whispered ominously, he made the discovery that his lone sailor-interpreter was a weak brother and received his returned messenger.

The negro went over to the turtle-catchers and talked with a friendliness and subservience, the tones of which Francis did not like. The messenger handed him his note, across which was scrawled in pencil:

"Vamos."

"Guess I'll have to go across myself," Francis told the negro whom he had beckoned back to him.

"Better be very careful and utmostly cautious, sir," the negro warned him. "These animals without reason are very problematically likely to act most unreasonably, sir."

"Get into the boat and row me over," Francis commanded shortly.

"No, sir, I regret much to say, sir," was the black sailor's answer. "I signed on, sir, as a sailor to Captain Trefethen, but I didn't sign on for no suicide, and I can't see my way to rowin' you over, sir, to certain death. Best thing we can do is to get out of this hot place that's certainly and without peradventure of a doubt goin' to get hotter for us if we remain, sir."

In huge disgust and scorn Francis pocketed his automatic, turned his back on the sacking-clad savages, and walked away through the palms. Where a great boulder of coral rock had been upthrust by some ancient restlessness of the earth, he came down to the beach. On the shore of the Calf, across the narrow channel, he 'made out a dinghy drawn up. Drawn up on his own side was a crank-looking and manifestly leaky dug-out canoe. As he tilted the water out of it, he noticed that the turtle -catchers had followed and were peering at him from the edge of the coconuts, though his weak-hearted sailor was not in sight.

To paddle across the channel was a matter of moments, but scarcely was he on the beach of the Calf when further inhospitality greeted him on the part of a tall , barefooted young man, who stepped from behind a palm, automatic pistol in hand, and shouted:

"Vamos! Get out! Scut!"

"Ye gods and little fishes!" Francis grinned, half-humorously, half-seriously. "A fellow can't move in these parts without having a gun shoved in his face. And everybody says get out pronto."

"Nobody invited you," the stranger retorted. "You're intruding. Get off my island. I'll give you half a minute."

"I'm getting sore, friend," Francis assured him truthfully, at the same time, out of the corner of his eye, measuring the distance to the nearest palm-trunk. "Everybody I meet around here is crazy and discourteous, and peevishly anxious to be rid of my presence, and they've just got me feeling that way myself. Besides, just because you tell me it's your island is no proof."

The swift rush he made to the shelter of the palm left his sentence unfinished. His arrival behind the trunk was simultaneous with the arrival of a bullet that thudded into the other side of it.

"Now, just for that!" he called out, as he centered a bullet into the trunk of the other man's palm.

The next few minutes they blazed away, or waited for calculated shots, and when Francis' eighth and last had been fired, he was unpleasantly certain that he had counted only seven shots for the stranger. He cautiously exposed part of his sun-helmet, held in his hand, and had it perforated.

"What gun are you using?" he asked with cool politeness.

"Colt's," came the answer.

Francis stepped boldly into the open, saying: "Then you're all out. I counted 'em. Eight. Now we can talk."

The stranger stepped out, and Francis could not help admiring the fine figure of him, despite the fact that a dirty pair of canvas pants, a cotton undershirt, and a floppy sombrero constituted his garmenting. Further, it seemed he had previously known him, though it did not enter his mind that he was looking at a replica of himself.

"Talk!" the stranger sneered, throwing down his pistol and drawing a knife. "Now we'll just cut off your ears, and maybe scalp you."

"Gee! You're sweet-natured and gentle animals in this neck of the woods," Francis retorted, his anger and disgust increasing. He drew his own hunting knife, brand new from the shop and shining. "Say, let's wrestle, and cut out this ten-twenty-and-thirty knife stuff."

"I want your ears," the stranger answered pleasantly, as he slowly advanced.

"Sure. First down, and the man who wins the fall gets the other fellow's ears."

"Agreed." The young man in the canvas trousers sheathed his knife.

"Too bad there isn't a moving picture camera to film this," Francis girded, sheathing his own knife. "I'm sore as a boil. I feel like a heap bad Injun. Watch out! I'm coming in a rush! Anyway and everyway for the first fall!"

Action and word went together, and his glorious rush ended ignorainiously, for the stronger, apparently braced for the shock, yielded the instant their bodies met and fell over on his back, at the same time planting his foot in Francis' abdomen and, from the back purchase on the ground, transforming Francis' rush into a wild forward somersault.

The fall on the sand knocked most of Francis' breath out of him, and the flying body of his foe, impacting on him, managed to do for what little breath was left him. As he lay speechless on his back, he observed the man on top of him gazing down at him with sudden curiosity.

"What d' you want to wear a mustache for?" the stranger muttered.

"Go on and cut 'em off," Francis gasped, with the first of his returning breath. "The ears are yours, but the mustache is mine. It is not in the bond. Besides, that fall was straight jiu jiutsu."

"You said 'anyway and everyway for the first fall,'" the other quoted laughingly. "As for your ears, keep them. I never intended to cut them off, and now that I look at them closely the less I want them. Get up and get out of here. I've licked you. Vamos! And don't come sneaking around here again! Git! Scut!"

In greater disgust than ever, to which was added the humiliation of defeat, Francis turned down to the beach toward his canoe.

"Say, Little Stranger, do you mind leaving your card?" the victor called after him.

"Visiting cards and cut-throating don't go together," Francis shot back across his shoulder, as he squatted in the canoe and dipped his paddle. "My name's Morgan."

Surprise and startlement were the stranger's portion, as he opened his mouth to speak, then changed his mind and murmured to himself, "Same stock — no wonder we look alike."

Still in the throes of disgust, Francis regained the shore of the Butt, sat down on the edge of the dugout, filled and lighted his pipe, and gloomily meditated. "Crazy, everybody," was the run of his thought. "Nobody acts with reason. I'd like to see old Regan try to do business with these people. They'd get his ears."

Could he have seen, at that moment, the young man of the canvas pants and of familiar appearance, he would have been certain that naught but lunacy resided in Latin America; for the young man in question, inside a grassthatched hut in the heart of his island, grinning to himself as he uttered aloud, "I guess I put the fear of God into that particular member of the Morgan family," had just begun to stare at a photographic reproduction of an oil painting on the wall of the original Sir Henry Morgan.

"Well, Old Pirate," he continued grinning, "two of your latest descendants came pretty close to getting each other with automatics that would make your antediluvian horsepistols look like thirty cents."

He bent to a battered and worm-eaten sea-chest, lifted the lid that was monogramed with an "M," and again addressed the portrait:

"Well, old pirate Welshman of an ancestor, all you've left me is the old duds and a face that looks like yours. And I guess, if I was really fired up, I could play your Port-au-Prince stunt about as well as you played it yourself."

A moment later, beginning to dress himself in the ageworn and moth-eaten garments of the chest, he added:

"Well, here's the old duds on my back. Come, Mister Ancestor, down out of your frame, and dare to tell me a point of looks in which we differ."

Clad in Sir Henry Morgan's ancient habiliments, a cutlass strapped on around the middle and two flint-lock pistols of huge and ponderous design thrust into his waist-scarf, the resemblance between the living man and the pictured semblance of the old buccaneer who had been long since resolved to dust, was striking.

"Back to back against the mainmast, Held at bay the entire crew ... "

As the young man, picking the strings of a guitar, began to sing the old buccaneer rouse, it seemed to him that the picture of his forebear faded into another picture and that he saw:

The old forebear himself, back to a mainmast, cutlass out and flashing, facing a semi-circle of fantastically clad sailor cutthroats, while behind him, on the opposite side of the mast, another similarly garbed and accoutred man, with cutlass flashing, faced the other semi-circle of cutthroats that completed the ring about the mast.

The vivid vision of his fancy was broken by the breaking of a guitar-string which he had thrummed too passionately. And in the sharp pause of silence, it seemed that a fresh vision of old Sir Henry came to him, down out of. the frame and beside him, real in all seeming, plucking at his sleeve to lead him out of the hut and whispering a ghostly repetition of:

"Back to back against the mainmast
Held at bay the entire crew."

The young man obeyed his shadowy guide, or some prompting of his own profound of intuition, and went out the door and down to the beach, where, gazing across the narrow channel, on the beach of the Bull, he saw his late antagonist, backed up against the great boulder of coral rock, standing off an attack of sack-clouted, machetewielding Indians with wide sweeping strokes of a driftwood timber.

And Francis, in extremity, swaying dizzily from the blow of a rock on his head, saw the apparition, that almost convinced him he was already dead and in the realm of the shades, of Sir Henry Morgan himself, cutlass in hand, rushing up the beach to his rescue. Further, the apparition, brandishing the cutlass and laying out Indians right and left, was bellowing:

"Back to back against the mainmast, Held at bay the entire crew."

As Francis' knees gave under him and he slowly crumpled and sank down, he saw the Indians scatter and flee before the onslaught of the weird pirate figure and heard their cries of:

"Heaven help us!" "The Virgin protect us!" "It's the ghost of old Morgan!"

Francis next opened his eyes inside the grass hut in the midmost center of the Calf. First, in the glimmering sight of returning consciousness, he beheld the pictured lineaments of Sir Henry Morgan staring down at him from the wall. Next, it was a younger edition of the same, in three dimensions of living, moving flesh, who thrust a mug of brandy to his lips and bade him drink. Francis was on his feet ere he touched lips to the mug; and both he and the stranger man, moved by a common impulse, looked squarely into each other's eyes, glanced at the picture on the wall find touched mugs in a salute to the picture and to each other ere they drank.

"You told me you were a Morgan," the stranger said. "I am a Morgan. That man on the wall fathered my breed. Your breed?"

"The old buccaneer's," Francis returned. "My first name is Francis. And yours?"

"Henry straight from the original. We must be remote cousins or something or other. I'm after the foxy old niggardly old Welshman's loot."

"So'm I," said Francis, extending his hand. "But to hell with sharing."

"The old blood talks in you," Henry smiled approbation. "For him to have who finds. I've turned most of this island upside down in the last six months, and all I've found are these old duds. I'm with you to beat you if I can, but to put my back against the mainmast with you any time the needed call goes out."

"That song's a wonder," Francis urged. "I want to learn it. Lift the stave again."

And together, clanking their mugs, they sang:
"Back to back against the mainmast,
Held at bay the entire crew … "

Chapter 3

BUT a splitting headache put a stop to Francis' singing and made him glad to be swung' in a cool hammock by Henry, who rowed off to the Angelique with orders from his visitor to the skipper to stay at anchor but not to permit any of his sailors to land on the Calf. Not until late in the morning of the following day, after hours of heavy sleep, did Francis get on his feet and announce that his head was clear again.

"I know what it is got bucked off a horse once," his strange relative sympathised, as he poured him a huge cup of fragrant black coffee. "Drink that down. It will make a new man of you. Can't offer you much for breakfast except bacon, sea biscuit, and some scrambled turtle eggs. They're fresh. I guarantee that, for I dug them out this morning while you slept."

"That coffee is a meal in itself," Francis praised, meanwhile studying his kinsman and ever and anon glancing at the portrait of their relative.

"You're just like him, and in more than mere looks," Henry laughed, catching him in his scrutiny. "When you refused to share yesterday, it was old Sir Henry to the fife. He had a deep-seated antipathy against sharing, even with his own crews. It's what caused most of his troubles. And he's certainly never shared a penny of his treasure with any of his descendants. Now I'm different. Not only will I share the Calf with you; but I'll present you with my half as well, lock, stock, and barrel, this grass hut, all these nice furnishings, tenements, hereditaments, and everything, and what's left of the turtle eggs. When do you want to move in?"

"You mean… ?" Francis asked.

"Just that. There's nothing here. I've just about dug the island upside down and all I found was the chest there full of old clothes."

"It must have encouraged you."

"Mightily. I thought I had a hammerlock on it. At any rate, it showed I'm on the right track."

"What's the matter with trying the Bull?" Francis queried.

"That's my idea right now," was the answer, "though I've got another clue for over on the mainland. Those oldtimers had a way of noting down their latitude and longitude whole degrees out of the way."

"Ten North and Ninety East on the chart might mean Twelve North and Ninety-two East," Francis concurred. "Then again it might mean Eight North and Eighty-eight East. They carried the correction in their heads, and if they died unexpectedly, which was their custom, it seems, the secret died with them."

"I've half a notion to go over to the Bull and chase those turtle-catchers back to the mainland," Henry went on. "And then again I'd almost like to tackle the mainland clue first. I suppose you've got a stock of clues, too?"

"Sure thing," Francis nodded. "But say, I'd like to take back what I said about not sharing."

"Say the word," the other encouraged.

"Then I do say it."

Their hands extended and gripped in ratification.

"Morgan and Morgan strictly limited," chortled Francis.

"Assets, the whole Caribbean Sea, the Spanish Main, most of Central America, one chest full of perfectly no good old clothes, and a lot of holes in the ground," Henry joined in the other's humor.

"Liabilities, snake-bite, thieving Indians, malaria, yellow fever—"

"And pretty girls with a habit of kissing total strangers one moment, and of sticking up said total strangers with shiny silver revolvers the next moment," Francis cut in. "Let me tell you about it. Day before yesterday, I rowed ashore over on the mainland. The moment I landed, the prettiest girl in the world pounced out upon me and dragged me away into the jungle. Thought she was going to eat me or marry me. I didn't know which. And before I could find out, what's the pretty damsel do but pass uncomplimentary remarks on my mustache and chase me back to the boat with a revolver. Told me to beat it and never come back, or words to that effect."

"Whereabouts on the mainland was this?" Henry demanded, with a tenseness which Francis, chuckling his reminiscence of the misadventure, did not notice.

"Down' toward the other end of Chiriqui Lagoon," he replied. "It was the stamping ground of the Solano family, I learned; and they are a red peppery family, as I found out. But I haven't told you all. Listen. First she dragged me into the vegetation and insulted my mustache ; next she chased me to the boat with a drawn revolver ; and then she wanted to know why I didn't kiss her. Can you beat that?"

"And did you?" Henry demanded, his hand unconsciously clinching by his side.

"What could a poor stranger in a strange land do? It was some armful of pretty girl—"

The next fraction of a second Francis had sprung to his feet and blocked before his jaw a crushing blow of Henry's fist.

"I … I beg your pardon," Henry mumbled, and slumped down on the ancient sea chest. I'm a fool, I know, but I'll be hanged if I can stand for—"

"There you go again," Francis interrupted resentfully. "As crazy as everybody else in this crazy country. One moment you bandage up my cracked head, and the next moment you want to knock that same head clean off of me. As bad as the girl taking turns at kissing me and shoving a gun into my midrif."

"That's right, fire away, I deserve it," Henry admitted ruefully, but involuntarily began to fire up as he continued with: "Confound you, that was Leoncia."

"What if it was Leoncia? Or Mercedes? Or Dolores? Can't a fellow kiss a pretty girl at a revolver's point without having his head knocked off by the next ruffian he meets in dirty canvas pants on a notorious sand-heap of an island?"

"When the pretty girl is engaged to marry the ruffian in the dirty canvas pants."

"You don't mean to tell me," the other broke in excitedly.

"It isn't particularly amusing to said ruffian to be told that his sweetheart has been kissing a ruffian she never saw before from off a disreputable Jamaica nigger's schooner," Henry completed his sentence.

"And she took me for you," Francis mused, glimpsing the situation. "I don't blame you for losing your temper, though you must admit it's a nasty one. Wanted to cut off my ears yesterday, didn't you?"

"Yours is just as nasty, Francis, my boy. The way you insisted that I cut them off when I had you down ha! ha!" Both young men laughed in hearty amity.

"It's the old Morgan temper," Henry said. "He was by all the accounts a peppery old cuss."

"No more peppery than those Solanos you're marrying into. Why, most of the family came down on the beach and peppered me with rifles on my departing way. And your Leoncia pulled her little popgun on a long-bearded old fellow who might have been her father and gave him to understand she'd shoot him full of holes if he didn't stop plugging away at me."

"It was her father, I'll wager, old Enrico himself," Henry exclaimed. "And the other chaps were her brothers."

"Lovely lizards!" ejaculated Francis. "Say, don't you think life is liable to become a trifle monotonous when you're married into such a peaceful, dove-like family as that!" He broke off, struck by a new idea. "By the way, Henry, since they all thought it was you, and not I, why in thunderation did they want to kill you? Some more of your crusty Morgan temper that peeved your prospective wife's relatives?"

Henry looked at him a moment, as if debating with himself, and then answered.

"I don't mind telling you. It is a nasty mess, and I suppose my temper was to blame. I quarreled with her uncle. He was her father's youngest brother."

"Was?" interrupted Francis with significant stress on the past tense.

"Was, I said," Henry nodded. "He isn't now. His name was Alfaro Solano, and he had some temper himself. They claim to be descended from the Spanish conquistadores, and they are prouder than hornets. He'd made money in logwood, and he had just got a big henequen plantation started farther down the coast. And then we quarreled. It was in the little town over there San Antonio. It may have been a misunderstanding, though I still maintain he was wrong. He always was looking for trouble with me didn't want me to marry Leoncia, you see.

"Well, it was a hot time. It started in a pulqueria where Alfaro had been drinking more mescal than was good for him. He insulted me all right. They had to hold us apart and take our guns away, and we separated swearing death and destruction. That was the trouble our quarrel and our threats were heard by a score of witnesses.

"Within two hours the Comisario himself and two gendarmes found me bending over Alfaro's body in a back street in the town. He'd been knifed in the back, and I'd stumbled over him on the way to the beach. Explain? No such thing. There were the quarrel and the threats of vengeance, and there I was, not two hours afterward, caught dead to right with his warm corpse. I haven't been back in San Antonio since, and I didn't waste any time in getting away. Alfaro was very popular, you know the dashing type that catches the rabble's fancy. Why, they couldn't have been persuaded to give me even the semblance of a trial. Wanted my blood there and then, and I departed very pronto.

"Next, up at Bocas del Toro, a messenger from Leoncia delivered back the engagement ring. And there you are. I developed a real big disgust, and, since I didn't dare go back with all the Solanos and the rest of the population thirsting for my life, I came over here to play hermit for a while and dig for Morgan's treasure… Just the same, I wonder who did stick that knife into Alfaro. If ever I find him, then I clear myself with Leoncia and the rest of the Solanos and there isn't a doubt in the world that there'll be a wedding. And now that it's all over I don't mind admitting that Alfaro was a good scout, even if his temper did go off at half-cock."

"Clear as print," Francis murmured. "No wonder her father and brothers wanted to perforate me. Why, the more I look at you, the more I see we're as like as two peas, except for my mustache—"

"And for this… " Henry rolled up his sleeve, and on the left forearm showed a long, thin white scar. "Got that when I was a boy. Fell oft a windmill and through the glass roof of a hothouse."

"Now listen to me," Francis said, his face beginning to light with the project forming in his mind. "Somebody's got to straighten you out of this mess, and the chap's name is Francis, partner in the firm of Morgan and Morgan. You stick around here, or go over and begin prospecting on the Bull, while I go back and explain things to Leoncia and her people."

"If only they don't shoot you first before you can explain you are not I," Henry muttered bitterly. "That's the trouble with those Solanos. They shoot first and talk afterward. They won't listen to reason unless it's post mortem."

"Quess I'll take a chance, old man," Francis assured the other, himself all fire with the plan of clearing up the distressing situation between Henry and the girl.

But the thought of her perplexed him. He experienced more than a twinge of regret that the lovely creature belonged of right to the man who looked so much like him, and he saw again the vision of her on the beach, when, with conflicting emotions, she had alternately loved him and yearned toward him and blazed her scorn and contempt on him. He sighed involuntarily.

"What's that for?" Henry demanded quizzically.

"Leoncia is an exceedingly pretty girl," Francis answered with transparent frankness. "Just the same, she's yours, and I'm going to make it my business to see that you get her. Where's that ring she returned? If I don't put it on her finger for you and be back here in a week with the good news, you can cut off my mustache along with my ears."

An hour later, Captain Trefethen having sent a boat to the beach from the Angelique in response to signal, the two young men were saying good-bye.

"Just two things more, Francis. First, and I forgot to tell you, Leoncia is not a Solano at all, though she thinks she is. Alfaro told me himself. She is an adopted child, and old Enrico fairly worships her, though neither his blood nor his race runs in her veins. Alfaro never told me the ins and outs of it, though he did say she wasn't Spanish at all. I don't even know whether she's English or American. She talks good enough English, though she got that at convent. You see, she was adopted when she was a wee thing, and she's never known anything else than that Enrico was her father."

"And no wonder she scorned and hated me for you," Francis laughed, "believing, as she did, as she still does, that you knifed her full blood-uncle in the back."

Henry nodded, and went on.

"The other thing is fairly important. And that's the law. Or the absence of it, rather. They make it whatever they want it, down in this out-of-the-way hole. It's a long way to Panama, and the gobernador of this state, or district, or whatever they call it, is a sleepy old Silenus. The Jefe Politico at San Antonio is the man to keep an eye on. He's the little czar of that neck of the woods, and he's some crooked hombre, take it from yours truly. Graft is too weak a word to apply to some of his deals, and he's as cruel and blood-thirsty as a weasel. And his one crowning delight is an execution. He dotes on a hanging. Keep your weather eye on him, whatever you do … And, well, so long. And half of whatever I find on the Bull is yours:… and see you get that ring back on Leoncia's finger."

15

Two days later, after the half-breed skipper had reconnoitered ashore and brought back the news that all the men of Leoncia's family were away, Francis had himself landed on the beach where he had first met her. No maidens with silver revolvers nor men with rifles were manifest. All was placid, and the only person on the beach was a ragged little Indian boy who at sight of a coin readily consented to carry a note up to the young senorita at the big hacienda. As Francis scrawled on a sheet of paper from his notebook, "I am the man whom ,you mistook for Henry Morgan, and I have a- message for you from him," he little dreamed that untoward happenings were about to occur with as equal rapidity and frequence as on his first visit.

For that matter, could he have peeped over the outjut of rock against which he leaned his back while composing the note to Leonica, he would have been star bled by a vision of the young lady herself, emerging like a sea-goddess fresh from a swim in the sea. But he wrote calmly on, the Indian lad even more absorbed than himself in the operation, so that it was Leonica, coming around the rock from behind, who first caught sight of him. Stifling an exclamation, she turned and fled blindly into the green screen of jungle.

His first warning of her proximity was immediately thereafter, when a startled scream of fear aroused him. Note and pencil fell to the sand as he sprang toward the direction of the cry and collided with a wet and scantily dressed young woman who was recoiling backward from whatever had caused her scream. The unexpectedness of the collision was provocative of a second startled scream from her ere she could turn and recognize that it was not a new attack but a rescuer.

She darted past him, her face colorless from the fright, stumbled over the Indian boy, nor paused until she was out on the open sand.

"What is it?" Francis demanded. "Are you hurt? What's happened?"

She pointed at her bare knee, where two tiny drops of blood oozed forth side by side from two scarcely perceptible lacerations.

"It was a viperine," she said. "A deadly viperine. I shall be a dead woman in five minutes, and I am glad, glad, for then my heart will be tormented no more by you."

She leveled an accusing finger at him, gasped the beginning of denunciation she could not utter, and sank down in a faint.

Francis knew about the snakes of Central America merely by hearsay, but the hearsay was terrible enough. Men talked of even mules and dogs dying in horrible agony five to ten minutes after being struck by tiny reptiles fifteen to twenty inches long. Small wonder she had fainted, was his thought, with so terribly rapid a poison doubtlessly beginning to work. His knowledge of the treatment of snake-bite was likewise hearsay, but flashed through his mind the recollection of the need of a tourniquet to shut off the circulation above the wound and prevent the poison from reaching the heart.

He pulled out his handkerchief and tied it loosely around her leg above the knee, thrust in a short piece of driftwood stick, and twisted the handkerchief to savage tightness. Next, and all by hearsay, working swiftly, he opened the small blade of his pocket-knife, burned it with several matches to make sure against germs, and cut carefully but remorsely into the two lacerations made by the snake's fangs.

He was in a fright himself, working with feverish deftness and apprehending at any moment that the pangs of dissolution would begin to set in on the beautiful form before him. From all he had heard, the bodies of snake- victims began to swell quickly and prodigiously. Even as he finished excoriating the fang-wounds, his mind was made up to his next two acts. First, he would suck out all poison he possibly could; and, next, light a cigarette and with its rive end proceed to cauterize the flesh.

But while he was still making light, criss-cross cuts with the point of his knife-blade, she began to move restlessly.

"Lie down," he commanded, as she sat up, and just when he was bending his lips to the task.

In response, he received a resounding slap alongside of his face from her little hand. At the same instant the Indian lad danced out of the jungle, swinging a small dead snake by the tail and crying exultingly:

"Labarri! Labarri!"

At which Francis assumed the worst.

"Lie down, and be quiet!" he repeated harshly. "You haven't a second to lose."

But she had eyes only for the dead snake. Her relief was patent; but Francis was no witness to it, for he was bending again to perform the classic treatment of snake-bite.

"You dare!" she threatened him. "It's only a baby labarri, and its bite is harmless. I thought it was a viperine. They look alike when the labarri is small."

The constriction of the circulation by the tourniquet pained her, and she glanced down and discovered his handkerchief knotted around her leg.

"Oh, what have you done?"

A warm blush began to suffuse her face.

"But it was only a baby labarri," she reproached him.

"You told me it was a viperine," he retorted.

She hid her face in her hands, although the pink of flush burned furiously in her ears. Yet he could have sworn, unless it were hysteria, that she was laughing ; and he knew for the first time how really hard was the task he had undertaken to put the ring of another man on her finger. So he deliberately hardened his heart against the beauty and fascination of her, and said bitterly:

"And now, I suppose some of your gentry will shoot me full of holes because I don't know a labarri from a viperine. You might call some of the farm hands down to do it. Or maybe you'd like to take a shot at me yourself."

But she seemed not to have heard, for she had arisen with the quick litheness to be expected of so gloriously fashioned a creature, and was stamping her foot on the sand.

"It's asleep my foot," she explained with laughter unhidden this time by her hands.

"You're acting perfectly disgracefully," he assured her wickedly, "when you consider that I am the murderer of your uncle."

Thus reminded, the laughter ceased and the color receded from her fa^e. She made no reply, but bending, with fingers that trembled with anger she strove to unknot the handkerchief as if it were some loathsome thing.

"Better let me help," he suggested pleasantly.

"You beast!" she flamed at him. "Step aside. Your shadow falls upon me."

"Now you are delicious, charming," he girded, belying the desire that stirred compellingly within him to clasp her in his arms. "You quite revive my last recollection of you here on the beach, one second reproaching me for not kissing you, the next second kissing me yes, you did, too —and the third second threatening to destroy my digestion forever with that little tin toy pistol of yours. No; you haven't changed an iota from last time. You're the same spitfire of a Leoncia. You'd better let me untie that for you. Don't you see the knot is jammed? Your little fingers can never manage it."

She stamped her foot in sheer inarticulateness of rage.

"Lucky for me you don't make a practice of taking your tin toy pistol in swimming with you," he teased on, "or else there 'd be a funeral right here on the beach pretty pronto of a perfectly nice young man whose intentions are never less than the best."

The Indian boy returned at this moment running with her bathing wrap, which she snatched from him and put on hastily. Next, with the boy's help, she attacked the knot again. When the handkerchief came off she flung it from her as if in truth it were a viperine.

"It was contamination," she flashed, for his benefit.

But Francis, still engaged in hardening his heart against her, shook his head slowly and said:

"It doesn't save you, Leoncia. I've left my mark on you that never will come off."

He pointed to the excoriations he had made on her knee and laughed.

"The mark of the beast," she came back, turning to go. "I warn you to take yourself off, Mr. Henry Morgan."

But he stepped in her way.

"And now we'll talk business, Miss Solano," he said in changed tones. "And you will listen. Let your eyes flash all they please, but don't interrupt me." He stooped and picked up the note he had been engaged in writing. "I was just sending that to you by the boy when you screamed. Take it. Read it. It won't bite you. It isn't a viperine."

Though she refused to receive it, her eyes involuntarily scanned the opening line:

I am the man whom you mistook for Henry Morgan...

She looked at him with startled eyes that could not comprehend much but which were guessing many vague things.

"On my honor," he said gravely.

"You... are... not... Henry?" she gasped.

"No, I am not. Won't you please take it and read."

This time she complied, while he gazed with all his eyes upon the golden pallor of the sun on her tropic-touched blonde face which colored the blood beneath, or which was touched by the blood beneath, to the amazingly beautiful golden pallor.

Almost in a dream he discovered himself looking into her startled, questioning eyes of velvet brown.

"And who should have signed this?" she repeated.

He came to himself and bowed.

"But the name? your name?"

"Morgan, Francis Morgan. As I explained there, Henry and I are some sort of distant relatives forty-fifth cousins, or something like that."

To his bewilderment, a great doubt suddenly dawned in her eyes, and the old familiar anger flashed.

"Henry," she accused him. "This is a ruse, a devil's trick you're trying to play on me. Of course you are Henry."

Francis pointed to his mustache.

"You've grown that since," she challenged.

He pulled up his sleeve and showed her his left arm from wrist to elbow. But she only looked her incomprehension of the meaning of his action.

"Do you remember the scar?" he asked.

She nodded.

"Then find it."

She bent her head in swift vain search, then shook it slowly as she faltered:

"I... I ask your forgiveness. I was terribly mistaken, and when I think of the way I... I've treated you... "

"That kiss was delightful," he naughtily disclaimed.

She recollected more immediate passages, glanced down at her knee and stifled what he adjudged was a most adorable giggle.

"You say you have a message from Henry," she changed the subject abruptly. "And that he is innocent... ? This is true? Oh, I do want to believe you!"

"I am morally certain that Henry no more killed your uncle than did I."

"Then say no more, at least not now," she interrupted joyfully. "First of all I must make amends to you, though you must confess that some of the things you have done and said were abominable. You had no right to kiss me."

"If you will remember," he contended, "I did it at the pistol point. How was I to know but what I would get shot if I didn't."

"Oh, hush, hush," she begged. "You must go with me now to the house. And you can tell me about Henry on the way."

Her eyes chanced upon the handkerchief she had flung so contemptuously aside. She ran to it and picked it up.

"Poor, ill-treated kerchief," she crooned to it. "To you also must I make amends. I shall myself launder you, and... " Her eyes lifted to Francis as she addressed him. "And return it to you, sir, fresh and sweet and all wrapped around my heart of gratitude... "

"And the mark of the beast?" he queried.

"I am so sorry," she confessed penitently.

"And may I be permitted to rest my shadow upon you?"

"Do! Do!" she cried gaily. "There! I am in your shadow now. And we must start."

Francis tossed a peso to the grinning Indian boy, and, in high elation, turned and followed her into the tropic growth on the path that led up to the white hacienda.

Seated on the broad piazza of the Solano Hacienda, Alvarez Torres saw through the tropic shrubs the couple approaching along the winding drive-way. And he saw what made him grit his teeth and draw v^-ry erroneous conclusions. He muttered imprecations to himself- and forgot his cigarette.

What he saw was Leoncia and Francis in such deep and excited talk as to be oblivious of everything else. He saw Francis grow so urgent of speech and gesture as to cause Leoncia to stop abruptly and listen further to his pleading. Next and Torres could scarcely believe the evidence of his eyes, he saw Francis produce a ring, and Leoncia, with averted face, extend her left hand and receive the ring upon her third finger. Engagement finger it was, and Torres could have sworn to it.

What had really occurred was the placing of Henry's engagement ring back on Leoncia's hand. And Leoncia, she knew not why, had been vaguely averse to receiving it.

Torres tossed the dead cigarette away, twisted his mustache fiercely, as if to relieve his own excitement, and advanced to meet them across the piazza. He did not return the girl's greeting at the first. Instead, with the wrathful face of the Latin, he burst out at Francis:

"One does not expect shame in a murderer, but at leastone does expect simple decency."

Francis smiled whimsically.

"There it goes again," he said. "Another lunatic in this lunatic land. The last time, Leoncia, that I saw this gentleman was in New York. He was really anxious to do business with me. Now I meet him here and the first thing he tells me is that I am an indecent, shameless murderer."

"Senor Torres, you must apologize," she declared angrily. "The house of Solano is not accustomed to having its guests insulted."

"The house of Solano, I then understand, is accustomed to having its men murdered by transient adventurers," he retorted. "No sacrifice is too great when it is in the name of hospitality."

"Get off your foot, Senor Torres," Francis advised him pleasantly. "You are standing on it. I know what your mistake is. You think I am Henry Morgan. I am Francis Morgan, and you and I, not long ago, transacted business together in Regan's office in New York. There's my hand. Your shaking of it will be sufficient apology under the circumstances."

Torres, overwhelmed for the moment by his mistake, took the extended hand and uttered apologies both to Francis and Leoncia.

"And now," she beamed through laughter, clapping her hands to call a house-servant, "I must locate Mr. Morgan, and go and get some clothes on. And after that, Senor Torres, if you will pardon us, we will tell you about Henry."

While she departed, and while Francis followed away to his room on the heels of a young and pretty mestizo woman, Torres, his brain resuming its functions, found he was more amazed and angry than ever. This, then, was a newcomer and stranger to Leoncia whom he had seen putting a ring on her engagement finger. He thought quickly and passionately for a moment. Leoncia, whom to himself he always named the queen of his dreams, had, on an instant's notice, engaged herself to a strange Gringo from New York. It was unbelievable, monstrous.

He clapped his hands, summoned his hired carriage from San Antonio, and was speeding down the drive when Francis strolled forth to have a talk with him about further details of the hiding place of old Morgan's treasure.

After lunch, when a land-breeze sprang up, which meant fair wind and a quick run across Chiriqui Lagoon and along the length of it to the Bull and the Calf, Francis, eager to bring to Henry the good word that his ring adorned Leoncia's finger, resolutely declined her proffered hospitality to remain for the night and meet Enrico Solano and his tall sons. Francis had a further reason for hasty departure. He could not endure the presence of Leoncia and this in no sense uncomplimentary to her. She charmed him, drew him, to such extent that he dared not endure her charm and draw if he were to remain man-faithful to the man in the canvas pants even then digging holes in the sands of the Bull.

So Francis departed, a letter to Henry from Leoncia in his pocket. The last moment, ere he departed, was abrupt. With a sigh so quickly suppressed that Leoncia wondered whether. or not she had imagined it, he tore himself away. She gazed after his retreating form down the driveway until it was out of sight, then stared at the ring on her finger with a vaguely troubled expression.

From the beach, Francis signaled the Angelique, riding at anchor, to send a boat ashore for him. But before it had been swung into the water, half a dozen horsemen, revolverbelted, rifles across their pommels, rode down the beach upon him at a gallop. Two men led. The following four were hang-dog half-castes. Of the two leaders, Francis recognized Torres. Every rifle came to rest on Francis, and he could not but obey the order snarled at him by the unknown leader to throw up his hands. And Francis opined aloud:

"To think of it! Once, only the other day or was it a million years ago? I thought auction bridge, at a dollar a point, was some excitement. Now, sirs, you on your horses, with your weapons threatening the violent introduction of foreign substances into my poor body, tell me what is doing now. Don't I ever get off this beach without gunpowder complications? Is it my ears, or merely my mustache, you want?"

"We want you," answered the stranger leader, whose mustache bristled as magnetically as his crooked black eyes.

"And in the name of original sin and of all lovely lizards, who might you be?"

"He is the honorable Senor Mariano Vercara e Hijos, Jefe Politico of San Antonio," Torres replied.

"Good night," Francis laughed, remembering the man's description as given to him by Henry. "I suppose you think I've broken some harbor rule or sanitary regulation by anchoring here. But you must settle such things with my captain, Captain Trefethen, a very estimable gentleman. I am only the charterer of the schooner just a passenger. You will find Captain Trefethen right up in maritime law and custom."

"You are wanted for the murder of Alfaro Solano," was Torres' answer. "You didn't fool me, Henry Morgan, with your talk up at the hacienda that you were some one else. I know that some one else. His name is Francis Morgan, and I do not hesitate to add that he is not a murderer, but a gentleman."

"Ye gods and little fishes!" Francis exclaimed. "And yet you ahook hands with me, Senor Torres."

"I was fooled," Torres admitted sadly. "But only for a moment. Will you come peaceably?"

"As if," Francis shrugged his shoulders eloquently at the six rifles. "I suppose you'll give me a pronto trial and hang me at daybreak."

"Justice is swift in Panama," the Jefe Politico replied, his English queerly accented but understandable. "But not so quick as that. We will not hang you at daybreak. Ten o'clock in the morning

19

is more comfortable all around, don't you think?"

"Oh, by all means," Francis retorted. "Make it eleven, or twelve noon I won't mind."

"You will kindly come with us, Senor," Mariano Vercara e Hijos, said, the suavity of his diction not masking the iron of its intention. "Juan! Ignacio!" he ordered in Spanish. "Dismount! Take his weapons. No, it will not be necessary to tie his hands. Put him on the horse behind Gregorio."

Francis, in a venerably whitewashed adobe cell with walls five feet thick, its earth floor carpeted with the forms of half a dozen sleeping peon prisoners, listened to a dim hammering not very distant, remembered the trial from which he had just emerged, and whistled long and low. The hour was half-past eight in the evening. The trial had begun at eight. The hammering was the hammering together of the scaffold beams, from which place of eminence he was scheduled at ten next morning to swing off into space supported from the ground by a rope around his neck. The trial had lasted half an hour by his watch. Twenty minutes would have covered it had Leoncia not burst in and prolonged it by the ten minutes courteously accorded her as the great lady of the Solano family.

"The Jefe was right," Francis acknowledged to himself in a matter of soliloquy. "Panama justice does move swiftly."

The very possession of the letter given him by Leoncia and addressed to Henry Morgan had damned him. The rest had been easy. Half a dozen witnesses had testified to the murder and identified him as the murderer. The Jefe Politico himself had so testified. The one cheerful note had been the eruption on the scene of Leoncia, chaperoned by a palsied old aunt of the Solano family. That had been sweet the fight the beautiful girl had put up for his life, despite the fact that it was foredoomed to futility.

When she had made Francis roll up the sleeve and expose his left forearm, he had seen the Jefe Politico shrug his shoulders contemptuously. And he had seen Leoncia fling a passion of Spanish words, too quick for him to follow, at Torres. And he had seen and heard the gesticulation and the roar of the mob-filled court-room as Torres had taken the stand.

But what he had not seen was the whispered colloquy between Torres and the Jefe, as the former was in the thick of forcing his way through the press to the witness box. He no more saw this particular side-play than did he know that Torres was in the pay of Regan to keep him away from New York as long as possible, and as long as ever if possible, nor than did he know that Torres himself, in love with Leoncia, was consumed with a jealousy that knew no limit to its ire.

All of which had blinded Francis to the play under the interrogation of Torres by Leoncia, which had compelled Torres to acknowledge that he had never seen a scar on Francis Morgan's left forearm. While Leoncia had looked at the little old judge in triumph, the Jefe Politico had advanced and demanded of Torres in stentorian tones:

"Can you swear that you ever saw a scar on Henry Morgan's arm?"

Torres had been baffled and embarrassed, had looked bewilderment to the judge and pleadingness to Leoncia, and, in the end, without speech, shaken his head that he could not so swear.

The roar of triumph had gone up from the crowd of ragamuffins. The judge had pronounced sentence, the roar had doubled on itself, and Francis had been hustled out and to his cell, not entirely unresistingly, by the gendarmes and the Comisario, all apparently solicitous of saving him from the mob that was unwilling to wait till ten next morning for his death.

"That poor dub, Torres, who fell down on the scar on Henry!" Francis was meditating sympathetically, when the bolts of his cell door shot back and he arose to greet Leoncia.

But she declined to greet him for the moment, as she flared at the Comisario in rapid-fire Spanish, with gestures of command to which he yielded when he ordered the jailer to remove the peons to other cells, and himself, with a nervous and apologetic bowing, went out and closed the door.

And then Leoncia broke down, sobbing on his shoulder, in his arms: "It is a cursed country, a cursed country. There is no fair play."

And as Francis held her pliant form, meltingly exquisite in its maddeningness of woman, he remembered Henry, in his canvas pants, bare-footed, un^er his floppy sombrero, digging holes in the sand of the Bull.

He tried to draw away from the armful of deliciousness, and only half succeeded. Still, at such slight removal of distance, he essayed the intellectual part, rather than the emotional part he desired all too strongly to act.

"And now I know at last what a frame-up is," he assured her, farthest from the promptings of his heart. "If these Latins of your country thought more coolly instead of acting so passionately, they might be building railroads and developing their country. That trial was a straight passionate frame-up. They just knew I was guilty and were so eager to punish me that they wouldn't even bother for mere evidence or establishment of identity. Why delay? They knew Henry Morgan had knifed Alfaro. They knew I was

Henry Morgan. When one knows, why bother to find out?"

Deaf to his words, sobbing and struggling to cling closer while he spoke, the moment he had finished she was deep again in his arms, against him, to him, her lips raised to his; and, ere he was aware, his own lips to hers. "I love you, I love you," she whispered brokenly.

"No, no," he denied what he most desired. "Henry and I are too alike. It is Henry you love, and I am not Henry."

She tore herself away from her own clinging, drew Henry's ring from her finger, and threw it on the floor. Francis was so beyond himself that he knew not what was going to happen the next moment, and was only saved from whatever it might be by the entrance of the Comisario, watch in hand, with averted face striving to see naught else than the moments registered by the second-hand on the dial.

She stiffened herself proudly, and all but broke down again as Francis slipped Henry's ring back on her finger and kissed her hand in farewell. Just ere she passed out the door she turned and with a whispered movement of the lips that was devoid of sound told him: "I love you."

Promptly as the stroke of the clock, at ten o'clock Francis was led out into the jail patio where stood the gallows. All San Antonio was joyously and shoutingly present,' including much of the neighboring population and Leoncia, Enrico Solano, and his five tall sons. Enrico and his sons fumed and strutted, but the Jefe Politico, backed by the Comisario and his gendarmes, was adamant. In vain, as Francis was forced to the foot of the scaffold, did Leoncia strive to get to him and did her men strive to persuade her to leave the patio. In vain, also, did her father and brothers protest that Francis was not the man. The Jefe Politico smiled contemptuously and ordered the execution to proceed.

On top of the scaffold, standing on the trap, Francis declined the ministrations of the priest, telling him in Spanish that no innocent man being hanged needed intercessions with the next world, but that the men who were doing the hanging were in need of just such intercessions.

They had tied Francis' legs, and were in the act of tying his arms, with the men who held the noose and the black cap hovering near to put them on him, when the voice of a singer was heard approaching from without; and the song he sang was:

"Back to back against the mainmast,
Held at bay the entire crew… "

Leoncia, almost fainting, recovered at the sound of the voice, and cried out with sharp delight as she descried Henry Morgan entering, thrusting aside the guards at the gate who tried to bar his way.

At sight of him the only one present who suffered chagrin was Torres, which passed unnoticed in the excitement. The populace was in accord with the Jefe, who shrugged his shoulders and announced that one man was as good as another so long as the hanging went on. And here arose hot contention from the Solano men that Henry was likewise innocent of the murder of Alfaro. But it was Francis, from the scaffold, while his arms and legs were being untied, who shouted through the tumult:

"You tried me! You have not tried him! You cannot hang a man without trial! He must have his trial!"

And when Francis had descended from the scaffold and was shaking Henry's hand in both his own, the Comisario, with the Jefe at his back, duly arrested Henry Morgan for the murder of Alfaro Solano.

Chapter 4

"WE must work quickly that is the one thing sure," Francis said to the little conclave of Solanos on the piazza of the Solano hacienda.

"One thing sure! " Leoncia cried out scornfully ceasing from her anguished pacing up and down. "The one thing sure is that we must save him."

As she spoke, she shook a passionate finger under Francis' nose to emphasize her point. Not content, she shook her finger with equal emphasis under the noses of all and sundry of her father and brothers.

"Quick!" she flamed on. "Of course we must be quick. It is that, or… "Her voice trailed off into the unvoiceable horror of what would happen to Henry if they were not quick.

"All Gringos look alike to the Jefe," Francis nodded sympathetically. She was splendidly beautiful and wonderful, he thought. "He certainly runs all San Antonio, and short shrift is his motto. He'll give Henry no more time than he gave us. We must get him out to-night."

"Now listen," Leoncia began again. "We Solanos cannot permit this… this execution. Our pride… our honor. We cannot permit it. Speak! any of you. Father you. Suggest something… "

And while the discussion went on, Francis, for the time being silent, wrestled deep in the throes of sadness. Leoncia's fervor was magnificent, but it was for another man and it did not precisely exhilarate him. Strong upon him was the memory of the jail patio after he had been released and Henry had been

21

arrested. He could still see, with the same stab at the heart, Leoncia in Henry's arms, Henry seeking her hand to ascertain if his ring was on it, and the long kiss of the embrace that followed.

Ah, well, he sighed to himself, he had done his best. After Henry had been led away, had he not told Leoncia, quite deliberately and coldly, that Henry was her man and lover, and the wisest of choices for the daughter of the Solanos?

But the memory of it did not make him a bit happy. Nor did the rightness of it. Right it was. That he never questioned, and it strengthened him into hardening his heart against her. Yet the right, he found in his case, to be the sorriest of consolation.

And yet what else could he expect? It was his misfortune to have arrived too late in Central America, that was all, and to find this flower of woman already annexed by a previous comer a man as good as himself, and, his heart of fairness prompted, even better. And his heart of fairness compelled loyalty to Henry from him to Henry Morgan, of the breed and blood ; to Henry Morgan, the wild-fire descendant of a wild-fire ancestor, in canvas pants, and floppy sombrero, with a penchant for the ears of strange young men, living on sea biscuit and turtle eggs and digging up the Bull and the Calf for old Sir Henry's treasure.

And while Enrico Solano and his sons talked plans and projects on their broad piazza, to which Francis lent only half an ear, a house servant came, whispered in Leoncia" ear, and led her away around the ell of the piazza, where occurred a scene that would have excited Francis' risibilities and wrath.

Around the ell, Alvarez Torres, in all the medieval Spanish splendor of dress of a great haciendado-owner, such as still obtains in Latin America, greeted her, bowed low with doffed sombrero in hand, and seated her in a rattan settee. Her own greeting was sad, but shot through with curiousness, as if she hoped he brought some word of hope.

"The trial is over, Leoncia," he said softly, tenderly, as one speaks of the dead. "He is sentenced. To-morrow at ten o'clock is the time. It is all very sad, most very sad. But... "He shrugged his shoulders. "No, I shall not speak harshly of him. He was an honorable man. His one fault was his temper. It was too quick, too fiery. It led him into a mischance of honor. Never, in a cool moment of reasonableness, would he have stabbed Alfaro—"

"He never killed my uncle!" Leoncia cried, raising her averted face.

"And it is regrettable," Torres proceeded gently and sadly, avoiding any disagreement. "The judge, the people, the Jefe Politico, unfortunately, are all united in believing that he did. Which is most regrettable. But which is not what I came to see you about. I came to offer my service in any and all ways you may command. My life, my honor, are at your disposal. Speak. I am your slave."

Dropping suddenly and gracefully on one knee before her, he caught her hand from her lap, and would have instantly flooded on with his speech, had not his eyes lighted on the diamond ring on her engagement finger. He frowned, but concealed the frown with bent face until he could drive it from his features and begin to speak.

"I knew you when you were small, Leoncia, so very, very charmingly small, and I loved you always. No, listen! Please. My heart must speak. Hear me out. I loved you always. But when you returned from your convent, from schooling abroad, a woman, a grand and noble lady fit to rule in the house of the Solanos, I was burnt by your beauty. I have been patient. I refrained from speaking. But you may have guessed. You surely must have guessed. I have been on fire for you ever since. I have been consumed by the flame of your beauty, by the flame of you that is deeper than your beauty."

He was not to be stopped, as she well knew, and she listened patiently, gazing down on his bent head and wondering idly why his hair was so unbecomingly cut, and whether it had been last cut in New York or San Antonio.

"Do you know what you have been to me ever since your return?"

She did not reply, nor did she endeavour to withdraw her hand, although his was crushing and bruising her flesh against Henry Morgan's ring. She forgot to listen, led away by a chain of thought that linked far. Not in such rhodomontade of speech had Henry Morgan loved and won her, was the beginning of the chain. Why did those of Spanish blood always voice their emotions so exaggeratedly? Henry had been so different. Scarcely had he spoken a word. He had acted. Under her glamor, himself glamoring her, without warning, so certain was he not to surprise and frighten her, he had put his arms around her and pressed his lips to hers. And hers had been neither too startled nor altogether unresponsive. Not until after that first kiss, arms still around her, had Henry begun to speak at all.

And what plan was being broached around the corner of the ell by her men and Francis Morgan? her mind strayed on, deaf to the suitor at her feet. Francis! Ah she almost sighed, and marveled, what of her self -known love for Henry, why this stranger Gringo so enamored her heart. Was she a wanton? Was it one man? Or another man? Or any man? No! No! She was not fickle nor unfaithful. And yet?...

Perhaps it was because Francis and Henry were so much alike, and her poor stupid loving woman's heart failed properly to distinguish between them. And yet while it had seemed she would have followed Henry anywhere over the world, in any luck or fortune, it seemed to her now that she would follow Francis even farther. She did love "Henry, her heart solemnly proclaimed. But also did she love Francis, and almost did she divine that Francis loved her the fervor of his lips on hers in his prison cell was inerasable; and there was a difference in her love for the two men that confuted her powers of reason and almost drove her to the shameful conclusion that she, the latest and only woman of the house of Solano, was a wanton.

A severe pinch of her flesh against Henry's ring, caused by the impassioned grasp of Torres, brought her back to him, so that she could hear the spate of his speech pouring on:

"You have been the delicious thorn in my side, the spiekd rowel of the spur forever prodding the sweetest and most poignant pangs of love into my breast. I have dreamed of you... and for you. And I have my own name for you. Ever the one name I have had for you: the Queen of my Dreams. And you will marry me, my Leoncia. We will forget this mad Gringo who is as already dead. I shall be gentle, kind. I shall love you always. And never shall any vision of him arise between us. For myself, I shall not permit it. For you ... I shall love you so that it will be impossible for the memory of him to arise between us and give you one moment's heart-hurt."

Leoncia debated in a long pause that added fuel to Torres' hopes. She felt the need to temporise. If Henry were to be saved... and had not Torres offered his services? Not lightly could she turn him away when a man's life might depend upon him.

"Speak! I am consuming!" Torres urged in a choking voice.

"Hush! Hush!" she said softly. "How can I listen to love from a live man, when the man I loved is yet alive?"

Loved! The past tense of it startled her. Likewise it startled Torres, fanning his hopes to fairer flames. Almost was she his. She had said loved. She no longer bore love for Henry. She had loved him, but no longer. And she, a maid and woman of delicacy and sensibility, could not, of course, give name to her love for him while the other man still lived. It was subtle of her. He prided himself on his own subtlety, and he flattered himself that he had interpreted her veiled thought aright. And... well, he resolved, he would see to it that the man who was to die at ten next morning should have neither reprieve nor rescue. The one thing clear, if he were to win Leoncia quickly, was that Henry Morgan should die quickly.

"We will speak of it no more... now," he said with chivalric gentleness, as he gently pressed her hand, rose to his feet, and gazed down on her.

She returned a soft pressure of thanks with her own hand ere she released it and stood up.

"Come," she said. "We will join the others. They are planning now, or trying to find some plan, to save Henry Morgan."

The conversation of the group ebbed away as they joined it, as if out of half -suspicion of Torres.

"Have you hit upon anything yet?" Leoncia asked.

Old Enrico, straight and slender and graceful as any of his sons despite his age, shook his head.

"I have a plan, if you will pardon me," Torres began, but ceased at a warning glance from Alesandro, the eldest son.

On the walk, below the piazza, had appeared two scarecrows of beggar boys. Not more than ten years of age, by their size, they seemed much older when judged by the shrewdness of their eyes and faces. Each wore a single marvelous garment, so that between them it could be said they shared a shirt and pants. But such a shirt! And such pants! The latter, man-size, of ancient duck, were buttoned around the lad's neck, the waistband reefed with knotted twine so as not to slip down over his shoulders. His arms were thrust through the holes where the side-pockets had been. The legs of the pants had been hacked off with a knife to suit his own diminutive length of limb. The tails of the man's shirt on the other boy dragged on the ground.

"Vamos!" Alesandro shouted fiercely at them to be gone.

But the boy in the pants gravely removed a stone which he had been carrying on top of his bare head, exposing a letter which had been thus carried. Alesandro leaned over, took the letter, and with a glance at the inscription passed it to Leoncia, while the boys began whining for money. Francis, smiling despite himself at the spectacle of them, tossed them a few pieces of small silver, whereupon the shirt and the pants toddled away down the path.

The letter was from Henry, and Leoncia scanned it hurriedly. It was not precisely in farewell, for he wrote in the tenour of a man who never expected to die save by some inconceivable accident. Nevertheless, on the chance of such inconceivable thing becoming possible, Henry did manage to say good-bye and to include a facetious recommendation to Leoncia not to forget Francis, who was well worth remembering because he was so much like himself, Henry.

Leoncia's first impulse was to show the letter to the others, but the portion about Francis withstrained her.

"It's from Henry," she said, tucking the note into her bosom. "There is nothing of importance. He seems to have not the slightest doubt that he will escape somehow." "We shall see that he does," Francis declared positively.

With a grateful smile to him, and with one of interrogation to Torres, Leoncia said:

"You were speaking of a plan, Senor Torres?"

Torres smiled, twisted his mustache, and struck an attitude of importance.

"There is one way, the Gringo, Anglo-Saxon way, and it is simple, straight to the point. That is just what it is, straight to the point. We will go and take Henry out of jail in forthright, brutal and direct Gringo fashion. It is the one thing they will not expect. Therefore, it will succeed. There are enough unhung rascals on the beach with which, to storm the jail. Hire them, pay them well, but only partly in advance, and the thing is accomplished."

Leoncia nodded eager agreement. Old Enrico's eyes flashed and his nostrils distended as if already sniffing gunpowder. The young men were taking fire from his example. And all looked to Francis for his opinion or agreement. He shook his head slowly, and Leoncia uttered a sharp cry of disappointment in him.

"That way is hopeless," he said. "Why should all of you risk your necks in a madcap attempt like that, doomed to failure from the start?" As he talked, he strode across from Leoncia's side to the railing in such way as to be for a moment between Torres and the other men, and at the same time managed a warning look to Enrico and his sons. "As for Henry, it looks as if it were all up with him—"

"You mean you doubt me?" Torres bristled.

"Heavens, man," Francis protested.

But Torres dashed on: "You mean that I am forbidden by you, a man I have scarcely met, from the councils of the Solanos who are my oldest and most honored friends."

Old Enrico, who had not missed the rising wrath against Francis in Leoncia's face, succeeded in conveying a warning to her, ere, with a courteous gesture, he hushed Torres and began to speak.

"There are no councils of the Solanos from which you are barred, Senor Torres. You are indeed an old friend of the family. Your late father and I were comrades, almost brothers. But that and you will pardon an old man's judgment does not prevent Senor Morgan from being right when he says your plan is hopeless. To storm the jail is truly madness. Look at the thickness of the walls. They could stand a siege of weeks. And yet, and I confess it, almost was I tempted when you first broached the idea. Now when I was a young man, fighting the Indians in the high Cordilleras, there was a very case in point. Come, let us all be seated and comfortable, and I will tell you the tale … "

But Torres, busy with many things, declined to wait, and with soothed amicable feelings shook hands all around, briefly apologized to Francis, and departed astride his silversaddled and silver-bridled horse for San Antonio. One of the things that busied him was the cable correspondence maintained between him and Thomas Regan's Wall Street office. Having secret access to the Panamanian government wireless station at San Antonio, he was thus able to relay messages to the cable station at Vera Cruz. Not alone was his relationship with Regan proving lucrative, but it was jibing in with his own personal plans concerning Leoncia and the Morgans.

"What have you against Senor Torres, that you should reject his plan and anger him?" Leoncia demanded of Francis.

"Nothing," was the answer, "except that we do not need him, and that I'm not exactly infatuated with him. He is a fool and would spoil any plan. Look at the way he fell down on testifying at my trial. Maybe he can't be trusted. I don't know. Anyway, what's the good of trusting him when we don't need him? Now his plan is all right. We'll go straight to the jail and take Henry out, if all you are game for it. And we don't need to trust to a mob of unhung rascals and beach-sweepings. If the six men of us can't do it, we might as well quit."

"There must be at least a dozen guards always hanging out at the jail," Ricardo, Leoncia's youngest brother, a lad of eighteen, objected.

Leoncia, her eagerness alive again, frowned at him; but Francis took his part.

"Well taken," he agreed. "But we will eliminate the guards."

"The five-foot walls," said Martinez Solano, twin brother to Alvarado.

"Go through them," Francis answered.

"But how?" Leoncia cried.

"That's what I am arriving at. You, Senor Solano, have plenty of saddle horses? Good. And you, Alesandro, does it chance you could procure me a couple of sticks of dynamite from around the plantation? Good, and better than good. And you, Leoncia, as the lady of the hacienda, should know whether you have in your store-room a plentiful supply of that three-star rye whiskey?

"Ah, the plot thickens," he laughed, on receiving her assurance. "We've all the properties for a Eider Haggard or Eex Beach adventure tale. Now listen. But wait. I want to talk to you, Leoncia, about private theatricals.

Chapter 5

IT was in the mid-afternoon, and Henry, at his barred cell- window, stared out into the street and wondered if any sort of breeze would ever begin to blow from off Chiriqui Lagoon and cool the stagnant air. The street was dusty and filthy filthy, because the only scavengers it had ever known since the town was founded centuries before were the carrion dogs and obscene buzzards even then prowling and hopping about in the debris. Low, white-washed buildings of stone and adobe made the street a furnace.

The white of it all, and the dust, was almost achingly intolerable to the eyes, and Henry would have withdrawn his gaze, had not the several ragged mosos, dozing in a doorway opposite, suddenly aroused and looked interestedly up the street. Henry could not see, but he could hear the rattling spokes of some vehicle coming at speed. Next, it surged into view, a rattle-trap light wagon drawn by a runaway horse. In the seat a gray-headed, gray-bearded ancient strove vainly to check the animal.

Henry smiled and marveled that the rickety wagon could hold together, so prodigious were the bumps imparted to it by the deep ruts. Every wheel, half-dished and threatening to dish, wobbled and revolved out of line with every other wheel. And if the wagon held intact, Henry judged", it was a miracle that the crazy harness did not fly to pieces. When directly opposite the window, the old man made a last effort, half -standing up from the seat as he pulled on the reins. One was rotten, and broke. As the driver fell backward into the seat, his weight on the remaining rein caused the horse to swerve sharply to the right. What happened then whether a wheel dished, or whether a wheel had come off first and dished afterward Henry could not determine. The one incontestable thing was that the wagon was a wreck. The old man, dragging in the dust and stubbornly hanging on to the remaining rein, swung the horse in a circle until it stopped, facing him and snorting at him.

By the time he gained his feet a crowd of mosos was forming about him. These were roughly shouldered right and left by the gendarmes who erupted from the jail. Henry remained at the window and, for a man with but a few hours to live, was an amused spectator and listener to what followed.

Giving his horse to a gendarme to hold, not stopping to brush the filth from his person, the old man limped hurriedly to the wagon and began an examination of the several packing cases, large and small, which composed its load. Of one case he was especially solicitous, even trying to lift it and seeming to listen as he lifted.

He straightened up, on being addressed by one of the gendarmes, and made voluble reply.

"Me? Alas senors, I am an old man, and far from home. I am Leopoldo Narvaez. It is true, my mother was German, may the Saints preserve her rest ; but my father was Baltazar de Jesus y Cervallos e Narvaez, son of General Narvaez of martial memory, who fought under the great Bolivar himself. And now I am half ruined and far from home.

Prompted by other questions, interlarded with the courteous expressions of sympathy with which even the humblest mo so is over generously supplied, he managed to be politefully grateful and to run on with his tale.

"I have driven from Bocas del Toro. It has taken me five days, and business has been poor. My home is in Colon, and I wish I were safely there. But even a noble Narvaez may be a peddler, and even a peddler must live, eh, senors, is it not so? But tell me, is there not a Tomas Eomero who dwells in this pleasant city of San Antonio?"

"There are any God's number of Tomas Komeros who dwell everywhere in Panama," laughed Pedro Zurita, the assistant jailer. "One would need fuller description."

"He is the cousin of my second wife," the ancient answered hopefully, and seemed bewildered by the roar of laughter from the crowd.

"And a dozen Tomas Komeros live in and about San Antonio," the assistant jailer went on, "any one of which may be your second wife's cousin, Senor. There is Tomas Romero, the drunkard. There is Tomas Romero, the thief. There is Tomas Romero but no, he was hanged a month back for murder and robbery. There is the rich Tomas Romero who owns many cattle on the hills. There is... "

To each suggested one, Leopoldo Narvaez had shaken his head dolefully, until the cattle-owner was mentioned. At this he had become hopeful and broken in:

"Pardon me, senor, it must be he, or some such a one as he. I shall find him. If my precious stock-in-trade can be safely stored, I shall seek him now. It is well my misfortune came upon me where it did. I shall be able to trust it with you, who are, one can see with half an eye, an honest and an honorable man." As he talked, he fumbled forth from his pocket two silver pesos and handed them to the jailer. "There, I wish you and your men to have some pleasure of assisting me."

Henry grinned to himself as he noted the access of interest in the old man and of consideration for him, on the part of Pedro Zurita and the gendarmes, caused by the present of the coins. They shoved the more curious of the crowd roughly back from the wrecked wagon and began to carry the boxes into the jail.

"Careful, senors, careful," the old one pleaded, greatly anxious, as they took hold of the big box. Handle it gently. It is of value, and it is fragile, most fragile."

While the contents of the wagon were being carried into the jail, the old man removed and deposited in the wagon all harness from the horse save the bridle.

Pedro Zurita ordered the harness taken in as well, explaining, with a glare at the miserable crowd: "Not a strap or buckle would remain the second after our backs were turned."

Using what was left of the wagon for a stepping block, and ably assisted by the jailer and his crew, the peddler managed to get astride his animal.

"It is well," he said, and added gratefully: "A thousand thanks, senors. It has been my good fortune to meet with honest men with whom my goods will be safe only poor goods, peddler's goods, you understand; but to me, everything, my way upon the road. The pleasure has been mine to meet you. To-morrow I shall return with my kinsman, whom I certainly shall find, and relieve from you the burden of safeguarding my inconsiderable property." He doffed his hat. "Adios, senors, adios!"

He rode away at a careful walk, timid of the animal he bestrode which had caused his catastrophe. He halted and turned his head at a call from Pedro Zurita.

"Search the graveyard, Senor Narvaez," the jailer advised. "Full a hundred Tomas Bomeros lie there."

"And be vigilant, I beg of you, senor, of the heavy box," the peddler called back.

Henry watched the street grow deserted as the gendarmes and the populace fled from, the scorch of the sun. Small wonder, he thought to himself, that the old peddler's voice had sounded vaguely familiar. It had been because he had possessed only half a Spanish tongue to twisf~around the language the other half being the German tongue of the mother. Even so, he talked like a native, and he would be robbed like a native if there was anything of value in the heavy box deposited with the jailers, Henry concluded, ere dismissing the incident from his mind.

In the guardroom, a scant fifty feet away from Henry's cell, Leopoldo Narvaez was being robbed. It had begun by Pedro Zurita making a profound and wistful survey of the large box. He lifted one end of it to sample its weight, and sniffed like a hound at the crack of it as if his nose might give him some message of its contents.

"Leave it alone, Pedro," one of the gendarmes laughed at him. "You have been paid two pesos to be honest."

The assistant jailer sighed, walked away and sat down, looked back at the box, and sighed again. Conversation languished. Continually the eyes of the men roved to the box. A greasy pack of cards could not divert them. The game languished. The gendarme who had twitted Pedro himself went to the box and sniffed.

"I smell nothing," he announced. "Absolutely in the box there is nothing to smell. Now what can it be? The caballero said that it was of value!"

"Caballero!" sniffed another of the gendarmes. "The old man's father was more like to have been peddler of rott'en fish on the streets of Colon and his father before him. Every lying beggar claims descent from the conquistadores."

"And why not, Eafael?" Pedro Zurita retorted. "Are we not all descended?"

"Without doubt," Eafael readily agreed. "The conquistadores slew many… "

"And were the ancestors of those that survived," Pedro completed for him and aroused a general laugh. "Just the same, almost would I give one of these pesos to know what is in that box."

"There is Ignacio," Rafael greeted the entrance of a turnkey whose heavy eyes tokened he was just out of his siesta. "He was not paid to be honest. Come, Ignacio, relieve our curiosity by letting us know what is in the box."

"How should I know?" Ignacio demanded, blinking at the object of interest. "Only now have I awakened."

"You have not been paid to be honest, then?" Eafael asked.

"Merciful Mother of God, who is the man who would pay me to be honest?" the turnkey demanded.

26

"Then take the hatchet there and open the box," Eafael drove his point home. "We may not, for as surely as Pedro is to share the two pesos with us, that surely have we been paid to be honest. Open the box, Ignacio, or we shall perish of our curiosity."

We will look, we will only look," Pedro muttered nervously, as the turnkey prized off a board with the blade of the hatchet. "Then we will close the box again and Put your hand in, Ignacio. What is it you find?… eh? what does it feel like? Ah!"

After pulling and tugging, Ignacio's hand had reappeared, clutching a cardboard cdrton.

"Remove it carefully, for it must be replaced," the jailer cautioned.

And when the wrappings of paper and tissue paper were removed, all eyes focused on a quart bottle of rye whiskey.

"How excellently is it composed," Pedro murmured in tones of awe. "It must be very good that such care be taken of it."

"It is Americano whiskey," sighed a gendarme. "Once, only, have I drunk Americano whiskey. It was wonderful. Such was the courage of it, that I leaped into the bull-ring at Santos and faced a wild bull with my hands. It is true, the bull rolled me, but did I not leap into the ring?"

Pedro took the bottle and prepared to knock its neck off. "Hold!" cried Rafael. "You were paid to be honest." By a man who was not himself honest," came the retort. "The stuff is contraband. It has never paid duty. The old man was in possession of smuggled goods. Let us now gratefully and with clear conscience invest ourselves in its possession. We will confiscate it. We will destroy it."

Not waiting for the bottle to pass, Ignacio and Rafael unwrapped fresh ones and broke off the necks.

"Three stars most excellent," Pedro Zurita orated in a pause, pointing to the trade mark. "You see, all Gringo whiskey is good. One star shows that it is very good; two stars that it is excellent; three stars that it is superb, the best, and better than beyond that. Ah, I know. The Gringos are strong on strong drink. No pulque for them."

"And four stars?" queried Ignacio, his voice husky from the liquor, the moisture glistening in his eyes.

"Four stars? Friend Ignacio, four stars would be either sudden death or translation into paradise."

In not many minutes, Eafael, his arm around another gendarme, was calling him brother and proclaiming that it took little to make men happy here below.

"The old man was a fool, three times a fool, and thrice that," volunteered Augustino, a sullen-faced gendarme, who for the first time gave tongue to speech.

"Viva Augustino! "cheered Eafael. "The three stars have worked a miracle. Behold! Have they not unlocked Augustino's mouth?"

"'And thrice times thrice again was the old man a fool!" Augustino bellowed fiercely. "The very drink of the gods was his, all his, and he has been five days alone with it on the road from Bocas del Toro, and never taken one little sip. Such fools as he should be stretched out naked on an ant-heap, say I."

"The old man was a rogue," quoth Pedro. "And when he comes back to-morrow for his three stars I shall arrest him for a smuggler. It will be a feather in all our caps." If we destroy the evidence thus?" queried Augustino, knocking off another neck.

"We will save the evidence thus!" Pedro replied, smashing an empty bottle on the stone flags. "Listen, comrades. The box was very heavy we are all agreed. It fell. The bottles broke. The liquor ran out, and so were we made aware of the contraband. The box and the broken bottles will be evidence sufficient."

The uproar grew as the liquor diminished. One gendarme quarreled with Ignacio over a forgotten debt of ten centavos. Two others sat upon the floor, arms around each other's necks, and wept over the miseries of their married lot. Augustino, like a very spendthrift of speech, explained his philosophy that silence was golden. And Pedro Zurita became sentimental on brotherhood.

"Even my prisoners," he maundered. "I love them as brothers. Life is sad." A gush of tears in his eyes made him desist while he took another drink. " My prisoners are my very children. My heart bleeds for them. Behold! I weep. Let us share with them. Let them have a moment's happiness. Ignacio, dearest brother of my heart.

Do me a favor. See, I weep on your hand. Carry a bottle of this elixir to the Gringo Morgan. Tell him my sorrow that he must hang to-morrow. Give him my love and bid him drink and be happy to-day."

And as Ignacio passed out on the errand, the gendarme who had once leapt into the bull-ring at Santos, began roaring:

"I want a bull! I want a bull!"

"He wants it, dear soul, that he may put his arms around it and love it," Pedro Zurita explained, with a fresh access of weeping. "I, too, love bulls. I love all things. I love even mosquitoes. All the world is love. That is the secret of the world. I should like to have a lion to play with… "

The unmistakable air of "Back to Back Against the Mainmast "being whistled openly in the street, caught Henry's attention, and he was crossing his big cell to the window when the grating of a key in the door made him lie down quickly on the floor and feign sleep. Ignacio staggered drunkenly in, bottle in hand, which he gravely presented to Henry.

"With the high compliments of our good jailer, Pedro Zurita," he mumbled. "He says to drink and forget that he must stretch your neck to-morrow."

"My high compliments to Senor Pedro Zurita, and tell him from me to go to hell along with his whiskey," Henry replied.

The turnkey straightened up and ceased swaying, as if suddenly become sober.

"Very well, senor," he said, then passed out and locked the door.

In a rush Henry was at the window just in time to encounter Francis face to face and thrusting a revolver to him through the bars.

"Greetings, camarada," Francis said. "We'll have you out of here in a jiffy." He held up two sticks of dynamite, with fuse and caps complete. "I have brought this pretty crowbar to pry you out. Stand well back in your cell, because real pronto there's going to be a hole in this wall that we could sail the Angelique through. And the Ang clique is right off the beach waiting for you. Now, stand back. I'm going to touch her off. It's a short fuse."

Hardly had Henry backed into a rear corner of his cell, when the door was clumsily unlocked and opened to a babel of cries and imprecations, chief est among which he could hear the ancient and invariable war-cry of Latin-America,

"Kill the Gringo!"

Also, he could hear Rafael and Pedro, as they entered, babbling, the one: "He is the enemy of brotherly love "; and the other, "He said I was to go to hell is not that what he said, Ignacio?"

In their hands they carried rifles, and behind them urged the drunken rabble, variously armed, from cutlasses and horse-pistols to hatchets and bottles. At sight of Henry's revolver, they halted, and Pedro, fingering his rifle unsteadily, maundered solemnly:

"Senor Morgan, you are about to take up your rightful abode in hell."

But Ignacio did not wait. He fired wildly and widely from his hip, missing Henry by half the width of the cell and going down the next moment under the impact of Henry's bullet. The rest retreated precipitately into the jail corridor, where, themselves unseen, they began discharging their weapons into the room.

Thanking his fortunate stars for the thickness of the walls, and hoping no ricochet would get him, Henry sheltered in a protecting angle and waited for the explosion.

It came. The window and the wall beneath it became all one aperture. Struck on the head by a flying fragment, Henry sank down dizzily, and, as the dust of the mortar and the powder cleared, with wavering eyes he saw Francis apparently swim through the hole. By the time he had been dragged out through the hole, Henry was himself again. He could see Enrico Solano and Ricardo, his youngest born, rifles in hand, holding back the crowd forming up the street, while the twins, Alvarado and Martinez, similarly held back the crowd forming down the street.

But the populace was merely curious, having its lives to lose and nothing to gain if it attempted to block the way of such masterful men as these who blew up walls and stormed jails in open day. And it gave back respectfully before the compact group as it marched down the street. "The horses are waiting up the next alley," Francis told Henry, as they gripped hands. "And Leoncia is waiting with them. Fifteen minutes' gallop will take us to the beach, where the boat is waiting."

"Say, that was some song I taught you," Henry grinned. "It sounded like the very best little bit of all right when I heard you whistling it. The dogs were so previous they couldn't wait till to-morrow to hang me. They got full of whiskey and decided to finish me off right away. Funny thing that whiskey. An old caballero turned peddler wrecked a wagon-load of it right in front of the jail—"

"For even a noble Narvaez, son of Baltazar de Jesus y Cervallos e Narvaez, son of General Narvaez of martial memory, may be a peddler, and even a peddler must live, eh, senors, is it not so?" Francis mimicked.

Henry looked his gleeful recognition, and added soberly:

"Francis, I'm glad for one thing, most damn glad … "

"Which is?" Francis queried in the pause, just as they swung around the corner to the horses.

"That I didn't cut off your ears that day on the Calf when I had you down and you insisted."

Chapter 6

MARIANO VERCARA E HIJOS, Jefe Politico of San Antonio, leaned back in his chair in the courtroom and with a quiet smile of satisfaction proceeded to roll a cigarette. The case had gone through as prearranged. He had kept the little old judge away from his mescal all day, and had been rewarded by having the judge try the case and give judgment according to program. He had not made a slip. The six peons, fined heavily, were ordered back to the plantation at Santos. The working out of the fines was added to the time of their contract slavery. And the Jefe was two hundred dollars good American gold richer for the transaction. Those Gringos at Santos, he smiled to himself, were men to tie to. True, they were developing the country with their henequen plantation. But, better than that, they possessed money in untold quantity and paid well for such little services as he might be able to render.

His smile was even broader as he greeted Alvarez Torres.

"Listen," said the latter, whispering low in his ear. "We can get both these devils of Morgans. The Henry pig hangs to-morrow. There is no reason that the Francis pig should not go out to-day."

The Jefe remained silent, questioning with a lift of his eyebrows.

"I have advised him to storm the jail. The Solanos have listened to his lies and are with him. They will surely attempt to do it this evening. They could not do it sooner. It is for you to be ready for the event, and to see to it that Francis Morgan is especially shot and killed in the fight."

"For what and for why?" the Jefe temporised. "It is Henry I want to see out of the way. Let the Francis one go back to his beloved New York."

"He must go out to-day, and for reasons you will appreciate. As you know, from reading my telegrams through the government wireless—"

"Which was our agreement for my getting you your permission to use the government station," the Jefe reminded.

"And of which I do not complain," Torres assured him. "But as I was saying, you know my relations with the New York Regan are confidential and important." He touched his hand to his breast pocket. "I have just received another wire. It is imperative that the Francis pig be kept away from New York for a month if forever, and I do not misunderstand Senor Regan, so much the better. In so far as I succeed in this, will you fare well."

"But you have not told me how much you have received, nor how much you will receive," the Jefe probed.

"It is a private agreement, and it is not so much as you may fancy. He is a hard man, this Senor Regan, a hard man. Yet will I divide fairly with you out of the success of our venture."

The Jefe nodded acquiescence, then said:

"Will it be as much as a thousand gold you will get?"

"I think so. Surely the pig of an Irish stock-gambler could pay me no less a sum, and five hundred is yours if pig Francis leaves his bones in San Antonio."

"Will it be as much as a hundred thousand gold?" was the Jefe's next query.

Torres laughed as if at a joke.

"It must be more than a thousand," the other persisted.

"And he may be generous," Torres responded. , "He may even give me five hundred over the thousand, half of which, naturally, as I have said, will be yours as well."

"I shall go from here immediately to the jail," the Jefe announced. "You may trust me, Se,nor Torres, as I trust you. Come. We will go at once, now, you and I, and you may see for yourself the preparation I shall make for this Francis Morgan's reception. I have not yet lost my cunning with a rifle. And, as well, I shall tell off three of the gendarmes to fire only at him. So this Gringo dog would storm our jail, eh? Come. We will depart at once."

He stood up, tossing his cigarette away with a show of determined energy. But, half way across the room, a ragged boy, panting and sweating, plucked his sleeve and whined:

"I have information. You will pay me for it, most high Senor? I have run all the way."

"I'll have you sent to San Juan for the buzzards to peck your carcass for the worthless carrion that you are," was the reply.

The boy quailed at the threat, then summoned courage from his emptiness of belly and meagerness of living and from his desire for the price of a ticket to the next bull-fight. "You will remember I brought you the information, Senor. I ran all the way until I am almost dead, as you can behold, Senor. I will tell you, but you will remember it was I who ran all the way and told you first."

"Yes, yes, animal, I will remember. But woe to you if I remember too well. What is the trifling information? It may not be worth a centavo. And if it isn't I'll make you sorry the sun ever shone on you. And buzzard-picking of you at San Juan will be paradise compared with what I shall visit on you."

"The jail," the boy quavered. "The strange Gringo, the one who was to be hanged yesterday, has blown down the side of the jail. Merciful Saints! The hole is as big as the steeple of the cathedral! And the other Gringo, the one who looks like him, the one who was to hang to-morrow, has escaped with him out of the hole. He dragged him out of the hole himself. This I saw, myself, with my two eyes, and then I ran here to you all the way, and you will remember... "

But the Jefe Politico had alread turned on Torres wither-

"And if this Senor Regan be princely generous, he may give you and me the munificent sum that was mentioned, eh? Five times the sum, or ten times, with this Gringo tiger blowing down law and order and our good jail-walls, would be nearer the mark."

"At any rate, the thing must be a false alarm, merely the straw that shows which way blows the wind of this Francis Morgan's intention," Torres murmured with a sickly smile. "Remember, the suggestion was mine to him to storm the jail."

"In which case you and Senor Regan will pay for the good jail wall?" the Jefe demanded, then, with a pause, added: " Not that I believe it has been accomplished. It is not possible. Even a fool Gringo would not dare."

Bafael, the gendarme, rifle in hand, the blood still oozing down his face from a scalp-wound, came through the courtroom door and shouldered aside the curious ones who had begun to cluster around Torres and the Jefe. "We are devastated," were Rafael's first words. "The jail is 'most destroyed. Dynamite! A hundred pounds of it: A thousand! We came bravely to save the jail. But it exploded the thousand pounds of dynamite. I fell unconscious, rifle in hand. When sense came back to me, I looked about. All others, the brave Pedro, the brave Ignacio, the brave Augustino all, all, lay around me dead!" Almost could he have added, "drunk"; but, his Latin- American nature so compounded, he sincerely stated the catastrophe as it most valiantly and tragically presented itself to his imagination. "They lay dead. They may not be dead, but merely stunned. I crawled. The cell of the , Gringo Morgan was empty. There was a huge and monstrous hole in the wall. I crawled through the hole into the street. There was a great crowd. But the Gringo Morgan was gone. I talked with a moso who had seen and who knew. They had horses waiting. They rode toward the beach. There is a schooner that is not anchored. It sails back and forth waiting for them. The Francis Morgan rides with a sack of gold on his saddle. The moso saw it. It is a large sack.' r

"And the hole?" the Jefe demanded. "The hole in the wall?"

"Is larger than the sack, much larger," was Rafael's reply. "But the sack is large. So the moso said. And he rides with it on his saddle."

"My jail!" the Jefe cried. He slipped a dagger from inside his coat under the left arm-pit and held it aloft by the blade so that the hilt showed as a true cross on which a finely modeled 'Christ hung crucified. "I swear by all the Saints the vengeance I shall have. My jail! Our justice! Our law! Horses! Horses! Gendarme, horses!" He whirled about upon Torres as if the latter Bad spoken, shouting: "To hell with Senor Regan! I am after my own! I have been defied! My jail is desolated! My law our law, good friends has been mocked. Horses! Horses! Commandeer them on the streets. Haste! Haste!"

Captain Trefethen, owner of the Angelique, son of a Maya Indian mother and a Jamaica negro father, paced the narrow after-deck of his schooner, stared shoreward toward San Antonio, where he could make out his crowded long-boat returning, and meditated flight from his mad American =charterer. At the same time he meditated remaining in order to break his charter and give a new one at three times the price ; for he was strangely torn by his conflicting bloods. The negro portion counseled prudence and observance of Panamanian law. The Indian portion was urgent to unlawfulness and the promise of conflict.

It was the Indian mother who decided the issue and made him draw his jib, ease his mainsheet, and begin to reach in-shore the quicker to pick up the oncoming boat. When he made out the rifles carried by the Solanos and the Morgans, almost he put up his helm to run for it and leave them. When he made out a woman in the boat's sternsheets, romance and thrift whispered in him to hang on and take the boat on board. For he knew wherever woman entered into the transactions of men that peril and pelf as well entered hand in hand.

And aboard came the woman, the peril and the pelf Leoncia, the rifles, and a sack of money all in a scramble; for, the wind being light, the captain had not bothered to stop way on the schooner.

"Glad to welcome you on board, sir," Captain Trefethen greeted Francis with a white slash of teeth between his smiling lips. "But who is this man?" He nodded his head to indicate Henry.

"A friend, captain, a guest of mine, in fact, a kinsman."

"And who, sir, may I make bold to ask, are those gentlemen riding along the beach in fashion so lively?"

Henry looked quickly at the group of horsemen galloping along the sand, unceremoniously took the binoculars from the skipper's hand, and gazed through them.

"It's the Jefe himself in the lead," he reported to Leoncia and her menfolk, "with a bunch of gendarmes." He uttered a sharp exclamation, stared through the glasses intently, then shook his head. "Almost I thought I made out our friend Torres."

"With our enemies!" Leoncia cried incredulously, remembering Torres' proposal of marriage and proffer of service and honor that very day on the hacienda piazza.

"I must have been mistaken," Francis acknowledged. "They are riding so bunched together. But it's the Jefe all right, two jumps ahead of the outfit."

"Who is this Torres duck?" Henry asked harshly. "I've never liked his looks from the first, yet he seems always welcome under your roof, Leoncia."

—"I beg jour parson, sir, most gratifiedly, and with my humilious respects," Captain Trefethen interrupted suavely. "But I must call your attention to the previous question, sir, which is: who and what is that cavalcade disporting itself with such earnestness along the sand?"

"They tried to hang me yesterday," Francis laughed. "And to-morrow they were going to hang my kinsman there. Only we beat them to it. And here we are. Now, Mr. Skipper, I call your attention to your head-sheets flapping in the wind. You are standing still. How much longer do you expect to stick around here?"

"Mr. Morgan, sir," came the answer, "it is with dumbfounded respect that I serve you as the charterer of my vessel. Nevertheless, I must inform you that I am a British subject. King George is my king, sir, and I owe obedience first of all to him and to his laws of maritime between all nations, sir. It is lucid to my comprehension that you have broken laws ashore, or else the officers ashore would not be so assiduously in quest of you, sir. And it is also lucid to clarification that it is now your wish to have me break the laws of maritime by enabling you to escape. So, in honor bound, I must stick around here until this little difficulty that you may have appertained ashore is adjusted to the satisfaction of all parties concerned, sir, and to the satisfaction of my lawful sovereign."

"Fill away and get out of this, skipper!" Henry broke in angrily.

"Sir, assuring you of your gratification of pardon, it is my unpleasant task to inform you of two things. Neither are you my charterer ; nor are you the noble King George to whom I give ambitious allegiance."

"Well, I'm your charterer, skipper," Francis said pleasantly, for he had learned to humor the man of mixed words and parentage. "So just kindly put up your helm and sail us out of this Chiriqui Lagoon as fast as God and this failing wind will let you."

"It is not in the charter, sir, that my Angelique shall break the laws of Panama and King George."

"I'll pay you well," Francis retorted, beginning to lose his temper. "Get busy."

"You will then recharter, sir, at three times the present charter?"

Francis nodded shortly.

"Then wait, sir, I entreat. I must procure pen and paper from the cabin and make out the document."

"Oh, Lord," Francis groaned. "Square away and get a move on first. We can make out the paper just as easily while we are running as standing still. Look! They are beginning to fire."

The half-breed captain heard the report, and, searching his spread canvas, discovered the hole of the bullet high up near the peak of the mainsail.

"Very well, sir," he conceded. "You are a gentleman and an honorable man. I trust you to affix your signature to the document at your early convenience Hey, you nigger! Put up your wheel! Hard up! Jump, you black rascals, and slack away mainsheetf Take a hand there, you, Percival, on the boom-tackle!"

All obeyed, as did Percival, a grinning shambling Kingston negro who was as black as his name was white, and as did another, addressed more respectfully as Juan, who was more Spanish and Indian than negro, as his light yellow skin attested, and whose fingers, slacking the foresheet, were as slim and delicate as a girl's.

"Knock the nigger on the head if he keeps up this freshness," Henry growled in an undertone to Francis. "For two cents I'll do it right now."

But Francis shook his head.

"He's all right, but he's a Jamaica nigger, and you know what they are. And he's Indian as well. We might as well humor him, since it's the nature of the beast. He means all right, but he wants the money, he's risking his schooner against confiscation, and he's afflicted with vocabularitis. He just must get those long words out of his system or else bust."

Here Enrico Solano, with quivering nostrils and fingers restless on his rifle as with half an eye he kept track of the wild shots being fired from the beach, approached Henry and held out his hand.

31

"I have been guilty of a grave mistake, Senor Morgan," he said. "In the first hurt of my affliction at the death of my beloved brother, Alfaro, I was guilty of thinking you guilty of his murder." Here old Enrico's eyes flashed with anger consuming but unconsumable. "For murder it was, dastardly and cowardly, a thrust in the dark in the back. I should have known better. But I was overwhelmed, and the evidence was all against you. I did not take pause of thought to consider that my dearly beloved and only daughter was betrothed to you; to remember that all I had known of you was straightness and man-likeness and courage such as never stabs from behind the shield of the dark. I regret. I am sorry. And I am proud once again to welcome you into my family as the husband-to-be of my Leoncia."

And while this whole-hearted restoration of Henry Morgan into the Solano family went on, Leoncia was irritated because her father, in Latin-American fashion, must use so many fine words and phrases, when a single phrase, a handgrip, and a square look in the eyes were all that was called for and was certainly all that either Henry or Francis would have vouchsafed had the situation been reversed. Why, why, she asked of herself, must her Spanish stock, in such extravagance of diction, seem to emulate the similar extravagance of the Jamaica negro?

While this reiteration of the betrothal of Henry and Leoncia was taking place, Francis, striving to appear uninterested, could not help taking note of the pale-yellow sailor called Juan, conferring for'ard with others of the crew, shrugging his shoulders significantly, gesticulating passionately with his hands.

Chapter 7

"AND now we've lost both the Gringo pigs," Alvarez Torres lamented on the beach as, with a slight freshening of the breeze and with booms winged out to port and starboard, the Ang clique passed out of range of their rifles.

"Almost would I give three bells to the cathedral," Mariano Vercara e Hijos proclaimed, "to have them within a hundred yards of this rifle. And if I had will of all Gringos they would depart so fast that the devil in hell would be compelled to study English."

Alvarez Torres beat the saddle pommel with his hand in sheer impotence of rage and disappointment.

"The Queen of my Dreams!" he almost wept. "She is gone and away, off with the two Morgans. I saw her climb up the side of the schooner. And there is the New York Regan. Once out of Chiriqui Lagoon, the schooner may sail directly to New York. And the Francis pig will not have been delayed a month, and the Senor Regan will remit no money."

"They will not get out of Chiriqui Lagoon," the Jefe said solemnly. "I am no animal without reason. I am a man. I know they will not get out. Have I not sworn eternal vengeance? The sun is setting, and the promise is for a night of little wind. The sky tells it to one with half an eye. Behold those trailing wisps of clouds. What wind may be, and little enough of that, will come from the north-east. It will be a head beat to the Chorrera Passage. They will not attempt it. That nigger captain knows the lagoon like a book. He will try to make the long tack and go out past Bocas del Toro, or through the Cartago Passage. Even so, we will outwit him. I have brains, reason. Reason. Listen. It is a long ride. We will make it straight down the coast to Las Palmas. Captain Rosaro is there with the Dolores—"

"The second-hand old tugboat? that cannot get out of her own way?" Torres queried.

"But this night of calm and morrow of calm she will capture the Angelique," the Jefe replied. "On, comrades! We will ride! Captain Rosaro is my friend. Any favor is but mine to ask."

At daylight, the worn-out men, on beaten horses, straggled through the decaying village of Las Palmas and down to the decaying pier, where a very decayed-looking tugboat, sadly in need of paint, welcomed their eyes. Smoke rising from the stack advertised that steam was up, and the Jefe was wearily elated.

"A happy morning, Senor Capitan Rosaro, and well met," he greeted the hard-bitten Spanish skipper, who was reclined on a coil of rope and who sipped black coffee from a mug that rattled against his teeth.

"It would be a happier morning if the cursed fever had not laid its chill upon me," Captain Rosaro grunted sourly, "the hand that held the mug, the arm, and all his body shivering so violently as to spill the hot liquid down his chin and into the black-and-gray thatch of hair that covered his half-exposed chest. "Take that, you animal of hell!" he cried, flinging mug and contents at a splinter of a half-breed boy, evidently his servant, who had been unable to repress his glee.

But the sun will rise and the fever will work its will and shortly depart," said the Jefe, politely ignoring the display of spleen. "And you are finished here, and you are bound for Bocas del Toro, and we shall go with you, all of us, on a rare adventure. We will pick up the schooner Angelique, calm-bound all last night in the lagoon, and I shall make many arrests, and all Panama will so ring with your courage and ability, Capitan, that you will forget that the fever ever whispered in you."

"How much?" Capitan Rosaro demanded bluntly.

Much?" the Jefe countered in surprise. "This is an affair of government, good friend. And it is right on your way to Bocas del Toro. It will not cost you an extra shovelful of coal."

"Muchacho! More coffee!" the tug-skipper roared at the boy.

A pause fell, wherein Torres and the Jefe and all the draggled following yearned for the piping hot coffee brought by the boy. Captain Rosaro played the rim of the mug against his teeth like a rattling of castanets, but managed to sip without spilling and so to burn his mouth.

A vacant-faced Swede, in filthy overalls, with a soiled cap on which appeared "Engineer," came up from below, lighted a pipe, and seemingly went into a trance as he sat on the tug's low rail.

"How much?" Captain Eosaro repeated.

"Let us get under way, dear friend," said the Jefe. "And then, when the fever-shock has departed, we will discuss the matter with reason, being reasonable creatures ourselves and not animals."

"How much?" Captain Eosaro repeated again. "I am never an animal. I always am a creature of reason, whether the sun is up or not up, or whether this thrice-accursed fever is upon me. How much?"

"Well, let us start, and for how much?" the Jefe conceded wearily.

"Fifty dollars gold," was the prompt answer.

"You are starting anyway, are you not, Capitan?" Torres queried softly.

"Fifty gold, as I have said."

The Jefe Politico threw up his hands with a hopeless gesture and turned on his heel to depart.

"Yet you swore eternal vengeance for the crime committed, on your jail," Torres reminded him.

"But not if it costs fifty dollars," the Jefe snapped back, out of the corner of his eye watching the shivering captain for some sign of relenting.

"Fifty gold," said the Captain, as he finished draining the mug and with shaking fingers strove to roll a cigarette. He nodded his head in the direction of the Swede, and added, "and five gold extra for my engineer. It is our custom."

Torres stepped closer to the Jefe and whispered:

"I will pay for the tug myself and charge the Gringo Regan a hundred, and you and I will divide the difference. We lose nothing. We shall make. For this Regan pig instructed me well not to mind expense."

As the sun slipped brazenly above the eastern horizon, one gendarme went back into Las Palmas with the jaded horses, the rest of the party descended to the deck of the tug, the Swede dived down into the engine-room, and Captain Eosaro, shaking off his chill in the sun's beneficent rays, ordered the deck-hands to cast off the lines, and put one of them at the wheel in the pilot-house.

And the same day-dawn found the Ang clique, after a night of almost perfect calm, off the mainland from which she had failed to get away, although she had made sufficient northing to be midway between San Antonio and the passages of Bocas del Toro and Cartago. These two passages to the open sea still lay twenty-five miles away, and the schooner truly slept on the mirror surface of the placid lagoon. Too stuffy below for sleep in the steaming tropics, the deck was littered with the sleepers. - On top the small house of the cabin, in solitary state, lay Leoncia. On the narrow runways of deck on either side lay her brothers and her father. Aft, between the cabin companionway and the wheel, side by side, Francis' arm across Henry's shoulder, as if still protecting him, were the two Morgans. On one side the wheel, sitting, with arms on knees and head on arms, the negro-Indian skipper slept, and just as precisely postured, on the other side of the wheel, slept the helmsman, who was none other than Percival, the black Kingston negro. The waist of the schooner was strewn with the bodies of the mixed-breed seamen, while for'ard, on the tiny forecastlehead, prone, his face buried upon his folded arms, slept the lookout.

Leoncia, in her high place on the cabin-top, awoke first. Propping her head on her hand, the elbow resting on a bit of the poncho on which she lay, she looked down past one side of the hood of the companionway upon the two young men. She yearned over them, who were so alike, and knew love for both of them, remembered the kisses of Henry on her mouth, thrilled till the blush of her own thoughts mantled her cheek at memory of the kisses of Francis, and was puzzled and amazed that she should have it in her to love two men at the one time. As she had already learned of herself, she would follow Henry to the end of the world and Francis even farther. And she could not understand such wantonness of inclination.

Fleeing from her own thoughts, which frightened her, she stretched out her arm and dangled the end of her silken scarf to a tickling of Francis' nose, who, after restless movements, still in the heaviness of sleep, struck with his hand at what he must have thought to be a mosquito or a fly, and hit Henry on the chest. So it was Henry who was first awak-ened. He sat up with such abruptness as to awaken

33

Francis.

"Good morning, merry kinsman," Francis greeted. "Why such violence?"

"Morning, morning, and the morning's morning, comrade," Henry muttered. "Such was the violence of your sleep that it was you who awakened me with a buffet on my breast. I thought it was the hangman, for this is the morning they planned to kink my neck." He yawned, stretched his arms, gazed out over the rail at the sleeping sea, and nudged Francis to observance of the sleeping skipper and helmsman.

They looked so bonny, the pair of Morgans, Leoncia thought; and at the same time wondered why the English word had arisen unsummoned in her mind rather than a Spanish equivalent. Was it because her heart went out so generously to the two Gringos that she must needs think of them in their language instead of her own?

To escape the perplexity of her thoughts, she dangled the scarf again, was discovered, and laughingly confessed that it was she who had caused their violence of waking.

Three hours later, breakfast of coffee and fruit over, she found herself at the wheel taking her first lesson of steering and of the compass under Francis' tuition. The Any clique, under a crisp little breeze which had hauled around well to north 'ard, was for the moment heeling it through the water at a six - knot clip. Henry, swaying on the weather side of the after-deck and searching the sea through the binoculars, was striving to be all unconcerned at the lesson, although secretly he was mutinous with himself for not having first thought of himself introducing her to the binnacle and the wheel. Yet he resolutely refrained from looking around or from even stealing a corner-of-the-eye glance at the other two.

But Captain Trefethen, with the keen cruelty of Indian curiosity and the impudence of a negro subject of King George, knew no such delicacy. He stared openly and missed nothing of the chemic drawing together of his charterer and the pretty Spanish girl. When they leaned over the wheel to look into the binnacle, they leaned toward each other and Leoncia's hair touched Francis' cheek. And the three of them, themselves and the breed skipper, knew the thrill induced by such contact. But the man and woman knew immediately what the breed skipper did not know, and what they knew was embarrassment. Their eyes lifted to each other in a flash of mutual startlement, and drooped away and down guiltily. Francis talked very fast and loud enough for half the schooner to hear, as he explained the lubber's point of the compass. But Captain Trefethen grinned.

A rising puff of breeze made Francis put the wheel up. His hand to the spoke rested on her hand already upon it. Again they thrilled, and again the skipper grinned.

Leoncia's eyes lifted to Francis', then dropped in confusion. She slipped her hand out from under and terminated the lesson by walking slowly away with a fine assumption of casualness, as if the wheel and the binnacle no longer interested her. But she had left Francis afire with what he knew was lawlessness and treason as he glanced at Henry's shoulder and profile and hoped he had not seen what had occurred. Leoncia, apparently gazing off across the lagoon to the jungle-clad shore, was seeing nothing as she thoughtfully turned her engagement ring around and around on her finger.

But Henry, turning to tell them of the smudge of smoke he had discovered on the horizon, had inadvertently seen. And the negro-Indian captain had seen him see. So the captain lurched close to him, the cruelty of the Indian dictating the impudence of the negro, as he said in a low voice:

"Ah, be not downcast, sir. The senorita is generously hearted. There is room for both you gallant gentlemen in her heart."

And the next fraction of a second he learned the inevitable and invariable lesson that white men must have their privacy of intimate things ; for he lay on his back, the back of his head sore from contact with the deck, the front of his head, between the eyes, sore from contact with the knuckles of Henry Morgan's right hand.

But the Indian in the skipper was up and raging as he sprang to his feet, knife in hand. Juan, the pale-yellow mixed breed, leaped to the side of his skipper flourishing another knife, while several of the nearer sailors joined in forming a s^mi-circle of attack on Henry, who, with a quick step back and an upward slap of his hand, under the pin-rail, caused an iron belaying pin to leap out and up into the air. Catching it m mid-flight, he was prepared to defend himself. Francis, abandoning the wheel and drawing his automatic as he sprang, was through the circle and by the side of Henry. "What did he say?" Francis demanded of his kinsman.

"I will say what I said," the breed skipper threatened, the negro side of him dominant as he built for a compromise of blackmail. "I said... "

"Hold on, skipper!" Henry interrupted. "I'm sorry I struck you. Hold your hush. Put a stopper on your jaw. Saw wood. Forget. I'm sorry I struck you. I... "

Henry Morgan could not help the pause in speech during which he swallowed his gorge rising at

34

what he was about, to say. And it was because of Leoncia, and because she was looking on and listening, that he said it. "I... I apologize, skipper."

"It is an injury," Captain Trefethsn stated aggrievedly. "It is a physical damage. No man can perpetrate a physical damage on a subject of King George's, God bless him, without furnishing a money requital."

At this crass statement of the terms cf the blackmail, Henry was for forgetting himself and for leaping upon the creature. But, restrained by Francis' hand on his shoulder, he struggled to self-control, made a noise like hearty laughter, dipped into his pocket for two ten-dollar gold-pieces, and, as if they stung him, thrust them into Captain Trefethen's palm.

"Cheap at the price," he could not help muttering aloud.

"It is a good price," the skipper averred. "Twenty gold is always a good price for a sore head. I am yours to command, sir. You are a sure-enough gentleman. You may hit me any time for the price."

"Me, sir, me!" the Kingston black named Percival volunteered with broad and prideless chucklings of subservience. "Take a swat at me, sir, for the same price, any time, now. And you may swat me as often as you please to pay... "

But the episode was destined to terminate at that instant, for at that instant a sailor called from amidships:

"Smoke! A steamer-smoke dead aft!"

The passage of an hour determined the nature and import of the smoke, for the Angelique, falling into a calm, was overhauled with such rapidity that the tugboat Dolores, at half a mile distance through the binoculars, was seen fairly to bristle with armed men crowded on her tiny for'ard deck. Both Henry and Francis could recognize the faces of the Jefe Politico and of several of the gendarmes. Old Enrico Solano's nostrils began to dilate, as, with his four sons who were aboard, he stationed them aft with him and prepared for the battle. Leoncia, divided between Henry and Francis, was secretly distracted, though outwardly she joined in laughter at the unkemptness of the little tug, and in glee at a flaw of wind that tilted the Angelique's port rail flush to the water and foamed her along at a nine-knot clip.

But weather and wind were erratic. The face of the lagoon was vexed with squalls and alternate streaks of calm. "We cannot escape, sir, I regret to inform you," Captain Trefethen informed Francis. "If the wind would hold, sir, yes. But the wind baffles and breaks. We are crowded down upon the mainland. We are cornered, sir, and as good as captured."

Henry, who had been studying the near shore through the glasses, lowered them and looked at Francis.

"Shout!" cried the latter. "You have a scheme. It's sticking out all over you. Name it."

"Eight there are the two Tigres islands," Henry elucidated. "They guard the narrow entrance to Juchitan Inlet, which is called El Tigre. Oh, it has the teeth of a tiger, believe me. On either side of them, between them and the shore, it is too shoal to float a whaleboat unless you know the winding channels, which I do know. But between them is deep water, though the El Tigre Passage is so pinched that there is no room to come about. A schooner can only run it with the wind abaft or abeam. Now, the wind favors. We will run it. Which is only half my scheme—"

"And if the wind baffles or fails, sir and the tide of the inlet runs out and in like a race, as I well know my beautiful schooner will go on the rocks," Captain Trefethen protested.

"For which, if it happens, I will pay you full value," Francis assured him shortly and brushed him aside. "And now, Henry, what's the other half of your scheme?"

"I'm ashamed to tell you," Henry laughed. "But it will be provocative of more Spanish swearing than has been heard in Chiriqui Lagoon since old Sir Henry sacked San Antonio and Bocas del Toro. You just watch."

Leoncia clapped her hands, as with sparkling eyes she cried:

"It must be good, Henry. I can see it by your face. You must tell me."

And, aside, his arm around her to steady her on the reeling deck, Henry whispered closely in her ear, while Francis, to hide his perturbation at the sight of them, made shift through the binoculars to study the faces on the pursuing tug. Captain Trefethen grinned maliciously and exchanged significant glances with the pale-yellow sailor."

"Now, skipper," said Henry, returning. "We're just opposite El Tigre. Put up your helm and run for the passage. Also, and pronto, I want a coil of half -inch, old, soft, manila rope, plenty of rope-yarns and sail twine, that case of beer from the lazarette, that five-gallon kerosene can that was emptied last night, and the coffee-pot from the galley."

But I am distrained to remark to your attention that that rope is worth good money, sir," Captain Trefethen complained, as Henry set to work on the heterogeneous gear. "You will be paid," Francis hushed him.

"And the coffee-pot it is almost new."

"You will be paid."

The skipper sighed and surrendered, although he sighed again at Henry's next act, which was to uncork the bottles and begin emptying the beer out into the scuppers.

"Please, sir," begged Percival. "If you must empty the beer please empty it into me."

No further beer was wasted, and the crew swiftly laid the empty bottles beside Henry. At intervals of six feet he fastened the recorked bottles to the half -inch line. Also, he cut off two-fathom lengths of the line and attached them like streamers between the beer bottles. The coffee-pot and two empty coffee tins were likewise added among the bottles. To one end of the main-line he made fast the kerosene can, to the other end the empty beer-case, and looked up to Francis, who replied:

"Oh, I got you five minutes ago. El Tigre must be narrow, or else the tug will go around that stuff."

"El Tigre is just that narrow," was the response. "There's one place where the channel isn't forty feet between the shoals. If the skippers-misses our trap, he'll go around, aground. Say, they'll be able to wade ashore from the tug if that happens. Come on, now, we'll get the stuff aft and ready to toss out. You take starboard and I'll take port, and when I give the word you shoot that beer case out to the side as far as you can."

Though the wind eased down, the Angelique, square before it, managed to make five knots, while the Dolores, doing six, slowly overhauled her. As the rifles began to speak from the Dolores, the skipper, under the direction of Henry and Francis, built up on the schooner's stern a low barricade of sacks of potatoes and onions, of old sails, and of hawser coils. Crouching low in the shelter of this, the helmsman managed to steer. Leoncia refused to go below as the firing became more continuous, but compromised by lying down behind the cabin-house. The rest of the sailors sought similar shelter in nooks and corners, while the Solano men, lying aft, returned the fire of the tug.

Henry and Francis, in their chosen positions and waiting until the narrowness of El Tigre was reached, took a hand in the free and easy battle.

"My congratulations, sir," Captain Trefethen said to Francis, the Indian of him compelling him to raise his head to peer across the rail, the negro of him flattening his body down until almost it seemed to bore into the deck. "That was Captain Rosaro himself that was steering, and the way he jumped and grabbed his hand would lead one to conclude that you had very adequately put a bullet through it. That Captain Rosaro is a very hot-tempered hombre, sir. I can almost hear him blaspheming now."

"Stand ready for the word, Francis," Henry said, laying down his rifle and carefully studying the low shores of the islands of El Tigre on either side of them. "We're almost ready. Take your time when I give the word, and at three let her go."

The tug was two hundred yards away and overtaking fast, when Henry gave the word. He and Francis stood up, and at "three "made their fling. To either side can and beercase flew, dragging behind them through the air the beaded rope of pots and cans and bottles and rope-streamers.

In their interest, Henry and Francis remained standing in order to watch the maw of their trap as denoted by the spread of miscellaneous objects on the surface of their troubled wake. A fusillade of rifle shots from the tug made them drop back flat to the deck; but, peering over the rail, they saw the tug's forefoot press the floated rope down and under. A minute later they saw the tug slow down to a stop.

"Some mess wrapped around that propeller," Francis applauded. "Henry, salute."

"Now, if the wind holds... " said Henry modestly.

The Angelique sailed on, leaving the motionless tug to grow smaller in the distance, but not so small that they could not see her drift helplessly onto the shoal, and see men going over the side and wading about.

"We just must sing our little song," Henry cried jubilantly, starting up the stave of "Back to Back Against the Mainmast."

"Which is all very nice, sir," Captain Trefethen interrupted at the conclusion of the first chorus, his eyes glistening and his shoulders still jiggling to the rhythm of the song. "But the wind has ceased, sir. We are becalmed. How are we to get out of Juchitan Inlet without wind? The Dolores is not wrecked. She is merely delayed. Some nigger will go down and clear her propeller, and then she has us right where she wants us."

"It's not so far to shore," Henry adjudged with a measuring eye as he turned to Enrico.

"What kind of a shore have they got ashore here, Senor Solano?" he queried. "Maya Indians and haciendados which?"

"Haciendados and Mayas, both," Enrico answered. "But I know the country well. If the schooner is not safe, we should be safe ashore. We can get horses and saddles and beef and corn. The Cordilleras are beyond. What more should we want?"

"But Leoncia?" Francis asked solicitously.

"Was born in the saddle, and in the saddle there are few Americanos she would not weary," came Enrico's answer. "It would be we", with your acquiescence, to swing out the long boat in case the Dolores appears upon us."

Chapter 8

IT'S all right, skipper, it's all right," Henry assured the breed captain, who, standing on the beach with them, seemed loath to say farewell and pull back to the Angelique adrift half a mile away in the dead calm which had fallen on Juchitan Inlet.

"It is what we call a diversion," Francis explained. "That is a nice word diversion. And it is even nicer when you see it work."

"But if it don't work," Captain Trefethen protested, "then will it spell a confounded word, which I may name as catastrophe."

"That is what happened to the Dolores when we tangled her propeller," Henry laughed. "But we do not know the meaning of that word. We use diversion instead. The proof that it will work is that we are leaving Senor Solano's two sons with you. Alvarado and Martinez know the passages like a book. They will pilot you out with the first favoring breeze. The Jefe is not interested in you. He is after us, and when we take to the hills he'll be on our trail with every last man of his."

"Don't you see!" Francis broke in. "The Angelique is trapped. If we remain on board he will capture us and the Angelique as well. But we make the diversion of taking to the hills. He pursues us. The Angelique goes free. And of course he won't catch us."

"But suppose I do lose the schooner!" the swarthy skipper persisted. "If she goes on the rocks I will lose her, and the passages are very perilous."

"Then you will be paid for her, as I've told you before," Francis said, with a show of rising irritation.

"Also are there my numerous expenses—"

Francis pulled out a pad and pencil, scribbled a note, and passed it over, saying:

"Present that to Senor Melchor Gonzales at Bocas del Toro. It is for a thousand gold. He is the banker; he is my agent, and he will pay it to you."

Captain Trefethen stared incredulously at the scrawled bit of paper.

"Oh, he's good for it," Henry said.

"Yes, sir, I know, sir, that Mr. Francis Morgan is a wealthy gentleman of renown. But how wealthy is he? Is he as wealthy as I modestly am? I own the Angelique, free of all debt. I own two town lots, unimproved, in Colon. And I own four water-front lots in Belen that will make me very wealthy when the Union Fruit Company begins the building of the warehouses—"

"How much, Francis, did your father leave you?" Henry quipped teasingly. "Or, rather, how many?"

Francis shrugged his shoulders as he answered vaguely: "More than I have fingers and toes."

"Dollars, sir?" queried the captain.

Henry shook his head sharply.

"Thousands, sir?"

Again Henry shook his head.

"Millions, sir?"

"Now you're talking," Henry answered. "Mr. Francis Morgan is rich enough to buy almost all of the Eepublic of Panama, with the Canal cut out of the deal."

The negro -Indian mariner looked his unbelief to Enrico Solano, who replied:

"He is an honorable gentleman. I know. I have cashed his paper, drawn on Senor Melchor Gonzales at Bocas del Toro, for a thousand pesos. There it is in the bag there."

He nodded his head up the beach to where Leoncia, in the midst of the dunnage landed with them, was toying with trying to slip cartridges into a Winchester rifle. The bag, which the skipper had long since noted, lay at her feet in the sand.

"I do hate to travel strapped," Francis explained embarrassedly to the white men of the group. "One never knows when a dollar mayn't come in handy. I got caught with a broken machine at Smith Biver Corners, up New York way, one night, with nothing but a check book, and, d'you know, I couldn't get even a cigarette in the town."

"I trusted a white gentleman in Barbadoes once, who chartered my boat to go fishing flying fish," the captain began.

"Well, so long, skipper," Henry shut him off. "You'd better be getting on board, because we're going to hike."

And for Captain Trefethen, staring at the backs of his departing passengers, remained naught but to obey. Helping to shove the boat oft, he climbed in, took the steering sweep, and directed his course toward the Angelique. Glancing back from time to time, he saw the party on the beach shoulder the baggage and disappear into the dense green wall of vegetation.

They came out upon an inchoate clearing, and saw gangs of peons at work chopping down and grubbing out the roots of the virgin tropic forest so that rubber trees for the manufacture of automobile tires might be planted to replace it. Leoncia, beside her father, walked in the lead. Her brothers, Ricardo and Alesandro, in the middle, were burdened with the dunnage, as were Francis and Henry, who brought up the rear. And this strange procession was met by a slender, straight-backed, hidalgo-appearing, elderly gentleman, who leaped his horse across tree-trunks and stump-holes in order to gain to them.

He was off his horse, at sight of Enrico, sombrero in hand in recognition of Leoncia, his hand extended to Enrico in greeting of ancient friendship, his lips wording words and his eyes expressing admiration to Enrico's daughter.

The talk was in rapid-fire Spanish, and the request for horses preferred and qualifiedly granted, ere the introduction of the two Morgans took place. The haciendado's horse, after the Latin fashion, was immediately Leoncia's, and, without ado, he shortened the stirrups and placed her astride in the saddle. A murrain, he explained, had swept his plantation of riding animals ; but his chief overseer still possessed a fair-conditioned one which was Enrico's as soon as it could be procured.

His handshake to Henry and Francis was hearty as well as dignified, as he took two full minutes ornately to state that any friend of his dear friend Enrico was his friend. When Enrico asked the haciendado about the trails up toward the Cordilleras and mentioned oil, Francis pricked up his ears.

"Don't tell me, Senor," he began, "that they have located oil in Panama?"

"They have," the haciendado nodded gravely. 'We knew of the oil ooze, and had known of it for generations. But it was the Hermosillo Company that sent its Gringo engineers in secretly and then bought up the land. They say it is a great field. But I know nothing of oil myself. They have many wells, and have bored much, and so much oil have they that it is running away over the landscape. They say they cannot choke it entirely down, such is the volume and pressure. What they need is the pipe-line to ocean-carriage, which they have begun to build. In the meantime it flows away down the canyons, an utter loss of incredible proportion."

"Have they built any tanks?" Francis demanded, his mind running eagerly on Tampico Petroleum, to which most of his own fortune was pledged, and of which, despite the rising stock-market, he had heard nothing since his departure from New York.

The haciendado shook his head.

"Transportation," he explained. "The freight from tide-water to the gushers by mule-back has been prohibitive. But they have impounded much of it. They have lakes of oil, great reservoirs in the hollows of the hills, earthendammed, and still they cannot choke down the flow, and still the precious substance flows down the canyons."

"Have they roofed these reservoirs?" Francis inquired, remembering a disastrous fire in the early days of Tampico Petroleum.

"No, Senor."

Francis shook his head disapprovingly.

"They should be roofed," he said. "A match from the drunken or revengeful hand of any peon could set the whole works off. It's poor business, poor business."

"But I am not the Hermosillo," the haciendado said.

"For the Hermosillo Company, I meant, Senor," Francis explained. "I am an oil-man. I have paid through the nose to the tune of hundreds of thousands for similar accidents or crimes. One never knows just how they happen What one does know is that they do happen—"

What more Francis might have said about the expediency of protecting oil reservoirs from stupid or wilful peons, was never to be known; for, at the moment, the chief overseer of the plantation, stick in hand, rode up, half his interest devoted to the newcomers, the other half to the squad of peons working close at hand.

"Senor Ramirez, will you favor me by dismounting," his employer, the haciendado, politely addressed him, at the same time introducing him to the strangers as soon as he had dismounted. "The animal is yours, friend Enrico," the haciendado said. "If it dies, please return at your easy convenience the saddle and gear. And if your convenience be not easy, please do not remember that there is to be any return, save ever and always, of your love for me. I regret that you and your party cannot now partake of my hospitality. But the Jefe is a bloodhound, I know. We shall do our best to send him astray."

With Leoncia and Enrico mounted, and the gear made fast to the saddles by. leather thongs, the cavalcade started, Alesandro and Ricardo clinging each to a stirrup of their father's saddle and trotting alongside. This was for making greater haste, and was emulated by Francis and Henry, who clung to Leoncia's stirrups. Fast to the pommel of her saddle was the bag of silver dollars.

"It is some mistake," the haciendado was explaining to his overseer. "Enrico Solano is an honorable man. Anything to which he pledges himself is honorable. He has pledged himself to this, whatever it may be, and yet is Mariano Vercara e" Hijos on their trail. We shall mislead him if he comes this way."

"And here he comes," the overseer remarked, "without luck so far in finding horses." Casually he turned on the laboring peons and with horrible threats urged them to do at least half a day's decent work in a day.

From the corner of his eye, the haciendado observed the fast-walking group of men, with Alvarez Torres in the lead; but, as if he had not noticed, he conferred with his overseer about the means of grubbing out the particular stump the peons were working on.

He returned the greeting of Torres pleasantly, and inquired politely, with a touch of devilry, if he led the party of men on some oil-prospecting adventure.

"No, Senor," Torres answered. "We are in search of Senor Enrico Solano, his daughter, his sons, and two tall Gringos with them. It is the Gringos we want. They have passed this way, Senor?"

"Yes, they have passed. I imagined they, too, were in some oil excitement, such was their haste that prevented them from courteously passing the time of day and stating their destination. Have they committed some offence? But I should not ask. Senor Enrico Solano is too honorable a man... "

"Which way did they go?" the Jefe demanded, thrusting himself breathlessly forward from the rear of his gendarmes with whom he had just caught up.

And while the haciendado and his overseer temporized and prevaricated, and indicated an entirely different direction, Torres noted one of the peons, leaning on his spade, listen intently. And still while the Jefe was being misled and was giving orders to proceed on the false scent, Torres flashed a silver dollar privily to the listening peon. The peon nodded his head in the right direction, caught the coin unobserved, and applied himself to his digging at the root of the huge stump.

Torres countermanded the Jefe's order.

"We will go the other way," Torres said, with a wink to the Jefe. "A little bird has told me that our friend here is mistaken and that they have gone the other way."

As the posse departed on the hot trail, the haciendado and his overseer looked at each other in consternation and amazement. The overseer made a movement of his lips for silence, and looked swiftly at the group of laborers. The offending peon was working furiously and absorbedly, but another peon, with a barely perceptible nod of head, indicated him to the overseer.

"There's the little bird," the overseer cried, striding to the traitor and shaking him violently.

Out of the peon's rags flew the silver dollar.

"Ah, ha," said the haciendado, grasping the situation. "He has become suddenly affluent. This is horrible, that my peons should be wealthy. Doubtless, he has murdered some one for all that sum. Beat him, and make him confess."

The creature, on his knees, the stick of the overseer raining blows on his head and back, made confession of what he had done to earn the dollar.

"Beat him, beat him some more, beat him to death, the beast who betrayed my dearest friends," the haciendado urged placidly. "But no caution. Do not beat him to death, but nearly so. We are short of labor now and cannot afford the full measure of our just resentment. Beat him to hurt him much, but that he shall be compelled to lay off work no more than a couple of days."

Of the immediately subsequent agonies, adventures, and misadventures of the peon, a volume might be written which w%ould be the epic of his life. Besides, to be beaten nearly to death is not nice to contemplate or dwell upon. Let it suffice to tell that when he had received no more than part of his beating; he wrenched free, leaving half his rags in the overseer's grasp, and fled madly for the jungle, outfooting the overseer who was unused to rapid locomotion save when on a horse's back.

Such was the speed of the wretched creature's flight, spurred on by the pain of his lacerations and the fear of the overseer, that, plunging wildly on, he overtook the Solano party and plunged out of the jungle and into them as they were crossing a shallow stream, and fell upon his knees, whimpering for mercy. He whimpered because of his betrayal of them. But this they did not know, and Francis, seeing his pitiable condition, lingered behind long enough to unscrew the metal top from a pocket flask and revive him with a drink of half the contents. Then Francis hastened on, leaving the poor devil muttering inarticulate thanks ere he dived off into the sheltering jungle in a different direction. But, underfed, overworked, his body gave way, and he sank down in collapse in the green covert. Next, Alvarez Torres in the lead and tracking lika a hound, the gendarmes at his back, the Jefe panting in the rear from shortness of breath, the pursuit arrived at the stream. The foot-marks of the peon, still wet on the dry stones beyond the margin of the stream, caught Torres' eye. In a trice, by what little was left of his garments, tne peon was dragged out. On his knees, which portion of his anatomy he was destined to occupy much this day, he begged for mercy and received his interrogation. And he denied knowledge of the Solano party. He, who had betrayed and been beaten, but who had received only succor from those he had betrayed, felt stir in him some atom of gratitude and good. He denied knowledge of the Solanos since in the clearing where he had sold them for the silver dollar. Torres' stick fell upon his head, five times, ten times, and went on falling with the certitude that in all eternity there would be no cessation unless he told the truth. And, after all, he was a miserable and wretched thing, spirit-broken by beatings from the cradle, and the sting of Torres' stick, with the threat of the plenitude of the stick that meant the death his own owner, the haciendado, could not afford, made him give in and point the way of the chase.

But his day of tribulation had only begun. Scarcely had be betrayed the Solanos the second time, and still on his knees, when the haciendado, with the posse of neighboring haciendados and overseers he had called to his help, burst upon the scene astride sweating horses.

"My peon, senors," announced the haciendado, itching to be at him. "You maltreat him."

"And why not?" demanded the Jefe.

"Because he is mine to maltreat, and I wish to do it myself."

The peon crawled and squirmed to the Jefe's feet and begged and entreated not to be given up. But he begged for mercy where was no mercy.

"Certainly, senor," the Jefe said to the haciendado. "We give him back to you. We must uphold the law, and he is your property. Besides, we have no further use for him. Yet is he a most excellent peon, senor. He has done what no peon has ever done in the history of Panama. He has told the truth twice in one day."

His hands tied together in front of him and hitched by a rope to the horn of the overseer's saddle, the peon was towed away on the back-track with a certain apprehension that the worst of his beatings for that day was very imminent. Nor was he mistaken. Back at the plantation, he was tied like an animal to a post of a barbed wire fence, while his owner and the friends of his owner who had helped in the capture went into the hacienda to take their twelve o'clock breakfast. After that, he knew what he was to receive. But the barbed wire of the fence, and the lame mare in the paddock behind it, built an idea in the desperate mind of the peon. Though the sharp barbs of the wire again and again cut his wrist, he quickly sawed through his bonds, free save for the law, crawled under the fence, led the lame mare through the gate, mounted her barebacked, and, with naked heels tattooing her ribs, galloped her away toward the safety of the Cordilleras.

Chapter 9

IN the meantime the Solanos were being overtaken, and Henry teased Francis with:

"Here in the jungle is where dollars are worthless. They can buy neither fresh horses, nor can they repair these two spineless creatures, which must likewise be afflicted with the murrain that carried off the rest of the haciendado's riding animals."

"I've never been in a place yet where money wouldn't work," Francis replied.

"I suppose it could even buy a drink of water in hell," was Henry's retort.

Leoncia clapped her hands.

"I don't know," Francis observed. "I have never been there."

Again Leoncia clapped her hands.

"Just the same I have an idea I can make dollars work in the jungle, and I am going to try it right now," Francis continued, at the same time untying the coin-sack from Leoncia's pommel. "You go ahead and ride on."

"But you must tell me," Leoncia insisted; and, aside, in her ear as she leaned to him from the saddle, he whispered what made her laugh again, while Henry, conferring with Enrico and his sons, inwardly berated himself for being a jealous fool.

Before they were out of sight, looking back, they saw Francis, with pad and pencil out, writing something. What he wrote was eloquently brief, merely the figure "50." Tearing off the sheet, he laid it conspicuously in the middle of the trail and weighted it down with a silver dollar. Counting out forty-nine other dollars from the bag, he sowed them very immediately about the first one and ran up the trail after his party.

Augustino, the gendarme who rarely spoke when he was sober, but who when drunk preached volubly the wisdom of silence, was in the lead, with bent head nosing the track of the quarry, when his keen eyes lighted on the silver dollar holding down the sheet of paper. The first he appropriated; the second he turned over to the Jefe. Torres looked over his shoulder, and together they read the mystic

"50." The Jefe tossed the scrap of paper aside as of little worth, and was for resuming the chase, but Augustino picked up and pondered the "50 "thoughtfully. Even as he pondered it, a shout from Rafael advertised the finding of another dollar. Then Augustino knew. There were fifty of the coins to be had for the picking up. Flinging the note to the wind, he was on hands and knees overhauling the ground. The rest of the party joined in the scramble, while Torres and the Jefe screamed curses on them in a vain effort to make them proceed.

When the gendarmes could find no more, they counted up what they had recovered. The toll came to forty-seven.

"There are three more," cried Rafael, whereupon all flung themselves into the search again. Five minutes more were lost, ere the three other coins were found. Each pocketed what he had retrieved and obediently swung into the pursuit at the heels of Torres and the Jefe.

A mile farther on, Torres tried to trample a shining dollar into the dirt, but Augustino's ferret eyes had been too quick, and his eager fingers dug it out of the soft earth. Where was one dollar, as they had already learned, there were more dollars. The posse came to a halt, and while the two leaders fumed and imprecated, the rest of the members cast about right and left from the trail.

Vicente, a moon -faced gendarme, who looked more like a Mexican Indian than a Maya or a Panamanian "breed," lighted first on the clue. All gathered about, like hounds around a tree into which the 'possum has been run. In truth, it was a tree, or a rotten and hollow stump of one, a dozen feet in height and a third as many feet in diameter. Five feet from the ground was an opening. Above the opening, pinned on by a thorn, was a sheet of paper the same size as the first they had found. On it was written "100."

In the scramble that ensued, half a dozen minutes were lost as half a dozen right arms strove to be first in dipping into the hollow heart of the stump to the treasure. But the hollow extended deeper than their arms were long. "We will chop down the stump," Rafael cried, sounding with the back of his machete against the side of it to locate the base of the hollow. "We will all chop, and we will count what we find inside and divide equally."

By this time their leaders were frantic, and the Jefe had begun threatening, the moment they were back in San Antonio, to send them to San Juan where their carcasses would be picked by the buzzards.

"But we are not back in San Antonio, thank God," said Augustino, breaking his sober seal of silence in order to enunciate wisdom.

"We are poor men, and we will divide in fairness," spoke up Rafael. "Augustino is right, and thank God for it that we are not back in San Antonio. This rich Gringo scatters more money along the way in a day for us to pick up than could we earn in a year where we come from. I, for one, am for revolution, where money is so plentiful."

"With the rich Gringo for a leader," Augustino supplemented. "For as long as he leads this way could I follow forever."

"If," Rafael nodded agreement, with a pitch of his head toward Torres and the Jefe, "if they do not give us opportunity to gather what the gods have spread for us, then to the last and deepest of the roasting hells of hell for them. We are men, not slaves. The world is wide. The Cordilleras are just beyond. We will all be rich, and free men, and live in the Cordilleras where the Indian maidens are wildly beautiful and desirable—"

"And we will be well rid of our wives, back in San Antonio," said Vicente. "Let us now chop down this treasure tree."

Swinging their machetes with heavy, hacking blows, the wood, so rotten that it was spongy, gave way readily before their blades. And when the stump fell over, they counted and divided, in equity, not one hundred silver dollars, but one hundred and forty-seven.

"He is generous, this Gringo," quoth Vicente. "He leaves more than he says. May there not be still more?"

And, from the debris of rotten wood, much of it crumbled to powder under their blows, they recovered five more coins, in the doing of which they lost ten more minutes that drove Torres and Jefe to the verge of madness.

"He does not stop to count, the wealthy Gringo," said Rafael. "He must merely open that sack and pour it out. And that is the sack with which he rode to the beach of San Antonio when he blew up with dynamite the wall of our jail."

The chase' was resumed, and all went well for half an hour, when they came upon an abandoned freehold, already half -overrun with the returning jungle. A dilapidated, strawthatched house, a fallen-in labor barracks, a broken-down corral the very posts of which had sprouted and leaved into growing trees, and a well showing recent use by virtue of a fresh length of riata attaching bucket to well-sweep, showed where some man had failed to tame the wild. And, conspicuously on the well-sweep, was pinned a familiar sheet of paper on which was written "300."

"Mother of God! a fortune!" cried Rafael.

"May the devil forever torture him in the last and deepest hell!" was Torres' contribution.

"He pays better than your Senor Regan," the Jefe sneered in his despair and disgust.

"His bag of silver is only so large," Torres retorted. "It seems we must pick it all up before we catch him. But when we have picked it all up, and his bag is empty, then will we catch him."

"We will go on now, comrades," the Jefe addressed his posse ingratiatingly. "Afterwards, we will return at our leisure and recover the silver."

Augustino broke his seal of silence again.

"One never knows the way of one's return, if one ever returns," he enunciated pessimistically. Elated by the pearl of wisdom he had dropped, he essayed another. "Three hundred in hand is better than three million in the bottom of a well we may never see again."

"Some one must descend into the well," spoke Rafael, testing the braided rope with his weight. "See! The riata is strong. We will lower a man by it. Who is the brave one who will go down?"

"I," said Vicente. "I will be the brave one to go down—"

"And steal half that you find," Rafael uttered his instant suspicion. "If you go down, first must you count over to us the pesos you already possess. Then, when you come up, we can search you for all you have found. After that, when we have divided equitably, will your other pesos be returned to you."

"Then will I not go down for comrades who have no trust in me," Vicente said stubbornly. "Here, beside the well, I am as wealthy as any of you. Then why should I go down? I have heard of men dying in the bottom of wells."

"In God's name go down!" stormed the Jefe. "Haste! Haste!"

"I am too fat, the rope is not strong, and I shall not go down," said Vicente.

All looked to Augustino, the silent one, who had already spoken more than he was accustomed to speak in a week. "Guillermo is the thinnest and lightest," said Augustino. "Guillermo will go down!" the rest chorused. But Guillermo, glaring apprehensively at the mouth of the well, backed away, shaking his head and crossing himself.

"Not for the sacred treasure in the secret city of the Mayas," he muttered.

The Jefe pulled his revolver and glanced to the remainder of the posse for confirmation. With eyes and head-nods they gave it.

"In heaven's name go down," he threatened the little gendarme. "And make haste, or I shall put you in such a fix that never again will you go up or down, but you will remain here and rot forever beside this hole of perdition. Is it well, comrades, that I kill him if he does not go down?" "It is well," they shouted.

And Guillermo, with trembling fingers, counted out the coins he had already retrieved, and, in the throes of fear, crossing himself repeatedly and urged on by the handthrusts of his companions, stepped upon the bucket, sat down on it with legs wrapped about it, and was lowered away out of the light of day.

"Stop!" he screamed up the shaft. "Stop! Stop! The water! I am upon it!"

Those on the sweep held it with their weight. "I should receive ten pesos extra above my share," he called up.

"You shall receive baptism," was called down to him, and, variously: "You will have your fill of water this day "; "We will let go "; "We will cut the rope "; "There will be one less with whom to share."

"The water is not nice," he replied, his voice rising like a ghost's out of the dark depth. "There are sick lizards, and a dead bird that stinks. And there may be snakes. It is well worth ten pesos extra what I must do."

"We will drown you!" Rafael shouted.

"I shall shoot down upon you and kill you!" the Jefe bullied.

"Shoot or drown me," Guillermo's voice floated up; "but it will buy you nothing, for the treasure will still be in the well."

There was a pause, in which those at the surface questioned each other with their eyes as to what they should do.

"And the Gringos are running away farther and farther," Torres fumed. "A fine discipline you have, Senor Mariano -Vercara e Hijos, over your gendarmes!"

"This is not San Antonio," the Jefe flared back. "This is the bush of Juchitan. My dogs are good dogs in San Antonio. In the bush they must be handled gently, else may they become wild dogs, and what then will happen to you and me?"

"It is the curse of gold," Torres surrendered sadly. "It is almost enough to make one become a socialist, with a Gringo thus tying the hands of justice with ropes of gold."

"Of silver," the Jefe corrected.

"You go to hell," said Torres. "As you have pointed out, this is not San Antonio but the bush of Juchitan, and here I may well tell you to go to hell. Why should you and I quarrel because of your bad temper, when our prosperity depends on standing together?"

"Besides," the voice of Guillermo drifted up, "the water is not two feet deep. You cannot drown me in it. I have just felt the bottom and I have four round silver pesos in my hand right now. The bottom is carpeted with pesos. Do you want to let go? Or do I get ten pesos extra for the filthy job? The water stinks like a fresh graveyard."

"Yes! Yes!" they shouted down.

"Which? Let go? Or the extra ten?"

"The extra ten!" they chorused.

"In God's name, haste! haste!" cried the Jefe.

They heard splashings and curses from the bottom of the well, and, from the lightening of the strain on the riata, knew that Guillermo had left the bucket and was floundering for the coin.

"Put it in the bucket, good Guillermo," Rafael called down.

"I am putting it in my pockets," up came the reply. "Did I put it in the bucket you might haul it up first and well forget to haul me up afterward."

"The double weight might break the riata," Rafael cautioned.

"The riata may not be so strong as my will, for my will in this matter is most strong," said Guillermo.

"If the riata should break … " Eafael began again.

"I have a solution," said Guillermo. "Do you come down. Then shall I go up first. Second, the treasure shall go up in the bucket. And, third and last, shall you go up. Thus will justice be triumphant."

Rafael, with dropped jaw of dismay, did not reply.

"Are you coming, Rafael?"

"No," he answered. "Put all the silver in your pockets and come up together with it."

"I could curse the race that bore me," was the impatient observation of the Jefe.

"I have already cursed it," said Torres.

"Haul away I " shouted Guillermo. " I have everything in my pockets save the stench ; and I am suffocating. Haul quick, or I shall perish, and the three hundred pesos will perish with me. And there are more than three hundred. He must have emptied his bag."

Ahead, on the trail, where the way grew steep and the horses without stamina rested and panted, Francis overtook his party.

"Never again shall I travel without minted coin of the realm," he exulted, as he described what he had remained behind to see from the edge of the deserted plantation. "Henry, when I die and go to heaven, I shall have a stout bag of cash along with me. Even there could it redeem me from heaven alone knows what scrapes. Listen! They fought like cats and dogs about the mouth of the well. Nobody would trust anybody to descend into the well unless he deposited what he had previously picked up with those that remained at the top. They were out of hand. The Jefe, at the point of his gun, had to force the littlest and leanest of them to go down. And when he was down he blackmailed them before he would come up. And when he came up they broke their promises and gave him a beating. They were still beating him when I left."

"But now your sack is empty," said Henry.

"Which is our present and most pressing trouble," Francis agreed. "Had I sufficient pesos I could keep the pursuit well behind us forever. I'm afraid I was too generous. I did not know how cheap the poor devils were. But I'll tell you something that will make your hair stand up. Torres, Senor Torres, Senor Alvarez Torres, the elegant gentleman and old-time friend of you Solanos, is leading the pursuit along with the Jefe. He is furious at the delay. They almost had a rupture because the Jefe couldn't keep his men in hand. Yes, sir, and he told the Jefe to go to hell. I distinctly heard him tell the Jefe to go to hell."

Five miles farther on, the horses of Leoncia and her father in collapse, where the trail plunged into and ascended a dark ravine, Francis urged the others on and dropped behind. Giving them a few minutes' start, he followed on behind, a self-constituted rearguard. Part way along, in an open space where grew only a thick sod of grass, he was dismayed to find the hoof-prints of the two horses staring at him as large as dinner plates from out of the sod. Into the hoofprints had welled a dark, slimy fluid that his eye told him was crude oil. This was but the beginning, a sort of seepage from a side stream above off from the main flow. A hundred yards beyond he came upon the flow itself, a river of oil that on such a slope would have been a cataract had it been water. But being crude oil, as thick as molasses, it oozed slowly down the hill like so much molasses. And here, preferring to make his stand rather than to wade through the sticky mess, Francis sat down on a rock, laid his rifle on one side of him, his automatic pistol on the other side, rolled a cigarette, and kept his ears pricked for the first sounds of the pursuit.

And the beaten peon, threatened with more beatings and belaboring his over-ridden mare, rode across the top of the ravine above Francis, and, at the oil-well itself, had his exhausted animal collapse under him. With his heels he kicked her back to her feet, and with a stick belabored her to stagger away from him and on and into the jungle. And the first day of his adventures, although he did not know it, was not yet over. He, too, squatted on a stone, his feet out of the oil, rolled a cigarette, and, as he smoked it, contemplated the flowing oil-well. The noise of approaching men startled him, and he fled into the immediately adjacent jungle, from which he peered forth and saw two strange men appear. . They came directly to the well, and, by an iron wheel turning the valve, choked down the flow still further.

"No more," commanded the one who seemed to be leader. "Another turn, and the pressure will blow out the pipes for so the Gringo engineer has warned me most carefully."

And a slight flow, beyond the limited safety, continued to run from the mouth of the gusher down the mountain side. Scarcely had the two men accomplished this, when a body of horsemen rode up, whom the peon in hiding recognized as the haciendado who owned him and the overseers and haciendados of neighboring plantations who delighted in running down a fugitive laborer in much the same way that the English delight in chasing the fox.

No, the two oil-men had seen nobody. But the haciendado who led saw the footprints of the mare, and spurred his horse to follow, his crowd at his heels.

The peon waited, smoked his cigarette quite to the finish, and cogitated. When all was clear, he ventured forth, turned the mechanism controlling the well wide open t watched the oil fountaining upward under the subterranean pressure and flowing down the mountain in a veritable river. Also, he listened to and noted the sobbing, and gasping, and bubbling of the escaping gas. This he did not comprehend, and all that saved him for his further adventures was the fact that he had used his last match to light his cigarette. In vain he searched his rags, his ears, and his hair. He was out of matches.

So, chuckling at the river of oil he was wantonly running to waste, and, remembering the canyon trail below, he plunged down the mountainside and upon Francis, who received him with extended automatic. Down went the peon on his frayed and frazzled knees in terror and supplication to the man he had twice betrayed that day. Francis studied him, at first without recognition, because of the bruised and lacerated face and head on which the blood had dried like a mask.

"Amigo, amigo," chattered the peon. But at that moment, from below on the ravine trail, Francis heard the clatter of a stone dislodged by some man's foot. The next moment he identified what was left of the peon as the pitiable creature to whom he had given half the contents of his whiskey flask.

"Well, amigo," Francis said in the native language, "it looks as if they are after you."

"They will kill me, they will beat me to death, they are very angry," the wretch quavered. "You are my only friend, my father and my mother, save me."

"Can you shoot?" Francis demanded.

"I was a hunter in the Cordilleras before I was sold into slavery, Senor," was the reply.

Francis passed him the automatic, motioned him to take shelter, and told him not to fire until sure of a hit. And to himself he mused: The golfers are out on the links right now at Tarrytown. And Mrs. Bellingham is on the clubhouse veranda wondering how she is going to pay the three thousand points she's behind and praying for a change of luck. And here am I, Lord! Lord, backed up to a river of oil ...

His musing ceased as abruptly as appeared the Jefe, Torres, and the gendarmes down the trail. As abruptly he fired his rifle, and as abruptly they fell back out of sight. He could not tell whether he had hit one, or whether the man had merely fallen in precipitate retreat. The pursuers did not care to make a rush of it, contenting themselves with bushwhacking. Francis and the peon did the same, sheltering behind rocks and bushes and frequently changing their positions.

At the end of an hour, the last cartridge in Francis' rifle was all that remained. The peon, under his warnings and threats, still retained two cartridges in the automatic. But the hour had been an hour saved for Leoncia and her people, and Francis was contentedly aware that at any moment he could turn and escape by wading across the river of oil. So all was well, and would have been well, had not, from above, come an eruption of another body of men, who, from behind trees, fired as they descended. This was the haciendado and his fellow haciendados, in chase of the fugitive peon although Francis did not know it. His conclusion was that it was another posse that was after him. The shots they fired at him were strongly confirmative.

The peon crawled to his side, showed him that two shots remained in the automatic he was returning to him, and impressively begged from him his box of matches. Next, the peon motioned him to cross the bottom of the canyon and climb the other side. With half a guess of the creature's intention, Francis complied, from his new position of vantage emptying his last rifle cartridge at the advancing posse and sending it back into shelter down the ravine.

The next moment, the river of oil flared into flame from where the peon had touched a match to it. In the following moment, clear up the mountainside, the well itself sent a fountain of ignited gas a hundred feet into the. air. And, in the moment after, the ravine itself poured a torrent of flame down upon the posse of Torres and the Jefe.

Scorched by the heat of the conflagration, Francis and the peon clawed up the opposite side of the ravine, circled around and past the blazing trail, and, at a dog-trot, raced up the recovered trail.

Chapter 10

WHILE Francis and the peon hurried up the ravine-trail in safety, the ravine itself, below where the oil flowed in, had become a river of flame, which drove the Jefe, Torres, and the gendarmes to scale the steep wall of the ravine. At the same time the party of haciendados in pursuit of the peon was compelled to claw back and up to escape out of the roaring canyon.

Ever the peon glanced back over his shoulder, until, with a cry of joy, he indicated a second black-smoke pillar rising in the air beyond the first burning well.

"More," he chuckled. "There are more wells. They will all burn. And so shall they and all their race pay for the many blows they have beaten on me. And there is a lake of oil there, like the sea, like Juchitan Inlet it is so big."

And Francis recollected the lake of oil about which the haciendado had told him that, containing at least five million barrels which could not yet be piped to sea transport, lay open to the sky, merely in a natural depression in the ground and contained by an earth dam.

"How much are you worth?" he demanded of the peon with apparent irrelevance.

But the peon could not understand.

"How much are your clothes worth all you've got on?"

"Half a peso, nay, half of a half peso," the peon admitted ruefully, surveying what was left of his tattered rags.

"And other property?"

The wretched creature shrugged his shoulders in token of his utter destitution, then added bitterly:

"I possess nothing but a debt. I owe two hundred and fifty pesos. I am tied to it for life, damned with it for life like a man with a cancer. That is why I am a slave to the haciendado."

"Huh!" Francis could not forbear to grin. "Worth two hundred and fifty pesos less than nothing, not even a cipher, a sheer abstraction of a minus quantity without existence save in the mathematical imagination ol man, and yet here you are burning up not less than millions of pesos' worth of oil. And if the strata is loose and erratic and the oil leaks up outside the tubing, the chances are that the oil-body of the entire field is ignited say a billion dollars' worth. Say, for an abstraction enjoying two hundred and fifty dollars' worth of non-existence, you are some hombre, believe me."

Nothing of which the peon understood save the word "hombre."

"I am a man," he proclaimed, thrusting out his chest and straightening up his bruised head. "I am a hombre and I am a Maya."

"Maya Indian you?" Francis scoffed.

"Half Maya," was the reluctant admission. "My father is pure Maya. But the Maya women of the Cordilleras did not satisfy him. He must love a mixed-breed woman of the tierra calient e. I was so born; but she afterward betrayed him for a Barbadoes nigger, and he went back to the Cordilleras to live. And, like my father, I was born to love a mixed breed of the tierra calient e. She wanted money, and my head was fevered with want of her, and I sold myself to be a peon for two hundred pesos. And I saw never her nor the money again. For five years I have been a peon. For five years I have slaved and been beaten, and behold, at the end of five years my debt is not two hundred but two hundred and fifty pesos."

And while Francis Morgan and the long -suffering Maya half-breed plodded on deeper into the Cordilleras to overtake their party, and while the oil fields of Juchitan continued to go up in increasing smoke, still farther on, in the heart of the Cordilleras, were preparing other events destined to bring together all pursuers and all pursued Francis and Henry and Leoncia and their party; the peon; the party of the haciendados; and the gendarmes of the Jefe, and, along with them, Alvarez Torres, eager to win for himself not only the promised reward of Thomas Regan but the possession of Leoncia Solano.

In a cave sat a man and a woman. Pretty the latter was, and young, a mestizo,, or half-caste woman. By the light of a cheap kerosene lamp she read aloud from a calf-bound tome which was a Spanish translation of Blackstone. Both were barefooted and bare-armed, clad in hooded gabardines of sack-cloth. Her hood lay back on her shoulders, exposing her black and generous head of hair. But the old man's hood was cowled about his head after the fashion of a monk. The face, lofty and ascetic, beaked with power, was pure Spanish. Don Quixote might have worn precisely a similar face. But there was a difference. The eyes of this old man were closed in the perpetual dark of the blind. Never could he behold a windmill at which to tilt.

He sat, while the pretty mestizo, read to him, listening and brooding, for all the world in the pose of Bodin's "Thinker." Nor was he a dreamer, nor a tilter of windmills, like Don Quixote. Despite his blindness, that ever veiled the apparent face of the world in invisibility, he was a man of action, and his soul was anything but blind, penetrating unerringly beneath the show of things to the heart and the soul of the world and reading its inmost sins and rapacities and noblenesses and virtues.

He lifted his hand and put a pause in the reading, while he thought aloud from the context of the reading.

"The law of man," he said with slow certitude, "is to-day a game of wits. Not equity, but wit, is the game of law to-day. The law in its inception was good; but the way of the law, the practice of it, has led men off into false pursuits. They have mistaken the way for the goal, the means for the end. Yet is law law, and necessary, and food. Only, law, in its practice to-day, has gone astray, udges and lawyers engage in competitions and affrays of wit and learning, quite forgetting the plaintiffs and defendants, before them and paying them, who are seeking equity and justice and not wit and learning.

"Yet is old Blackstone right. Under it all, at the bottom of it all, at the beginning of the building of the edifice of the law, is the quest, the earnest and sincere quest of righteous men, for justice and equity. But what is it that the Preacher said? 'They made themselves many inventions.' And the law, good in its beginning, has been invented out of all its intent, so that it serves neither litigants nor injured ones, but merely the fatted judges and the lean and hungry lawyers who achieve names and paunches if they prove themselves cleverer than their opponents and than the judges who render decision."

He paused, still posed as Bodin's "Thinker," and meditated, while the mestizo, woman waited his customary signal to resume the reading. At last, as out of a profound of thought in which universes had been weighed in the balance, he spoke:

"But we have law, here in the Cordilleras of Panama, that is just and right and all of equity. We work for no man and serve not even paunches. Sack-cloth and not broadcloth conduces to the equity of judicial decision. Read on, Mercedes. Blackstone is always right if always rightly read which is what is called a paradox, and is what modern law ordinarily is, a paradox. Read on. Blackstone is the very foundation of human law but, oh, how many wrongs are cleverly committed by clever men in his name!"

Ten minutes later, the blind thinker raised his head, sniffed the air, and gestured the girl to pause. Taking her cue from him, she, too, sniffed:

"Perhaps it is the lamp, Just One," she suggested.

"It is burning oil," he said. "But it is not the lamp. It is from far away. Also, have I heard shooting in the canyons."

"I heard nothing" she began.

"Daughter, you who see have not the need to hear that I have. There have been many shots fired in the canyons. Order my children to investigate and make report."

Bowing reverently to the old man who could not see but who, by keen-trained hearing and conscious timing of her every muscular action, knew that she had bowed, the young woman lifted the curtain of blankets and passed out into the day. At either side the cave-mouth sat a man of the peon class. Each was armed with rifle and machete, while through their girdles were thrust naked-bladed knives. At the girl's order, both arose and bowed, not to her, but to the command and the invisible source of the command. One of them tapped with the back of his machete against the stone upon which he had been sitting, then laid his ear to the stone and listened. In truth, the stone was but the out-jut of a vein of metalliferous ore that extended across and through the heart of the mountain. And beyond, on the opposite slope, in an eyrie commanding the magnificent panorama of the descending slopes of the Cordilleras, sat another peon who first listened with his ear pressed to similar metalliferous quartz, and next tapped response with his machete. After that, he stepped half a dozen paces to a tall tree, half-dead, reached into the hollow heart of it, and pulled on the rope within as a man might pull who was ringing a steeple bell.

But no sound was evoked. Instead, a lofty branch, fifty feet above his head, sticking out from the main-trunk like a semaphore arm, moved up and down like the semaphore arm it was. Two miles away, on a mountain crest, the branch of a similar semaphore tree replied. Still beyond that, and farther down the slopes, the flashing of a hand-mirror in the sun heliographed the relaying of the blind man's message from the cave. And all that portion of the Cordilleras became voluble with coded speech of vibrating ore-veins, sun-flashings, and waving tree-branches.

While Enrico Sola-no, slenderly erect on his horse as an Indian youth and convoyed on either side by his sons, Alesandro and Kicardo, hanging to his saddle trappings, made the best of the time afforded them by Francis' rearguard battle with the gendarmes, Leoncia, on her mount, and Henry Morgan, lagged behind. One or the other was continually glancing back for the sight of Francis overtaking them. Watching his opportunity, Henry took the backtrail. Five minutes afterward, Leoncia, no less anxious than he for Francis' safety, tried to turn her horse about. But the animal, eager for the companionship of its mate ahead, refused to obey the rein, cut up and pranced, and then deliberately settled into a balk. Dismounting and throwing her reins on the ground in the Panamanian method of tethering a saddle horse, Leoncia took the back trail on foot. So rapidly did she follow Henry, that she was almost treading on his heels when he encountered Francis and the peon. The next moment, both Henry and Francis were chiding her for her conduct; but in both their voices was the involuntary tenderness of love, which pleased neither to hear the other uttering.

Their hearts more active than their heads, they were caught in total surprise by the party of haciendados that dashed out upon them with covering rifles from the surrounding jungle. Despite the fact that they had thus captured the runaway peon, whom they proceeded to kick and cuff, all would have been well with Leoncia and the two Morgans had the owner of the peon, the old-time friend of the Solano family, been present. But an attack of the malarial fever, which was his due every third day, had stretched him out in a chill near the burning oilfield.

Nevertheless, though by their blows they reduced the peon to weepings and pleadings on his knees, the haciendados were courteously gentle to Leoncia and quite decent to Francis and Henry, even though they tied the hands of the latter two behind them in preparation for the march up the ravine slope to where the horses had been left. But upon the peon, with Latin-American cruelty, they continued to reiterate their rage.

Yet were they destined to arrive nowhere, by themselves, with their captives. Shouts of joy heralded the debouchment upon the scene of the Jefe's gendarmes and of the Jefe and Alvarez Torres. Arose at once the rapid-fire, staccato, bastard-Latin of all men of both parties of pursuers, trying to explain and demanding explanation at one and the same time. And while the farrago of all talking simultaneously and of no one winning anywhere in understanding, made anarchy of speech, Torres, with a nod to Francis and a sneer of triumph to Henry, ranged before Leoncia and bowed low to her in true and deep hidalgo courtesy and respect.

"Listen!" he said, low-voiced, as she rebuffed him with an arm movement of repulsion. "Do not misunderstand me. Do not mistake me. I am here to save you, and, no matter what may happen, to protect you. You are the lady of my dreams. I will die for you yes, and gladly, though far more gladly would I live for you."

"I do not understand," she replied curtly. "I do not see life or death in the issue. We have done no wrong. I have done no wrong, nor has my father. Nor has Francis Morgan, nor has Henry Morgan. Therefore, sir, the matter is not a question of life or death."

Henry and Francis, shouldering close to Leoncia, on either side, listened and caught through the hubble-bubble of many voices the conversation of Leoncia and Torres.

"It is a question absolute of certain death by execution for Henry Morgan," Torres persisted. "Proven beyond doubt is his conviction for the murder of Alfaro Solano, who was your own full-blood uncle and your father's own fullblood brother. There is no chance to save Henry Morgan. But Francis Morgan can I save in all surety, if—"

"If?" Leoncia queried, with almost the snap of jaws of a she-leopard.

"If… you prove kind to me, and marry me," Torres said with magnificent steadiness, although two Gringos, helpless, their hands tied behind their backs, glared at him through their eyes their common desire for his immediate extinction.

Torres, in a genuine outburst of his passion, though his rapid glances had assured him of the helplessness of the two Morgans, seized her hands in his and urged:

"Leoncia, as your husband I might be able to do something for Henry. Even may it be jpossible for me to save his life and his neck, if he will yield to leaving Panama immediately."

"You Spanish dog!" Henry snarled at him, struggling with his tied hands behind his back in an effort to free them.

"Gringo cur!" Torres retorted, as, with an open backhanded blow, he struck Henry on the mouth.

On the instant Henry's foot shot out, and the kick in Torres' side drove him staggering in the direction of Francis, who was no less quick with a kick of his own. Back and forth like a shuttlecock between the battledores, Torres was kicked from one man to the other, until the gendarmes seized the two Gringos and began to beat them in their helplessness. Torres not only urged the gendarmes on, but

47

himself drew a knife; and a red tragedy might have happened with offended Latin-American blood up and raging, had not a score or more of armed men silently appeared and silently taken charge of the situation. Some of the mysterious newcomers were clad in cotton singlets and trousers, and others were in cowled gabardines of sackcloth.

The gendarmes and haciendados recoiled in fear, crossing themselves, muttering prayers and ejaculating: "The Blind Brigand! ""The Cruel Just One! "' They are his people I" "We are lost."

But the much-beaten peon sprang forward and fell on his bleeding knees before a stern-faced man who appeared to be the leader of the Blind Brigand's men. From the mouth of the peon poured forth a stream of loud lamentation and outcry for justice.

"You know that justice to which you appeal?" the leader spoke gutturally.

"Yes, the Cruel Justice," the peon replied. "I know what it means to appeal to the Cruel Justice, yet do I appeal, for I seek justice and my cause is just."

"I, too, demand the Cruel Justice!" Leoncia cried with flashing eyes, although she added in an undertone to Francis and Henry: "Whatever the Cruel Justice is."

"It will have to go some to be unfairer than the justice we can expect from Torres and the Jefe," Henry replied in similar undertones, then stepped forward boldly before the cowled leader and said loudly: "And I demand the Cruel Justice."

The leader nodded.

"Me, too," Francis murmured low, and then made loud demand.

The gendarmes did not seem to count in the matter, while the haciendados signified their willingness to abide by whatever justice the Blind Brigand might mete out to them. Only the Jefe objected.

"Maybe you don't know who I am," he blustered. "I am Mariano Vercara e Hijos, of long illustrious name and long and honorable career. I am Jefe Politico of San Antonio, the highest friend of the governor, and high in the confidence of the government of the Republic of Panama. I am the law. There is but one law and one justice, which is of Panama and not the Cordilleras. I protest against this mountain law you call the Cruel Justice. I shall send an army against your Blind Brigand, and the buzzards will peck his bones in San Juan."

"Remember," Torres sarcastically warned the irate Jefe, "that this is not San Antonio, but the bush of Juchitan. Also, you have no army."

"Have these two men been unjust to any one who has appealed to the Cruel Justice?" the leader asked abruptly.

"Yes," asseverated the peon. "They have beaten me. Everybody has beaten me. They, too, have beaten me and without cause. My hand is bloody. My body is bruised and torn. Again I appeal to the Cruel Justice, and I charge these two men with injustice."

The leader nodded and to his own men indicated the disarming of the prisoners and the order of the march.

"Justice! I demand equal justice!" Henry cried out. "My hands are tied behind my back. All hands should be so tied, or no hands be so tied. Besides, it is very difficult to walk when one is so tied."

The shadow of a smile drifted the lips of the leader as he directed his men to cut the lashings that invidiously advertised the inequality complained of.

"Huh!" Francis grinned to Leoncia and Henry. "I have a vague memory that somewhere around a million years ago I used to live in a quiet little old burg called New York, where we foolishly thought we were the wildest and wickedest that ever cracked at a golf ball, electrocuted an

Inspector of Police, battled with Tammany, or bid four nullos with five sure tricks in one's own hand."

"Huh!" Henry vouchsafed half an hour later, as the trail, from a lesser crest, afforded a view of higher crests beyond. "Huh! and hell's bells! These gunny-sack chaps are not animals of savages. Look, Henry! They are semaphoring! See that near tree there, and that big one across the canyon. Watch the branches wave."

Blindfold for a number of miles at the last, the prisoners, still blindfolded, were led into the cave where the Cruel Justice reigned. When the bandages were removed, they found themselves hi a vast and lofty cavern, lighted by many torches, and, confronting them, a blind and white-haired man in sackcloth seated on a rock-hewn throne, with, beneath him, her shoulder at his knees, a pretty mestiza woman.

The blind man spoke, and in his voice was the thin and bell-like silver of age and weary wisdom.

"The Cruel Justice has been invoked. Speak! Who demands decision and equity?"

All held back, and not even the Jefe could summon heart of courage to protest against Cordilleras law.

"There is a woman present," continued the Blind Brigand. "Let her speak first. All mortal men and women are guilty of something or else are charged by their fellows with some guilt."

Henry and Francis were for withstraining her, but with an equal smile to them she addressed the Cruel Just One in clear and ringing tones:

"I only have aided the man I am engaged to marry to escape from death for a murder he did not commit."

"You have spoken," said the Blind Brigand. "Come forward to me."

Piloted by sackcloth men, while the two Morgans who loved her were restless and perturbed, she was made to kneel at the blind man's knees. The mestiza girl placed his hand on Leoncia's head. For a full and solemn minute silence obtained, while the steady fingers of the Blind One rested about her forehead and registered the pulse-beats of her temples. Then he removed his hand and leaned back to decision.

"Arise, Senorita," he pronounced. "Your heart is clean of evil. You go free. Who else appeals to the Cruel Justice?"

Francis immediately stepped forward.

"I likewise helped the man to escape from an undeserved death. The man and I are of the same name, and, distantly, of the same blood."

He, too, knelt, and felt the soft finger-lobes play delicately over his brows and temples and come to rest finally on the pulse of his wrist.

"It is not all clear to me," said the Blind One. "You are not at rest nor at peace with your soul. There is trouble within you that vexes you."

Suddenly the peon stepped forth and spoke unbidden, his voice evoking a thrill as of the shock of blasphemy from the sackcloth men.

"Oh, Just One, let this man go," said the peon passionately. "Twice was I weak and betrayed him to his enemy this day, and twice this day has he protected me from my enemy and saved me."

And the peon, once again on his knees, but this time at the knees of justice, thrilled and shivered with superstitious awe, as he felt wander over him the light but firm fingertouches of the strangest judge man ever knelt before. Bruises and lacerations were swiftly explored even to the shoulders and down the back.

"The other man goes free," the Cruel Just One announced. "Yet is there trouble and unrest within him. It one here who knows and will speak up?"

And Francis knew on the instant the trouble the blind man had divined within him the full love that burned in him for Leoncia and that threatened to shatter the full loyalty he must ever bear to Henry. No less quick was Leoncia in knowing, and could the blind man have beheld the involuntary glance of knowledge the man and woman threw at each other and the immediate embarrassment of averted eyes, he could have unerringly diagnosed Francis' trouble. The mestiza girl saw, and with a leap at her heart scented a love affair. Likewise had Henry seen and unconsciously scowled.

The Just One spoke:

"An affair of heart undoubtedly," he dismissed the matter. "The eternal vexation of woman In the heart of man. Nevertheless, this man stands free. Twice, in the one day, has he succored the man who twice betrayed him. Nor has the trouble within him aught to do with the aid he rendered the man said to be sentenced to death undeserved. Remains to question this last man; also to settle for this beaten creature before me who twice this day has proved weak out of selfishness, and who has just now proved bravely strong out of unselfishness for another."

He leaned forward and played his fingers searchingly over the face and brows of the peon.

"Are you afraid to die?" he asked suddenly.

"Great arid Holy One, I am sore afraid to die," was the peon's reply.

"Then say that you have lied about this man, say that his twice succoring of you was a lie, and you shall live."

Under the Blind One's fingers the peon cringed and wilted.

"Think well," came the solemn warning. "Death is not good. To be forever unmoving, as the clod and rock, is not good. Say that you have lied and life is yours. Speak!"

But, although his voice shook from the exquisiteness of his fear, the peon rose to the full spiritual stature of a man.

"Twice this day did I betray him, Holy One. But my name is not Peter. Not thrice in this day will I betray him. I am sore afraid, but I cannot betray him thrice."

The blind judge leaned back and his face beamed and glowed as if transfigured.

"Well spoken," he said. "You have the makings of a man. I now lay my sentence upon you: From now on, through all your days under the sun, you shall always think like a man, act like a man, be a man. Better to die a man any time, than live a beast forever in time. The Ecclesiast was wrong. A dead lion is always better than a live dog. Go free, regenerate son, go free."

But, as the peon, at a signal from the mestiza, started to rise, the blind judge stopped him.

"In the beginning, O man who but this day has been born man, what was the cause of all your troubles?"

"My heart was weak and hungry, Holy One, for a mixed-breed woman of the tierra caliente. I myself am mountain born. For her I put myself in debt to the haciendado for the sum of two hundred pesos. She fled with the money and another man. I remained the slave of the haciendado, who is not a bad man,- but who, first and always, is a haciendado. I have toiled, been beaten, and have suffered for five long years, and my debt is now become two hundred and fifty pesos, and yet I possess naught but these rags and a body weak from insufficient food."

"Was she wonderful? this woman of the tierra caliente?" the blind judge queried softly.

"I was mad for her, Holy One. I do not think now that she was wonderful. But she was wonderful then. The fever of her burned my heart and brain and made a taskslave of me, though she fled in the night and I knew her never again."

The peon waited, on his knees, with bowed head, while, to the amazement of all, the Blind Brigand sighed deeply and seemed to forget time and place. His hand strayed involuntarily and automatically to the head of the mestiza, caressed the shining black hair and continued to caress it while he spoke.

"The woman," he said, with such gentleness that his voice, still clear and bell-like, was barely above a whisper. "Ever the woman wonderful. All women are wonderful ... to man. They love our fathers; they birth us; we love them; they birth our sons to love their daughters and to call their daughters wonderful ; and this has always beefa and shall continue always to be until the end of man's time and man's loving on earth."

A profound of silence fell within the cavern, while the Cruel Just One meditated for a space. At the last, with a touch dared of familiarity, the pretty mestiza touched him and roused him to remembrance of the peon still crouching at his feet.

"I pronounce judgment," he spoke. "You have received many blows. Each blow on your body is quittance in full of the entire debt to the haciendado. Go free. But remain in the mountains, and next time love a mountain woman, since woman you must have, and since woman is inevitable and eternal in the affairs of men. Go free. You are half Maya?"

"I am half Maya," the peon murmured. "My father is a Maya."

"Arise and go free. And remain in the mountains with your Maya father. The tierra caliente is no place for the Cordilleras-born. The haciendado is not present, and therefore cannot be judged. And after all he is but a haciendado. His fellow haciendados, too, go free."

The Cruel Just One waited, and, without waiting, Henry stepped forward.

"I am the man," he stated boldly, "sentenced to the death undeserved for the killing of a man I did not kill. He was the blood-uncle of the girl I love, whom I shall marry if there be true justice here in this cave in the Cordilleras."

But the Jefe interrupted.

"Before a score of witnesses he threatened to his face to kill the man. Within the hour we found him bending over the man's dead body that was yet warm and limber with departing life."

"He speaks true," Henry affirmed. "I did threaten the man, both of us heady from strong drink and hot blood. I was so found, bending over his dead warm body. Yet did I not kill him. Nor do I know, nor can I guess, the coward hand in the dark that knifed out his life through the back from behind."

"Kneel both of you, that I may interrogate you," the Blind Brigand commanded.

Long he interrogated with his sensitive, questioning fingers. Long, and still longer, unable to attain decision, his fingers played over the faces and pulses of the two men.

"Is there a woman?" he asked Henry Morgan pointedly.

"A woman wonderful. I love her."

"It is good to be so vexed, for a man unvexed by woman is only half a man," the blind judge vouchsafed. He addressed the Jefe. "No woman vexes you, yet are you troubled. But this man "indicating Henry "I cannot tell if all his vexation be due to woman. Perhaps, in part, it may be due to you, or to what some prompting of evil may make him meditate against you. Stand up, both men of you. I cannot judge between you. Yet is there the test infallible, the test of the Snake and the Bird. Infallible it is, as God is infallible, for by such ways does God still maintain truth in the affairs of men. As well does Blackstone mention just such methods of determining the truth by trial and ordeal."

Chapter 11

To all intents it might have been a tiny bull-ring, that pit in the heart of the Blind Brigand's domain.

Ten feet in depth and thirty in diameter, with level floor and perpendicular wall, its natural formation had required little work at the hands of man to complete its symmetry. The sackcloth men, the haciendados, the gendarmes all were present, save for the Cruel Just One and the mestiza, and all were lined about the rim of the pit, as an audience, to gaze down upon some bullfight or gladiatorial combat within the pit.

At command of the stern-faced leader of the sackcloth men who had captured them, Henry and the Jefe descended down a short ladder into the pit. The leader and several of the brigands accompanied them.

"Heaven alone knows what's going to happen," Henry laughed up in English to Leoncia and Francis. "But if it's rough and tumble, bite and gouge, or Marquis of Queensbury or London Prize Eing, Mister Fat Jefe is my meat. But that old blind one is clever, and the chances are he's going to put us at each other on some basis of evenness. In which case, do you, my audience, if he gets me down,, stick your thumbs up and make all the noise you can. Depend upon it, if it's he that's down, all his crowd will be thumbs up."

The Jefe, overcome by the trap into which he had descended, in Spanish addressed the leader.

"I shall not fight with this man. He is younger than I, and has better wind. Also, the affair is illegal. It is not according to the law of the Eepublic of Panama. It is extra-territorial and entirely unjudicial."

"It is the Snake and the Bird," the leader shut him off. "You shall be the Snake. This rifle shall be in your hands. The other man shall be the Bird. In his hand shall be the bell. Behold! Thus may you understand the ordeal."

At his command, one of the brigands was given the rifle and was blindfolded. To another brigand, not blindfolded, was given a silver bell.

"The man with the rifle is the Snake," said the leader. "He has one shot at the Bird who carries the bell."

At signal to begin, the bandit with the bell, tinkled it at extended arm's length and sprang swiftly aside. The man with the rifle lowered it as if to fire at the space just vacated and pretended to fire.

"You understand?" the leader demanded of Henry and the Jefe.

The former nodded, but the latter cried exultantly:

"And I am the Snake?"

"You are the Snake," affirmed the leader.

And the Jefe was eager for the rifle, making no further protests against the extra-territoriality of the proceedings.

"Are you going to try to get me?" Henry warned the Jefe.

"No, Senor Morgan. I am merely going to get you. I am one of the two best shots in Panama. I have two score and more of medals. I can shoot with my eyes shut. I can shoot in the dark. I have often shot, and with precision, in the dark. Already may you count yourself a dead man."

Only one cartridge was put into the rifle, ere it was handed to the Jefe after he was blindfolded. Next, while Henry, equipped with the tell-tale bell, was stationed directly across the pit, the Jefe was faced to the wall and kept there while the brigands climbed out of the pit and drew the ladder up after them. The leader, from above, spoke down:

"Listen carefully, Senor Snake, and make no move until you have heard. The Snake has but one shot. The Snake cannot tamper with his blindfold. If he so tampers it is our duty to see that he immediately dies. The Snake has no time limit. He may take the rest of the day, and all of the night, and the remainder of eternity ere he fires his one shot. As for the Bird, the one rule is that never must the bell leave his hand, and never may he stop the clapper of it from making the full noise intended of the clapper against the sides of the bell. Should he do so, then will he immediately die. We are here above you, both of you Senors, rifles in hand, to see that you die the second you infract any of the rules. And now, God be with the right, proceed!"

The Jefe turned slowly about and listened, while Henry, essaying gingerly to move with the bell, caused it to tinkle. The rifle was quick to bear upon the sound, and to pursue it as Henry ran. With a quick shift he transferred the bell to the other extended hand and ran back in the opposite direction, the rifle sweeping after him in inexorable pursuit. But the Jefe was too cunning to risk all on a chance shot, and slowly advanced across the arena. Henry stood still, and the bell made no sound.

So unerringly had the Jefe's ear located the last silvery tinkle, and so straightly did he walk despite his blindfold, that he advanced just to the right of Henry and directly at the bell. With infinite caution, provoking no tinkle, Henry slightly raised his arm and permitted the Jefe's head to go under the bell with a bare inch of margin.

His rifle pointed, and within a foot of the pit-wall, the Jefe halted in indecision, listened vainly for a moment, then made a further stride that collided the rifle muzzle with the wall. He whirled about, and, with the rifle extended, like any blind man felt out the air-space for his enemy. The muzzle would have touched Henry had he not sprung away on a noisy and zig-zag course.

In the center of the pit he came to a frozen pause. The Jefe stalked past a yard to the side and collided with the opposite wall. He circled the wall, walking cat-footed, his rifle forever feeling out into the empty air. Next he ventured across the pit. After several such crossings, during which the stationary bell gave him no clue, he adopted a clever method. Tossing his hat on the ground for the mark of his starting point, he crossed the edge of the pit on a shallow chord, extended the chord by a pace farther along the wall, and felt his way back along the new and longer chord. Again against the wall, he verified the correctness of the parallelness of the two chords, by pacing back to his hat. This time, with three paces along the wall from the hat, he initiated his third chord.

Thus he combed the area of the pit, and Henry saw that he could not escape such combing. Nor did he wait to be discovered. Tinkling the bell as he ran and zigzagged and exchanging it from one hand to the other, he froze into immobility in a new place.

The Jefe repeated the laborious combing out process ; but Henry was not minded longer to prolong the tension. He waited till the Jefe's latest chord brought him directly upon him. He waited till the rifle muzzle, breast high, was within half a dozen inches of his heart. Then he exploded into two simultaneous actions. He ducked lower than the rifle and yelled "Fire!" in stentorian command.

So startled, the Jefe pulled the trigger, and the bullet sped above Henry's head. From above, the sackcloth men applauded wildly. The Jefe tore off his blindfold and saw the smiling face of his foe.

"It is well God has spoken," announced the sackcloth leader, as he descended into the pit. "The man uninjured is innocent. Remains now to test the other man."

"Me?" the Jefe almost shouted in his surprise and consternation.

"Greetings, Jefe," Henry grinned. "You did try to get me. It's my turn now. Pass over that rifle."

But the Jefe, with a curse, in his disappointment and rage forgetting that the rifle had contained only one cartridge, thrust the muzzle against Henry's heart and pulled the trigger. The hammer fell with a metallic click.

"It is well," said the leader, taking away the rifle and recharging it. "Your conduct shall be reported. The test for you remains, yet must it appear that you are not acting like God's chosen man."

Like a beaten bull in the ring seeking a way to escape and gazing up at the amphitheatre of pitiless faces, so the Jefe looked up and saw only the rifles of the sackcloth men, the triumphing faces of Leoncia and Francis, the curious looks of his own gendarmes, and the blood-eager faces of the haciendados that were like the faces of any bull-fight audience.

The shadowy smile drifted the stern lips of the leader as he handed the rifle to Henry and started to blindfold him.

"Why don't you make him face the wall until I'm ready?" the Jefe demanded, as the silver bell tinkled in his passion-convulsed hand.

"Because he is proven God's man," was the reply. "He has stood the test. Therefore he cannot do a treacherous deed. You now must stand the test of God. If you are true and honest, no harm can befall you from the Snake. For such is God's way."

Far more successful as the hunter than as the hunted one, did the Jefe prove. Across the pit from Henry, he strove to stand motionless; but out of nervousness, as Henry's rifle swept around on him, his hand trembled and the bell tinkled. The rifle came almost to rest and wavered ominously about the sound. In vain the Jefe tried to control his flesh and still the bell.

But the bell tinkled on, and, in despair, he flung it away and threw himself on the ground. But Henry, following the sound of his enemy's fall, lowered the rifle and pulled trigger. The Jefe yelled out in sharp pain as the bullet perforated his shoulder, rose to his feet, cursed, sprawled back on the ground, and lay there cursing.

Again in the cave, with the mestiza beside him at his knee, the Blind Brigand gave judgment.

"This man who is wounded and who talks much of the law of the tierra caliente, shall now learn Cordilleras law. By the test of the Snake and the Bird has he been proven guilty. For his life a ransom of ten thousand dollars gold shall be paid, or else shall he remain here, a hewer of wood and a carrier of water, for the remainder of the time God shall grant him to draw breath on earth. I have spoken, and I know that my voice is God's voice, and I know that God will not grant him long to draw breath if the ransom be not forthcoming."

A long silence obtained, during which even Henry, who could slay a foe in the heat of combat, advertised that such cold-blooded promise of murder was repugnant to him.

"The law is pitiless," said the Cruel Just One; and again silence fell.

"Let him die for want of a ransom," spoke one of the haciendados. "He has proved a treacherous dog. Let him die a dog's death."

"What say you?" the Blind Brigand asked solemnly. "What say you, peon of the many beatings, man new-born this day, half-Maya that you are and lover of the woman wonderful? Shall this man die the dog's death for want of a ransom?"

"This man is a hard man," spoke the peon. "Yet is my heart strangely soft this day. Had I ten thousand gold I would pay his ransom myself. Yea, O Holy One and Just, and had I two hundred and fifty pesos, even would I pay off my debt to the haciendado of which I am absolved."

The old man's blind face lighted up to transfiguration.

"You, too, speak with God's voice this day, regenerate one," he approved.

But Francis, who had been scribbling hurriedly in his check book, handed a check, still wet with the ink, to the mestiza.

"I, too, speak," he said. "Let not the man die the dog's death he deserves, proven treacherous hound that he is."

The mestiza read the check aloud.

"It is not necessary to explain," the Blind Brigand shut Francis off. "I am a creature of reason, and have not lived always in the Cordilleras. I was trained in business in Barcelona. I know the Chemical National Bank of New York, and through my agents have had dealings with it aforetime. The sum is for ten thousand dollars gold. This man who writes it has told the truth already this day. The check is good. Further, I know he will not stop payment. This man who thus pays the ransom of a foe is one of three things: a very good man ; a fool ; or a very rich man. Tell me, Man, is there a woman wonderful?"

And Francis, not daring to glance to right or left, at Leoncia or Henry, but gazing straight before him on the Blind Brigand's face, answered because he felt he must so answer:

"Yes, Cruel Just One, there is a woman wonderful."

Chapter 12

AT the precise spot where they had been first blindfolded by the sackcloth men, the cavalcade halted. It was composed of a number of the sackcloth men; of Leoncia, Henry, and Francis, blindfolded and mounted on mules; and of the peon, blindfolded and on foot. Similarly escorted, the haciendados, and the Jefe and Torres with their gendarmes, had preceded by half an hour.

At permission given by the stern-faced leader, the captives, about to be released, removed their blindfolds.

"Seems I've been here before," Henry laughed, looking about and identifying the place.

"Seems the oil-wells are still burning," Francis said, pointing out half the field of day that was eaten up by the black smoke-pall. "Peon, look upon your handiwork. For a man who possesses nothing, you are the biggest spender I ever met. I have heard of drunken oil-kings lighting cigars with thousand dollar bank-notes, but here are you burning up a million dollars a minute.

"I am not a poor man," the peon boasted in proud mysteriousness.

"A millionaire in disguise!" Henry twitted.

"Where do you deposit?" was Leoncia's contribution. "In the Chemical National Bank?"

The peon did not understand the allusions, but knew that he was being made fun of, and drew himself up in proud silence.

The stern leader spoke:

"From this point you may now go your various ways. The Just One has so commanded. You, senors, will dismount and turn over to me your mules. As for the senorita, she may retain her mule as a present from the Just One, who would not care to be responsible for compelling any senorita to walk. The two senors, without hardship, may walk. Especially has the Just One recommended walking for the rich senor. The possession of riches, he advised, leads to too little walking. Too little walking leads to stoutness; and stoutness does not lead to the woman wonderful. Such is the wisdom of the Just One.

"Further, he has repeated his advice to the peon to remain in the mountains. In the mountains he will find his woman wonderful, since woman he must have ; and it is wisest that such woman be of his own breed. The woman of the tierra caliente are for the men of the tierra caliente. The Cordilleras women are for the Cordilleras men. God dislikes mixed breeds. A mule is abhorrent under the sun. The world was not intended for mixed breeds, but man has made for himself many inventions. Pure races interbred leads to impurity. Neither will oil nor water congenially intermingle. Since kind begets kind, only kind should mate. Such are the words of the Just One which I have repeated as commanded. And he has especially impressed upon me to add that he knows whereof he speaks, for he, too, has sinned in just such ways."

And Henry and Francis, of Anglo-Saxon stock, and Leoncia of the Latin, knew perturbation and embarrassment as the vicarious judgment of the Blind Brigand sank home. And Leoncia, with her splendid eyes of woman, would have appealed protest to either man she loved, had the other been absent; while both Henry and Francis would have voiced protest to Leoncia had either of them been alone with her. And yet, under it all, deep down, uncannily, was a sense of the correctness of the Blind Brigand's thought. And heavily, on the heart of each, rested the burden of the conscious oppression of sin.

A crashing and scrambling in the brush diverted their train of thought, as descending the canyon slope on desperately slipping and sliding horses, appeared on the scene the haciendado with several followers. His greeting of the daughter of the Solanos was hidalgo-like and profound, and only less was the heartiness of his greeting to the two men for whom Enrico Solano had stood sponsor.

"Where is your noble father?" he asked Leoncia. "I have good news for him. In the week since I last saw you, I have been sick with fever and encamped. But by swift messengers, and favoring winds across Chiriqui Lagoon to Bocas del Toro, I have used the government wireless the Jefe of Bocas del Toro is my friend and have communicated with the President of Panama who is my ancient comrade whose nose I rubbed as often in the dirt as did he mine in the boyhood days when we were schoolmates and cubicle-mates together at Colon. And the word has come back that all is well; that justice has miscarried in the court at San Antonio from the too great but none the less worthy zeal of the Jefe Politico ; and that all is forgiven, pardoned, and forever legally and politically forgotten against all of the noble Solano family and their two noble Gringo friends—"

Here, the haciendado bowed low to Henry and Francis. And here, skulking behind Leoncia's uncle, his eyes chanced to light on the peon; and, so lighting, his eyes blazed with triumph.

"Mother of God, fhou has net forgotten me!" he breathed fervently, then turned to the several friends who accompanied him. "There he is, the creature without reason or shame who has fled his debt of me. Seize him! I shall put him on his back for a month from the beating he shall receive!"

So speaking, the haciendado sprang around the rump of Leoncia's mule; and the peon, ducking under the mule's nose, would have won to the freedom of the jungle, had not another of the haciendados, with quick spurs to his horse's sides, cut him off and run him down. In a trice, used to just such work, the haciendados had the luckless wight on his feet, his hands tied behind him, a lead-rope made fast around his neck.

In one voice Francis and Henry protested.

"Senors," the haciendado replied, "my respect and consideration and desire to serve you are as deep as for the noble Solano family under whose protection you are. Your safety and comfort are sacred to me. I will defend you from harm with my life. I am yours to command. My hacienda is yours, likewise all I possess. But this matter of this peon is entirely another matter. He is none of yours. He is my peon, in my debt, who has run away from my hacienda. You will understand and forgive me, I trust. This is a mere matter of property. He is my property."

Henry and Francis glanced at each other in mutual perplexity and indecision. It was the law of the land, as they thoroughly knew.

"The Cruel Just One did remit my debt, as all here will witness," the peon whispered.

"It is true, the Cruel Justice remitted his debt," Leoncia verified.

The haciendado smiled and bowed low.

"But the peon contracted with me," he smiled. "And who is the Blind Brigand that his foolish law shall operate on my plantation and rob me of my rightful two hundred and fifty pesos?"

"He's right, Leoncia," Henry admitted.

"Then will I go back to the high Cordilleras," the peon asserted. "Oh, you men of the Cruel Just One, take me back to the Cordilleras."

But the stern leader shook his head.

"Here you were released. Our orders went no further. No further jurisdiction have we over you. We shall now bid farewell and depart."

"Hold on!" Francis cried, pulling out his check book and beginning to write. "Wait a moment. I must settle for this peon now. Next, before you depart, I have a favor to ask of you."

He passed the check to the haciendado, saying:

"I have allowed ten pesos for the exchange."

The haciendado glanced at the check, folded it away in his pocket, and placed the end of the rope around the wretched creature's neck in Francis' hand.

"The peon is now yours," he said.

Francis looked at the rope and laughed.

"Behold! I now own a human chattel. Slave, you are mine, my property now, do you understand?"

"Yes, Senor," the peon muttered humbly. "It seems, when I became mad for the woman I gave up my freedom for, that God destined me always afterward to- be the property of some man. The Cruel

Just One is right. It is God's punishment for mating outside my race."

"You made a slave of yourself for what the world has always considered the best of all causes, a woman," Francis observed, cutting the thongs that bound the peon's hands. "And so, I make a present of you to yourself." So saying, he placed the neck-rope in the peon's hand. "Henceforth, lead yourself, and put not that rope in any man's hand."

While the foregoing had been taking place, a lean old man, on foot, had noiselessly joined the circle. Maya Indian he was, pure-blooded, with ribs that corrugated plainly through his parchment -like skin. Only a breechclout covered his nakedness. His unkempt hair hung in dirty -gray tangles about his face, which was high-cheeked, and emaciated to cadaverousness. Strings of muscles showed for his calves and biceps. A few scattered snags of teeth were visible between his withered lips. The hollows under his check-bones were prodigious. While his eyes, beads of black, deep-sunk in their sockets, burned with the wild light of a patient in fever.

He slipped eel-like through the circle and clasped the peon in his skeleton-like arms.

"He is my father," proclaimed the peon proudly. "Look at him. He is pure Maya, and he knows the secrets of the Mayas."

And while the two re-united ones talked endless explanations, Francis preferred his request to the sackcloth leader to find Enrico Solano and his two sons, wandering somewhere in the mountains, and to tell them that they were free of all claims of the law and to return home.

"They have done no wrong?" the leader demanded. "No; they have done no wrong," Francis assured him. "Then it is well. I promise you to find them immediately, for we know the direction of their wandering, and to send them down to the coast to join you."

"And in the meantime shall you be my guests while you wait," the haciendado invited eagerly. "There is a freight schooner at anchor in Juchitan Inlet now oS my plantation, and sailing for San Antonio. I can hold her until the noble Enrico and his sons come down from the Cordilleras."

"And Francis will pay the demurrage, of course," Henry interpolated with a sly sting that Leoncia caught, although it missed Francis, who cried joyously:

"Of course I will. And it proves my contention that a checkbook is pretty good to have anywhere."

To their surprise, when they had parted from the sackcloth men, the peon and his Indian father attached themselves to the Morgans, and journeyed down through the burning oil-fields to the plantation which had been the scene of the peon's slavery. Both father and son were unremitting in their devotion, first of all to Francis, and, next, to Leoncia and Henry. More than once they noted father and sen in long and earnest conversations; and, after Enrico and his sons had arrived, when the party went down to the beach to board the waiting schooner, the peon and his Maya parent followed along. Francis essayed to say farewell to them on the beach, but the peon stated that the pair of them were likewise journeying on the schooner.

"I have told you that I was not a poor man," the peon explained, after they had drawn the party aside from the waiting sailors. "This is true. The hidden treasure of the Mayas, which the conquistadores and the priests of the Inquisition could never find, is in my keeping. Or, to be very true, is in my father's keeping. He is the descendant, in the straight line, from the ancient high priest of the Mayas. He is the last high priest. He and I have talked much and long. And we are agreed that riches do not make life. You bought me for two hundred and fifty pesos, yet you made me free, gave me back to myself. The gift of a man's life is greater than all the treasure in the world. So are we agreed, my father and I. And so, since it is the way of Gringos and Spaniards to desire treasure, we will lead you to the Maya treasure, my father and I, my father knowing the way. And the way into the mountains begins from San Antonio and not from Juchitan."

"Does your father know the location of the treasure? just where it is?" Henry demanded, with an aside to Francis that this was the very Maya treasure that had led him to abandon the quest for Morgan's gold on the Calf and to take to the mainland.

The peon shook his head.

"My father has never been to it. He was not interested in it, caring not for wealth for himself. Father, bring forth the tale written in our ancient language which you alone of living Mayas can read."

From within his loin-cloth the old man drew forth a dirty and much-frayed canvas bag. Out ot this he pulled what looked like a snarl of knotted strings. But the strings were twisted sennit of some fibrous forest bark, so ancient that they threatened to crumble as he handled them, while from under the touch and manipulation of his fingers a fine powder of decay arose. Muttering and mumbling prayers in the ancient Maya tongue, he held up the snarl of knots, and bowed reverently before it ere he shook it out.

"The knot-writing, the lost written language of the Mayas," Henry breathed softly. "This is the real thing, if only the old geezer hasn't forgotten how to read it."

All heads bent curiously toward it as it was handed to Francis. It was in the form of a crude tassel, composed of many thin, long strings. Not alone were the knots, and various kinds of knots, tied at irregular intervals in the strings, but the strings themselves were of varying lengths and diameters. He ran them through his fingers, mumbling and muttering.

"He reads!" cried the peon triumphantly. "All our old language is there in those knots, and he reads them as any man may read a book."

Bending closer to observe, Francis and Leoncia's hair touched, and, in the thrill of the immediately broken contact, their eyes met, producing the second thrill as they separated. But Henry, all eagerness, did not observe. He had eyes only for the mystic tassel.

"What d'you say, Francis?" he murmured. "It's big! It's big!"

"But New York is beginning to call," Francis demurred. "Oh, not its people and its fun, but its business," he added hastily, as he sensed Leoncia's unuttered reproach and hurt. "Don't forget, I'm mixed up in Tampico Petroleum and the stock market, and I hate to think how many millions are involved."

"Hell's bells!" Henry ejaculated. "The Maya treasure, if a tithe of what they say about its immensity be true, could be cut three ways between Enrico, you and me, and make each of us richer than you are now."

Still Francis was undecided, and, while Enrico expanded on the authenticity of the treasure, Leoncia managed to query in an undertone in Francis' ear:

"Have you so soon tired of ... of treasure-hunting?"

He looked at her keenly, and down at her engagement ring, as he answered in the same low tones:

"How can I stay longer in this country, loving you as I do, while you love Henry?"

It was the first time he had openly avowed his love, and Leoncia knew the swift surge of joy, followed by the no less swift surge of mantling shame that she, a woman who had always esteemed herself good, could love two men at the same time. She glanced at Henry, as if to verify her heart, and her heart answered yes. As truly did she love Henry as she did Francis, and the emotion seemed similar where the two were similar, different where they were different.

"I'm afraid I'll have to connect up with the Angelique, most likely at Bocas del Toro, and get away," Francis told Henry. "You and Enrico can find the treasure and split it two ways."

But the peon, having heard, broke into quick speech with his father, and, next, with Henry.

"You hear what he says, Francis," the latter said, holding up the sacred tassel. "You've got to go with 'us. It is you he feels grateful to for his son. He isn't giving the treasure to us, but to you. And if you don't go, he won't read a knot of the writing."

But it was Leoncia, looking at Francis with quiet wistfulness of pleading, seeming all but to say, "Please, for my sake," who really caused Francis to reverse his decision.

Chapter 13

A WEEK later, out of San Antonio on a single day, three separate expeditions started for the Cordilleras. The first, mounted on mules, was composed of Henry, Francis, the peon and his ancient parent, and of several of the Solano peons, each leading a pack-mule, burdened with supplies and outfit. Old Enrico Solano, at the last moment, had been prevented from accompanying the party because of the bursting open of an old wound received hi the revolutionary fighting of his youth.

Up the main street of San Antonio the cavalcade proceeded, passing the jail, the wall of which Francis had dynamited, and which was only even then being tardily rebuilt by the Jefe's prisoners. Torres, sauntering down the street, the latest wire from Regan tucked in his pocket, saw the Morgan outfit with surprise. "Whither away, senors?" he called.

So spontaneous that it might have been rehearsed, Francis pointed to the sky, Henry straight down at the earth, the peon to the right, and his father to the left. The curse from Torres at such impoliteness, caused all to burst into laughter, in which the mule-peons joined as they rode along.

Within the morning, at the time of the siesta hour, while all the town slept, Torres received a second surprise. This time it was the sight of Leoncia and her youngest brother, Ricardo, on mules', leading a third that was evidently loaded with a camping outfit.

The third expedition was Torres' own, neither more nor less meager than Leoncia's, for it was composed only of himself and one, Jose Mancheno, a notorious murderer of the place whom Torres, for private reasons, had saved from the buzzards of San Juan. But Torres' plans, in the matter of an expedition, were more ambitious than they appeared. Not far up the slopes of the Cordilleras dwelt the strange tribe of the Caroos. Originally founded by runaway negro slaves of Africa and Carib slaves of the Mosquito Coast, the renegades had perpetuated themselves with stolen women of the tierra caliente and with fled women slaves like themselves. Between the Mayas beyond, and the government of the

56

coast, this unique colony had maintained itself in semi-independence. Added to, in later days, by runaway Spanish prisoners, the Caroos had become a hotchpotch of, bloods and breeds, possessing a name and a taint so bad that the then governing power of Colombia, had it not been too occupied with its own particular political grafts, would have sent armies to destroy the pest-hole. And in this pest-hole of the Caroos Jose" Mancheno had been born of a Spanish -murderer father and a mestizamurderess mother. And to this pest-hole Jose Mancheno was leading Torres in order that the commands of Thomas Regan of Wall Street might be carried out.

"Lucky we found him when we did," Francis told Henry, as they rode at the rear of the last Maya priest.

"He's pretty senile," Henry nodded. "Look at him."

The old man, as he led the way, was forever pulling out the sacred tassel and mumbling and muttering as he fingered it.

"Hope the old gentleman doesn't wear it out," was Henry's fervent wish. "You'd think he'd read the directions once and remember them for a little while instead of continually pawing them over."

They rode out through the jungle into a clear space that looked as if at some time man had hewn down the jungle and fought it back. Beyond, by the vista afforded by the clearing, the mountain called Blanco Kovalo towered high in the sunny sky. The old Maya halted his mule, ran over certain strings in the tassel, pointed at the mountain, and spoke in broken Spanish:

"It says: In the foot-steps of the God wait till the eyes of Chia flash."

He indicated the particular knots of a particular string as the source of his information.

"Where are the foot-steps, old priest?" Henry demanded, staring about him at the unbroken sward.

But the old man started his mule, and, with a tattoo of bare heels on the creature's ribs, hastened it on across the clearing and into the jungle beyond.

"He's like a hound on the scent, and it looks as if the scent is getting hot," Francis remarked.

At the end of half a mile, where the jungle turned to grass-land on swift-rising slopes the old man forced his mule into a gallop which he maintained until he reached a natural depression in the ground. Three feet or more in depth, of area sufficient to accommodate a dozen persons in comfort, its form was strikingly like that which some colossal human foot could have made.

"The foot-step of the God," the old priest proclaimed solemnly, ere he slid off his mule and prostrated himself in prayer. "In the foot-step of the God must we wait till the eyes of Chia flash so say the sacred knots."

"Pretty good place for a meal," Henry vouchsafed, looking down into the depression. While waiting for the mumbo- jumbo foolery to come oft, we might as well stay our stomachs."

"If Chia doesn't object," laughed Francis. And Chia did not object, at least the old priest could not find any objection written in the knots.

While the mules were being tethered on the edge of the first break of woods, water, was fetched from a nearby spring and a fire built in the foot-step. The old Maya seemed oblivious of everything, as he mumbled endless prayers and ran the knots over and over.

"If only he doesn't blow up," Francis said. "I thought he was wild-eyed the first day we met him up in Juchitan," concurred Henry. "But it's nothing to the way his eyes are now."

Here spoke the peon, who, unable to understand a word of their English, nevertheless sensed the drift of it.

"This is very religious, very dangerous, to have anything to do with the old Maya sacred things. It is the death-road. My father knows. Many men have died. The deaths are sudden and horrible. Even Maya priests have died. My father's father so died. He, too, loved a woman of the tierra caliente. And for love of her, for gold, he sold the Maya secret and by the knot-writing led tierra caliente men to the treasure. He died. They all died. My father does not like the women of the tierra caliente now that he is old. He liked them too well in his youth, which was his sin. And he knows the danger of leading you to the treasure. Many men have sought during the centuries. Of those who found it, not one came back. It is said that even conquist adores and pirates of the English Morgan have won to the hiding-place and decorated it with their bones."

"And when your father dies," Francis queried, "then, being his son, you will be the Maya high priest?"

"No, senor," the peon shook his head. "I am only half -May a. I cannot read the knots. My father did not teach me because I was not of the pure Maya blood."

"And if he should die, right now, is there any other Maya who can read the knots?"

"No, senor. My father is the last living man who knows that ancient language."

But the conversation was broken in upon by Leoncia and Ricardo, who, having tethered their mules with the others, were gazing sheepishly down from the rim of the depression. The faces of Henry and Francis lighted with joy at the sight of Leoncia, while their mouths opened and their tongues articulated censure and scolding. Also, they insisted on her returning with Ricardo.

"But you cannot send me away before giving me something to eat," she persisted, slipping down the slope of the depression with pure feminine cunning in order to place the discussion on a closer and more intimate basis.

Aroused by their voices, the old Maya came out of a trance of prayer and observed her with wrath. And in wrath he burst upon her, intermingling occasional Spanish words and phrases with the flood of denunciation in Maya.

"He says that women are no good," the peon interpreted in the first pause. "He says women bring quarrels among men, the quick steel, the sudden death. Bad luck and God's wrath are ever upon them. Their ways are not God's ways, and they lead men to destruction. He says women are the eternal enemy of God and man, forever keeping God and man apart. He says women have ever cluttered the footsteps of God and have kept men away from travelling the path of God to God. He says this woman must go back."

With laughing eyes, Francis whistled his appreciation of the diatribe, while Henry said:

"Now will you be good, Leoncia? You see what a Maya thinks of your sex. This is no place for you. California's the place. Women vote there."

"The trouble is that the old man is remembering the woman who brought misfortune upon him in the heyday of his youth," Francis said. He turned to the peon. "Ask your father to read the knot-writing and see what it says for or against women traveling in the foot-steps of God."

In vain the ancient high priest fumbled the sacred writing. There was not to be found the slightest authoritative objection to woman.

"He's mixing his own experiences up with his mythology," Francis grinned triumphantly. "So I guess it's pretty near all right, Leoncia, for you to stay for a bite to eat. The coffee's made. After that… "

But "after that" came before. Scarcely had they seated themselves on the ground and begun to eat, when Francis, standing up to serve Leoncia with tortillas, had his hat knocked off.

"My word!" he said, sitting down. "That was sudden. Henry, take a squint and see who tried to pot-shoot me."

The next moment, save for the peon's father, all eyes were peeping across the rim of the foot-step. What they saw, creeping upon them from every side, was a nondescript and bizarrely clad horde of men who seemed members of no particular race but composed of all races. The breeds of the entire human family seemed to have moulded their lineaments and vari-colored their skins.

"The mangiest bunch I ever laid eyes on," was Francis' comment.

"They are the Caroos," the peon muttered, betraying fear.

"And who in," Francis began. Instantly he amended. "And who in Paradise are the Caroos?"

"They come from hell," was the peon's answer. "They are more savage than the Spaniard, more terrible than the Maya. They neither give nor take in marriage, nor does a priest reside among them. They are the devil's own spawn, and their ways are the devil's ways, only worse."

Here the Maya arose, and, with accusing finger, denounced Leoncia for being the cause of this latest trouble. A bullet creased his shoulder and half-whirled him about.

"Drag him down!" Henry shouted to Francis. "He's the only man who knows the knot-language; and the eyes of Chia, whatever that may mean, have not yet flashed."

Francis obeyed, with an out-reach of arm to the old fellow's legs, jerking him down in a crumpled, skeleton-like fall.

Henry loosed his rifle, and elicited a fusillade in response. Next, Ricardo, Francis, and the peon joined in. But the old man, still running his knots, fixed his gaze across the far rim of the foot-step upon a rugged wall of mountain beyond.

"Hold on!" shouted Francis, in a vain attempt to make himself heard above the shooting.

He was compelled to crawl from one to another and shake them into ceasing from firing. And to each, separately, he had to explain that all their ammunition was with the mules, and that they must be sparing with the little they had in their magazines and belts.

"And don't let them hit you," Henry warned. "They've got old muskets and blunderbuses that will drive holes through you the size of dinner-plates."

An hour later, the last cartridge, save several in Francis' automatic pistol, was gone; and to the irregular firing of the Caroos the pit replied with silence. Jose Mancheno was the first to guess the situation. He cautiously crept up to the edge of the pit to make sure, then signaled to the Caroos that the ammunition of the besieged was exhausted and to come on.

"Nicely trapped, senors," he exulted down at the defenders, while from all around the rim laughter arose from the Caroos.

But the next moment the change that came over the situation was as astounding as a transformation scene in a pantomime. With wild cries of terror the Caroos were fleeing. Such was their disorder and haste that numbers of them dropped their muskets and machetes.

"Anyway, I'll get you, Senor Buzzard," Francis pleasantly assured Mancheno, at the same time flourishing his pistol at him.

He leveled his weapon as Mancheno fled, but reconsidered and did not draw trigger.

"I've only three shots left," he explained to Henry, half in apology. "And in this country one can never tell when three shots will come in handiest, as I've found out, beyond a doubt, beyond a doubt."

"Look!" the peon cried, pointing to his father and to the distant mountainside. "That is why they ran away. They have learned the peril of the sacred things of Maya."

The old priest, running over the knots of the tassel in an ecstasy that was almost trance-like, was gazing fixedly at the distant mountainside, from which, side by side and close together, two bright flashes of light were repeating themselves.

"Twin mirrors could do it in the hands of a man," was Henry's comment.

"They are the eyes of Chia," the peon repeated. "It is so written in the knots as you have heard my father say. 'Wait in the foot-steps of the God till the eyes of Chia flash.'"

The old man rose to his feet and wildly proclaimed: "To find the treasure we must find the eyes!"

"All right, old top," Henry soothed him, as, with his small traveler's compass he took the bearings of the flashes.

"He's got a compass inside his head," Henry remarked an hour later of the old priest, who led on the foremost mule. "I check him by the compass, and, no matter how the natural obstacles compel him to deviate, he comes back to the course as if he were himself a magnetic needle."

Not since leaving the foot-step, had the flashings been visible. Only from that one spot, evidently, did the rugged landscape permit the seeing of them. Rugged the country was, broken into arroyos and cliffs, interspersed with forest patches and stretches of sand and of volcanic ash.

At last the way became impassable for their mounts, and Ricardo was left behind to keep charge of the mules and mule-peons and to make, a camp. The remainder of the party continued on, scaling the jungle-clad steep that blocked their way by hoisting themselves and one another up from root to root. The old Maya, still leading, was oblivious to Leoncia's presence.

Suddenly, half a mile farther on, he halted and shrank back as if stung by a viper. Francis laughed, and across the wild landscape came back a discordant, mocking echo. The last priest of the Mayas ran the knots hurriedly, picked out a particular string, ran its knots twice, and then announced:

"When the God laughs, beware! so say the knots."

Fifteen minutes were lost ere Henry and Francis succeeded in only partly convincing him, by repeated trials of their voices, that the thing was an echo.

Half an hour later, they debouched on a series of abruptrolling sand-dunes. Again the old man shrank back. From the sand in which they strode, arose a clamor of noise. When they stood still, all was still. A single step, and all the sand about them became vocal.

"When the God laughs, beware!" the old Maya warned.

Drawing a circle in the sand with his finger, which shouted at him as he drew it, he sank down within it on his knees, and as his knees contacted on the sand arose a very screaming and trumpeting of sound. The peon joined his father inside the noisy circle, where, with his fore-finger, the old man was tracing screeching cabalistic figures and designs.

Leoncia was overcome, and clung both to Henry and Francis. Even Francis was perturbed.

"The echo was an echo," he said. "But here is no echo. I don't understand it. Frankly, it gets my goat."

"Piffle!" Henry retorted, stirring the sand with his foot till it shouted again. "It's the barking sand. On the island of Kauai, down in the Hawaiian Islands, I have been across similar barking sands quite a place for tourists,

I assure you. Only this is a better specimen, and much noisier. The scientists have a score of high-brow theories to account for the phenomenon. It occurs in several other places in the world, as I have heard. There's only one thing to do, and that is to follow the compass bearing which leads straight across. Such sands do bark, but they have never been known to bite."

But the last of the priests could not be persuaded out of his circle, although they succeeded in disturbing him from his prayers long enough to spout a flood of impassioned Maya speech.

"He says," the son interpreted, "that we are bent on such sacrilege that the very sands cry out against us. He will go no nearer to the dread abode of Chia. Nor will I. His father died there, as is well known amongst the Mayas. He says he will not die there. He says he is not old enough to die."

"The miserable octogenarian!" Francis laughed, and was startled by the ghostly, mocking laugh of the echo, while all about them the sand-dunes bayed in chorus. "Too youthful to die! How about you, Leoncia? Are you too young to die yet a while?"

"Say," she smiled back, moving her foot slightly so as to bring a moan of reproach from the sand beneath it. "On the contrary, I am too old to die just because the cliffs echo our laughter back at us and because the sandhills bark at us. Come, let us go on. We are very close to those flashings. Let the old man wait within his circle until we come back."

She cast off their hands and stepped forward, and as they followed, all the dunes became inarticulate, while one, near to them, down the sides of which ran a slide of sand, rumbled and thundered. Fortunately for them, as they were soon to learn, Francis, at abandoning the mules, had equipped himself with a coil of thin, strong rope.

Once across the sands they encountered more echoes. On trials, they found their halloes distinctly repeated as often as six or eight times.

"Hell's bells," said Henry. "No wonder the natives fight shy of such a locality!"

Wasn't it Mark Twain who wrote about a man whose hobby was making a collection of echoes? "Francis queried.

"Never heard of him. But this is certainly some fine collection of Maya echoes. They chose the region wisely for a hiding place. Undoubtedly it was always sacred, even before the Spaniards came. The old priests knew the natural causes of the mysteries, and passed them over to the herd as mystery with a capital "M "and supernatural in origin."

Not many minutes afterward they emerged on an open, level space, close under a crannied 'and ledge-ribbed cliff, and exchanged their single-file mode of progression to threeabreast. The ground was a hard, brittle crust of surface, so crystalline and dry as never to suggest that it was aught else but crystalline and dry all the way down. In an ebullition of spirits, desiring to keep both men on an equality of favor, Leoncia seized their hands and started them into a run. At the end of half a dozen strides the disaster happened. Simultaneously Henry and Francis broke through the crust, sinking to their thighs, and Leoncia was only a second behind them in breaking through and sinking almost as deep.

"Hell's bells!" Henry muttered. "It's the very devil's own landscape."

And his low-spoken words were whispered back to him from the near-by cliffs on all sides and endlessly and sibilantly repeated.

Not at first did they fully apprehend their danger. It was when', by their struggles, they found themselves waistdeep and steadily sinking, that the two men grasped the gravity of the situation. Leoncia still laughed at the predicament, for it seemed no more than that to her.

"Quicksand," Francis gasped.

"Quicksand!" all the landscape gasped back at him, and continued to gasp it in fading ghostly whispers, repeating it and gossiping about it with gleeful unction.

"It's a pot-hole filled with quicksand," Henry corroborated.

"Maybe the old boy was right in sticking back there on the barking sands," observed Francis.

The ghostly whispering redoubled upon itself and was a long time in dying away.

By this time they were midway between waist and arm-pits and sinking as methodically as ever.

"Well, somebody's got to get out of the scrape alive," Henry remarked.

And, even without discussing the choice, both men began to hoist Leoncia up, although the effort and her weight thrust them more quickly down. When she stood, free and clear, a foot on the nearest shoulder of each of the two men she loved, Francis said, though the landscape mocked him:

"Now, Leoncia, we're going to toss you out^of this. At the word "Go! "let yourself go. And you must strike full length and softly on the crust. You'll slide a little. But don't let yourself stop. Keep on going. Crawl out to the solid land on your hands and knees. And, whatever you do, don't stand up until you reach the solid land. Beady, Henry?"

Between them, though it hastened their sinking, they swung her back and forth, free in the air, and, the third swing, at Francis' "Go!" heaved her shoreward.

Her obedience to their instructions was implicit, and, on hands and knees, she gained the solid rocks of the shore.

"Now for the rope!" she called to them.

But by this time Francis was too deep to be able to remove the coil from around his neck and under one arm. Henry did it for him, and, though the exertion sank him to an equal deepness, managed to fling one end of the rope to Leoncia.

At first she pulled on it. Next, she fastened a turn around a boulder the size of a motor car, and let Henry pull. But it was in vain. The strain or purchase was so lateral that it seemed only to pull him deeper. The quicksand was sucking and rising over his shoulders when Leoncia cried out, precipitating a very Bedlam of echoes:

"Wait! Stop pulling! I have an idea! Give me all the slack! Just save enough of the end to tie under your shoulders!"

The next moment, dragging the rope after her by the other end, she was scaling the cliff . Forty feet up, where a gnarled and dwarfed tree rooted in the crevices, shs paused. Passing the rope across the tree-trunk, as over a hook, she drew in the slack and made fast to a boulder of several hundred-weight.

"Good for the girl!" Francis applauded to Henry.

Both men had grasped her plan, and success depended merely on her ability to dislodge the boulder and topple it off the ledge. Five precious minutes were lost, until she could find a dead branch of sufficient strength to serve as a crowbar. Attacking the boulder from behind and working with tense coolness while her two lovers continued to sink, she managed at the last to topple it over the brink.

As it fell, the rope tautened with a jerk that fetched an involuntary grunt from Henry's suddenly constricted chest. Slowly, he arose out of the quicksand, his progress being accompanied by loud sucking reports as the sand reluctantly released him. But, when he cleared the surface, the boulder so outweighed him that he shot shoreward across the crust until directly under the purchase above, when the boulder came to rest on the ground beside him.

Only Francis' head, arms, and tops of shoulders were visible above the quicksand when the end of the rope was flung to him. And, when he stood beside them on terra firma, and when he shook his fist at the quicksand he had escaped by so narrow a shave, they joined with him in deriding it. And a myriad ghosts derided them back, and all the air about them was woven by whispering shuttles into an evil texture of mockery.

Chapter 14

"WE can't be a million miles away from it," Henry said, as the trio came to pause at the foot of a high steep cliff. "If it's any farther on, then the course lies right straight over the cliff, and, since we can't climb it and from the extent of it it must be miles around, the source of those flashes ought to be right here."

"Now could it have been a man with looking-glasses?" Leoncia ventured.

"Most likely some natural phenomenon," Francis answered. "I'm strong on natural phenomena since those barking sands."

Leoncia, who chanced to be glancing along the face of the cliff farther on, suddenly stiffened with attention and cried, "Look!" r

Their eyes followed hers, and rested on the same point. What they saw was no flash, but a steady persistence of white light that blazed and burned like the sun. Following the base of the cliff at a scramble, both men remarked, from the density of vegetation, that there had been no travel of humans that way in many years. Breathless from their exertions, they broke out through the brush upon an open-space where a not-ancient slide of rock from the cliff precluded the growth of vegetable life.

Leoncia clapped her hands. There was no need for her to point. Thirty feet above, on the face of the cliff, were two huge eyes. Fully a fathom across was each of the eyes, their surfaces brazen with some white reflecting substance.

"The eyes of Chia!" she cried.

Henry scratched his head with sudden recollection.

"I've a shrewd suspicion I can tell you what they're composed of," he said. "I've never seen it before, but I've heard old-timers mention it. It's an old Maya trick.

My share of the treasure, Francis, against a perforated dime, that I can tell you what the reflecting stuff is."

"Done!" cried Francis. "A man's a fool not to take odds like that, even if it's a question of the multiplication table. Possibly millions of dollars against a positive bad dime! I'd bet two times two made five on the chance that a miracle could prove it. Name it? What is it? The bet is on."

"Oysters," Henry smiled. "Oyster shells, or, rather, pearl-oyster shells. It's mother-of-pearl, cunningly mosaicked and cemented in so as to give a continuous reflecting surface. Now you have to prove me wrong, so climb up and see."

Beneath the eyes, extending a score of feet up and down the cliff, was a curious, triangular out-jut of rock. Almost was it like an excrescence on the face of the cliff. The apex of it reached within a yard of the space that intervened between the eyes. Rough inequalities of surface, and cat-like clinging on Francis' part, enabled him to ascend the ten feet to the base of the excrescence. Thence, up to the ridge of it, the way was easier. But a twenty-fivefoot fall and a broken arm or leg in the midst of such isolation was no pleasant thing to consider, and Leoncia, causing an involuntary jealous gleam to light Henry's eyes, called up:

"Oh, do be careful, Francis!"

Standing on the tip of the triangle he was gazing, now into one, and then into the other, of the eyes. He drew his hunting knife and began to dig and pry at the right-hand eye.

"If the old gentleman were here he'd have a fit at such sacrilege," Henry commented.

"The perforated dime is yours," Francis called down, at the same time dropping into Henry's outstretched palm the fragment he had dug loose.

Mother-of-pearl it was, a flat,; piece cut with definite purpose to fit in with the many other pieces to form the eye.

"Where there's smoke there's fire," Henry adjudged. "Not for nothing did the Mayas select this God-forsaken spot and stick these eyes of Chia on the cliff."

"Looks as if we'd made a mistake in leaving the old gentleman and his sacred knots behind," Francis said.

"The knots should tell all about it and what our next move should be."

"Where there are eyes there should be a nose," Leoncia contributed.

"And there is!" exclaimed Francis. "Heavens! That was the nose I just climbed up. We're too close up against it to have perspective. At a hundred yards' distance it would look like a colossal face."

Leoncia advanced gravely and kicked at a decaying deposit of leaves and twigs evidently blown there by tropic gales.

"Then the mouth ought to be where a mouth belongs, here -under the nose," she v said.

In a trice Henry and Francis had kicked the rubbish aside and exposed an opening too small to admit a man's body. It was patent that the rock-slide had partly blocked the way. A few rocks heaved aside gave space for Francis to insert his head and shoulders and gaze about with a lighted match.

"Watch out for snakes," warned Leoncia.

Francis grunted acknowledgment and reported:

"This is no natural cavern. It's all hewn rock, and well done, if I'm any judge." A muttered expletive announced the burning of his fingers by the expiring matchstub. And next they heard his voice, in accents of surprise: "Don't need any matches. It's got a lighting system of its own from somewhere above regular concealed lighting, though it's daylight all right. Those old Mayas were certainly some goers. Wouldn't be surprised if we found an elevator, hot and cold water, a furnace, and a Swede janitor. Well, so long."

His trunk, and legs, and feet disappeared, and then his voice issued forth:

"Come on in. The cave is fine.

"And now aren't you glad you let me come along?" Leoncia twitted, as she joined the two men on the level floor of the rock-hewn chamber, where, their eyes quickly accustoming to the mysterious gray-percolation of daylight, they could see about them with surprising distinctness. "First, I found the eyes for you, and, next, the mouth. If I hadn't been along, most likely, by this time, you'd have been 4 half a mile away, going around the cliff and going farther and farther every step you took.

"But the place is bare as old Mother Hubbard's cupboard," she added, the next moment.

"Naturally," said Henry. "This is only the antechamber. Not so sillily would the Mayas hide the treasure the conquistadores were so mad after. I'm willing to wager right now that we're almost as far from finding the actual treasure as we would be if we were not here but in San Antonio."

Twelve or fifteen feet in width and of an unascertainable height, the passage led them what Henry judged "forty paces, or well over a hundred feet. Then it abruptly narrowed, turned at a right angle to the right, and, with a similar right angle to the left, made an elbow into another spacious chamber.

Still the mysterious percolation of daylight guided the way for their eyes, and Francis, in the lead, stopped so suddenly that Leoncia and Henry, in a single file behind, collided with him. Leoncia in the center, and Henry on her left, they stood abreast and gazed down a long avenue of humans, long dead, but not dust.

"Like the Egyptians, the Mayas knew embalming and mummifying," Henry said, his voice unconsciously sinking to a whisper in the presence of so many unburied dead, who stood erect and at gaze, as if still alive.

All were European-clad, and all exposed the impassive faces of Europeans. About them, as to the life, were draped the ages-rotten habiliments of the conquistadores and of the English pirates. Two of them, with visors raised, were encased in rusty armor. Their swords and cutlasses were belted to them or held in their shriveled hands, and through their belts were thrust huge flintlock pistols of archaic model.

"The old Maya was right," Francis whispered. "They've decorated the hiding place with their mortal remains and been stuck up in the lobby as a warning to trespassers. Say! If that chap isn't a real Iberian!

I'll bet he played haia-lai, and his fathers before him."

"And that's a Devonshire man if ever I saw one," Henry whispered back. "Perforated dimes to pieces-ofeight that he poached the fallow deer and fled the king's wrath in the first forecastle for the Spanish Main."

"Br-r-r!" Leoncia shivered, clinging to both men. "The sacred things of the Mayas are dea'dly and ghastly. And there is a classic vengeance about it. The would-be robbers of the treasure-house have become its defenders, guarding it with their unperishing clay."

They were loath to proceed. The garmented spectres of the ancient dead held them temporarily spell-bound. Henry grew melodramatic.

"Even to this far, mad place," he said, "as early as the beginning of the Conquest, their true-hound noses led them on the treasure-scent. Even though they could not get away with it, they won unerringly to it. My hat is off to you, pirates and conquistadores! I salute you, old gallant plunderers, whose noses smelt out gold, and whose hearts were brave sufficient to fight for it!"

"Huh!" Francis concurred, as he urged the other two to traverse the avenue of the ancient adventurers. "Old Sir Henry himself ought to be here at the head of the procession."

Thirty paces they took, ere the passage elbowed as before, and, at the very end of the double-row of mummies, Henry brought his companions to a halt as he pointed and said:

"I don't know about Sir Henry, but there's Alvarez Torres."

Under a Spanish helmet, in decapitated medieval Spanish dress, a big Spanish sword in its brown and withered hand, stood a mummy whose lean brown face for all the world was the lean brown face of Alvarez Torres. Leoncia gasped, shrank back, and crossed herself at the sight.

Francis released her to Henry, advanced, and fingered the cheeks and lips and forehead of the thing, and laughed reassuringly:

"I only wish Alvarez Torres were as dead as this dead one is. I haven't the slightest doubt, however, but what Torres descended from him I mean before he came here to take up his final earthly residence as a member of the Maya Treasure Guard."

Leoncia passed the grim figure shudderingly. This time, the elbow passage was very dark, compelling Henry, who had changed into the lead, to light numerous matches.

"Hello!" he said, as he paused at the end of a couple of hundred feet. "Gaze on that for workmanship! Look at the dressing of that stone!"

From beyond, gray light streamed into the passage, making matches unnecessary to see. Half into a niche was thrust a stone the size of the passage. It was apparent that it had been used to block the passage. The dressing was exquisite, the sides and edges of the block precisely aligned with the place in the wall into which it was made to dovetail.

"I'll wager here's where the old Maya's father died," Francis exclaimed. "He knew the secret of the balances and leverages that pivoted the stone, and it was only partly pivoted, as you'll observe—"

"Hell's bells!" Henry interrupted, pointing before him on the floor at a scattered skeleton. "It must be what's left of him. It's fairly recent, or he would have been mummified. Most likely he was the last visitor before us."

"The old priest said his father led men of the tierra caliente here," Leoncia reminded Henry.

"Also," Francis supplemented, "he said that none returned."

Henry, who had located the skull and picked it up, uttered another exclamation and lighted a match to show the others what he had discovered-. Not only was the skull dented with what must have been a blow from a sword or a machete, but a shattered hole in the back of the skull showed the unmistakable entrance of a bullet. Henry shook the skull, was rewarded by an interior rattling, shook again, and shook out a partly flattened bullet. Francis examined it.

"From a horse-pistol," he concluded aloud. "With weak or greatly deteriorated powder, because, in a place like this, it must have been fired pretty close t9 point blank range and yet failed to go all the way through. And it's an aboriginal skull all right."

A right-angled turn completed the elbow and gave them access to a small but well-lighted rock chamber. From a window, high up and barred with vertical bars of stone a foot thick and half as wide, poured gray daylight. The floor of the place was littered with white-picked bones of men. An examination of the skulls showed them to be those of Europeans. Scattered among them were rifles, pistols, and knives, with, here and there, a machete.

"Thus far they won, across the very threshold to the treasure," Francis said, "and, from the looks, began to fight for its possession before they laid hands on it. Too bad the old man isn't here to see what happened to his father.

"Might there not have been survivors who managed to get away with the loot?" suggested Henry.

But at that moment, casting, his eyes from the bones to a survey of the chamber, Francis saw what

63

made him say: "Without doubt, no. See those gems in those eyes. Rubies, or I never saw a ruby!"

They followed his gaze to the stone statue of a squat and heavy female who stared at them red-eyed and openmouthed. So large was the mouth that it made a caricature of the rest of the face. Beside it, carved similarly of stone, and on somewhat more heroic lines, was a more obscene and hideous male statue, with one ear of proportioned size and the other ear as grotesquely large as the female's mouth.

"The beauteous dame must be Chia all right," Henry grinned. "But who's her gentleman friend with the elephant ear and the green eyes?"

"Search me," Francis laughed. "But this I do know: those green eyes of the elephant-eared one are the largest emeralds I've ever seen or dreamed of. Each of them is really too large to possess fair carat value. They should be crown jewels or nothing."

"But a couple of emeralds and a couple of rubies, no matter what size, should not constitute the totality of the Maya treasure," Henry contended. "We're across the threshold of it, and yet we lack the key—"

"Which the old Maya, back on the barking sands, undoubtedly holds in that sacred tassel of his," Leoncia said. "Except for these two statues and the bones on the floor, the place is bare."

As she spoke, she advanced to look the male statue over more closely. The grotesque ear centered her attention, and she pointed into it as she added: "I don't know about the key, but there is the key - hole."

True enough, the elephantine ear, instead of enfolding an orifice as an ear of such size should, was completely blocked up save for a small aperture that not too remotely resembled a key-hole. They wandered vainly about the chamber, tapping the walls and floor, seeking for cunninglyhidden passageways or unguessable clues to the hiding place of the treasure.

"Bones of tierra caliente men, two idols, two emeralds of enormous size, two rubies ditto, and ourselves, are all the place contains," Francis summed up. "Only a couple of things remain for us to do: go back and bring up Ricardo and the mules to make camp outside; and bring up the old gentleman and his sacred knots if we have to carry him."

"You wait with Leoncia, and I'll go back and bring them up," Henry volunteered, when they had threaded the long passages and the avenues of the erect dead and won to the sunshine and the sky outside the face of the cliff.

Back on the barking sands the peon and his father knelt in the circle so noisily drawn by the old man's forefinger. A local rain squall beat upon them, and, though the peon shivered, the old man prayed on oblivious to what might happen to his skin in the way of wind and water. It was because the peon shivered and was uncomfortable that he observed two things which his father missed. First, he saw Alvarez Torres and José Mancheno cautiously venture out from the jungle upon the sand. Next, he saw a miracle. The miracle was that the pair of them trudged steadily across the sand without causing the slightest sound to arise from their progress. When they had disappeared ahead, he touched his finger tentatively to the sand, and aroused no ghostly whisperings. He thrust his finger into the sand, yet all was silent, as was it silent when he buffeted the sand heartily with the flat of his palm. The passing shower had rendered the sand dumb.

He shook his father out of his prayers, announcing:

"The sand no longer is noisy. It is as silent as the grave. And I have seen the enemy of the rich Gringo pass across the sand without sound. He is not devoid of sin, this Alvarez Torres, yet did the sand make no sound. The sand has died. The voice of the sand is not. Where the sinful may walk, you and I, old father, may walk."

Inside the circle, the old Maya, with trembling forefinger in the sand, traced further cabalistic characters; and the sand did not shout back at him. Outside the circle it was the same because the sand had become wet, and because it was the way of the sand to be vocal only when it was bone-dry under the sun. He fingered the knots of the sacred writing tassel.

"It says," he reported, "that when the sand no longer talks it is safe to proceed. So far I have obeyed all instruction. In order to obey further instruction, let us now proceed."

So well did they proceed, that, shortly beyond the barking sands, they overtook Torres and Mancheno, which worthy pair slunk off into the brush on one side, watched the priest and his son go by, and took up their trail well in the rear. While Henry, taking a short cut, missed both couples of men.

Chapter 15

"EVEN so, it was a mistake and a weakness on my part to remain in Panama," Francis was saying to Leoncia, as they sat side by side on the rocks outside the cave entrance, waiting Henry's return.

"Does the stock market of New York then mean so much to you?" Leoncia coquettishly teased; yet only part of it was coquetry, the major portion of it being temporization. She was afraid of being alone with this man whom she loved so astoundingly and terribly.

Francis was impatient.

"I am ever a straight talker, Leoncia. I say what I mean, in the directest, shortest way—"

"Wherein you differ from us Spaniards," she interpolated, "who must garnish and dress the simplest thoughts with all decorations of speech."

But he continued undeterred what he had started to say.

"There you are a baffler, Leoncia, which was just what I was going to call you. I speak straight talk and true talk, which is a man's way. You baffle in speech, and flutter like a butterfly which, I grant, is a woman's way and to be expected. Nevertheless, it is not fair ... to me. I tell you straight out the heart of me, and you understand. You do not tell me your heart. You flutter and baffle, and I do not understand. Therefore, you have me at a disadvantage. You know I love you. I have told you plainly. I? What do I know about you?"

With downcast eyes and rising color in her cheeks, she sat silent, unable to reply.

"You see!" he insisted. "You do not answer. You look warmer and more beautiful and desirable than ever, more enticing, in short; and yet you baffle me and tell me nothing of your heart or intention. Is it because you are woman? Or because you are Spanish?"

She felt herself stirred profoundly. Beyond herself, yet in cool control of herself, she raised her eyes and looked steadily in his as steadily she said:

"I can be Anglo-Saxon, or English, or American, or whatever you choose to name the ability to look things squarely in the face and to talk squarely into the face of things." She paused and debated coolly with herself, and coolly resumed. "You complain that while you have told me that you love me, I have not told you whether or not I love you. I shall settle that forever and now. I do love you—"

She thrust his eager arms away from her.

"Wait!" she commanded. "Who is the woman now? Or the Spaniard? I had not finished. I love you. I am proud that I love you. Yet there is more. You have asked me for my heart and intention. I have told you part of the one. I now tell you all of the other: I intend to marry Henry."

Such Anglo-Saxon directness left Francis breathless.

"In heaven's name, why?" was all he could utter.

"Because I love Henry," she answered, her eyes still unshrinkingly on his.

"And you... you say you love me?" he quavered.

"And I love you, too. I love both of you. I am a good woman, at least I always used to think so. I still think so, though my reason tells me that I cannot love two men at the same time and be a good woman. I don't care about that. If I am bad, it is I, and I cannot help myself for being what I was born to be."

She paused and waited, but her lover was still speechless.

"And who's the Anglo-Saxon now?" she queried, with a slight smile, half of bravery, half of amusement at the dumbness of consternation her words had produced in him. "I have told you, without baffling, without fluttering, my full heart and my full intention."

"But you can't!" he protested wildly. "You can't love me and marry Henry."

"Perhaps you have not understood," she chided gravely. "I intend to marry Henry. I love you. I love Henry. But I cannot marry both of you. The law will not permit. Therefore I shall marry only one of you. It is my intention that that one be Henry."

"Then why, why," he demanded, "did you persuade me into remaining?"

"Because I loved you. I have already so told you."

"If you keep this up I shall go mad!" he cried.

"I have felt like going mad over it myself many times," she assured him. "If you think it is easy for me thus to play the Anglo-Saxon, you are mistaken. But no Anglo-Saxon, not even you whom I love so dearly, can hold me in contempt because I hide the shameful secrets of the impulses of my being. Less shameful I find it, for me to tell them, right out in meeting, to you. If this be Anglo-Saxon, make the most of it. If it be Spanish, and woman, and Solano, still make the most of it, for I am Spanish, and woman a Spanish woman of the Solanos—"

"But I don't talk with my hands," she added with a wan smile in the silence that fell.

Just as he was about to speak, she hushed him, and both listened to a crackling and rustling from the underbrush that advertised the passage of humans.

"Listen," she whispered hurriedly, laying her hand suddenly on his arm, as if pleading. "I shall be finally Anglo-Saxon, and for the last time, when I tell you what I am going to tell you. Afterward, and for always, I shall be the baffling, fluttering, female Spaniard you have chosen for my description. Listen:

I love Henry, it is true, very true. I love you more, much more. I shall marry Henry... because I love him and am pledged to him. Yet always shall I love you more."

Before he could protest, the old Maya priest and his peon son emerged from the underbrush close upon them. Scarcely noticing their presence, the pries,t went down on his knees, exclaiming, in Spanish:

"For the first Cirne have my eyes beheld the eyes of Chia."

He ran the knots of the sacred tassel and began a prayer in Maya, which, could they have understood, ran as follows:

"O immortal Chia, great spouse of the divine Hzatzl who created all things out of nothingness! O immortal spouse of Hzatzl, thyself the mother of the corn, the divinity of the heart of the husked grain, goddess of the rain and the fructifying sun-rays, nourisher of all the grains and roots and fruits for the sustenance of man! O glorious Chia, whose mouth ever commands the ear of Hzatzl, to thee humbly, thy priest, I make my prayer. Be kind to me, and forgiving. From thy mouth let issue forth the golden key that opens the ear of Hzatzl. Let thy faithful priest gain to Hzatzl's treasure Not for himself, Divinity, but for the sake of his son whom the Gringo saved. Thy children, the Mayas, pass. There is no need for them of the treasure. I am thy last priest. With me passes all understanding of thee and of thy great spouse, whose name I breathe only with my forehead on the stones. Hear me, O Chia, hear me! My head is on the stones before thee!"

For all of five minutes the old Maya lay prone, quivering and jerking as if in a catalepsy, while Leoncia and Francis looked curiously on, themselves half -swept by the unmistakable solemnity of the old man's prayer, non-understandable though it was.

Without waiting for Henry, Francis entered the cave a second time. With Leoncia beside him, he felt quite like a guide as he showed the old priest over the place. The latter, ever reading the knots and mumbling, followed behind, while the peon was left on guard outside. In the avenue of mummies the priest halted reverently not so much for the mummies as for the sacred tassel.

"It is so written," he announced, holding out a particular string of knots. "These men were evil, and robbers. Their doom here is to wait forever outside the inner room of Maya mystery."

Francis hurried him past the heap of bones of his father before him, and led him into the inner chamber, where first of all, he prostrated himself before the two idols and prayed long and earnestly. After that, he studied certain of the strings very carefully. Then he made announcement, first in Maya, which Francis gave him to know was unintelligible, and next in broken Spanish:

"From the mouth of Chia to the ear of Hzatzl so is it written."

Francis listened to the cryptic utterance, glanced into the dark cavity of the goddess' mouth, stuck the blade of his hunting-knife into the key-hole of the god's monstrous ear, then tapped the stone with the hilt of his knife and declared the statue to be hollow. Back to Chia, he was tapping her to demonstrate her hollo wness, when the old Maya muttered:

"The feet of Chia rest upon nothingness."

Francis caught by the idea, made the old man verify the message by the knots.

"Her feet are large," Leoncia laughed, "but they rest on the solid rock-floor and not on nothingness."

Francis pushed against the female deity with his hand and found that she moved easily. Gripping her with both hands, he began to wrestle, moving her with quick jerks and twists.

"For the strong men and unafraid will Chia walk," the priest read. "But the next three knots declare: Beware! Beware! Beware!"

"Well, I guess, that nothingness, whatever it is, won't bite me," Francis chuckled, as he released the statue after shifting it a yard from its original position.

There, old lady, stand there for a while, or sit down if that will rest your feet. They ought to be tired after standing on nothing for so many centuries."

A cry from Leoncia drew his gaze to the portion of the floor just vacated by the large feet of Chia. Stepping backward from the displaced goddess, he had been just about to fall into the rock-hewn hole her feet had concealed. It was circular, and a full yard in diameter. In vain he tested the depth by dropping lighted matches. They fell burning, and, without reaching bottom, still falling, were extinguished by the draught of their flight.

"It looks very much like nothingness without a bottom," he adjudged, as he dropped a tiny stone fragment.

Many seconds they listened ere they heard it strike.

"Even that may not be the bottom," Leoncia suggested. "It may have been struck against some projection from the side and even lodged there."

"Well, this will determine it," Francis cried, seizing an ancient musket from among the bones on the floor and preparing to drop it.

66

But the old man stopped him.

"The message of the sacred knots is: whoso violates the nothingness beneath the feet of Chia shall quickly and terribly die."

"Far be it from me to make a stir in the void," Francis grinned, tossing the musket aside. "But what are we to do now, old Maya man? From the mouth of Chia to the ear of Hzatzl sounds easy but how? and what? Run the sacred knots with thy fingers, old top, and find for us how and what."

For the son of the priest, the peon with the frayed knees, the clock had struck. All unaware, he had seen his last sun-rise. No matter what happened this day, no matter what blind efforts he might make to escape, the day was to be his last day. Had he remained on guard at the caveentrance, he would surely have been killed by Torres and Mancheno, who had arrived close on his heels.

But, instead of so remaining, it entered his cautious, timid soul to make a scout out and beyond for possible foes. Thus, he missed death in the daylight under the sky. Yet the pace of the hands of the clock was unalterable, and neither nearer nor farther was his destined end from him.

While he scouted, Alvarez Torres and Jose" Mancheno arrived at the cave-opening. The colossal, mother-of-pearl eyes of Chia on the wall of the cliff were too much for the superstition-reared Caroo.

"Do you go in," he told Torres. "I will wait here and watch and guard."

And Torres, with strong in him the blood of the ancient forebear who stood faithfully through the centuries in the avenue of the mummy dead, entered the Maya cave as courageously as that forebear had entered.

And the instant he was out of sight, Jose Mancheno, unafraid to murder treacherously any living, breathing man, but greatly afraid of the unseen world behind unexplainable phenomena, forgot the trust of watch and ward and stole away through the jungle. Thus, the peon, returning reassured from his scout and curious to learn the Maya secrets of his father and of the sacred tassel, found nobody at the cave mouth and himself entered into it close upon the heels of Torres.

The latter trod softly and cautiously, for fear of disclosing his presence to those he trailed. Also his progress was still further delayed by the spectacle of the ancient dead in the hall of mummies. Curiously he examined these men whom history had told about, and for whom history had stopped there in the antechamber of the Maya gods. Especially curious was he at the sight of the mummy at the end of the line. The resemblance to him was too striking for him not to see, and he could not but believe that he was looking upon some direct great-ancestor of his.

Still gazing and speculating, he was warned by approaching footsteps, and glanced about for some place to hide. A sardonic humor seized him. Taking the helmet from the head of his ancient kin, he placed it on his own head. Likewise did he drape the rotten mantle about his form, and equip himself with the great sword and the great floppy boots that almost fell to pieces as he pulled them on. Next, half tenderly, he deposited the nude mummy on its back in the dark shadows behind the other mummies. And, finally, in the same spot at the end of the line, his hand resting on the sword-hilt, he assumed the same posture he had observed of the mummy.

Only his eyes moved as he observed the peon venturing slowly and fearfully along the avenue of upright corpses. At sight of Torres he came to an abrupt stop and with wide eyes of dread muttered a succession of Maya prayers. Torres, so confronted, could only listen with closed eyes and conjecture. When he heard the peon move on he stole a look and saw him pause with apprehension at the narrow elbow-turn of the passage which he must venture next. Torres saw his chance and swung the sword aloft for the blow that would split the peon's head in twain.

Though this was the day and the very hour for the peon, the last second had not yet ticked. Not there, in the thoroughfare of the dead, was he destined to die under the hand of Torres. For Torres held his hand and slowly lowered the point of the sword to the floor, while the peon passed on into the elbow.

The latter met up with his father, Leoncia, and Francis, just as Francis was demanding the priest to run the knots again for fuller information of the how and what that would open the ear of Hzatzl.

"Put your hand into the mouth of Chia and draw forth the key," the old man commanded his reluctant son, who went about obeying him most gingerly.

"She won't bite you she's stone," Francis laughed at him in Spanish.

"The Maya gods are never stone," the old man reproved him. "They seem to be stone, but they are alive, and ever alive, and under the stone, and through the stone, and by the stone, as always, work their everlasting will."

Leoncia shuddered away from him and clung against Francis, her hand on his arm, as if for protection.

"I know that something terrible is going to happen," she gasped. "I don't like this place in the heart of a mountain among all these dead old things. I like the blue of the sky and the balm of the sunshine, and the wide-spreading sea. Something terrible is going to happen. I know that something terrible is going to happen."

While Francis reassured her, the last seconds of the last minute for the peon were ticking off. And when, summoning all his courage, he thrust his hand into the mouth of the goddess, the last second ticked and the clock struck. With a scream of terror he pulled back his hand and gazed at the wrist where a tiny drop of blood exuded directly above an artery. The mottled head of a snake thrust forth like a mocking, derisive tongue and drew back and disappeared in the darkness of the mouth of the goddess.

"A viperine!" screamed Leoncia, recognising the reptile.

And the peon, likewise recognising the viperine and knowing his certain death by it, recoiled backward in horror, stepped into the hole, and vanished down the nothingness which Chia had guarded with her feet for so many centuries.

For a full minute nobody spoke, then the old priest said: "I have angered Chia, and she has slain my son."

"Nonsense," Francis was comforting Leoncia. "The whole thing is natural and explainable. What more natural than that a viperine should choose a hole in a rock for a lair? It is the way of snakes. What more natural than that a man, bitten by a viperine, should step backward? And what more natural, with a hole behind him, than that he should fall into it-"

"That is then just natural!" she cried, pointing to a stream of crystal water which boiled up over the lips of the hole and fountained up in the air like a geyser. "He is right. Through stone itself the gods work their everlasting will. He warned us. He knew from reading the knots of the sacred tassel."

"Piffle!" Francis snorted. "Not the will of the gods, but of the ancient Maya priests who invented their gods as well as this particular device. Somewhere down that hole the peon's body struck the lever that opened stone flood-gates. And thus was released some subterranean body of water in the mountain. This is that water. No goddess with a monstrous mouth like that could ever have existed save in the monstrous imaginations of men. Beauty and divinity are one. A real and true goddess is always beautiful. Only man creates devils in all their ugliness." So large was the stream that already the water was about their ankles.

"It's all right," Francis said. "I noticed, all the way from the entrance, the steady inclined plane of the floors of the rooms and passages. Those old Mayas were engineers, and they built with an eye on drainage. See how the water rushes away out through the passage. Well, old man, read your knots, where is the treasure?"

Where is my son?" the old man counter-demanded in dull and hopeless tones. "Chia has slain my only born. For his mother I broke the Maya law and stained the pure Maya blood with the mongrel blood of a woman of the tierra caliente. Because I sinned for him that he might be, is he thrice precious to me. What care I for treasure? My son is gone. The wrath of the Maya gods is upon me."

With gurglings and burblings and explosive air-bubblings that advertised the pressure behind, the water fountained high as ever into the air. Leoncia was the first to notice the rising depth of the water on the chamber floor.

"It is half way to my knees," she drew Francis' attention.

"And time to get out," he agreed, grasping the situation. "The drainage was excellently planned, perhaps.

But that slide of rocks at the cliff entrance has evidently blocked the planned way of the water. In the other passages, being lower, the water is deeper, of course, than here. Yet is it already rising here on the general level. And that way lies the only way out. Come!"

Thrusting Leoncia to lead in the place of safety, he caught the apathetic priest by the hand and dragged him after. At the entrance of the elbow turn the water was boiling above their knees. It was to their waists as they emerged into the chamber of mummies.

And out of the water, confronting Leoncia's astounded gaze, arose the helmeted head and ancient-mantled body of a mummy. Not this alone would have astounded her, for other mummies were overtoppling, falling and being washed about in the swirling waters. But this mummy moved and made gasping noises for breath, and with eyes of life stared into her eyes.

It was too much for ordinary human nature to bear a four-centuries old corpse dying the second death by drowning. Leoncia screamed, sprang forward, and fled the way she had come, while Francis, in his own way equally startled, let her go past as he drew his automatic pistol. But the mummy, finding footing in the swift rush of the current, cried out:

"Don't shoot! It is I Torres! I have just come back from the entrance. Something has happened. The way is blocked. The water is over one's head and higher than the entrance, and rocks are falling."

"And your way is blocked in this direction," Francis said, aiming the revolver at him.

"This is no time for quarreling," Torres replied. "We must save all our lives, and, afterwards, if quarrel we must, then quarrel we will."

Francis hesitated.

"What is happening to Leoncia?" Torres demanded slyly. "I saw her run back. May she not be in danger by herself?"

Letting Torres live and dragging the old man by the arm, Francis waded back to the chamber of the idols, followed by Torres. Here, at sight of him, Leoncia screamed her horror again.

"It's only Torres," Francis reassured her. "He gave me a devil of a fright myself when I first saw him. But he's real flesh. He'll bleed if a knife is stuck into him. Come, old man! We don't want to drown here like rats in a trap. This is not all of the Maya mysteries. Read the tale of the knots and get us out of this!"

"The way is not out but in," the priest quavered.

"And we're not particular so long as we get away. But how can we get in?"

"From the mouth of Chia to the ear of Hzatzl, was the answer.

Francis was struck by a sudden grotesque and terrible thought.

"Torres," he said, "there is a key or something inside that stone lady's mouth there. You're the nearest. Stick your hand in and get it."

Leoncia gasped with horror as she divined Francis' vengeance. Of this Torres took no notice, and gaily waded toward the goddess, saying: "Only too glad to be of service."

And then Francis' sense of fair play betrayed him.

"Stop! "he commanded harshly, himself wading to the idol's side.

And Torres, at first looking on in puzzlement, saw what he had escaped. Several times Francis fired his pistol into the stone mouth, while the old priest moaned "Sacrilege!" Next, wrapping his coat around his arm and hand, he groped into the mouth and pulled out the wounded viper by the tail. With quick swings in the air he beat its head to a jelly against the goddess' side.

Wrapping his hand and arm against the possibility of a second snake, Francis thrust his hand into the mouth and drew forth a piece of worked gold of the shape and size of the hole in Hzatzl's ear. The old man pointed to the ear, and Francis inserted the key.

"Like a nickle-in-the-slot machine," he remarked, as the key disappeared from sight. "Now what's going to happen? Let's watch for the water to drain suddenly away."

But the great stream continued to spout unabated out of the hole. With an exclamation, Torres pointed to the wall, an apparently solid portion of which was slowly rising.

"The way out," said Torres.

"In, as the old man said," Francis corrected. "Well, anyway, let's start."

All were through and well along the narrow passage beyond, when the old Maya, crying, "My son!" turned and ran back.

The section of wall was already descending into its original place, and the priest had to crouch low in order to pass it. A moment later, it stopped in its old position. So accurately was it contrived and fitted that it immediately shut off the stream of water which had been flowing out of the idol room.

Outside, save for a small river of water that flowed out of the base of the cliff, there were no signs of what was vexing the interior of the mountain. Henry and Ricardo, arriving, noted the stream, and Henry observed:

"That's something new. There wasn't any stream of water here when I left."

A minute later he was saying, as he looked at a fresh slide of rock: "This was the entrance to the cave. Now there is no entrance. I wonder where the others are."

As if in answer, out of the mountain, borne by the spouting stream, shot the body of a man. Henry and Ricardo pounced upon it and dragged it clear. Recognizing it for the priest,

Henry laid him face downward, squatted astride of him, and proceeded to give him the first aid for the drowned.

Not for ten minutes did the old man betray signs of life, and not until after another ten minutes did he open his eyes and look wildly about.

"Where are they?" Henry asked.

The old priest muttered in Maya, until Henry shook more thorough consciousness into him.

"Gone all gone," he gasped in Spanish.

"Who?" Henry demanded, shook memory into the resuscitated one, and demanded again.

"My son; Chia slew him. Chia slew my son, as she slew them all.

"Who are the rest?"

Followed more shakings and repetitions of the question.

"The rich young Gringo who befriended my son, the enemy of the rich young Gringo whom men call Torres, and the young woman of the Solanos who was the cause of all that happened. I warned you. She should not have come. Women are always a curse in the affairs of men. By her presence, Chia, who is likewise a woman, was made angry. The tongue of Chia is a viperine. By her tongue Chia struck and slew my son, and the mountain vomited the ocean upon us there in the heart of the mountain, and all are dead, slain by Chia. Woe is me! I have angered the gods. Woe is me I Woe is me! And woe upon all who would seek the sacred treasure to filch it from the gods of Maya!"

Chapter 16

MIDWAY between the out-bursting stream of water and the rock-slide, Henry and Eicardo stood in hurried debate. Beside them, crouched on the ground, moaned and prayed the last priest of the Mayas. From him, by numerous shakings that served to clear his addled old head, Henry had managed to extract a rather vague account of what had occurred inside the mountain.

Only his son was bitten and fell into that hole," Henry reasoned hopefully.

"That's right," Eicardo concurred. "He never saw any damage, beyond a wetting, happen to the rest of them,"

And they may be, right now, high up above the floor in some chamber," Henry went on. "Now, if we could attack the slide, we might open up the cave and drain the water off. If they're alive they can last for many days, for lack of water is what kills quickly, and they've certainly more water than they know what to do with. They can get along without food for a long time. But what gets me is how Torres got inside with them."

Wonder if he wasn't responsible for that attack of the Caroos upon us," Eicardo suggested.

But Henry scouted the idea.

"Anyway," he said, "that isn't the present proposition which proposition is: how to get inside that mountain on the chance that they are still alive. You and I couldn't go through that slide in a month. If we could get fifty men to help, night and day shifts, we might open her up in fortyeight hours. So, the primary thing is to get the men. Here's what we must do. I'll take a mule and beat it back to that Caroo community and promise them the contents of one of Francis' check-books if they will come and help. Failing that, I can get up a crowd in San Antonio. So here's where I pull out on the run. In the meantime, you can work out trails and bring up all the mules, peons, grub and camp equipment. Also, keep your ears to the cliff they might start signalling through it with tappings."

Into the village of the Caroos Henry forced his mule much to the reluctance of the mule, and equally as much to the astonishment of the Caroos, who thus saw their stronghold invaded single-handed by one of the party they had attempted to annihilate. They squatted about their doors and loafed in the sunshine, under a show of lethargy hiding the astonishment that tingled through them and almost put them on their toes. As has been ever the way, the very daring of the white man, over savage and mongrel breeds, in this instance stunned the Caroos to inaction. Only a man, they could not help but reason in their slow way, a superior man, a noble or over-riding man, equipped with potencies beyond their dreaming, could dare to ride into their strength of numbers on a fagged and mutinous mule.

They spoke a mongrel Spanish which he could understand, and, in turn, they understood his Spanish; but what he told them concerning the disaster in the sacred mountain had no effect of rousing them. With impassive faces, shrugging shoulders of utmost indifference, they listened to his proposition of a rescue and promise of high pay for their time.

"If a mountain has swallowed up the Gringos, then is it the will of God, and who are we to interfere between God and His will?" they replied. "We are poor men, but we care not to work for any man, nor do we care to make war upon God. Also, it was the Gringos' fault. This is not their country. They have no right here playing pranks on our mountains. Their troubles are between them and God. We have troubles enough of our own, and our wives are unruly."

Long after the siesta hour, on his third and most reluctant mule, Henry rode into sleepy San Antonio. In the main street, midway between the court and the jail, he pulled up at sight of the Jefe Politico and the little fat old judge, with, at their heels, a dozen gendarmes and a couple of wretched prisoners runaway peons from the henequen plantations at Santos. While the judge and the Jefe listened to Henry's tale and appeal for help, the Jefe gave one slow wink to the judge, who was his judge, his creature, body and soul of him.

"Yes, certainly we will help you," the Jefe said at the end, stretching his arms and yawning. "How soon can we get the men together and start?" Henry demanded eagerly.

"As for that, we are very busy are we not, honorable judge?" the Jefe replied with lazy insolence.

"We are very busy," the judge yawned into Henry's face.

"Too busy for a time," the Jefe went on. "We regret that not to-morrow nor next day shall we be able to try and rescue your Gringos. Now, a little later... "

"Say next Christmas," the judge suggested.

"Yes," concurred the Jefe with a grateful bow. "About next Christmas come around and see us, and, if the pressure of our affairs has somewhat eased, then, maybe possibly, we shall find it convenient to go about beginning to attempt to raise the expedition you have requested. In the meantime, good day to you, Senor Morgan."

"You mean that?" Henry demanded with wrathful face.

"The very face he must have worn when he slew Senor Alfaro Solano treacherously from the back," the Jefe soliloquized ominously.

But Henry ignored the later insult.

"I'll tell you what you are," he flamed in righteous wrath.

"Beware!" the judge cautioned him.

"I snap my fingers at you,'" Henry retorted. "You have no power over me. I am a full-pardoned man by the President of Panama himself. And this is what you are. You are half-breeds. You are mongrel pigs."

"Pray proceed, Senor," said the Jefe, with the suave politeness of deathly rage.

"You've neither the virtues of the Spaniard nor of the Carib, but the vices of both thrice compounded. Mongrel pigs, that's what you are and all you are, the pair of you."

"Are you through Senor? quite through?" the Jefe queried softly.

At the same moment he gave a signal to the gendarmes, who sprang upon Henry from behind and disarmed him.

"Even the President of the Republic of Panama cannot pardon in anticipation of a crime not yet committed am I right, judge?" said the Jefe.

"This is afresh offense," the judge took the cue promptly. "This Gringo dog has blasphemed against the law."

"Then shall he be tried, and tried now, right here, immediately. We will not bother io go back and reopen court. We shall try him, and when we have disposed of him, we shall proceed. I have a very good bottle of wine—"

"I care not for wine," the judge disclaimed hastily. "Mine shall be mescal. And in the meantime, and now, having been both witness and victim of the offense and there being no need of evidence further than what I already possess, I find the prisoner guilty. Is there anything you would suggest, Senor Mariano Vercara e Hijos?"

"Twenty-four hours in the stocks to cool his heated Gringo head," the Jefe answered.

"Such is the sentence," the judge affirmed, "to begin at once. Take the prisoner away, gendarmes, and put him in the stocks."

Daybreak found Henry in the stocks, with a dozen hours of such imprisonment already behind him, lying on his back asleep. But the sleep was restless, being vexed subjectively by nightmare dreams of his mountain-imprisoned companions, and, objectively, by the stings of countless mosquitoes. So it was, twisting and squirming and striking at the winged pests, he awoke to full consciousness of his predicament. And this awoke the full expression of his profanity. Irritated beyond endurance by the poison from a thousand mosquito-bites, he filled the dawn so largely with his curses as to attract the attention of a man carrying a bag of tools. This was a trim-figured, eagle-faced young man, clad in the military garb of an aviator of the United States Army. He deflected his course so as to come by the stocks, and paused, and listened, and stared with quizzical admiration.

"Friend," he said, when Henry ceased to catch breath.

Last night, when I found myself marooned here with half my outfit left on board, I did a bit of swearing myself. But it was only a trifle compared with yours. I salute you, sir. You've an army teamster skinned a mile. Now if you don't mind running over the string again, I shall be better equipped the next time I want to do any cussing."

"And who in hell are you?" Henry demanded. "And what in hell are you doing here?"

"I don't blame you," the aviator grinned. "With a face swollen like that you've got a right to be rude. And who beat you up? In hell, I haven't ascertained my status yet. But here on earth I am known as Parsons, Lieutenant Parsons. I am not doing anything in hell as yet; but here in Panama I am scheduled to fly across this day from the Atlantic to the Pacific. Is there any way I may serve you before I start?"

"Sure," Henry nodded. "Take a tool out of that bag of yours and smash this padlock. Ill get rheumatism if I have to stick here much longer. My name's Morgan, and no man has beaten me up. Those are mosquito-bites."

With several blows of a wrench, Lieutenant Parsons smashed the ancient padlock and helped Henry to his feet. Even while rubbing the circulation back into his feet and ankles, Henry, in a rush, was telling the army aviator of the predicament and possibly tragic disaster to Leoncia and Francis.

"I love that Francis," he concluded. "He is the dead spit of myself. We're more like twins, and we must be distantly related. As for the senorita, not only do I love her but I am engaged to marry her. Now will you help? Where's the machine? It takes a long time to get to the Maya Mountain on foot or mule-back ; but if you give me a lift in your machine I'd be there in no time, along with a hundred sticks of dynamite, which you could procure for me and with which I could blow the side out of that mountain and drain off the water."

Lieutenant Parsons hesitated.

"Say yes, say yes," Henry pleaded.

Back in the heart of the sacred mountain, the three imprisoned ones found themselves in total darkness the instant the stone that blocked the exit from the idol chamber had settled into place. Francis and Leoncia groped for each other and touched hands. In another moment his arm was around her, and the deliciousness of the contact robbed the situation of half its terror. Near them they could hear Torres breathing heavily. At last he muttered:

"Mother of God, but that was a close shave! What next, I wonder?"

"There'll be many nexts before we get out of this neck of the woods," Francis assured him. "And we might as well start getting out."

The method of procedure was quickly arranged. Placing Leoncia behind him, her hand clutching the hem of his jacket so as to be guided by him, he moved ahead with his left hand in contact with the wall. Abreast of him, Torres felt his way along the right-hand wall. By their voices they could thus keep track of each other, measure the width of the passage, and guard against being separated into forked passages. Fortunately, the tunnel, for tunnel it truly was, had a smooth floor, so that, while they groped their way, they did not stumble. Francis refused to use his matches unless extremity arose, and took precaution against falling into a possible pit by cautiously advancing one foot at a time and ascertaining solid stone under it ere putting on his weight. As a result, their progress was slow. At no greater speed than half a mile an hour did they proceed.

Once only did they encounter branching passages. Here he lighted a precious match from his waterproof case, and found that between the two passages there was nothing to choose. They were as like as two peas.

"The only way is to try one," he concluded, "and, if it gets us nowhere, to retrace and try the other. There's one thing certain: these passages lead somewhere, or the Mayas wouldn't have gone to all the trouble of making them."

Ten minutes later he halted suddenly and cried warning. The foot he had advanced was suspended in emptiness where the floor should have been. Another match was struck, and they found themselves on the edge of a natural cavern of such proportions that neither to right nor left, nor up nor down, nor across, could the tiny flame expose any limits to it. But they did manage to make out a rough sort of stairway, half-natural, half-improved by man, which fell away beneath them into the pit of black.

In another hour, having followed the path down the length of the floor of the cavern, they were rewarded by a feeble glimmer of daylight, which grew stronger as they advanced.

Before they knew it, they had come to the source of it being much nearer than they had judged; and Francis, tearing away vines and shrubbery, crawled out into the blaze of the afternoon sun. In a moment Leoncia and Torres were beside him, gazing down into a valley from an eyrie on a cliff. Nearly circular was the valley, a full league in diameter, and it appeared to be mountain -walled and cliff-walled for its entire circumference.

"It is the Valley of Lost Souls," Torres utterly solemnly. "I have heard of it, but never did I believe."

"So have I heard of it and never believed," Leoncia

"And what of it?" demanded Francis. We're not lost souls, but good flesh-and-blood persons. We should worry." "But Francis, listen," Leoncia said. "The tales I have heard of it, ever since I was a little girl, all agreed that no person who ever got into it ever got out again."

"Granting that that is so," Francis could not help smiling, "then how did the tales come out? If nobody ever came out again to tell about it, how does it happen that everybody outside knows about it?"

"I don't know," Leoncia admitted. "I only tell you what I have heard. Besides, I never believed. But this answers all the descriptions of the tales."

"Nobody ever got out," Torres affirmed with the same solemn utterance.

"Then how do you know that anybody got in?" Francis persisted.

"All the lost souls live here," was the reply. "That is why we've never seen them, because they never got out. I tell you, Mr. Francis Morgan, that I am no creature without reason. I have been educated. I have studied in Europe, and I have done business in your own New York. I know science and philosophy; and yet do I know that this is the valley, once in, from which no one emerges."

"Well, we're not in yet, are we?" retorted Francis with a slight manifestation of impatience. "And we don't have to go in, do we?" He crawled forward to the verge of the shelf of loose soil and crumbling stone in order to get a better view of the distant object his eye had just picked out. "If that isn't a grass-thatched roof—"

At that moment the soil broke away under his hands. In a flash, the whole soft slope on which they rested broke away, and all three were sliding and rolling down the steep slope in the midst of a miniature avalanche of soil, gravel, and grass-tufts.

The two men picked themselves up first, in the thicket of bushes which had arrested them; but, before they could get to Leoncia, she, too, was up and laughing.

"Just as you were saying we didn't have to go into the valley!" she gurgled at Francis. "Now will you believe?"

But Francis was busy. Reaching out his hand, he caught and stopped a familiar object bounding down the steep slope after them. It was Torres' helmet purloined from the chamber of mummies, and to Torres he tossed it. "Throw it away," Leoncia said.

It's the only protection against the sun I possess," was his reply, as, turning it over in his hands, his eyes lighted upon an inscription on the inside. He showed it to his companions, reading it aloud:

"DA VASCO."

"I have heard," Leoncia breathed.

And you heard right," Torres nodded. "Da Vasco was my direct ancestor. My mother was a Da Vasco. He came over the Spanish Main with Cortez."

"He mutined," Leoncia took up the tale. "I remember it well from my father and from my Uncle Alfaro. With a dozen comrades he sought the Maya treasure. They led a sea-tribe of Caribs, an hundred strong including their women, as auxiliaries. Mendoza, under Cortez's instructions, pursued; and his report, in the archives, so Uncle Alfaro told me, says that they were driven into the Valley of the Lost Souls where they were left to perish miserably."

"And he evidently tried to get out by the way we've just come in," Torres continued, "and the Mayas caught him and made a mummy of him."

He jammed the ancient helmet down on his head, saying:

"Low as the sun is in the afternoon sky, it bites my crown like acid."

"And famine bites at me like acid," Francis confessed. "Is the valley inhabited?"

"I should know, Senor," Torres replied. "There is the narrative of Mendoza, in which he reported that Da Vasco and his party were left there "to perish miserably. "This I do know: they were never seen again of men."

"Looks as though plenty of food could be grown in a place like this," Francis began, but broke off at sight of Leoncia. picking berries from a bush. "Here! Stop that, Leoncia! We've got enough troubles without having a very charming but very much poisoned young woman on our hands."

"They're all right, she said, calmly eating. "You can see where the birds have been pecking and eating them."

"In which case I apologize and join you," Francis cried, filling his mouth with the luscious fruit. "And if I could catch the birds that did the pecking, I'd eat them too."

By the time they had eased the sharpest of their hungerpangs, the sun was so low that Torres removed the helmet of Da Vasco.

"We might as well stop here for the night," he said. "I left my shoes in the cave with the mummies, and lost Da Vasco's old boots during the swimming. My feet are cut to ribbons, and there's plenty of seasoned grass here out of which I can plait a pair of sandals."

While occupied with this task, Francis built a fire and gathered a supply of wood, for, despite the low latitude, the high altitude made fire a necessity for a night's lodging. Ere he had completed the supply, Leoncia, curled up on her side, her head in the hollow of her arm, was sound asleep. Against the side of her away from the fire, Francis thoughtfully packed a mound of dry leaves and dry forest mould.

Chapter 17

DAYBREAK in the Valley of the Lost Souls, and the Long House in the village of the Tribe of the Lost Souls. Fully eighty feet in length was the Long House, with half as much in width, built of adobe bricks, and rising thirty feet to a gable roof thatched with straw. Out of the house feebly walked the Priest of the Sun an old man, tottery on his legs, sandal-footed, clad in a long robe of rude homespun cloth, in whose withered Indian face were haunting reminiscences of the racial lineaments of the ancient

73

conquistadores. On his head was a curious cap of gold, arched over by a semi-circle of polished golden spikes. The effect was obvious, namely, the rising sun and the rays of the rising sun.

He tottered across the open space to where a great hollow log swung suspended between two posts carved with totemic and heraldic devices. He glanced at the eastern horizon, already red with the dawning, to reassure himself that he was on time, lifted a stick, the end of which was fiber-woven into a ball, and struck the hollow log. Feeble as he was, and light as was the blow, the hollow log boomed and reverberated like distant thunder.

Almost immediately, while he continued slowly to beat, from the grass-thatched dwellings that formed the square about the Long House, emerged the Lost Souls. Men and women, old and young, and children and babes in arms, they all came out and converged upon the Sun Priest. No more archaic spectacle could be witnessed in the twentieth-century world. Indians, indubitably they w T ere, yet in many of their faces were the racial reminiscences of the Spaniard. Some faces, to all appearance, were all Spanish. Others, by the same token, were all Indian. But betwixt and between, the majority of them betrayed the inbred blend of both races.

But more bizarre was their costume unremarkable in the women, who were garbed in long, discreet robes of homespun cloth, but most remarkable in the men, whose homespun was grotesquely fashioned after the style of Spanish dress that obtained in Spain at the time of Columbus' first voyage. Homely and sad-looking were the men and women as of a breed too closely interbred to retain joy of life. This was true of the youths and maidens, of the children, and of the very babes against breasts true, with the exception of two, one, a child-girl of ten, in whose face was fire, and spirit, and intelligence. Amongst the sodden faces of the sodden and stupid Lost Souls, her face stood out like a flaming flower. Only like hers was the face of the old Sun Priest, cunning, crafty, intelligent.

While the priest continued to beat the resounding log, the entire tribe formed about him in a semi-circle, facing the east. As the sun showed the edge of its upper rim, the priest greeted it and hailed it with a quaint and medieval Spanish, himself making low obeisance thrice repeated, while the tribe prostrated itself. And, when the full sun shone clear of the horizon, all the tribe, under the direction of the priest, arose and uttered a joyful chant. Just as he had dismissed his people, a thin pillar of smoke, rising in the quiet air across the valley, caught the priest's eye. He pointed it out, and commanded several of the young men.

"It rises in the Forbidden Place of Fear where no member of the tribe may wander. It is some devil of a pursuer sent out by our enemies who have vainly sought our hidingplace through the centuries. He must not escape to make report, for our enemies are powerful, and we shall be destroyed. Go. Kill him that we may not be killed."

About the fire, which had been replenished at intervals throughout the night, Leoncia, Francis, and Torres lay asleep, the latter with his new-made sandals on his feet and with the helmet of Da Vasco pulled tightly down on his head to keep off the dew. Leoncia was the first to awaken, and so curious was the scene that confronted her, that she watched quietly through her do wn- dropped lashes. Three of the strange Lost Tribe men, bows still stretched and arrows drawn in what was evident to her as the interrupted act of slaying her and her companions, were staring with amazement at the face of the unconscious Torres. They looked at each other in doubt, let their bows straighten, and shook their heads in patent advertisement that they were not going to kill. Closer they crept upon Torres, squatting on their hams the better to scrutinize his face and the helmet, which latter seemed to arouse their keenest interest.

From where she lay, Leoncia was able privily to nudge Francis' shoulder with her foot. He awoke quietly, and quietly sat up, attracting the attention of the strangers. Immediately they made the universal peace sign, laying down their bows and extending their palms outward in token of being weaponless.

"Good morning, merry strangers," Francis addressed them in English, which made them shake their heads while it aroused Torres.

"They must be Lost Souls," Leoncia whispered to Francis.

"Or real estate agents," he smiled back. "At least the valley is inhabited. Torres, who 're your friends? From the way they regard you, one would think they were relatives of yours."

Quite ignoring them, the three Lost Souls drew apart a slight distance and debated in low sibilant tones.

"Sounds like a queer sort of Spanish," Francis observed. "It's medieval, to say the least," Leoncia confirmed.

"It's the Spanish of the conquistadores pretty badly gone to seed," Torres contributed. "You see I was right. The Lost Souls never get away."

"At any rate they must give and be given in marriage," Francis quipped, "else how explain these three young huskies?"

74

But by this time the three huskies, having reached agreement, were beckoning them with encouraging gestures to follow across the valley.

"They're good-natured and friendly cusses, to say the least, despite their sorrowful mug," said Francis, as they prepared to follow. But did you ever see a sadder-faced aggregation in your life? They must have been born in the dark of the moon, or had all their sweet gazelles die, or something or other worse."

"It's just the kind of faces one would expect of lost souls," Leoncia answered.

"And if we never get out of here, I suppose we'll get to looking a whole lot sadder than they do," he came back. "Anyway, I hope they're leading us to breakfast. Those berries were better than nothing, but that is not saying much."

An hour or more afterward, still obediently following their guides, they emerged upon the clearings, the dwelling places, and the Long House of the tribe.

"These are descendants of Da Vasco's party and the Caribs," Torres affirmed, as he glanced over the assembled faces. "That is incontrovertible on the face of it."

"And they've relapsed from the Christian religion of Da Vasco to old heathen worship," added Francis. "Look at that altar there. It's a stone altar, and, from the smell of it, that is no breakfast, but a sacrifice that is cooking, in spite of the fact that it smells like mutton."

"Thank heaven it's only a lamb," Leoncia breathed. "The old Sun Worship included human sacrifice. And this is Sun Worship. See that old man there in the long shroud with the golden-rayed cap of gold. He's a sun priest. Uncle Alfaro has told me all about the sun-worshipers."

Behind and above the altar, was a great metal image of the sun.

"Gold, all gold," Francis whispered, "and without alloy. Look at those spikes, the size of them, yet so pure is the metal that I wager a child could bend them any way it wished and even tie knots in them."

Merciful God! look at that!" Leoncia gasped, indicating with her eyes a crude stone bust that stood to one side of the altar and slightly lower. "It is the face of Torres. It is the face of the mummy in the Maya cave."

"And there is an inscription… " Francis stepped closer to see and was peremptorily waved back by the priest. "It says, 'Da Vasco.' Notice that it has the same sort of helmet that Torres is wearing. And, say! Glance at the priest! If he doesn't look like Torres' full brother, I've never fancied a resemblance in my life!"

The priest, with angry face and imperative gesture, motioned Francis to silence, and made obeisance to the cooking sacrifice. As if in response, a flaw of wind put out the flame of the cooking.

"The Sun God is angry," the priest announced with great solemnity, his queer Spanish nevertheless being intelligible to the newcomers. "Strangers have come among us and remain unslain. That is why the Sun God is angry. Speak, you young men who have brought the strangers alive to our altar. Was not my bidding, which is ever and always the bidding of the Sun God, that you should slay them?"

One of the three young men stepped tremblingly forth, and with trembling forefingers pointed at the face of Torres and at the face of the stone bust.

"We recognised him," he quavered, "and we could not slay him for we remembered prophecy and that our great ancestor would some day return. Is this stranger he? We do not know. W T e dare not know nor judge. Yours, priest, is the knowledge, and yours be the judgment. Is this he?"

The priest looked closely at Torres and exclaimed incoherently. Turning his back abruptly, he rekindled the sacred cooking fire from a pot of fire at the base of an altar. But the fire flamed up, flickered down, and died.

"The Sun God is angry," the priest reiterated; whereat the Lost Souls beat their breasts and moaned and lamented. "The sacrifice is unacceptable, for the fire will not burn. Strange things are afoot. This is a matter of the deeper mysteries which I alone may know. We shall not sacrifice the strangers… now. I must take time to inform myself of the Sun God's will.

With his hands he waved the tribespeople away, ceasing the ceremonial half-completed, and directed that the three captives be taken into the Long House.

"I can't follow the play," Francis whispered in Leoncia's ear, but just the same I hope here's where we eat."

"Look at that pretty little girl," said Leoncia, indicating with her eyes the child with the face of fire and spirit.

"Torres has already spotted her," Francis whispered back. "I caught him winking at her. He doesn't know the play, nor which way the cat will jump, but he isn't missing a chance to make friends. We'll have to keep an eye on him, for he's a treacherous hound and capable of throwing us over any time if it would serve to save his skin."

Inside the Long House, seated on rough-plaited mats of grass, they found themselves quickly served with food. Clear drinking water and a thick stew of meat and vegetables were served in generous quantity in queer, unglazed pottery jars. Also, they were given hot cakes of ground Indian corn that were not altogether unlike tortillas.

After the women who served had departed, the little girl, who had led them and commanded them, remained. Torres resumed his overtures, but she, graciously ignoring him, devoted herself to Leoncia who seemed to fascinate her.

"She's a sort of hostess, I take it," Francis explained. "You know like the maids of the village in Samoa, who entertain all travellers and all visitors of no matter how high rank, and who come pretty close to presiding at all functions and ceremonials. They are selected by the high chiefs for their beauty, their virtue, and their intelligence. And this one reminds me very much of them, except that she's so awfully young."

Closer she came to Leoncia, and, fascinated though she patently was by the beautiful strange woman, in her bearing of approach there was no hint of servility nor sense of inferiority.

"Tell me," she said, in the quaint archaic Spanish of the valley, "is that man really Capitan Da Vasco returned from his home in the sun in the sky?"

Torres smirked and bowed, and proclaimed proudly: "I am a Da Vasco!"

"Not a Da Vasco, but Da Vasco himself," Leoncia coached him in English.

"It's a good bet play it!" Francis commanded, likewise in English. "It may pull us all out of a hole. I'm not particularly stuck on that priest, and he seems the high-cockalorum over these Lost Souls."

"I have at last come back from the sun," Torres told the little maid, taking his cue.

She favored him with a long and unwavering look, in which they could see her think, and judge, and appraise. Then, with expressionless face, she bowed to him respectfully, and, with scarcely a glance at Francis, turned to Leoncia and favored her with a friendly smile that was an illumination.

"I did not know that God made women so beautiful as you," the little maid said softly, ere she turned to go out. At the door she paused to add, "The Lady Who Dreams is beautiful, but she is strangely different from you."

But hardly had she gone, when the Sun Priest, followed by a number of young men, entered, apparently for the purpose of removing the dishes and the uneaten food. Even as some of them were in the act of bending over to pick up the dishes, at a signal -from the priest they sprang upon the three guests, bound their hands and arms securely behind them, and led them out to the Sun God's altar before the assembled tribe. Here, where they observed a crucible on a tripod over a fierce fire, they were tied to fresh-sunken posts, while many eager hands heaped fuel about them to their knees.

"Now buck up be as haughty as a real Spaniard!" Francis at the same time instructed and insulted Torres. "You're Da Vasco himself. Hundreds of years before, you were here on earth in this very valley with the ancestors of these mongrels."

"You must die," the Sun Priest was now addressing them, while the Lost Souls nodded unanimously. "For four hundred years, as we count our sojourn in this valley, have we slain all strangers. You were not slain, and behold the instant anger of the Sun God: our altar fire went out." The Lost Souls moaned and howled and pounded their chests. Therefore, to appease the Sun God, you shall now die."

"Beware!" Torres proclaimed, prompted in whispers, sometimes by Francis, sometimes by Leoncia. "I am Da Vasco. I have just come from the sun." He nodded with his head, because of his tied hands, at the stone bust. "I am that Da Vasco. I led your ancestors here four hundred years ago, and I left you here, commanding you to remain until my return."

The Sun Priest hesitated.

"Well, priest, speak up and answer the divine Da Vasco," Francis spoke harshly.

"How do I know that he is divine?" the priest countered quickly. "Do I not look much like him myself? Am I therefore divine? Am I Da Vasco? Is he Da Vasco? Or may not Da Vasco be yet in the sun? for truly I know that I am man born of woman three-score and eighteen years ago and that I am not Da Vasco."

"You have not spoken to Da Vasco!" Francis threatened, as he bowed in vast humility to Torres and hissed at him in English: "Be haughty, damn you, be haughty."

The priest wavered for the moment, and then addressed Torres.

"I am the faithful priest of the sun. Not lightly can I relinquish my trust. If you are the divine Da Vasco, then answer me one question."

Torres nodded with magnificent haughtiness. "Do you love gold?"

"Love gold!" Torres jeered. "I am a great captain in the sun, and the sun is made of gold. Gold? It is like to me this dirt beneath my feet and the rock of which your mighty mountains are composed."

"Bravo," Leoncia whispered approval.

"Then, divine Da Yasco," the Sun Priest said humbly, although he could not quite muffle the ring of triumph in his voice, "are you fit to pass the ancient and usual test. When you have drunk the drink of gold, and can still say that you are Da Vasco, then will I, and all of us, bow down and worship you. We have had occasional intruders in this valley. Always did they come athirst for gold. But when we had satisfied their thirst, inevitably they thirsted no more, for they were dead."

As he spoke, while the Lost Souls looked on eagerly, and while the three strangers looked on with no less keenness of apprehension, the priest thrust his hand into the open mouth of a large leather bag and began dropping handfuls of gold nuggets into the heated crucible of the tripod. So near were they, that they could see the gold melt into fluid and rise up in the crucible like the drink it was intended, to be.

The little maid, daring on her extraordinary position in the Lost Souls Tribe, came up to the Sun Priest and spoke that all might hear.

"That is Da Vasco, the Capitan Da Vasco, the divine Capitan da Vasco, who led our ancestors here the long long time ago."

The priest tried to silence her with a frown. But the maid repeated her statement, pointing eloquently from the bust to Torres and back again; and the priest felt his grip on the situation slipping, while inwardly he cursed the sinful love of the mother of the little girl which had made her his daughter.

"Hush!" he commanded sternly. "These are things of which you know nothing. If he be the Capitan Da Vasco, being divine he will drink the gold and be unharmed."

Into a rude pottery pitcher, which had been heated in the pot of fire at the base of the altar, he poured the molten gold. At a signal, several of the young men laid aside their spears, and, with the evident intention of prying her teeth apart, advanced on Leoncia.

"Hold, priest!" Francis shouted stentoriously. "She is not divine as Da Vasco is divine. Try the golden drink on Da Vasco."

Whereat Torres bestowed upon Francis a look of malignant anger.

"Stand on your haughty pride," Francis instructed him. "Decline the drink. Show them the inside of your helmet."

"I will not drink!" Torres cried, half in a panic as the priest turned to him.

"You shall drink. If you are Da Vasco, the divine capitan from the sun, we will then know it and we will fall down and worship you."

Torres looked appeal at Francis, which the priest's narrow eyes did not fail to catch.

"Looks as though you'll have to drink it," Francis said dryly. "Anyway, do it for the lady's sake and die like a hero."

With a sudden violent strain at the cords that bound him, Torres jerked one hand free, pulled off his helmet, and held it so that the priest could gaze inside.

"Behold what is graven therein," Torres commanded.

Such was the priest's startlement at sight of the inscription, DA VASCO, that the pitcher fell from his hand. The molten gold, spilling forth, set the dry debris on the ground afire-, while one of the spearmen, spattered on the foot, danced away with wild yells of pain. But the Sun Priest quickly recovered himself. Seizing the fire pot, he was about to set fire to the faggots heaped about his three victims, when the little maid intervened.

"The Sun God would not let the great captain drink the drink," she said. "The Sun God spilled it from your hand."

And when all the Lost Souls began to murmur that there was more in the matter than appeared to their priest, the latter was compelled to hold his hand. Nevertheless was he resolved on the destruction of the three intruders. So, craftily, he addressed his people.

"We shall wait for a sign. Bring oil. We will give the Sun God time for a sign. Bring a candle."

Pouring the jar of oil over the faggots to make them more inflammable, he set the lighted stub of a candle in the midst of the saturated fuel, and said: "The life of the candle will be the duration of the time for the sign. Is it well, People?"

And all the Lost Souls murmured, "It is well."

Torres looked appeal to Francis, who replied:

"The old brute certainly pinched on the length of the candle. It won't last five minutes at best, and, maybe, inside three minutes we'll be going up in smoke."

"What can we do?" Torres demanded frantically, while Leoncia looked bravely, with a sad brave smile of love, into Francis' eyes.

"Pray for rain," Francis answered. "And the sky is as clear as a bell. After that, die game. Don't squeal too loud."

And his eyes returned to Leoncia's and expressed what he had never dared express to her before his full heart of love. Apart, by virtue of the posts to which they were tied and which separated them, they had never been so close together, and the bond that drew them and united them was their eyes.

First of all, the little maid, gazing into the sky for the sign, saw it. Torres, who had eyes only for the candle stub, nearly burned to its base, heard the maid's cry and looked up. And at the same time he heard, as all of them heard, the droning flight as of some monstrous insect in the sky.

"An aeroplane," Francis muttered. "Torres, claim it for the sign."

But no need to claim was necessary. Above them not more than a hundred feet, it swooped and circled, the first aeroplane the Lost Souls had ever seen, while from it, like a benediction from heaven, descended the familiar:

"Back to back against the mainmast, Held at bay the entire crew."

Completing the circle and rising to an elevation of nearly a thousand feet, they saw an object detach itself directly overhead, fall like a plummet for three hundred feet, then expand into a spread parachute, with beneath i^ like a spider suspended on a web, the form of a man, which last, as it neared the ground, again began to sing:

"Back to back against the mainmast, Held at bay the entire crew."

And then event crowded on event with supremest rapidity. The stub of the candle fell apart, the flaming wick fell into the tiny lake of molten fat, the lake flamed, and the oil-saturated faggots about it flamed. And Henry, landing in the thick of the Lost Souls, blanketing a goodly portion of them under his parachute, in a couple of leaps was beside his friends and kicking the blazing faggots right and left. Only for a second did he desist. This was when the Sun Priest interfered. A right hook to the jaw put that aged confidant of God down on his back, and, while he slowly recuperated and crawled to his feet, Henry slashed clear the lashings that bound Leoncia, Francis, and Torres. His arms were out to embrace Leoncia, when she thrust him away with:

"Quick! There is no time for explanation. Down on your knees to Torres and pretend you are his slave and don't talk Spanish; talk English."

Henry could not comprehend, and, while Leoncia reassured him with her eyes, he saw Francis prostrate himself at the feet of their common enemy.

"Gee!" Henry muttered, as he joined Francis. "Here goes. But it's worse than rat poison."

Leoncia followed him, and all the Lost Souls went down prone before the Capitan Da Vasco who received in their midst celestial messengers direct from the sun. All went down, except the priest, who, mightily shaken, was meditating doing it, when the mocking devil of melodrama in Torres' soul prompted him to overdo his part.

As haughtily as Francis had coached him, he lifted his right foot and placed it down on Henry's neck, incidentally covering and pinching most of his ear.

And Henry literally went up in the air. "You can't step on my ear, Torres!" he shouted, at the same time dropping him, as he had dropped the priest with his right hook.

"And now the beans are spilled," Francis commented in dry and spiritless disgust. "The Sun God stuff is finished right here and now."

The Sun Priest, exultantly signaling his spearmen, grasped the situation. But Henry dropped the muzzle of his automatic pistol to the old priest's midrif; and the priest, remembering the legends of deadly missiles propelled by the mysterious substance called "gunpowder," smiled appeasingly and waved back his spearmen. "This is beyond my powers of wisdom and judgment," he addressed his tribespeople, while ever his wavering glance returned to the muzzle of Henry's pistol. "I shall appeal to the last resort. Let the messenger be sent to wake the Lady Who Dreams. Tell her that strangers from the sky, and, mayhap, the sun, are here in our valley. And that only the wisdom of her far dreams will make clear to us what we do not understand, and what even I do not understand."

Chapter 18

CONVOYED by the spearmen, the party of Leoncia, the two Morgans, and Torres, was led through the pleasant fields, all under a high state of primitive cultivation, and on across running streams and through woodland stretches and knee deep pastures where grazed cows of so miniature a breed that, full-grown, they were no larger than young calves.

"They're milch cows without mistake," Henry commented. "And they're perfect beauties. But did you ever see such dwarfs! A strong man could lift up the biggest specimen and walk off with it."

"Don't fool yourself," Francis spoke up. "Take that one over there, the black one. I'll wager it's not an ounce under three hundredweight."

"How much will you wager?" Henry challenged.

"Name the bet," was the reply.

78

"Then a hundred even," Henry stated, "that I can lift it up and walk away with it."

"Done."

But the bet was never to be decided, for the instant Henry left the path he was poked back by the spearmen, who scowled and made signs that they were to proceed straight ahead.

Where the way came to lead past the foot of a very rugged cliff, they saw above them many goats.

"Domesticated," said Francis. "Look at the herd boys."

"I was sure it was goat-meat in that stew," Henry nodded. "I always did like goats. If the Lady Who Dreams, whoever she may be, vetoes the priest and lets us live, and if we have to stay with the Lost Souls for the rest of our days, I'm going to petition to be made master goatherd of the realm, and I'll build you a nice little cottage, Leoncia, and you can become the Exalted Cheese-maker to the Queen."

But he did not whimsically wander farther, for, at that ejaculation of appreciation from Torres. Fully a mile in length it stretched, with more than half the same in width, and was a perfect oval. With one exception, no habitation broke the fringe of trees, bamboo thickets, and rushes that circled its shore, even along the foot of the cliff where the bamboo was exceptionally luxuriant. On the placid surface was so vividly mirrored the surrounding mountains that the eye could scarcely discern where reality ended and reflection began.

In the midst of her rapture over the perfect reflection, Leoncia broke off to exclaim her disappointment in that the water was not crystal clear:

"What a pity it is so muddy!"

"That's because of the wash of the rich soil of the valley floor," Henry elucidated. "It's hundreds of feet deep, that soil."

"The whole valley must have been a lake at some time," Francis concurred. "Run your eye along the cliff and see the old water-lines. I wonder what made it shrink."

"Earthquake, most likely opened up some subterranean exit and drained it off to its present level and keeps on draining it, too. Its rich chocolate color shows the amount of water that flows in all the time, and that it doesn't have much chance to settle. It's the catch-basin for the entire circling watershed of the valley."

"Well, there's one house at least," Leoncia was saying five minutes later, as they rounded an angle of the cliff and saw, tucked against the cliff and extending out over the water, a low-roofed bungalow-like dwelling.

The piles were massive tree-trunks, but the walls of the house were of bamboo, and the roof was thatched with grassstraw. So isolated was it, that the only access, except by boat, was a twenty-foot bridge so narrow that two could not walk on it abreast. At either end of the bridge, evidently armed guards or sentries, stood two young men of the tribe. They moved aside, at a gesture of command from the Sun Priest, and let the party pass, although the two Morgans did not fail to notice the spearmen who had accompanied them from the, Long House remained beyond the bridge.

Across the bridge and entered into the bungalow-like dwelling on stilts, they found themselves in a large room better furnished, crude as the furnishings were, than they would have expected in the Valley of Lost Souls. The grass mats on the floor were of fine and careful weave, and the shades of split bamboo that covered the window-openings were of patient workmanship. At the far end, against the wall, was a huge golden emblem of the rising sun similar to the one before the altar in the Long House. But by far most striking, were two living creatures who strangely inhabited the place and who scarcely moved. Beneath the rising sun, raised above the floor on a sort of dais, was a many-pillowed divan that was half -throne. And on the divan, among the pillows, clad in a softly-shimmering robe of some material no one of them had seen before, reclined a sleeping woman. Only her breast softly rose and softly fell to her breathing. No Lost Soul was she, of the inbred and degenerate mixture of Carib and Spaniard. On her head was a tiara of beaten gold and sparkling gems so large that almost it seemed a crown.

Before her, on the floor, were two tripods of gold the one containing smouldering fire, the other, vastly larger, a golden bowl fully a fathom in diameter. Between the tripods, resting with outstretched paws like the Sphinx, with unblinking eyes and without a quiver, a great dog, snowwhite of coat and resembling a Russian wolf-hound, stedfastly regarded the intruders.

"She looks like a lady, and seems like a queen, and certainly dreams to the queen's taste," Henry whispered, and earned a scowl from the Sun Priest.

Leoncia was breathless, but Torres shuddered and crossed himself, and said:

"This I have never heard of the Valley of Lost Souls. This woman who sleeps is a Spanish lady. She is of the pure Spanish blood. She is Castilian. I am as certain, as that I stand here, that her eyes are blue. And yet that pallor!" Again he shuddered. "It is an unearthly sleep. It is as if she tampered with drugs, and had long tampered with drugy—"

"The very thing!" Francis broke in with excited whispers. "The Lady Who Dreams drug dreams. They must keep her here doped up as a sort of super-priestess or super-oracle. That's all right, old priest," he broke off to say in Spanish. "If we wake her up, what of it? We have been brought here to meet her, and, I hope, awake."

The Lady stirred, as if the whispering had penetrated her profound of sleep, and, for the first time, the dog moved. turning his head toward her so that her down-dropping hand rested on his neck caressingly. The priest was imperative, now, in his scowls and gestured commands for silence. And in absolute silence they stood and watched the awakening of the oracle.

Slowly she drew herself half upright, paused, and recaressed the happy wolf hound, whose cruel fangs were exposed in a formidable, long- jawed laugh of joy. Awesome the situation was to them, yet more awesome it became to them when she turned her eyes full upon them for the first time. Never had they seen such eyes, in which smouldered the world and all the worlds. Half way did Leoncia cross herself, while Torres, swept away by his own awe, completed his own crossing of himself and with moving lips of silence enunciated his favorite prayer to the Virgin. Even Francis and Henry looked, and could not take their gaze away from the twin wells of blue that seemed almost dark in the shade of the long black eyelashes.

"A blue-eyed brunette," Francis managed to whisper.

But such eyes! Round they were, rather than long. And yet thy were not round. Square they might have been, had they not been more round than square. Such shape had they that they were as if blocked off in the artist's swift and sketchy way of establishing circles out of the sums of angles. The long, dark lashes veiled them and perpetuated the illusion of their darkness. Yet was there no surprise nor startlement in them at first sight of her visitors. Dreamily incurious were they, yet were they languidly certain of comprehension of what they beheld. Still further, to awe those who so beheld, her eyes betrayed a complicated totality of paradoxical alivenesses. Pain trembled its quivering anguish perpetually impending. Sensitiveness moistily hinted of itself like a spring rain-shower on the distant sea-horizon or a dew-fall of a mountain morning. Pain ever pain resided in the midst of languorous slumberousness. The fire of immeasurable courage threatened to glint into the electric spark of action and fortitude. Deep slumber, like a palpitant, tapestried background, seemed ever ready to obliterate all in sleep. And over all, through all, permeating all, brooded ageless wisdom'. This was accentuated by cheeks slightly hollowed, hinting of asceticism. Upon them was a flush, either hectic or of the paint-box.

When she stood up, she showed herself to be slender and fragile as a fairy. Tiny were her bones, not too generously flesh-covered; yet the lines of her were not thin. Had either Henry or Francis registered his impression aloud, he would have proclaimed her the roundest thin woman he had ever seen.

The Sun Priest prostrated his aged frame till he lay stretched flat out on the floor, his old forehead burrowing into the grass mat. The rest remained upright, although Torres evidenced by a crumpling at the knees that he would have followed the priest's action had his companions shown signs of accompanying him. As it was, his knees did partly crumple, but straightened again and stiffened under the controlled example of Leoncia and the Morgans.

At first the Lady had no eyes for aught but Leoncia; and, after a careful looking over of her, with a curt upward lift of head she commanded her to approach. Too imperative by far was it, in Leoncia's thought, to proceed from so etherially beautiful a creature, and she sensed with immediacy an antagonism that must exist between them. So she did not move, until the Sun Priest muttered harshly that she must obey. She approached, regardless of the huge, long-haired hound, threading between the tripods and past the beast, nor would stop until commanded by a second nod as curt as the first. For a long minute the two women gazed steadily into each other's eyes, at the end of which, with a flicker of triumph, Leoncia observed the other's eyes droop. But the flicker was temporary, for Leoncia saw that the Lady was studying her dress with haughty curiosity. She even reached out her slender, pallid hand and felt the texture of the cloth and caressed it as only a woman can.

"Priest!" she summoned sharply. "This is the third day of the Sun in the House of Manco. Long ago I told you something concerning this day. Speak."

Writhing in excess of servility, the Sun Priest quavered:

"That on this day strange events were to occur. They have occurred, Queen."

Already had the Queen forgotten. Still caressing the cloth of Leoncia's dress, her eyes were bent upon it in curious examination.

"You are very fortunate," the Queen said, at the same time motioning her back to rejoin the others. "You are well loved of men. All is not clear, yet does it seem that you are too well loved of men." Her voice, mellow and low, tranquil as silver, modulated in exquisite rhythms of sound, was almost as a distant temple bell calling believers to worship or sad souls to quiet judgment. But to Leoncia it was not given to appreciate the wonderful voice. Instead, only was she aware of anger flaming up to her cheeks and burning in her pulse.

"I have seen you before, and often," the Queen went on.

"Never!" Leoncia cried out.

"Hush!" the Sun Priest hissed at her.

"There," the Queen said, pointing at the great golden bowl. "Before, and often, have I seen you there.

"You also, there," she addressed Henry.

"And you," she confirmed to Francis, although her great blue eyes opened wider and she gazed at him long too long to suit Leoncia, who knew the stab of jealousy that only a woman can thrust into a woman's heart.

The Queen's eyes glinted when they had moved on to rest on Torres.

"And who are you, stranger, so strangely apparelled, the helmet of a knight upon your head, upon your feet the sandals of a slave?"

"I am Da Vasco," he answered stoutly.

"The name has an ancient ring," she smiled.

"I am the ancient Da Vasco," he pursued, advancing unsummoned. She smiled at his temerity but did not stay him. "This is the helmet I wore four hundred years ago when I led the ancestors of the Lost Souls into this valley." The Queen smiled quiet unbelief, as she quietly asked:

"Then you were born four hundred years ago?"

"Yes, and never. I was never born. I am Da Vasco. I have always been. My home is in the sun."

Her delicately stenciled brows drew quizzically to interrogation, though she said nothing. From a gold-wrought box beside her on the divan she pinched what seemed a powder between a fragile and almost transparent thumb and forefinger, and her thin beautiful lips curved to gentle mockery as she casually tossed the powder into the great tripod. A sheen of smoke arose and in a moment was lost to sight.

"Look!" she commanded.

And Torres, approaching the great bowl, gazed into it. What he saw, the rest of his party never learned. But the Queen herself leaned forward and gazing down from above, saw with him, her face a beautiful advertisement of gentle and pitying mockery. And what Torres himself saw was a bedroom and a birth in the second story of the Bocas del Tore house he had inherited. Pitiful it was, with its last secrecy exposed, as was the gently smiling pity in the Queen's face. And, in that flashing glimpse of magic vision, Torres saw confirmed about himself what he had always guessed and suspected.

"Would you see more," the Queen softly mocked. "I have shown you the beginning of you. Look now, and behold your ending."

But Torres, too deeply impressed by what he had already seen, shuddered away in recoil.

"Forgive me, Beautiful Woman," he pleaded. "And let me pass. Forget, as I shall hope ever to forget."

"It is gone," she said, with a careless wave of her hand over the bowl. "But I cannot forget. The record will persist always in my mind. But you, O Man, so young of life, so ancient of helmet, have I beheld before this day, there in my Mirror of the World. You have vexed me much of late with your portending. Yet not with the helmet." She smiled with quiet wisdom. "Always, it seems to me, I saw a chamber of the dead, of the long dead, upright on their unmoving legs and guarding through eternity mysteries alien to their faith and race. And in that dolorous company did it seem. that I saw one who wore your ancient helmet... Shall I speak further?"

"No, no," Torres implored.

She bowed and nodded him back. Next, her scrutiny centred on Francis, whom she nodded forward. She stood up upon the dais as if to greet him, and, as if troubled by the fact that she must gaze down on him, stepped from the dais to the floor so that she might gaze up into his face as she extended her hand. Hesitatingly he took her hand in his, then knew not what next to do. Almost did it appear that she read his thought, for she said:

"Do it. I have never had it done to me before. I have never seen it done, save in my dreams and in the visions shown me in my Mirror of the World."

And Francis bent and kissed her hand. And, because she did not signify to withdraw it, he continued to hold it, while, against his palm, he felt the faint but steady pulse of her pink finger-tips. And so they stood in pose, neither speaking, Francis embarrassed, the Queen sighing faintly, while the sex anger of woman tore at Leoncia's heart, until Henry blurted out in gleeful English:

"Do it again, Francis! She likes it!"

The Sun Priest hissed silencing command at him. But the Queen, half withdrawing her hand with a

81

startle like a maiden's, relumed it as deeply as before into Francis' clasp, and addressed herself to Henry.

"I, too, know the language you speak," she admonished. "Yet am I unashamed, I, who have never known a man, do admit that I like it. It is the first kiss that I have ever had. Francis for such your friend calls you obey your friend. I like it. I do like it. Once again kiss my hand."

Francis obeyed, waited while her hand still lingered in his, and while she, oblivious to all else, as if toying with some beautiful thought, gazed lingeringly up into his eyes. By a visible effort she pulled herself together, released his hand abruptly, gestured him back to the others, and addressed the Sun Priest.

"Well, priest," she said, with a return of the sharpness in her voice, "You have brought these captives here for a reason which I already know. Yet would I hear you state it yourself."

"Lady Who Dreams, shall we not kill these intruders as has ever been our custom? The people are mystified and in doubt of my judgment, and demand decision from you."

"And you would kill?"

"Such is my judgment. I seek now your judgment that yours and mine may be one."

She glanced over the faces of the four captives. For Torres, her brooding expression portrayed only pity. To Leoncia she extended a frown; to Henry, doubt. And upon Francis she gazed a full minute, her face growing tender, at least to Leoncia's angry observation.

"Are any of you unmarried?" the Queen asked suddenly. "Nay," she anticipated them. "It is given me to know that you are all unmarried." She turned quickly to Leoncia. "Is it well," she demanded, "that a woman should have two husbands?"

Both Henry and Francis could not refrain from smiling their amusement at so absurdly irrelevant a question. But to Leoncia it was neither absurd nor irrelevant, and in her cheeks arose the flush of anger again. This was a woman, she knew, with whom she had to deal, and who was dealing with her like a woman.

"It is not well," Leoncia answered, with clear, ringing voice.

"It is very strange," the Queen pondered aloud. "It is very strange. Yet is it not fair. Since there are equal numbers of men and women in the world, it cannot be fair for one woman to have two husbands, for, if so, it means that another woman shall have no husband."

Another pinch of dust she tossed into the great bowl of gold. The sheen of smoke arose and vanished as before.

"The Mirror of the World will tell me, priest, what disposition shall be made of our captives."

Just ere she leaned over to gaze into the bowl, a fresh thought deflected her. With an embracing wave of arm she invited them all up to the bowl.

"We may all look," she said. "I do not promise you we will see the same visions of our dreams. Nor shall I know what you will have seen. Each for himself will see and know. You, too, priest."

They found the bowl, six feet in diameter that it was, halffull of some unknown metal liquid.

It might be quicksilver, but it isn't," Henry whispered to Francis. "I have never seen the like of any similar metal. It strikes me as hotly molten."

"It is very cold," the Queen corrected him in English. "Yet is it fire. You, Francis, feel the bowl outside."

He obeyed, laying his full palm unhesitatingly to the yellow outer surface.

"Colder than the atmosphere of the room," he adjudged. But look!" the Queen, cried, tossing more powder upon the contents. "It is fire that remains cold."

"It is the powder that smokes with the heat of its own containment," Torres blurted out, at the same time feeling into the bottom of his coat pocket. He drew forth a pinch of crumbs of tobacco, match splinters, and cloth-fluff. "This will not burn," he challenged, inviting invitation by extending the pinch of rubbish over the bowl as if to drop it in.

The Queen nodded consent, and all saw the rubbish fall upon the liquid metal surface. The particles made no indentation on that surface. Only did they transform into smoke that sheened upward and was gone. No remnant of ash remained. "Still is it cold," said Torres, imitating Francis and feeling the outside of the bowl.

"Thrust your finger into the contents," the Queen suggested to Torres.

"No," he said.

"You are right," she confirmed. "Had you done so, you would now be with one finger less than the number with which you w r ere born." She tossed in more powder. "Now shall each behold what he alone will behold."

And it was so.

To Leoncia was it given to see an ocean separate her and Francis. To Henry was it given to see the Queen and Francis married by so strange a ceremony, that scarcely did he realise, until at the close, that it was a wedding taking place. The Queen, from a flying gallery in a great house, looked down into a magnificent drawing-room that Francis would have recognized as builded by his father had her vision been his. And, beside her, his arm about her, she saw Francis. Francis saw but one thing, vastly perturbing, the face of Leoncia, immobile as death, with thrust into it, squarely between the eyes, a slended-bladed dagger. Yet he did not see any blood flowing from the wound of the dagger. Torres glimpsed the beginning of what he knew must be his end, crossed himself, and alone of all of them shrank back, refusing to see further. While the Sun Priest saw the vision of his secret sin, the face and form of the woman for whom he had betrayed the Worship of the Sun, and th face and form of the maid of the village at the Long House.

As all drew back by common consent when the visions faded, Leoncia turned like a tigress, with flashing eyes, upon the Queen, crying:

"Your mirror lies! Your Mirror of the World lies!"

Francis and Henry, still under the heavy spell of what they had themselves beheld, were startled and surprised by Leoncia's outburst. But the Queen, speaking softly, replied: My Mirror of the World has never lied. I know not what you saw. But I do know, whatever it was, that it is truth."

"You are a monster!" Leoncia cried on. "You are a vile witch that lies!"

You and I are women," the Queen chided with sweet gentleness, "and may not know of ourselves, being women. Men will decide whether or not I am a witch that lies or a woman with a woman's heart of love. In the meanwhile, being women and therefore weak, let us be kind to each other."

"And now, Priest of the Sun, to judgment. You, as priest under the Sun God, know more of the ancient rule and procedure than do I. You know more than do I about myself and how I came to be here. You know that always, mother and daughter, and by mother and daughter, has the tribe maintained a Queen of Mystery, a Lady of Dreams. The time has come when we must consider the future generations. The strangers have come, and they are unmarried. This must be the wedding day decreed, if the generations to come after of the tribe are to possess a Queen to dream for them. It is well, and time and need and place are met. I have dreamed to judgment. And the judgment is that I shall marry, of these strangers, the stranger alloted to me before the foundations of the world were laid. The test is this: If no one of these will marry, then shall they die and their warm blood be offered up by you before the altar of the Sun. If one will marry me, then all shall live, and Time hereafter will register our futures."

The Sun Priest, trembling with anger, strove to protest, but she commanded:

"Silence, priest! By me. only do you rule the people. At a word from me to the people well, you know. It is not any easy way to die."

She turned to the three men, saying:

"And who will marry me?"

They looked embarrassment and consternation at one another, but none spoke.

"I am a woman," the Queen went on teasingly. "And therefore am I not desirable to men? Is it that I am not young? Is it, as women go, that I am not beautiful? Is it that men's tastes are so strange that no man cares to clasp the sweet of me in his arms and press his lips on mine as good Francis there did on my hand?"

She turned her eyes on Leoncia.

You be judge. You are a woman well loved of men.

Am I not such a woman as you, and shall I not be loved?"

You will ever be kinder to men than to women, " Leoncia answered cryptically as regarded the three men who heard, but clearly to the woman's brain of the Queen. "And as a woman," Leoncia continued, "you are strangely beautiful and luring ; and there are men in this world, many men, who could be made mad to clasp you in their arms. But I warn you, Queen, that in this world are men, and men, and men."

Having heard and debated this, the Queen turned abruptly to the priest.

"You have heard, priest. This day a man shall marry me. If no man marries me, these three men shall be offered up on your altar. So shall be offered up this woman, who, it would seem, would put shame upon me by having me less than she."

Still, she addressed the priest, although her message was for the others.

"There are three men of them, one of whom, long cycles before he was born, was destined to marry me. So, priest, I say, take the captives away into some other apartment, and let them decide among themselves which is the man."

"Since it has been so long destined," Leoncia flamed forth, "then why put it to the chance of their decision? You know the man. Why put it to the risk? Name the man, Queen, and name him now."

M The man shall be selected in the way I have indicated," the Queen replied, as, at the same time, absently she tossed a pinch of powder into the great bowl and absently glanced therein. "So now depart, and let the inevitable choice be made."

They were already moving away out of the room, when a cry from the Queen stopped them.

"Wait!" she ordered. "Come, Francis. I have seen something that concerns you. Come, gaze with me upon the Mirror of the World."

And while the others paused, Francis gazed with her upon the strange liquid metal surface. He saw himself in the library of his New York house, and he saw beside him the Lady Who Dreams, his arm around her. Next, he saw her curiosity at sight of the stock-ticker. As he tried to explain it to her, he glanced at the tape and read such disturbing information thereon that he sprang to the nearest telephone and, as the vision faded, saw himself calling up his broker.

"What was it you saw?" Leoncia questioned, as they passed out.

And Francis lied. He did not mention seeing the Lady Who Dreams in his New York library. Instead, he replied:

"It was a stock-ticker, and it showed a bear market on Wall Street somersaulting into a panic. Now how did she know I was interested in Wall Street and stock-tickers?"

Chapter 19

"SOMEBODY'S got to marry that crazy woman," Leoncia spoke up, as they lolled upon the mats of the room to which the priest had taken them. "Not only will he be a hero by saving our lives, but he will save his own life as well. Now, Senor Torres, is your chance to save all our lives and your own."

"Br-r-r!" Torres shivered. "I would not marry her for ten million gold. She is too wise. She is terrible. She how shall I say? she, as you Americans say, gets my goat. I am a brave man. But before her I am not brave. The flesh of me melts in a sweat of fear. Not for less than ten million would I dare to overcome my fear. Now Henry and Francis are braver than I. Let one of them marry her."

But I am engaged to marry Leoncia," Henry spoke up promptly. "Therefore, I cannot marry the Queen."

And their eyes centered on Francis, but, before he could reply, Leoncia broke in.

"It is not fair, "she said. "No one of you wants to marry her. The only equitable way to settle it will be by drawing lots." As she spoke, she pulled three straws from the mat on which she sat and broke one off very short. "The man who draws the short straw shall be the victim. You; Senor Torres, draw first."

"Wedding bells for the short straw," Henry grinned.

Torres crossed himself, shivered, and drew. So patently long was the straw, that he executed a series of dancing steps as he sang:

"No wedding bells for me,
I'm as happy as can be... "

Francis drew next, and an equally long straw was his portion. To Henry there, was no choice. The remaining straw in Leoncia's hand was the fatal one. All tragedy was in his face as he looked instantly at Leoncia. And she, observing, melted in pity, while Francis saw her pity and did some rapid thinking. It was the way out. All the perplexity of the situation could be thus easily solved. Great as was his love for Leoncia, greater was his man's loyalty to Henry. Francis did not hesitate. With a merry slap of his hand on Henry's shoulder, he cried:

"Well, here's the one unattached bachelor who isn't afraid of matrimony. I'll marry her."

Henry's relief was as if he had been reprieved from impending death. His hand shot out to Francis' hand, and, while they clasped, their eyes gazed squarely into each other's as only decent, honest men's may gaze. Nor did either see the dismay registered in Leoncia's face at this unexpected denouement. The Lady Who Dreams had been right. Leoncia, as a woman, was unfair, loving two men and denying the Lady her fair share of men.

But any discussion that might have taken place, was prevented by the little maid of the village, who entered with women to serve them the midday meal. It was Torres' sharp eyes that first lighted upon the string of gems about the maid's neck. Rubies they were, and magnificent.

"The Lady Who Dreams just gave them to me," the maid said, pleased with their pleasure in her new possession.

"Has she any more?" Torres asked.

"Of course," was the reply. "Only just now did she show me a great chest of them. And they were all kinds, and much larger; but they were not strung. They were like so much shelled corn."

While the others ate and talked, Torres nervously smoked a cigarette. After that, he arose and claimed a passing indisposition that prevented him from eating.

"Listen," he quoth impressively. "I speak better Spanish than either of you two Morgans. Also, I know, I am confident, the Spanish woman character better. To show you my heart's in the right place,

I'll go in to her now and see if I can talk her out of this matrimonial proposition."

One of the spearmen barred Torres' way, but, after going within, returned and motioned him to enter. The Queen, reclined on the divan, nodded him to her graciously.

You do not eat?" she queried solicitously; and added, after he had reaffirmed his loss of appetite, "Then will you drink?"

Torres' eyes sparkled. Between the excitement he had gone through for the past several days, and the new adventure he was resolved upon, he knew not how, to achieve, he felt the important need of a drink. The Queen clapped her hands, and issued commands to the waiting woman who responded.

"It is very ancient, centuries old, as you will recognize, Da Vasco, who brought it here yourself four centuries ago," she said, as a man carried in and broached a small wooden

About the age of the keg there could be no doubt, and Torres, knowing that it had crossed the Western Ocean twelve generations before, felt his throat tickle with desire to taste its contents. The drink poured by the waiting woman was a big one, yet was Torres startled by the mildness of it. But quickly the magic of four-centuries-old spirits began to course through his veins and set the maggots crawling in his brain.

The Queen bade him sit on the edge of the divan at her feet, where she could observe him, and asked:

"You came unsummoned. What is it you have to tell me or ask of me?"

"I am the one selected," he replied, twisting his moustache and striving to look the enticingness of a male man on love adventure bent.

"Strange," she said. "I saw not your face in the Mirror of the World. There is … some mistake, eh?"

"A mistake," he acknowledged readily, reading certain knowledge in her eyes. "It was the drink. There is magic in it that made me speak the message of my heart to you, I want you so."

Again, with laughing eyes, she summoned the waiting woman and had his pottery mug replenished.

"A second mistake, perhaps will now result, eh?" she teased, when he had downed the drink.

"No, O Queen," he replied. "Now all is clarity. My true heart I can master. Francis Morgan, the one who kissed your hand, is the man selected to be your husband."

"It is true," she said solemnly. "His was the face I saw, and knew from the first."

Thus encouraged, Torres continued.

"I am his friend, his very good best friend. You, who know all things, know the custom of the marriage dowry. He has sent me, his best friend, to inquire into and examine the dowry of his bride. You must know that he is among the richest of men in his own country, where men are very rich."

So suddenly did she arise on the divan that Torres cringed and half shrank down, in his panic expectance of a knifeblade between his shoulders. Instead, the Queen walked swiftly, or, rather, glided, to the doorway to an inner apartment.

"Come!" she summoned imperiously. Once inside, at the first glance around, Torres knew the room for what it was, her sleeping chamber. But his eyes had little space for such details. Lifting the lid of a heavy chest of ironwood, brass-bound, she motioned him to look in. He obeyed, and saw the amazement of the world. The little maid had spoken true. Like so much shelled corn, the chest was filled with an incalculable treasure of gems diamonds, rubies, emeralds, sapphires, the most precious, the purest and largest of their kinds.

"Thrust in your arms to the shoulders," she said, "and make sure that these baubles be real and of the adamant of flint, rather than illusions and reflections of unreality dreamed real in a dream. Thus may you make certain report to your very rich friend who is to marry me."

And Torres, the madness of the ancient drink like fire in his brain, did as he was told.

"These trifles of glass are such an astonishment?" she plagued. "Your eyes are as if they were witnessing great wonders."

"I never dreamed in all the world there was such a treasure," he muttered in his drunkenness. "They are beyond price?"

"They are beyond price."

"They are beyond the value of valor, and love, and honor?"

"They are beyond all things. They are a madness."

"Can a woman's or a man's true love be purchased by them?"

"They can purchase all the world."

"Come," the Queen said. "You are a man. You have held women in your arms. Will they purchase women?"

"Since the beginning of time women have been bought and sold for them, and for them women have sold themselves."

"Will they buy me the heart of your good friend Francis?" For the first time Torres looked at her, and nodded and muttered, his eyes swimming with drink and wild-eyed with sight of such array of gems.

"Will good Francis so value them?" Torres nodded speechlessly.

Do all persons so value them?" Again he nodded emphatically.

She began to laugh in silvery derision. Bending, at haphazard she clutched a priceless handful of the pretties.

Come," she commanded. "I will show you how I value them."

She led him across the room and out on a platform that extended around three sides of a space of water, the fourth side being the perpendicular cliff. At the base of the cliff the water formed a whirlpool that advertised the drainage exit for the lake which Torres had heard the Morgans speculate about.

With another silvery tease of laughter, the Queen tossed the handful of priceless gems into the heart of the whirlpool. "Thus I value them," she said.

Torres was aghast, and, for the nonce, well-nigh sobered by such wantonness.

And they never come back," she laughed on. "Nothing ever comes back. Look!"

She flung in a handful of flowers that raced around and around the whirl and quickly sucked down from sight in the center of it.

If nothing comes back, where does everything go?" Torres asked thickly.

The Queen shrugged her shoulders, although he knew that she knew the secret of the waters.

"More than one man has gone that way," she said dreamily. "No one of them has ever returned. My mother went that way, after she was dead. I was a girl then." She roused. "But you, helmeted one, go now. Make report to your master your friend, I mean. Tell him what I possess for dowry. And, if he be half as mad as you about the bits of glass, swiftly will his arms surround me. I shall remain here and in dreams await his coming. The play of the water fascinates me."

Dismissed, Torres entered the sleeping chamber, crept back to steal a glimpse of the Queen, and saw her sunk down on the platform, head on hand, and gazing into the whirlpool. Swiftly he made his way to the chest, lifted the lid, and stowed a scooping handful into his trousers' pocket. Ere he could scoop a second handful, the mocking laughter of the Queen was at his back.

Fear and rage mastered him to such extent, that he sprang toward her, and pursuing her out upon the platform, was only prevented from seizing her by the dagger she threatened him with.

"Thief," she said quietly. "Without honor are you. And the way of all thieves in this valley is death. I shall summon my spearmen and have you thrown into the whirling water."

And his extremity gave Torres cunning. Glancing apprehensively at the water that threatened him, he ejaculated a cry of horror as if at what strange thing he had seen, sank down on one knee, and buried his convulsed face of simulated fear hi his hands. The Queen looked sidewise to see wfiat he had seen. Which was his moment. He rose in the air upon her like a leaping tiger, clutching her wrists and wresting the dagger from her.

He wiped the sweat from his face and trembled while he slowly recovered himself. Meanwhile she gazed upon him curiously, without fear.

"You are a woman of evil," he snarled at her, still shaking with rage, "a witch that traffics with the powers of darkness and all devilish things. Yet are you woman, born of woman, and therefore mortal. The weakness of mortality and of woman is yours, wherefore I give you now your choice of two things. Either you shall be thrown into the whirl of water and perish, or… " "Or?" she prompted.

"Or… " He paused, licked his dry lips, and burst forth. "No! By the Mother of God, I am not afraid. Or marry me this day, which is the other choice."

You would marry me for me? Or for the treasure?" For the treasure," he admitted brazenly. "But it is written in the Book of Life that I shall marry Francis," she objected.

Then will we rewrite that page in the Book of Life." "As if it could be done!" she laughed. "Then will I prove your mortality there in the whirl, whither I shall fling you as you flung the flowers."

Truly intrepid Torres was for the time intrepid because of the ancient drink that burned in his blood and brain, and because he was master of the situation. Also, like a true Latin- American, he loved a scene wherein he could strut and elocute.

Yet she startled him by emitting a hiss similar to the Latin way of calling a servitor. He regarded her suspiciously, glanced at the doorway to the sleeping chamber, then returned his gaze to her.

Like a ghost, seeing it only vaguely out of the corner of his eye, the great white hound erupted through the doorway. Startled again, Torres involuntarily stepped to the side. But his foot failed to come to rest on the emptiness of air it encountered, and the weight of his body toppled him down off the platform into the water. Even as he fell and screamed his despair, he saw the hound in mid-air leaping after him.

Swimmer that he was, Torres was like a straw in the grip of the current; and the Lady Who Dreams, gazing down upon him fascinated from the edge of the platform, saw him disappear, and the hound after him, into the heart of the whirlpool from which there was no return.

Chapter 20

LONG the Lady Who Dreams gazed down at the playing waters. At last, with a sighed "My poor dog," she arose. The passing of Torres had meant nothing to her. Accustomed from girlhood to exercise the high powers of life and death over her semi-savage and degenerate people, human life, per se, had no sacredness to her. If life were good and lovely, then, naturally, it was the right thing to let it live. But if life were evil, ugly, and dangerous to other lives, then the thing was to let it die or make it die. Thus, to her,

Torres had been an episode unpleasant, but quickly over.

But it was too bad about the dog.

Clapping her hands loudly as she entered her chamber, to summon one of her women, she made sure that the lid of the jewel chest was raised. To the woman she gave a command, and herself returned to the platform, from where she could look into the room unobserved.

A few minutes later, guided by the woman, Francis entered the chamber and was left alone. He was not in a happy mood. Fine as had been his giving up of Leoncia, he got no pleasure from the deed. Nor was there any pleasure in looking forward to marrying the strange lady who ruled over the Lost Souls and resided in this weird lake -dwelling. Unlike Torres, however, she did not arouse in him fear or animosity. Quite to the contrary, Francis' feeling toward her was largely that of pity. He could not help but be impressed by the tragic pathos of the ripe and lovely woman desperately seeking love and a mate, despite her imperious and cavalier methods.

At a glance he recognized the room for what it was, and idly wondered if he were already considered the bridegroom, sans discussion, sans acquiescence, sans ceremony. In his brown study, the chest scarcely caught his attention. The Queen, watching, saw him evidently waiting for her, and, after a few minutes, walk over to the chest. He gathered up a handful of the gems, dropped them one by one carelessly back as if they had been so many marbles, and turned and strolled over to examine the leopard skins on her couch. Next, he sat down upon it, oblivious equally of couch or treasure. All of which was provocative of such delight to the Queen that she could no longer withstrain herself to mere spying. Entering the room and greeting him, she laughed: "Was Senor Torres a liar?"

"Was?" Francis queried, for the need of saying something, as he arose before her.

"He no longer is," she assured him. "Which is neither here nor there," she hastened on as Francis began to betray interest in the matter of Torres' end. "He is gone, and it is well that he is gone, for he can never come back. But he did lie, didn't he?"

"Undoubtedly," Francis replied. "He is a confounded liar."

He could not help noticing the way her face fell when he so heartily agreed with her concerning Torres' veracity. "What did he say?" Francis questioned.

"That he was the one selected to marry me."

"A liar," Francis commented dryly.

"Next he said that you were the selected one which was also a lie," her voice trailed off.

Francis shook his head.

The involuntary cry of joy the Queen uttered touched his heart to such tenderness of pity that almost did he put his arms around her to soothe her. She waited for him to speak.

"I am the one to marry you," he went on steadily. "You are very, beautiful. When shall we be married?"

The wild joy in her face was such that he swore to himself that never would he willingly mar that face with marks of sorrow. She might be ruler over the Lost Souls, with the wealth of Ind and with supernatural powers of mirrorgazing ; but most poignantly she appealed to him as a lonely and naïve woman, overspilling of love and totally unversed in love,

"And I shall tell you of another lie this Torres animal told to me," she burst forth exultantly. "He told me that you were rich, and that, before you married me, you desired to know what wealth was mine. He told me you had sent him to inquire into what riches I possessed. This I know was a lie. You are not marrying me for that!" with a scornful gesture at the jewel chest. Francis shook his head.

"You are marrying me for myself," she rushed on in triumph.

"For yourself," Francis could not help but lie.

And then he beheld an amazing thing. The Queen, this Queen who was the sheerest autocrat, who said come here and go there, who dismissed the death of Torres with its mere announcement, and who selected her royal spouse without so much as consulting his prenuptial wishes, this Queen began to blush. Up her neck, flooding her face to her ears and forehead, welled the pink tide of maidenly modesty and embarrassment. And such sight of faltering made Francis likewise falter. He knew not what to do, and felt a warmth of blood rising under the sun-tan of his own face. Never, he thought, had there been a inan-and-woman situation like it in all the history of men and women. The mutual embarrassment of the pair of them was appalling, and to save his life he could not have summoned a jot of initiative. Thus, the Queen was compelled to speak first.

"And now," she said, blushing still more furiously, "you must make love to me."

Francis strove to speak, but his lips were so dry that he licked them and succeeded only in stammering incoherently.

"I never have been loved," the Queen continued bravely. "The affairs of my people are not love. My people are animals without reason. But we, you and I, are man and woman. There must be wooing, and tenderness that much I have learned from my Mirror of the World. But I am unskilled. I know not how. But you, from out of the great world, must surely know. I wait. You must love me."

She sank down upon the couch, drawing Francis beside her, and true to her word, proceeded to wait. While he, bidden to love at command, was paralyzed by the preposterous impossibility of so obeying.

"Am I not beautiful?" the Queen queried after another pause. "Are not your arms as mad to be about me as I am mad to have them about me? Never have a man's lips touched my lips. What is a kiss like on the lips, I mean? Your lips on my hand were ecstasy. You kissed then, not alone my hand, but my soul. My heart was there, throbbing against the press of your lips. Did you not feel it?"

"And so," she was saying, half an hour later, as they sat on the couch hand in hand, "I have told you the little I know of myself. I do not know the past, except what I have been told of it. The present I see clearly in my Mirror of the World. The future I can likewise see, but vaguely; nor can I always understand what I see. I was born here. So was my mother, and her mother. How it chanced is that always into the life of each queen came a lover. Sometimes, as you, they came here. My mother's mother, so it was told me, left the valley to find her lover and was gone a long time for years. So did my mother go forth. The secret is known to me, where the long dead conquistadores guard the Maya mysteries, and where Da Vasco himself stands whose helmet this Torres animal had the impudence to steal and claim for his own. Had you not come, I should have been compelled to go forth and find you, for you were my appointed one and had to be."

A woman entered, followed by a spearman, and Francis could scarce make his way through the quaint antiquated Spanish of the conversation that ensued. In commingled anger and joy, the Queen epitomized it to him.

"We are to depart now to the Long House for our wedding. The Priest of the Sun is stubborn, I know not why, save that he has been balked of the blood of all of you on his altar. He is very bloodthirsty. He is the Sun Priest, but he is possessed of little reason. I have report that he is striving to turn the people against our wedding the dog!" She clinched her hands, her face set, and her eyes blazed with royal fury. "He shall marry us, by the ancient custom, before the Long House, at the Altar of the Sun."

"It's not too late, Francis, to change your mind," Henry urged. "Besides, it is not fair. The short straw was mine. Am I not right, Leoncia?"

Leoncia could not reply. They stood in a group, at the forefront of the assembled Lost Souls, before the altar. Inside the Long House the Queen and the Sun Priest were closeted.

"You wouldn't want to see Henry marry her, would you, Leoncia?" Francis argued.

"Nor you, either," Leoncia countered. "Torres is the only one I'd like to have seen marry her. I don't like her. I would not care to see any friend of mine her husband."

"You're almost jealous," commented Henry. "Just the same, Francis doesn't seem so very cast down over his fate."

"She's not at all bad," Francis retorted. "And I can accept my fate with dignity, if not with equanimity. And I'll tell you something else, Henry, now that you are harping on this strain: she wouldn't marry you if you asked her."

"Oh, I don't know," Henry began.

"Then ask her," was the challenge. "Here she comes now. Look at her eyes. There's trouble brewing. And the priest's black as thunder. You just propose, to her and see what chance you've got while I'm around."

Henry nodded his head stubbornly.

"I will but not to show you what kind of a woman-conqueror I am, but for the sake of fair play. I wasn't playing the game when I accepted your sacrifice of yourself, but I am going to play the game now."

Before they could prevent him, he had thrust his way to the Queen, shouldered in between her and the priest, and began to speak earnestly. And the Queen laughed as she listened. But her laughter was not for Henry. With shining triumph she laughed across at Leoncia.

Not many moments were required to say no to Henry's persuasions, whereupon the Queen joined Leoncia and Francis, the priest tagging at her heels, and Henry, following more slowly, trying to conceal the gladness that was his at being rejected.

"What do you think," the Queen addressed Leoncia directly. "Good Henry has just asked me to marry him, which makes the fourth this day. Am I not well loved? Have you ever had four lovers, all desiring to marry you on your wedding day?"

"Four!" Francis exclaimed.

The Queen looked at him tenderly.

"Yourself, and Henry whom I have just declined. And, before either of you, this day, the insolent Torres; and, just now, in the Long House, the priest here." Wrath began to fire her eyes and cheeks at the recollection. "This Priest of the Sun, this priest long since renegade to his vows, this man who is only half a man, wanted me to marry him! The dog! The beast! And he had the insolence to say, at the end, that I should not marry Francis. Come. I will show him."

She nodded her own private spearmen up about the group, and with her eyes directed two of them behind the priest to include him. At sight of this, murmurs began to arise in the crowd.

"Proceed, priest," the Queen commanded harshly. "Else will my men kill you now."

He turned sharply about, as if to appeal to the people, but the speech that trembled to his lips died unuttered at sight of the spear-points at his breast. He bowed to the inevitable, and led the way close to the altar, placing the Queen and Francis facing him, while he stood above on the platform of the altar, looking at them and over them at the Lost Souls.

"I am the Priest of the Sun," he began. "My vows are holy. As the vowed priest I am to marry this woman, the Lady Who Dreams, to this stranger and intruder, whose blood is already forfeit to our altar. My vows are holy. I cannot be false to them. I refuse to marry this woman to this man. In the name of the Sun God I refuse to perform this ceremony—"

"Then shall you die, priest, here and now," the Queen hissed at him, nodding the near spearmen to lift their spears against him, and nodding the other spearmen to face the murmuring and semi-mutinous Lost Souls.

Followed a pregnant pause. For less than a minute, but for nearly a minute, no word was uttered, no thought was betrayed by a restless movement. All stood, like so many statues; and all gazed upon the priest against whose heart the poised spears rested.

He, whose blood of heart and life was nearest at stake in the issue, was the first to act. He gave in. Calmly he turned his back to the threatening spears, knelt, and, in archaic Spanish, prayed an invocation of fruitfulness to the Sun. Returning to the Queen and Francis, with a gesture he made them fully bow and almost half kneel before him. As he touched their hands with his finger-tips he could not forbear the involuntary scowl that convulsed his features.

As the couple arose, at his indication, he broke a small corn-cake in two, handing a half to each.

"The Eucharist," Henry whispered to Leoncia, as the pair crumbled and ate their portions of cake.

"The Roman Catholic worship Da Vasco must have brought in with him, twisted about until it is now the marriage ceremony," she whispered back comprehension, although, at sight of Francis thus being lost to her, she was holding herself tightly for control, her lips bloodless and stretched to thinness, her nails hurting into her palms.

From the altar the priest took and presented to the Queen a tiny dagger and a tiny golden cup. She spoke to Francis, who rolled up his sleeve and presented to her his bared left forearm. About to scarify his flesh, she paused, considered till all could see her visibly think, and, instead of breaking his skin, she touched the dagger point carefully to her tongue.

And then arose rage. At the taste of the blade she threw the weapon from her, half sprang at the priest, half gave command to her spearmen for the death of him, and shook and trembled in the violence of her effort for self-possession. Following with her eyes the flight of the dagger to assure herself that its poisoned point should not strike the flesh of another and wreak its evilness upon it, she drew from the breast-fold of her dress another tiny dagger. This, too, she tested with her tongue, ere she broke Francis' skin with the point of it and caught in the cup of gold the several red blooddrops that exuded from the incision. Francis repeated the same for her and on her, whereupon, under her flashing eyes, the priest took the cup and offered the commingled blood upon the altar.

Came a pause. The Queen frowned.

"If blood is to be shed this day on the altar of the Sun God" she began threateningly.

And the priest, as if recollecting what he was loath to do, turned to the people and made solemn pronouncement that the twain were man and wife. The Queen turned to Francis with glowing invitation to his arms. As he folded her to him and kissed her eager lips, Leoncia gasped and leaned closely to Henry for support. Nor did Francis fail to observe and understand her passing indisposition, although when the flush-faced Queen next sparkled triumph at her sister woman, Leoncia was to all appearance proudly indifferent.

Chapter 21

Two thoughts flickered in Torres' mind as he was sucked down. The first was of the great white hound which had leaped after him. The second was that the Mirror of the World told lies. That this was his end he was certain, yet the little he had dared permit himself to glimpse in the Mirror had given no hint of an end anything like this.

A good swimmer, as he was engulfed and sucked on in rapid, fluid darkness, he knew fear that he might have his brains knocked out by the stone walls or roof of the subterranean passage through which he was being swept. But the freak of the currents was such that not once did he collide with any part of his anatomy. Sometimes he was aware of being banked against water-cushions that tokened the imminence of a wall or boulder, at which times he shrank as it were into smaller compass, like a sea-turtle drawing in its head before the onslaught of sharks.

Less than a minute, as he measured the passage of time by the holding of his breath, elapsed, ere, in an easier-flowing stream, his head emerged above the surface and he refreshed his lungs with great inhalations of cool air. Instead of swimming, he contented himself with keeping afloat, and with wondering what had happened to the hound and with what next excitement would vex his underground adventure. Soon he glimpsed light ahead, the dim but unmistakable light of day; and, as the way grew brighter, he turned his face back and saw what made him proceed to swim with a speed-stroke. What he saw was the hound, swimming high, with the teeth of its huge jaws gleaming in the increasing light. Under the source of the light, he saw a shelving bank and climbed out. His first thought, which he half carried out, was to reach into his pocket for the gems he had stolen from the Queen's chest. But a reverberant barking that grew to thunder in the cavern reminded him of his fanged pursuer, and he drew forth the Queen's dagger instead.

Again two thoughts divided his judgment for action. Should he try to kill the swimming brute ere it landed? Or should he retreat up the rocks toward the light on the chance that the stream might carry the hound past him? His judgment settled on the second course of action, and he fled upw r ard along a narrow ledge. But the dog landed and followed with such four-footed certainty of speed that it swiftly overtook him. Torres turned at bay on the cramped footing, crouched, and brandished the dagger against the brute's leap.

But the hound did not leap. Instead, playfully, with jaws widespread of laughter, it sat down and extended its right paw in greeting. As he took the paw in his hand and shook it, Torres almost collapsed in the revulsion of relief. He laughed with exuberant shrilliness that advertised semihysteria, and continued to pump the hound's leg up and down, while the hound, with wide jaws and gentle eyes, laughed as exuberantly back.

Pursuing the shelf, the hound contentedly at heel and occasionally sniffing his calves, Torres found that the narrow track, paralleling the river, after an ascent descended to it again. And then Torres saw two things, one that made him pause and shudder, and one that made his heart beat high with hope. The first was the underground river. Rushing straight at the wall of rock, it plunged into it in a chaos of foam and turbulence, with stiffly serrated and spitefully spitting waves that advertised its' swiftness and momentum. The second was an opening to one side, through which streamed white daylight. Possibly fifteen feet in diameter was this opening, but across it was stretched a spider web more monstrous than any product of a madman's fancy. Most ominous of all was the debris of bones that lay beneath. The threads of the web were of silver and of the thickness of a lead pencil. He shuddered as he touched a thread with his hand. It clung to his flesh like glue, and only by an effort that agitated the entire web did he succeed in freeing his hand. Upon his clothes and upon the coat of the dog he rubbed off the stickiness from his skin.

Between two of the lower guys of the great web he saw that there was space for him to crawl through the opening to the day; but, ere he attempted it, caution led him to test the opening by helping and shoving the hound ahead of him. The white beast crawled and scrambled out of sight, and Torres was about to follow when it returned. Such was the panic haste of its return that it collided with him and both fell. But the man managed to save himself by clinging with his hands to the rocks, while the four-footed brute, not able so to check itself, fell into the churning water. Even as Torres reached a hand out to try to save it, the dog was carried under the rock.

Long Torres debated. That farther subterranean plunge of the river was dreadful to contemplate.

Above was the open way to the day, and the life of him yearned towards the day as a bee or a flower toward the sun. Yet what had the hound encountered to drive it back in such precipitate retreat? As he pondered, he became aware that his hand was resting on a rounded surface. He picked the object up, and gazed into the eyeless, noseless features of a human skull. His frightened glances played over the carpet of bones, and, beyond all idoubt, he made out the ribs and spinal columns and thigh bones of what had once been men. This inclined him toward the water as the way out, but at sight of the foaming madness of it plunging through solid rock he recoiled.

Drawing the Queen's dagger, he crawled up between the web-guys with infinite carefulness, saw what the hound had seen, and came back in such vertigo of retreat that he, too, fell into the water, and, with but time to fill his lungs with air, was drawn into the opening and into darkness.

In the meanwhile, back at the lake dwelling of the Queen, events no less portentous were occurring with no less equal rapidity. Just returned from the ceremony at the Long House, the wedding party was in the action of seating itself for what might be called the wedding breakfast, when an arrow, penetrating an interstice in the bamboo wall, flashed between the Queen and Francis and transfixed the opposite wall, where its feathered shaft vibrated from the violence of its suddenly arrested flight. A rush to the windows looking out upon the narrow bridge, showed Henry and Francis the gravity of the situation. Even as they looked, they saw the Queen's spearman who guarded the approach to the bridge, midway across it in flight, falling into the water with the shaft of an arrow vibrating out of his back in similar fashion to the one in the wall of the room. Beyond the bridge, on the shore, headed by their priest and backed by their women and children, all the male Lost Souls were arching the air full with feathered bolts from their bows.

A spearman of the Queen tottered into the apartment, his limbs spreading vainly to support him, his eyes glazing, his lips beating a soundless message which his fading life could not utter, as he fell prone, his back bristling with arrow shafts like a porcupine. Henry sprang to the door that gave entrance from the bridge, and, with his automatic, swept it clear of the charging Lost Souls who- could advance only in single file and who fell as they advanced before his fire.

The siege of the frail house was brief. Though Francis, protected by Henry's automatic, destroyed the bridge, by no method could the besieged put out the blazing thatch of roof ignited in a score of places by the fire-arrows discharged under the Sun Priest's directions.

"There is but one way to escape," the Queen panted, on the platform overlooking the whirl of waters, as she clasped one hand of Francis in hers and threatened to precipitate herself clingingly into his arms. "It wins to the world." She pointed to the sucking heart of the whirlpool. "No one has ever returned from that. In my Mirror I have beheld them pass, dead always, and out to the wider world. Except for Torres, I have never seen the living go. Only the dead. And they never returned.. Nor has Torres returned."

All eyes looked to all eyes at sight of the dreadfumess of the way.

"There is no other way?" Henry demanded, as he drew Leoncia close to him.

The Queen shook her head. About them already burning portions of the thatch were falling, while their ears were deafened by the blood-lust chantings of the Lost Souls on the lake-shore. The Queen disengaged her hand from Francis', with the evident intention of dashing into her sleeping room, then caught his hand and led him in. As he stood wonderingly beside her, she slammed down the lid on the chest of jewels and fastened it. Next, she kicked aside the floor matting and lifted a trap door that opened down to the water. At her indication, Francis dragged over the chest and dropped it through.

"Even the Sun Priest does not know that hiding place," she whispered, ere she caught his hand again, and, running, led him back to the others on the platform.

"It is now time to depart from this place," she announced.

"Hold me in your arms, good Francis, husband of mine, and lift me and leap with me," she commanded. "We will lead the way."

And so they leapt. As the roof was crashing down in a wrath of fire and flying embers, Henry caught Leoncia to him, and sprang after into the whirl of waters wherein Francis and the Queen had already disappeared.

Like Torres, the four fugitives escaped injury against the rocks and were borne onward by the underground river to the daylight opening where the great spider-web guarded the way. Henry had an easier time of it, for Leoncia knew how to swim. But Francis' swimming prowess enabled him to keep the Queen up. She obeyed him implicitly, floating low in the water, nor clutched at his arms nor acted as a drag on him in any way. At the ledge, all four drew out of the water and rested. The two women devoted themselves to wringing out their hair, which had been flung adrift all about them by the swirling currents.

"It is not the first mountain I have been in the heart of with you two, "Leoncia laughed to the Morgans, although more than for them was her speech intended for the Queen.

"It is the first time I have been in the heart of 9. mountain with my husband," the Queen laughed back, and the barb of her dart sank deep into Leoncia.

"Seems as though your wife, Francis, and my wife-to-be, aren't going to hit it off too well together," Henry said, with the sharpness of censure that man is wont to employ to conceal the embarrassment caused by his womankind.

And. as inevitable result of such male men's ways, all that Henry gained was a silence more awkward and more embarrassing. The two women almost enjoyed the situation. Francis cudgeled his brains vainly for some remark that wquld ameliorate matters; while Henry, in desperation, arose suddenly with the observation that he was going to "explore a bit," and invited, by his hand out to help her to her feet, the Queen to accompany him. Francis and Leoncia sat on for a moment in stubborn silence. He was the first to break it.

"For two cents I'd give you a thorough shaking, Leoncia."

"And what have I done now?" she countered.

"As if you didn't know. You've been behaving abominably." "It is you who have behaved abominably," she halfsobbed, in spite of her determination to betray no such feminine signs of weakness. "Who asked you to marry her? You did not draw the short straw. Yet you must volunteer, must rush in where even angels would fear to tread? Did I ask you to? Almost did my heart stop beating when I heard you tell Henry you would marry her. I thought I was going to faint. You had not even consulted me; yet it was on my suggestion, in order to save you from her, that the straws were drawn yes, and I am not too little shameless to admit that it was because I wanted to save you for myself . Henry does not love me as you led me to believe you loved me. I never loved Henry as I loved you, as I do love you even now, God forgive me."

Francis was swept beyond himself. He caught her and pressed her to him in a crushing embrace.

And on your very wedding day," she gasped reproachfully in the midmost of his embrace.

His arm died away from about her.

"And this from you, Leoncia, at such a moment," he murmured sadly.

And why not?" she flared. "You loved me. You gave me to understand, beyond all chance of misunderstanding, that you loved me; yet here, to-day, you went out of your way, went eagerly and gladly, and married yourself to the first woman with a white skin who presented herself."

"You are jealous," he charged, and knew a heart-throb of joy as she nodded. "And I grant you are jealous; but at the same time, exercising the woman's prerogative of lying, you are lying now. What I did, was not done eagerly nor gladly. I did it for your sake and my sake or for Henry's sake, rather. Thank God, I have a man's honor still left to me!"

"Man's honour does not always satisfy woman," she replied.

"Would you prefer me dishonorable?" he was swift on the uptake.

"I am only a woman who loves," she pleaded.

"You are a stinging, female wasp," he raged, "and you are not fair."

"Is any woman fair when she loves?" she made the great confession and acknowledgment. "Men may succeed in living in their heads of honor; but know, and as a humble woman I humbly state my womanhood, that woman lives only in her heart of love."

"Perhaps you are right. Honor, like arithmetic, can be reasoned and calculated. Which leaves a woman no morality, but only... "

"Only moods," Leoncia completed abjectly for him.

Calls from Henry and the Queen put an end to the conversation, for Leoncia and Francis quickly joined the others in gazing at the great web.

"Did you ever see so monstrous a web!" Leoncia exclaimed.

"I'd like to see the monster that made it," said Henry.

"And I'd rather see than be it," Francis paraphrased from the "Purple Cow."

"It is our good fortune that we do not have to go that way," the Queen said.

All looked inquiry at her, and she pointed down to the stream.

"That is the way," she said. "I know it. Often and often, in my Mirror of the World, have I seen the way. When my mother died and was buried in the whirlpool, I followed her body in the Mirror, and I saw it come to this place and go by this place still in the water." But she was dead," Leoncia objected quickly.

The rivalry between them fanned instantly.

"One of my spearmen," the Queen went on quietly, "a handsome youth, alas, dared to look at me as a lover. He was flung in alive. I watched him, too, in the Mirror. When he came to this place he climbed out. I saw him crawl under the web to the day, and I saw him retreat backward from the day and throw himself into the stream."

"Another dead one," Henry commented grimly.

"No; for I followed him on in the Mirror, and though all was darkness for a time and I could see nothing, in the end, and shortly, under the sun he emerged into the bosom of a large river, and swam to the shore, and climbed the bank it was the left hand bank as I remember well and disappeared among large trees such as do not grow in the Valley of the Lost Souls."

But, like Torres, the rest of them recoiled from thought of the dark plunge through the living rock.

"These are the bones of animals and of men," the Queen warned, "who were daunted by the way of the water and who strove to gain the sun. Men there are there behold! Or at least what remains of them for a space, the bones, ere, in time, the bones, too, pass into nothingness."

"Even so," said Francis, "I suddenly discover a pressing need to look into the eye of the sun. Do the rest of you remain here while I investigate."

Drawing his automatic, the water-tightness of the cartridges a guarantee, he crawled under the web. The moment he had disappeared from view beyond the web, they heard him begin to shoot. Next, they saw him retreating backward, still shooting. And, next, falling upon him, two yards across from black-haired leg-tip to black-haired leg-tip, the denizen of the web, a monstrous spider, still wriggling with departing life, shot through and through again and again. The solid center of its body, from which the legs radiated, was the size of a normal waste-basket, and the substantial density of it crunched audibly as it struck on Francis' shoulders and back, rebounded, the hairy legs still helplessly quivering, and pitched down into the wave-crisping water. All four pair of eyes watched the corpse of it plunge against the wall of rock, suck down, and disappear.

"Where there's one, there are two," said Henry, looking dubiously up toward the daylight.

"It is the only way," said the Queen. "Come, my husband, each in the other's arms let us win through the darkness to the sun-bright world. Remember, I have never seen it, and soon, with you, shall I for the first time see it."

Her arms open in invitation, Francis could not decline. "It is a hole in the sheer wall of a precipice a thousand feet deep," he explained to the others the glimpse he had caught from beyond the spider web, as he clasped the Queen in his arms and leaped off.

Henry had gathered Leoncia to him and was about to leap, when she stopped him.

Why did you accept Francis' sacrifice?" she demanded. Because... He paused and looked at her wonderingly.

"Because I wanted you," he completed. "Because I was engaged to you as well, while Francis was unattached. Besides, if I'm not greatly mistaken, Francis appears to be a pretty well satisfied bridegroom."

"No," she shook her head emphatically. "He has a chivalrous spirit, and he is acting his part in order not to hurt her feelings."

Oh, I don't know. Remember, before the altar, at the Long House, when I said I was going to ask the Queen to marry me, that he bragged she wouldn't marry me if I did ask? Well, the conclusion's pretty obvious that he wanted her himself. And why shouldn't he? He's a bachelor. And she's some nice woman herself."

But Leoncia scarcely heard. With a quick movement, leaning back in his arms away from him so that she could look him squarely in the eyes, she demanded:

"How do you love me? Do you love me madly? Do you love me badly madly? Do I mean that to you, and more, and more, and more?"

He could only look his bewilderment.

"Do you? do you?" she urged passionately.

"Of course I do," he made slow answer, "but it would never have entered my head to describe it that way. Why, you're the one woman for me. Rather would I describe it as loving you deeply, and greatly, and enduringly. W 7 hy, you seem so much a part of me that I feel almost as if I had always, known you. It was that way from the first."

"She is an abominable woman!" Leoncia broke forth irrelevantly. "I hated her from the first."

"My! What a spitfire! I hate to think how much you would have hated her had I married her instead of Francis."

"We'd better follow them," she put an end to the discussion.

And Henry, very much bepuzzled, clasped her tightly and leaped off into the white turmoil of water.

On the bank of the Gualaca River sat two Indian girls fishing. Just up-stream from them arose the precipitous cliff of one of the buttresses of the lofty mountains. The main stream flowed past in chocolate-colored spate; but, directly beneath them, where they fished, was a quiet eddy. No less quiet was the fishing. No bites jerked their rods in token that the bait was enticing. One of them, Nicoya, yawned, ate ja banana, yawned again, and held the skin she was about to cast aside suspended in her hand.

"We have been very quiet, Concordia," she observed to her companion, "and it has won us no fish. Now shall I make a noise and a splash. Since they say 'what goes up must come down,' why should not something come up after something has gone down? I am going to try. There!" She threw the banana peel into the water and lazily watched the point where it had struck.

"If anything comes up I hope it will be big," Concordia murmured with equal laziness.

And upon their astonished gaze, even as they looked, arose up out of the brown depths a great white hound. They jerked their poles up and behind them on the bank, threw their arms about each other, and watched the hound gain the shore at the lower end of the eddy, climb the sloping bank, pause to shake himself, and then disappear among the trees.

Nicoya and Concordia giggled.

"Try it again," Concordia urged.

"No; you this time. And see what you can bring up."

Quite unbelieving, Concordia tossed in a clod of earth. And almost immediately a helmeted head arose on the flood. Clutching each other very tightly, they watched the man under the helmet gain the shore where the hound had landed and disappear into the forest.

Again the two Indian girls giggled ; but this time, urge as they would, neither could raise the courage to throw anything into the water.

Some time later, still giggling over the strange occurrences, they were espied by two young Indian men, who were hugging the bank as they paddled their canoe up against the stream.

"What makes you laugh," one of them greeted.

"We have been seeing things," Nicoya gurgled down to them.

"Then have you been drinking pulque," the young man charged.

Both girls shook their heads, and Concordia said:

"We don't have to drink to see things. First, when Nicoya threw in a banana skin, we saw a dog come up out of the water a white dog that was as big as a tiger of the mountains—"

"And when Concordia threw in a clod," the other girl took up the tale, "up came a man with a head of iron. It is magic. Concordia and I can work magic."

"Jose," one of the Indians addressed his mate, "this merits a drink."

And each, in turn, while the other with his paddle held the canoe in place, took a swig from a square-face Holland gin bottle part full of pulque.

"No," said Jose, when the girls had begged him for a drink. "One drink of pulque and you might see more white dogs as big as tigers or more iron-headed men."

"All right," Nicoya accepted the rebuff. "Then do you throw in your pulque bottle and see what you will see. We drew a dog and a man. Your prize may be the devil."

"I should like to see the devil," said Jose, taking another drain at the bottle. "The pulque is a true fire of bravery. I should very much like to see the devil."

He passed the bottle to his companion with a gesture to finish it.

"Now throw it into the water," Jose commanded.

The empty bottle struck with a forceful splash, and the evoking was realized with startling immediacy, for up to the surface floated the monstrous, hairy body of the slain spider. Which was too much for ordinary Indian flesh and blood. So suddenly did both young men recoil from the sight that they capsized the canoe. When their heads emerged from the water they struck out for the swift current, and were swiftly borne away down stream, followed more slowly by the swamped canoe.

Nicoya and Concordia had been too frightened to giggle. They held on to each other and waited, watching the magic water and out of the tails of their eyes observing the frightened young men capture the canoe, tow it to shore, and run out and hide on the bank.

The afternoon sun was getting low in the sky ere the girls summoned courage again to evoke the magic water. Only after much discussion did they agree both to fling in clods of earth at the same time. And up arose a man and a woman—Francis and the Queen. The girls fell over backward into the bushes, and were themselves unobserved as they watched Francis swim with the Queen to shore.

"It may just have happened all these things may just have happened at the very times we threw things into the water," Nicoya whispered to Concordia five minutes later.

"But when we threw one thing in, only one came up," Concordia argued. "And when we threw two, two came up."

"Very well," said Nicoya. "Let us now prove it. Let us try again, both of us. If nothing comes up, then have we no power of magic."

Together they threw in clods, and uprose another man and womaji But this pair, Henry and Leoncia, could swim, and they swam side by side to the natural landing place, and, like the rest that had preceded them, passed on out of sight among the trees.

Long the two Indian girls lingered. For they had agreed to throw nothing, and, if something arose, then would coincidence be proved. But if nothing arose, because nothing further was by them evoked, they could only conclude that the magic was truly theirs. They lay hidden and w r atched the water until darkness hid it from their eyes; and, slowly and soberly, they took the trail back to their village, overcome by an awareness of having been blessed by the gods.

Chapter 22

NOT until the day following his escape from the subterranean river, did Torres reach San Antonio. He arrived on foot, jaded and dirty, a small Indian boy at his heels carrying the helmet of Da Vasco. For Torres wanted to show the helmet to the Jefe and the Judge in evidence of the narrative of strange adventure he chuckled to tell them.

First on the main street he encountered the Jefe, who cried out loudly at his appearance.

"Is it truly you, Senor Torres?" The Jefe crossed himself solemnly ere he shook hands.

The solid flesh, and, even more so, the dirt and grit of the other's hand, convinced the Jefe of reality and substance.

Whereupon the Jefe became wrathful.

"And here I've been looking upon you as dead!" he exclaimed. "That Caroo dog of a JoseMancheno! He came back and reported you dead dead and buried until the Day of Judgment in the heart of the Maya Mountain."

"He is a fool, and I am possibly the richest man in Panama," Torres replied grandiosely. "At least, like the ancient and heroic conquistadores, I have braved all dangers and penetrated to the treasure. I have seen it. Nay—"

Torres' hand had been sunk into his trousers' pocket to bring forth the filched gems of the Lady Who Dreams; but he withdrew the hand empty. Too many curious eyes of the street were already centered upon him and the draggled figure he cut.

"I have much to say to you," he told the Jefe, "that cannot well be said now. I have knocked on the doors of the dead and worn the shrouds of corpses. And I have consorted with men four centuries dead but who were not dust, and I have beheld them drown in the second death. I have gone through mountains, as well as over them, and broken bread with lost souls, and gazed into the Mirror of the World. All of which I shall tell you, my best friend, and the honorable Judge, in due time, for I shall make you rich along with me."

"Have you looked upon the pulque when it was sour?" the Jefe quipped incredulously.

"I have not had drink stronger than water since I last departed from San Antonio," was the reply. "And I shall go now to my house and drink a long long drink, and after that I shall bathe the filth from me, and put on garments whole and decent."

Not immediately, as he proceeded, did Torres gain his house. A ragged urchin exclaimed out at sight of him, ran up to him, and handed him an envelope that he knew familiarly to be from the local government wireless, and that he was certain had been sent by Regan.

You are doing well. Imperative you keep party away from New York for three weeks more. Fifty thousand if you succeed.

Borrowing a pencil from the boy, Torres wrote a reply on the back of the envelope:

Send the money. Party will never come back from mountains where he is lost.

Two other occurrences delayed Torres' long drink and bath. Just as he was entering the jewelry store of old Kodriguez Fernandez, he was intercepted by the old Maya priest with whom he had last parted in the Maya mountain. He recoiled as from an apparition, for sure he was that the old man was drowned in the Boom of the Gods. Like the Jefe at sight of Torres, so Torres, at sight of the priest, drew back in startled surprise.

"Go away," he said. "Depart, restless old man. "You are a spirit. Thy body lies drowned and horrible in the heart of the mountain. You are an appearance, a ghost. Go away, nothing corporeal resides in this illusion of you, else would I strike you. You are a ghost. Depart at once. I should not like to strike a ghost."

But the ghost seized his hands and clung to them with ouch beseeching corporality as to unconvince him.

"Money," the ancient one babbled. "Let me have money. Lend me money. I will repay! I who know the secrets of the Maya treasure. My son is lost in the mountain with the treasure. The Gringos also are lost in the mountain. Help me to rescue my son. With him alone will I be satisfied, while the treasure shall all be yours. But we must take men, and much of the white man's wonderful powder and tear a hole out of the mountain so that the water will run away. He is not drowned. He is a prisoner of the water in the room where stand the jewel-eyed Chia and Hzatzl. Their eyes of green and red alone will pay for all the wonderful powder in the world. So let me have the money with which to buy the wonderful powder."

But Alvarez Torres was a strangely constituted man. Some warp or slant or idiosyncrasy of his nature always raised insuperable obstacles to his parting with money when such parting was unavoidable. And the richer he got the more positively this idiosyncrasy asserted itself.

"Money!" he asserted harshly, as he thrust the old priest aside and pulled open the door of Fernandez's store. "Is it I who should have money . I who am all rags and tatters as a beggar. I have no money for myself, much less for you, old man. Besides, it was you, and not I, who led your son to the Maya mountain. On your head be it, not on mine, the death of your son who fell into the pit under the feet of Chia that was digged by your ancestors and not by mine."

Again the ancient one clutched at him and yammered for money with which to buy dynamite. So roughly did Torres thrust him aside that his old legs failed to perform their wonted duty and he fell upon the flagstones.

The shop of Rodriguez Fernandez was small and dirty, and contained scarcely more than a small and dirty showcase that rested upon an equally small and dirty counter. The place was grimy with the undusted and unswept filth of a generation. Lizards and cockroaches crawled along the walls. Spiders webbed in every corner, and Torres saw, crossing the ceiling above, what made him step hastily to the side. It was a seven-inch centipede which he did not care to have fall casually upon his head or down his back between shirt and skin. And, when he appeared crawling out like a huge spider himself from some inner den of an unventilated cubicle, Fernandez looked like an Elizabethan stage-representation of Shylock withal he was a dirtier Shylock than even the Elizabethan stage could have stomached.

The jeweler fawned to Torres and in a cracked falsetto humbled himself even beneath the dirt of his shop. Torres pulled from his pocket a haphazard dozen or more of the gems filched from the Queen's chest, selected the smallest, and, without a word, while at the same time returning the rest to his pocket, passed it over to the jeweler.

"I am a poor man," he cackled, the while Torres could not fail to see how keenly he scrutinised the gem.

He dropped it on the top of the show case as of little worth, and looked inquiringly at his customer. But Torres waited in a silence which he knew would compel the garrulity of covetous age to utterance.

"Do I understand that the honorable Senor Torres seeks advice about the quality of the stone?" the old jeweler finally quavered.

Torres did no more than nod curtly.

"It is a natural gem. It is small. It, as you can see for yourself, is not perfect. And it is clear that much of it will be lost in the cutting."

"How much is it worth?" Torres demanded with impatient bluntness.

"I am a poor man," Fernandez reiterated.

"I have not asked you to buy it, old fool. But now that you bring the matter up, how much will you give for it?"

"As I was saying, craving your patience, honorable senor, as I was saying, I am a very poor man. There are days when I cannot spend ten centavos for a morsel of spoiled fish. There are days when I cannot afford a sip of the cheap red wine I learned was tonic to my system when I was a lad, far from Barcelona, serving my apprenticeship in Italy. I am so very poor that I do not buy costly pretties"

"Not to sell again at a profit?" Torres cut in.

"If I am sure of my profit," the old man cackled. "Yes, then will I buy ; but, being poor, I cannot pay more than little." He picked up the gem and studied it long and carefully. "I would give," he began hesitatingly, "I would give but, please, honorable senor, know that I am a very poor man. This day only a spoonful of onion soup, with my morning coffee and a mouthful of crust, passed my lips—"

"In God's name, old fool, what will you give?" Torres thundered.

"Five hundred dollars but I doubt the profit that will remain to me."

"Gold?"

"Mex.," came the reply, which cut the offer in half and which Torres knew was a lie. "Of course, Mex., only Mex., all our transactions are in Mex."

Despite his elation at so large a price for so small a gem, Torres play-acted impatience as he reached to take back the gem. But the old man jerkgd his hand away, loath to let go of the bargain it contained.

"We are old' friends," he cackled shrilly. "I first saw you, when, a boy, you came to San Antonio from Boca del Toros. And, as between old friends, we will say the sum is gold."

And Torres caught a sure but vague glimpse of the enormousness, as well as genuineness, of the Queen's treasure which at some remote time the Lost Souls had ravished from its hiding place in the Maya Mountain.

"Very good," said Torres, with a quick, cavalier action recovering the stone. "It belongs to a friend of mine. He wanted to borrow money from me on it. I can now lend him up to five hundred gold on it, thanks to your information. And I shall be grateful to buy for you, the next time we meet in the pulqueria, a drink yes, as many drinks as you can care to carry of the thin, red, tonic wine."

And as Torres passed out of the shop, not in any way attempting to hide the scorn and contempt he felt for the fool he had made of the jeweler, he knew elation in that Fernandez, the Spanish fox, must have cut his estimate of the gem's value fully in half when he uttered it.

In the meanwhile, descending the Gualaca River by canoe, Leoncia, the Queen, and the two Morgans, had made better time than Torres to the coast. But ere their arrival and briefly pending it, a matter of moment that was not appreciated at the time, had occurred at the Solano hacienda. Climbing the winding pathway to the hacienda, accompanied by a decrepit old crone whose black shawl over head and shoulders could not quite hide the lean and withered face of blasted volcanic fire, came as strange a caller as the hacienda had ever received.

He was a Chinaman, middle-aged and fat, whose moonlace beamed the beneficent good nature that seems usual with fat persons. By name, Yi Poon, meaning "the Cream of the Custard Apple," his manners were as softly and richly oily as his name. To the old crone, who tottered beside him and was half -supported by him, he was the quintessence of gentleness and consideration. When she faltered from sheer physical weakness and would have fallen, he paused and gave her chance to gain strength and breath. Thrice, at such times, on the climb to the hacienda, he fed her a spoonful of French brandy from a screw-cap pocket flask.

Seating the old woman in a selected, shady corner of the piazza, Yi Poon boldly knocked for admittance at the front door. To him, and in his business, back-stairs was the accustomed way; but his business and his wdt had taught him the times when front entrances were imperative.

The Indian maid who answered his knock, took his message into the living room wiiere sat the disconsolate Enrico Solano among his sons disconsolate at the report Bicardo had brought in of the loss of Leoncia in the Maya Mountain. The Indian maid returned to the door. The Senor Solano was indisposed and would see nobody, was her report, humbly delivered, even though the recipient was a Chinese.

"Huh!" observed Yi Poon, with braggart confidence for the purpose of awing the maid to carrying a second message. "I am no coolie. I am smart Chinaman. I go to school plenty much. I speak Spanish. I speak English. I write Spanish. I write English. See I write now in Spanish for the Senor Solano. You cannot write, so you cannot read what I write. I write that I am Yi Poon. I belong Colon. I come this place to see Senor Solano. Big business. Much important. Very secret. I write all this here on paper which you cannot read."

But he did not say that he had further written: "The Senorita Solano. I have great secret."

It was Alesandro, the eldest of the tall sons of Solano, who evidently had received the note, for he came bounding to the door, far outstripping the returning maid.

"Tell me your business!" he almost shouted at the fat Chinese. "What is it? Quick!"

"Very good business," was the reply, Yi Poon noting the other's excitement with satisfaction. "I make much money. I buy what you call secrets. I sell secrets. Very nice business."

"What do you know about the Senorita Solano?" Alesandro shouted, gripping him by the shoulder.

"Everything. Very important information… "

But Alesandro could no longer control himself. He almost hurled the Chinaman into the house, and, not relaxing his grip, rushed him on into the living room and up to Enrico.

"He has news of Leoncia!" Alesandro shouted.

"Where is she?" Enrico and his sons shouted in chorus.

Hah! was Yi Poon's thought. Such excitement, although it augured well for his business, was rather exciting for him as well.

Mistaking his busy thinking for fright, Enrico stilled his sons back with an upraised hand, and addressed the visitor quietly.

"Where is she?" Enrico asked.

Hah! thought Yi Poon. The senorita was lost. That was a new secret. It might be worth something some day, or any day. A nice girl, of high family and wealth such as the Solanos, lost in a Latin-American country, was information well worth possessing. Some day she might be married there was that gossip he had heard in Colon and some later day she might have trouble with her husband or her husband have trouble with her - at which time, she or her husband, it mattered not which, might be eager to pay high for the secret.

"This Senorita Leoncia," he said, finally, with sleek suavity. "She is not your girl. She has other papa and mama."

But Enrico's present grief at her loss was too great to permit startlement at this explicit statement of an old secret. "Yes," he nodded. "Though it is not known outside my family, I adopted her when she was a baby. It is strange that you should know this. But I am not interested in having you tell me what I have long since known. What I want to know now is: where is she now?"

Yi Poon gravely and sympathetically shook his head.

"That is different secret," he explained. "Maybe I find that secret. Then I sell it to you. But I have old secret. You do not know the name of the Senorita Leoncia's papa and mama. I know."

And old Enrico Solano could not hide his interest at the temptation of such information.

"Speak," he commanded. "Name the names, and prove them, and I shall reward."

"No," Yi Poon shook his head. "Very poor business. I no do business that way. You pay me I tell you. My secrets good secrets. I prove my secrets. You give me five hundred pesos and big expenses from Colon to San Antonio and back to Colon and I tell you name of papa and mama."

Enrico Solano bowed acquiescence, and was just in the act of ordering Alesandro to go and fetch the money, when the quiet, spirit-subdued Indian maid created a diversion. Bunning into the room and up to Enrico as they had never seen her run before, she wrung her hands and wept so incoherently that they knew her paroxysm was of joy, not of sadness.

"The Senorita!" she was finally able to whisper hoarsely, as she indicated the side piazza with a nod of head and glance of eyes. "The Senorita!"

And Yi Poon and his secret were forgotten. Enrico and his sons streamed out to the side piazza to behold Leoncia and the Queen and the two Morgans, dropping dust-covered off the backs of riding mules recognizable as from the pastures of the mouth of the Gualaca Kiver. At the same time two Indian man-servants, summoned by the maid, cleared the house and grounds of the fat Chinaman and his old crone of a companion.

"Come some other time," they told him. "Just now the Senor Solano is very importantly busy."

"Sure, I come some other time," Yi Poon assured them pleasantly, without resentment and without betrayal of the disappointment that was his at his deal interrupted just ere the money was paid into his hand.

But he departed reluctantly. The place was good for his business. It was sprouting secrets. Never was there a riper harvest in Canaan out of which, sickle in hand, a husbandman was driven! Had it not been for the zealous Indian attendants, Yi Poon would have darted around the corner of the hacienda to note the newcomers. As it was, half way down the hill, finding the weight of the crone too fatiguing, he put into her life and ability to carry her own weight a little farther by feeding her a double teaspoonf ul of brandy from his screw-top flask.

Enrico swept Leoncia off her mule ere she could dismount, so passionately eager was he to fold her in his arms. For several minutes ensued naught but noisy Latin affection as her brothers all strove to greet and embrace her at once. When they recollected themselves, Francis had already helped the Lady Who Dreams from her mount, and beside her, her hand in his, was waiting recognition.

"This is my wife," Francis told Enrico. "I went into the Cordilleras after treasure, and behold what I found. Was there ever better fortune?"

And she sacrificed a great treasure herself," Leoncia murmured bravely.

"She was queen of a little kingdom," Francis added, with a grateful and admiring flash of eyes to Leoncia, who quickly added:

"And she saved all our lives but sacrificed her little kingdom in so doing."

And Leoncia, in an exaltation of generousness, put her arm around the Queen's waist, took her away from Francis, and led the way into the hacienda.

Chapter 23

IN all the magnificence of medieval Spanish and New World costume such as was still affected by certain of the great haciendados of Panama, Torres rode along the beach-road to the home of the Solanos. Running with him, at so easy a lope that it promised an extension that would outspeed the best of Torres' steed, was the great white hound that had followed him down the subterranean river. As Torres turned to take the winding road up the hill to the hacienda, he passed Yi Poon, who had paused to let the old crone gather strength. He merely noticed the strange couple as dirt of the common people. The hauteur that he put on with his magnificence of apparel forbade that he should betray any interest further than an unseeing glance.

But him Yi Poon noted with slant Oriental eyes that missed no details. And Yi Poon thought: He looks very rich. He is a friend of the Solanos. He rides to the house. He may even be a lover of the Senorita Leoncia. Or a worsted rival for her love. In almost any case, he might be expected to buy the secret of the Senorita Leoncia's birth, and he certainly looks rich, most rich.

Inside the hacienda, assembled in the living room, were the returned adventurers and all the Solanos. The Queen, taking her turn in piecing out the narrative of all that had occurred, with flashing eyes was denouncing Torres for his theft of her jewels and describing his fall into the whirlpool before the onslaught of the hound, when Leoncia, at the window with Henry, uttered a sharp exclamation.

"Speak of the devil!" said Henry. "Here comes Torres himself."

"Me first!" Francis cried, doubling his fist and flexing his biceps significantly.

"No," decreed Leoncia. "He is a wonderful liar. He is a very Wonderful liar, as we've all found out. Let us have some fun, He is dismounting now. Let the four of us dis- appear. Father!" With a wave of hand she indicated Enrico and all his sons. "You will sit around desolated over the loss of me. This scoundrel Torres will enter. You will be thirsty for information. He will tell you no one can guess what astounding lies about us. As for us, we'll hide behind the screen there. Come! All of you!"

And, catching the Queen by the hand and leading the way, with her eyes she commanded Francis and Henry to follow to the hiding place.

And Torres entered upon a scene of sorrow which had been so recently real that Enrico and his sons had no difficulty in acting it. Enrico started up from his chair in eagerness of welcome and sank weakly back. Torres caught the other's hand in both his own and manifested deep sympathy and could not speak from emotion.

"Alas!" he finally managed heart-brokenly. "They are dead. She is dead, your beautiful daughter, Leoncia. And the two Gringo Morgans are dead with her. As Eicardo, there, must know, they died in the heart of the Maya Mountain.

"It is the home of mystery," he continued, after giving due time for the subsidence of the first violent outburst of Enrico's grief. "I was with them when they died. Had they followed my counsel, they would all have lived. But not even Leoncia would listen to the old friend of the Solanos. No, she must listen to the two Gringos. After incredible dangers I won my way out through the heart of the mountain, gazed down into the Valley of Lost Souls, and returned into the mountain to find them dying—"

Here, pursued by an Indian man-servant, the white hound bounded into the room, trembling and whining in excitement as with its nose it quested the multitudinous scents of the room that advertised his mistress. Before he could follow up to where the Queen hid behind the screen, Torres caught him, by the neck and turned him over to a couple of the Indian house-men to hold.

"Let the brute remain," said Torres. "I will tell you about him afterward. But first look at this." He pulled forth a handful of gems. "I knocked on the doors of the dead, and, behold, the Maya treasure is mine. I am the richest man in Panama, in all the Americas. I shall be powerful—"

"But you were with my daughter when she died." Enrico interrupted to sob, "Had she no word for me?" "Yes," Torres sobbed back, genuinely affected by the death-scene of his fancy. "She died with your name on her lips. Her last words were—"

But, with bulging eyes, he failed to complete his sentence, for he was watching Henry and Leoncia, in the most natural, casual manner in the world stroll down the room, immersed in quiet conversation. Not noticing Torres, they crossed over to the window still deep in talk.

"You were telling me her last words were… ?" Enrico prompted.

"I… I have lied to you," Torres stammered, while he sparred for time in which to get himself out of the scrape. "I was confident that they were as good as dead and would never find their way to the world again. And I thought to soften the blow to you, Senor Solano, by telling what I am confident would be her last words were she dying. Also, this man Francis, whom you have elected to like. I thought it better for you to believe him dead than know him for the Gringo cur he is."

Here the hound barked joyfully at the screen, giving the two Indians all they could do to hold him back. But Torres, instead of suspecting, blundered on to his fate.

In the Valley there is a silly weak demented creature who pretends to read the future by magic. An altogether atrocious and blood-thirsty female is she. I am not denying that in physical beauty she is beautiful. For beautiful she is, as a centipede is beautiful to those who think centipedes are beautiful. You see what has happened. She has sent Henry and Leoncia out of the Valley by some secret way, while Francis has elected to remain there with her in sin for sin it is, since there exists in the valley no Catholic priest to make their relation lawful. Oh, not that Francis is infatuated with the terrible creature.

But he is infatuated with a paltry treasure the creature possesses. And this is the Gringo Francis you have welcomed into the bosom of your family, the slimy snake of a Gringo Francis who has even flared to sully the fair Leoncia by casting upon her the looks of a lover. Oh, I know of what I speak. I have seen—"

A joyous outburst from the hound drowned his voice, and he beheld Francis and the Queen, as deep in conversation as the two who had preceded them, walk down the room. The Queen paused to caress the hound, who stood so tall against her that his forepaws, on her shoulders, elevated his head above hers; while Torres licked his suddenly dry lips and vainly cudgeled his brains for some fresh lie with which to extricate himself from the impossible situation.

Enrico Solano was the first to break down in mirth. All his sons joined him, while tears of sheer delight welled out of his eyes.

"I could have married her myself," Torres sneered malignantly. "She begged me on her knees."

"And now," said Francis, "I shall save you all a dirty job by throwing him out."

But Henry, advancing swiftly, asserted:

"I like dirty jobs equally. And this is a dirty job particularly to my liking."

Both the Morgans were about to fall on Torres, when the Queen held up her hand.

"First," she said, "let him return to me, from there in his belt, the dagger he stole from me."

"Ah," said Enrico, when this had been accomplished. "Should he not also return to you, lovely lady, the gems he filched?"

Torres did not hesitate. Dipping into his pocket, he laid a handful of the jewels on the table. Enrico glanced at the Queen, who merely waited expectantly.

"More," said Enrico.

And three more of the beautiful uncut stones Torres added to the others on the table.

"Would you search me like a common pickpocket?" he demanded in frantic indignation, turning both trousers' pockets emptily inside out.

"Me," said Francis.

"I insist," said Henry.

"Oh, all very well," Francis conceded. "Then we'll do it together. We can throw him farther off the steps."

Acting as one, they clutched Torres by collar and trousers and started in a propulsive rush for the door.

All others in the room ran to the windows to behold Torres' exjt; but Enrico, quickest of all, gained a window first. And, afterward, into the middle of the room, the Queen scooped the gems from the table into both her hands, and gave the double handful to Leoncia, saying:

"From Francis and me to you and Henry your wedding present."

Yi Poon, having left the crone by the beach and crept back to peer at the house from the bushes, chuckled gratifiedly to himself when he saw the rich caballero thrown off the steps with such a will as to be sent sprawling far out into the gravel. But Yi Poon was too clever to let on that he had seen. Hurrying away, he was half down the hill ere overtaken by Torres on his horse.

The celestial addressed him humbly, and Torres, in his general rage, lifted his riding whip savagely to slash him across the face. But Yi Poon did not quail.

"The Senorita Leoncia," he said quickly, and arrested the blow. "I have great secret." Torres waited, the whip still lifted as a threat. "You like 'm some other man marry that very nice Senorita Leoncia?"

Torres dropped the whip to his side.

"Go on," he commanded harshly. "What is the secret?"

"You no want 'm other man marry that Senorita Leoncia?"

"Suppose I don't?"

"Then, suppose you have secret, you can stop other man."

"Well, what is it? Spit it out."

"But first," Yi Poon shook his head, "you pay me six hundred dollars gold. Then I tell you secret."

"I'll pay you," Torres said readily, although without the slightest thought of keeping his word. "You tell me first, then, if no lie, I'll pay you. See!"

From his breast pocket he drew a wallet bulging with paper bills; and Yi Poon, uneasily acquiescing, led him down the road to the crone on the beach.

"This old woman," he explained, "she no lie. She sick woman. Pretty soon she die. She is afraid. She talk to priest along Colon. Priest say she must tell secret, or die and go to hell. So she no lie."

"Well, if she doesn't lie, what is it she must tell?" You pay me?"

"Sure. Six hundred gold."

"Well, she born Cadiz in old country. She number one servant, number one baby nurse. One time she take job with English family that come traveling in her country. Long time she work with that family. She go back along England. Then, bime by you know Spanish blood very hot she get very mad. That family have one little baby girl. She steal little baby girl and run away to Panama. That little baby girl Senor Solano he adopt just the same his own daughter. He have plenty sons and no daughter, So that little baby girl he make his daughter. But that old woman she no tell what name belong little girl's family. That family very high blood, very rich, everybody in England know that family. That family's name "Morgan.' You know that name? In Colon comes San Antonio men who say Senor Solano's daughter marry English Gringo named Morgan. That Gringo Morgan the Senorita Leoncia's brother."

"Ah!" said Torres with maleficent delight.

"You pay me now six hundred gold," said Yi Poon.

"Thank you for the fool you are," said Torres with untold mockery in his voice. "You will learn better perhaps some day the business of selling secrets. Secrets are not shoes or mahogany timber. A secret told is no more than a whisper in the air. It comes. It goes. It is gone. It is a ghost. Who has seen it? You can claim back shoes or mahogany timber. You can never claim back a secret when you have told it."

"We talk of ghosts, you and I," said Yi Poon calmly. "And the ghosts are gone. I have told you no secret. You have dreamed a dream. When you tell men they will ask you who told you. And you will say, 'Yi Poon.' But Yi Poon will say, 'No.' And they will say, 'Ghosts,' and laugh at you."

Yi Poon, feeling the other yield to his superior subtlety of thought, deliberately paused.

"We have talked whispers," he resumed after a few seconds. "You speak true when you say whispers are ghosts. When I sell secrets I do not sell ghosts. I sell shoes. I sell mahogany timber. My proofs are what I sell. They are solid. On the scales they will weigh weight. You can tear the paper of them, which is legal paper of record, on which they are written. Some of them, not paper, you can bite with your teeth and break your teeth upon. For the whispers are already gone like morning mists. I have proofs. You will pay me six hundred gold for the proofs, or men will laugh at you for lending your ears to ghosts."

"All right," Torres capitulated, convinced. "Show me the proofs that I can tear and bite."

"Pay me the six hundred gold."

"When you have shown me the proofs."

"The proofs you can tear and bite are yours after you have put the six hundred gold into my hand. You promise. A promise is a whisper, a ghost. I do not do business with ghost money. You pay me real money I can tear or bite." And in the end Torres surrendered, paying in advance for what did satisfy him when he had examined the documents, the old letters, the baby locket and the baby trinkets. And Torres not only assured Yi Poon that he was satisfied, but paid him in advance, on the latter's insistence, an additional hundred gold to execute a commission for him.

Meanwhile, in the bathroom which connected their bedrooms, clad in fresh undeiiinen and shaving with safety razors, Henry and Francis were singing:

"Back to back against the mainmast,
Held at bay the entire crew… "

In her charming quarters, aided and abetted by a couple of Indian seamstresses, Leoncia, half in mirth, half in sadness, and in all sweetness and wholesomeness of generosity, was initiating the Queen into the charmingness of civilized woman's dress. The Queen, a true woman to her heart's core, was wild with delight in the countless pretties of texture and adornment with which Leoncia's wardrobe was stored. It was a maiden frolic for the pair of them, and a stitch here and a take-up there modified certain of Leoncia's gowns to the Queen's slenderness.

No," said Leoncia judicially. "You will not need a corset. You are the one woman in a hundred for whom a corset is not necessary. You have the roundest lines for a thin woman that I ever saw. You… "Leoncia paused, apparently deflected by her need for a pin from her dressing table, for which she turned; but at the same time she swallowed the swelling that choked in her throat, so that she was able to continue: "You are a beautiful bride, and Francis can only grow prouder of you."

In the bathroom, Francis, finished shaving first, broke off the song to respond to the knock at his bedroom door and received a telegram from Fernando, the next to the youngest of the Solano brothers. And Francis read:

Important your immediate return. Need more margins. While market very weak but a strong attack on all your stocks except Tampico Petroleum, which is strong as ever. Wire me when to expect you. Situation is serious. Think I can hold out if you start to return at once. Wire me at once.

Bascom.

In the living room the two Morgans found Enrico and his sons opening wine.

"Having but had my daughter restored to me," Enrico said, "I now lose her again. But it is an easier

101

loss, Henry. To-morrow shall be the wedding. It cannot take place too quickly. It is sure, right now, that that scoundrel Torres is whispering all over San Antonio Leoncia's latest unprotected escapade with you."

Ere Henry could express his gratification, Leoncia and the Queen entered. He held up his glass and toasted: "To the bride!"

Leoncia, not understanding, raised a glass from the table and glanced to the Queen.

"No, no," Henry said, taking her glass with the intention of passing it to the Queen.

"No, no," said Enrico. "Neither shall drink the toast which is incomplete. Let me make it: "To the brides!"

You and Henry are to be married to-morrow," Alesandro explained to Leoncia.

Unexpected and bitter though the news was, Leoncia controlled herself, and dared with assumed jollity to look Francis in the eyes while she cried:

Another toast! To the bridegrooms!"

Difficult as Francis had found it to marry the Queen and maintain equanimity, he now found equanimity impossible at the announcement of the immediate marriage of Leoncia. Nor did Leoncia fail to observe how hard he struggled to control himself. His suffering gave her secret joy, and with a feeling almost of triumph she watched him take advantage of the first opportunity to leave the room.

Showing them his telegram and assuring them that his fortune was at stake, he! said he must get off an answer and asked Fernando to arrange for a rider to carry it to the government wireless at San Antonio.

Nor was Leoncia long in following him. In the library she came upon him, seated at the reading table, his telegram unwritten, while his gaze was fixed upon a large photograph of her which he had taken from its place on top the low bookshelves. All of which was too much for her. Her involuntary gasping sob brought him to his feet in time to catch her as she swayed into his arms. And before either knew it their lips were together in fervent expression. Leoncia struggled and tore herself away, gazing upon her lover with horror.

Tiiis must stop, Francis!" she cried. "More: you cannot remain here for my wedding. If you do, I shall not be responsible for my actions. There is a steamer leaves San Antonio for Colon. You and your wife must sail on it. You can easily catch passage on the fruit boats to New r Orleans and take train to New York. I love you! you know it."

"The Queen and I are not married!" Francis pleaded, beside himself, overcome by what had taken place. "That heathen marriage before the Altar of the Sun was no marriage. In neither deed nor ceremony are we married. I assure you of that, Leoncia. It is not too late

That heathen marriage has lasted you thus far," she interrupted him with quiet firmness. Let it last you to New York, or, at least, to … Colon."

"The Queen will not have any further marriage after our forms," Francis said. "She insists that all her female line before her has been so married and that the Sun Altar ceremony is sacredly binding."

Leoncia shrugged her shoulders non-committally, although her face was stern with resolution.

Marriage or no," she replied, "you must go to-night the pair of you. Else I shall go mad. I warn you: I shall not be able to withstand the presence of you. I cannot, I know I cannot, be able to stand the sight of you while I am being married to Henry and after I am married to Henry. Oh, please, please, do not misunderstand me. I do love Henry, but not in the… not in that way… not in the way I love you. I and I am not ashamed of the boldness with which I say it I love Henry about as much as you love the Queen; but I love you as I should love Henry, as you should love the Queen, as I know you do love me."

She caught his hand and pressed it against her heart. "There! For the last time! Now go!"

But his arms were around her, and she could not help but yield her lips. Again she tore herself away, this time fleeing to the doorway. Francis bowed his head to her decision, then picked up her picture.

"I shall keep this," he announced.

"You oughtn't to," she flashed a last fond smile at him. "You may," she added, as she turned and was gone.

Yet Yi Poon had a commission to execute, for which Torres had paid him one hundred gold hi advance. Next morning, with Francis and the Queen hours departed on their way to Colon, Yi Poon arrived at the Solano hacienda. Enrico, smoking a cigar on the veranda and very much pleased with himself and all the world and the way the world was going, recognized and welcomed Yi Poon as his visitor of the day before. Even ere they talked, Leoncia's father had dispatched Alesandro for the five hundred pesos agreed upon. And Yi Poon, whose profession was trafficking in secrets, was not averse to selling his secret the second time. Yet was he true to his salt, in so far as he obeyed Torres' instructions in refusing to tell the secret save in the presence of Leoncia and Henry.

"That secret has the string on it," Yi Poon apologized, after the couple had been summoned, as he began unwrapping the parcel of proofs. "The Senorita Leoncia and the man she is going to marry must first, before anybody else, look at these things. Afterward, all can look."

"Which is fair, since they are more interested than any of us," Enrico conceded grandly, although at the same time he betrayed his eagerness by the impatience with which ho motioned his daughter and Henry to take the evidence to one side for examination.

He tried to appear uninterested, but his side-glances missed nothing of what they did. To his amazement, he saw Leoncia suddenly cast down a legal -appear ing document, which she and Henry had read through, and throw her arms, whole-heartedly and freely about his neck, and wholeheartedly and freely kiss him on the lips. Next, Enrico saw Henry step back and exclaim in a dazed, heart-broken way.

"But, my God, Leoncia! This is the end of everything. Never can we be husband and wife!"

"Eh?" Enrico snorted. "When everything was arranged! What do you mean, sir? This is an insult! Marry you shall, and marry to-day!"

Henry, almost in stupefaction, looked to Leoncia to speak for him.

"It is against God's law and man's," she said, "for a man to marry his sister. Now I understand my strange love for Henry. He is my brother. We are full brother and sister, unless these documents lie."

And Yi Poon knew that he could take report to Torres that the marriage would not take place and would never take place.

Chapter 24

CATCHING a United Fruit Company boat at Colon within fifteen minutes after landing from the small coaster, the Queen's progress with Francis to New York had been a swift rush of fortunate connections. At New Orleans a taxi from the wharf to the station and a racing of porters with hand luggage had barely got them aboard the train just as it started. Arrived at New York, Francis had been met by Bascom, in Francis' private machine, and the rush had continued to the rather ornate palace R.H.M. himself, Francis' father, had built out of his millions on Riverside Drive.

So it was that the Queen knew scarcely more of the great world than when she first started her travels by leaping into the subterranean river. Had she been a lesser creature, she would have been stunned by this vast civilisation around her. As it was, she was royally inconsequential, accepting such civilization as an offering from her royal spouse. Royal he was, served by many slaves. Had she not, on steamer and train, observed it? And here, arrived at his palace, she took as a matter of course the showing of house servants that greeted them. The chauffeur opened the door of the limousine. Other servants carried in the hand baggage. Francis touched his hand to nothing, save to her arm to assist her to alight. Even Bascom a man she divined was no servitor she also divined as one who served Francis. And she could not but observe Bascom depart in Francis' limousine, under instruction and command of Francis.

She had been a queen, in an isolated valley, over a handful of salvages. Yet here, in this mighty land of kings, her husband ruled kings. It was all very wonderful, and she was deliciously aware that her queenship had suffered no diminishing by her alliance with Francis.

Her delight in the interior of the mansion was naive and childlike. Forgetting the servants, or, rather, ignoring them as she ignored her own attendants in her lake dwelling, she clapped her hands in the great entrance hall, glanced at the marble stairway, tripped in a little run to the nearest apartment, and peeped in. It was the library, which she had visioned in the Mirror of the World the first day she saw Francis. And the vision realized itself, for Francis entered with her into the great room of books, his arm about her, just as she had seen him on the fluid-metal surface of the golden bowl. The telephones, and the stock-ticker, too, she remembered; and, just as she had foreseen herself do, she crossed over to the ticker curiously to examine, and Francis, his arm still about her, stood by her side.

Hardly had he begun an attempted explanation of the instrument, and just as he realized the impossibility of teaching her in several minutes all the intricacies of the stock market institution, when his eyes noted on the tape that Frisco Consolidated was down twenty points a thing unprecedented in that little Iowa railroad which E.H.M. had financed and builded and to the day of his death maintained proudly as so legitimate a creation, that, though half the banks and all of Wall Street crashed, it would weather any storm.

The Queen viewed with alarm the alarm that grew on Francis' face.

It is magic liko my Mirror of the World?" she halfqueried, half-stated.

Francis nodded.

It tells you secrets, I know," she continued. "Like my golden bowl, it brings all the world, here within this very room, to you. It brings you trouble. That is very plain. But what trouble can this world bring you, who are one of its great kings?"

He opened his mouth to reply to her last question, halted, and said nothing, realizing the impossibility of conveying comprehension to her, the while, under his eyelids, or at the foreground of his brain, burned pictures of great railroad and steamship lines, of teeming terminals and noisy docks; of miners toiling in Alaska, in Montana, in Death Valley; of bridled rivers, and harnessed waterfalls, and of power-lines stilting across lowlands and swamps and marshes on twohundred-foot towers ; and of all the mechanics and economics and finances of the twentieth century machine-civilization.

It brings you trouble," she repeated. "And, alas! I cannot help you. My golden bowl is no more. Never again shall I see the world in it. I am no longer a ruler of the future. I am a woman merely, and helpless in this strange, colossal world to which you have brought me. I am a woman merely, and your wife, Francis, your proud wife."

Almost did he love her, as, dropping the tape, he pressed her closely for a moment ere going over to the battery of telephones. She is delightful, was his thought. There is neither guile nor malice in her, only woman, all woman, lovely and lovable alas, that Leoncia should ever and always arise in my thought between her whom I have and herself whom I shall never have!

"More magic," the Queen murmured, as Francis, getting Bascom's office, said:

"Mr. Bascom will undoubtedly arrive back in half an hour. This is Morgan talking Francis Morgan. Mr. Bascom left his office not five minutes ago. When he arrives, tell him that I have started for his office and shall not be more than five minutes behind him. This is important. Tell him I am on the way. Thank you. Good bye."

Very naturally, with all the wonders of the great house yet to be shown her, the Queen betrayed her disappointment when Francis told her he must immediately depart for a place called Wall Street.

What is it," she asked, with a pout of displeasure, "that drags you away from me like a slave?"

"It is business and very important," he told her with a smile and a kiss.

"And what is Business that it should have power over you who are a king? Is business the name of your god whom all of you worship as the Sun God is worshipped by my people?"

He smiled at the almost perfect appositeness of her idea, saying:

It is the great American god. Also, is it a very terrible god, and when it slays it slays terribly and swiftly."

"And you have incurred its displeasure?" she queried.

"Alas, yes, though I know not how. I must go to Wall Street—"

Which is its altar?" she broke in to ask.

Which is its altar," he answered, "and where I must find out wherein I have offended and wherein I may placate and make amends."

His hurried attempt to explain to her the virtues and functions of the maid he had wired for from Colon, scarcely interested her, and she broke him off by saying that evidently the maid was similar to the Indian women who had attended her in the Valley of Lost Souls, and that she had been accustomed to personal service ever since she was a little girl learning English and Spanish from her mother in the house on the lake.

But when Francis caught up his hat and kissed her, she relented and wished him luck before the altar.

After several hours of amazing adventures in her own quarters, where the maid, a Spanish-speaking Frenchwoman, acted as guide and mentor, and after being variously measured and gloated over by a gorgeous woman who seemed herself a queen and who was attended by two young women, and who, in the Queen's mind, was without doubt summoned to serve her and Francis, she came back down the grand stairway to investigate the library with its mysterious telephones and ticker.

Long she gazed at the ticker and listened to its irregular chatter. But she, who could read and write English and Spanish, could make nothing of the strange hieroglyphics that grew miraculously on the tape. Next, she explored the first of the telephones. Eemembering how Francis had listened, she put her ear to the transmitter. Then, recollecting his use of the receiver, she took it off its hook and placed it to her ear. The voice, unmistakably a woman's, sounded so near to her that in her startled surprise she dropped the receiver and recoiled. At this moment, Parker, Francis' old valet, chanced to enter the room. She had not observed him before, and, so immaculate was his dress, so dignified his carriage, that she mistook him for a friend of Francis rather than a servitor a friend similar to Bascom who had met them at the station with Francis' machine, ridden inside with them as an equal, yet departed with Francis' commands in his ears which it was patent he was to obey.

At sight of Parker's solemn face she laughed with embarrassment and pointed inquiringly to the telephone. Solemnly he picked up the receiver, murmured "A mistake," into the transmitter, and hung up. In those several seconds the Queen's thought underwent revolution. No god's nor spirit's voice had been that which she had heard, but a woman's voice.

"Where is that woman?" she demanded.

Parker merely stiffened up more stiffly, assumed a solemner expression, and bowed.

"There is a woman concealed in the house," she charged with quick words. "Her voice speaks there in that thing. She must be in the next room—"

"It was Central," Parker attempted to stem the flood of her utterance.

"I care not what her name is," the Queen dashed on. "I shall have no other woman but myself in my house. Bid her begone. I am very angry."

Parker was even stiffer and solemner, and a new mood came over her. Perhaps this dignified gentleman was higher than she had suspected in the hierarchy of the lesser kings, she thought. Almost might he be an equal king with Francis, and she had treated him peremptorily as less, as much less.

She caught him by the hand, in her impetuousness noting his reluctance, drew him over to a sofa, and made him sit beside her. To add to Parker's discomfiture, she dipped into a box of candy and began to feed him chocolates, closing his mouth with the sweets every time he opened it to protest.

"Come," she said, when she had almost choked him, "is it the custom of the men of this country to be polygamous?"

Parker was aghast at such rawness of frankness.

"Oh, I know the meaning of the word," she assured him. "So I repeat: is it the custom of the men of this country to be polygamous?"

"There is no woman in this house, besides yourself, madam, except servant women," he managed to enunciate. "That voice you heard is not the voice of a woman in this house, but the voice of a woman miles away who is your servant, or is anybody's servant who desires to talk over the telephone."

"She is the slave of the mystery?" the Queen questioned, beginning to get a dim glimmer of the actuality of the matter.

"Yes," her husband's valet admitted. "She is a slave of the telephone."

"Of the flying speech?"

"Yes, madam, call it that, of the flying speech." He was desperate to escape from a situation unprecedented in his entire career. "Come, I will show you, madam. This slave of the flying speech is yours to command both by night and day. If you wish, the slave will enable you to talk with your husband, Mr. Morgan… "

"Now?"

Parker nodded, arose, and led her to the telephone.

"First of all," he instructed, "you will speak to the slave. The instant you take this down and put it to your ear, the slave will respond. It is the slave's invariable way of saying 'Number?' Sometimes she says it, 'Number? Number?' And sometimes she is very irritable.

"When the slave has said 'Number,' then do you say "Eddystone 1292,' whereupon the slave will say 'Eddystone 1292?' and then you will say, 'Yes, please'… "

"To a slave I shall say 'please'?" she interrupted.

"Yes, madam, for these slaves of the flying speech are peculiar slaves that one never sees. I am not a young man, yet I have never seen a Central in all my life. Thus, next, after a moment, another slave, a woman, who is miles away from the first one, will say to you, 'This is Eddystone 1292,' and you will say, 'I am Mrs. Morgan. I wish to speak with Mr. Morgan, who is, I think, in Mr. Bascom's private office.' And then you wait, maybe for half a minute, or for a minute, and then Mr. Morgan will begin to talk to you."

"From miles and miles away?"

"Yes, madam just as if he were in the next room. And when Mr. Morgan says 'Goodbye,' you will say 'Goodbye,' and hang up-as you have seen me do."

And all that Parker had told her came to pass as she carried out his instructions. The two different slaves obeyed the magic of the number she gave them, and Francis talked and laughed with her, begged her not to be lonely, and promised to be home not later than five that afternoon.

Meanwhile, and throughout the day, Francis was a very busy and perturbed man.

"What secret enemy have you?" Bascom again and again demanded, while Francis shook his head in futility of conjecture.

For see, except where your holdings are concerned, the market is reasonable and right. But take your holdings. There's Frisco Consolidated. There is neither sense nor logic that it should be beared this way. Only your holdings are being beared. New York, Vermont and Connecticut, paid fifteen per cent, the last four quarters and is as solid as Gibraltar. Yet it's down, and down hard. The same with Montana Lode, Death Valley Copper, Imperial Tungsten, Northwestern Electric. Take Alaska Trodwell as solid as

105

the everlasting rock. The movement against it started only yesterday late. It closed eight points down, and to-day has slumped twice as much more. Every one, stock in which you are heavily interested. And no other stocks involved. The rest of the market is firm."

"So is Tampico Petroleum firm," Francis said, "and I'm interested in it heaviest of all."

Bascom shrugged his shoulders despairingly.

"Are you sure you cannot think of somebody who is doing this and who may be your enemy?"

"Not for the life of me, Bascom. Can't think of a soul. I haven't made any enemies, because, since my father died, I have not been active. Tampico Petroleum is the only thing I ever got busy with, and even now it's all right." He strolled over to the ticker. "There. Half a point up for five hundred shares."

"Just the same, somebody's after you," Bascom assured him. "The thing is clear as the sun at midday. I have been going over the reports of the different stocks at issue. They are colored, artfully and delicately colored, and the coloring matter is pessimistic and official. Why did Northwestern Electric pass its dividend? Why did they put that black-eye stuff into Mulhaney's report on Montana Lode? Oh, never mind the rest of the black-eying, but why all this activity of unloading? It's clear. There's a raid on, and it seems on you, and it's not a sudden rush raid. It's been slowly and steadily growing. And it's ripe to break at the first rumor of war, at a big strike, or a financial panic at anything that will bear the entire market.

"Look at the situation you're in now, when all holdings except your own are normal. I've covered your margins, and covered them. A grave proportion of your straight collateral is already up. And your margins keep on shrinking. You can scarcely throw them overboard. It might start a break. It's too ticklish."

There's Tampico Petroleum, smiling as pretty as you please it's collateral enough to cover everything," Francis suggested. "Though I've been chary of touching it," he amended.

Bascom shook his head.

There's the Mexican revolution, and our own spineless administration. If we involved Tampico Petroleum, and anything serious should break down there, you'd be finished, cleaned out, broke.

"And yet," Bascom resumed, "I see no other way out than to use Tampico Petroleum. You see, I have almost exhausted what you have placed in my hands. And this is no whirlwind raid. It's slow and steady as an advancing glacier. I've only handled the market for you all these years, and this is the first tight place we've got into. Now your general business affairs? Collins has the handling and knows. You must know. What securities can you let me have? Now? And to-morrow? And next week? And the next three weeks?"

"How much do you want?" Francis questioned back.

"A million before closing time to-day." Bascom pointed eloquently at the ticker. "At least twenty million more in the next three weeks, if and mark you that if well if the world remains at peace, and if the general market remains as normal as it has been for the past six months."

Francis stood up with decision and reached for his hat.

"I'm going to Collins at once. He knows far more about my outside business than I know myself. I shall have at least the million in your hands before closing time, and I've a shrewd suspicion that I'll cover the rest during the next several weeks."

Remember," Bascom warned him, as they shook hands, it's the very slowness of this raid that is ominous. It's directed against you, and it's no fly-by-night affair. Whoever is making it, is doing it big, and must be big."

Several times, late that afternoon and evening, the Queen was called up by the slave of the flying speech and enabled to talk with her husband. To her delight, in her own room, by her bedside, she found a telephone, through which, by calling up Collins' office, she gave her good night to Francis. Also, she essayed to kiss her heart to him, and received back, queer and vague of sound, his answering kiss.

She knew not how long she had slept, when she awoke. Not moving, through her half-open eyes she saw Francis peer into the room and across to her. When he had gone softly away, she leapt out of bed and ran to the door in time to see him start down the staircase.

More trouble with the great god Business was her surmise. He was going down to that wonderful room, the library, to read more of the dread god's threats and warnings that were so mysteriously made to take form of written speech to the clicking of the ticker. She looked at herself in the mirror, adjusted her hair, and with a little love-smile of anticipation on her lips put on a dressing-gown another of the marvelous pretties of Francis' forethought and providing.

At the entrance of the library she paused, hearing the voice of another than Francis. At first thought she decided it was the flying speech, but immediately afterward she knew it to be too loud and near and different. Peeping in, she saw two men drawn up in big leather chairs near to each other and facing.

Francis, tired of face from the day's exertions, still wore his business suit; but the other was clad in evening dress. And she heard him call her husband "Francis," who, in turn, called him "Johnny." That, and the familiarity of their conversation, conveyed to her that they were old, close friends.

"And don't tell me, Francis," the other was saying, "that you've frivoled through Panama all this while without losing your heart to the senoritas a dozen times."

"Only once," Francis replied, after a pause, in which the Queen noted that he gazed steadily at his friend.

Further," he went on, after another pause, "I really lost my heart but not my head. Johnny Pathmore, O Johnny Pathmore, you are a mere flirtatious brute, but I tell you that you've lots to learn. I tell you that in Panama I found the most wonderful woman in the world a woman that I was glad I had lived to know, a woman that I would gladly die for; a woman of fire, of passion, of sweetness, of nobility, a very queen of women."

And the Queen, listening and looking upon the intense exaltation of his face, smiled with proud fondness and certitude to herself, for had she not won a husband who remained a lover?

"And did the lady, er ah did she reciprocate?"

Johnny Pathmore ventured.

The Queen saw Francis nod as he solemnly replied.

"She loves me as I love her this I know in all absoluteness." He stood up suddenly. "Wait. I will show her to you."

And as he started toward the door, the Queen, in roguishness of a very extreme of happiness at her husband's confession she had overheard, fled trippingly to hide in the wide doorway of a grand room which the maid had informed her was the drawing room, whatever such room might be. Deliciously imagining Francis' surprise at not finding tier in bed, she watched him go up the wide marble staircase. In a few moments^ he descended. With a slight chill at the heart she observed that he betrayed no perturbation at not having found her. In his hand he carried a scroll or roll of thin, white cardboard. Looking neither to right nor left, he re-entered the library.

Peeping in, she saw him unroll the scroll, present it before Johnny Pathmore's eyes, and heard him say: Judge for yourself. There she is."

"But why be so funereal about it, old man?" Johnny Pathmore queried, after a prolonged examination of the photograph.

"Because we met too late. I was compelled to marry another. And I left her forever just a few hours before she was to marry another, which marriage had been compelled before either of us ever knew the other existed. And the woman I married, please know, is a good and splendid woman. She will have my devotion forever. Unfortunately, she will never posses my heart."

In a great instant of revulsion, the entire truth came to the Queen. Clutching at her heart with clasped hands, she nearly fainted of the vertigo that assailed her. Although they still talked inside the library, she heard no further word of their utterance as she strove with slow success to draw herself together. Finally, with indrawn shoulders, a little forlorn sort of a ghost of the resplendent woman and wife she had been but minutes before, she staggered across the hall and slowly, as if in a nightmare wherein speed never resides, dragged herself upstairs. In her room, she lost all control. Francis' ring was torn from her finger and stamped upon. Her boudoir cap and her turtle-shell hairpins joined the general havoc under her feet. Convulsed, shuddering, muttering to herself in her extremity, she threw herself upon her bed and only managed, in an ecstasy of anguish, to remain perfectly quiet when Francis peeped in on his way to bed.

An hour, that seemed a thousand centuries, she gave him to go to sleep. Then she arose, took in hand the crude jeweled dagger which had been hers in the Valley of the Lost Souls, and softly tiptoed into his room. There on the dresser it was, the large photograph of Leoncia. In thorough indecision, clutching the dagger until the cramp of her palm and fingers hurt her, she debated between her husband and Leoncia. Once, beside his bed, her hand raised to strike, an effusion of tears into her dry eyes obscured her seeing so that her dagger-hand dropped as she sobbed audibly.

Stiffening herself with changed resolve, she crossed over to the dresser. A pad and pencil lying handy, caught her attention. She scribbled two words, tore off the sheet, and placed it upon the face of Leoncia as it lay flat and upturned on the surface of polished wood. Next, with an unerring drive of the dagger, she pinned the note between the pictured semblance of Leoncia's eyes, so that the point of the blade penetrated the wood and left the haft quivering and upright.

Chapter 25

MEANWHILE, after the manner of cross purposes in New York, wherein Regan craftily proceeded with his gigantic raid on all Francis' holdings while Francis and Bascom vainly strove to find his identity, so in Panama were at work cross purposes which involved Leoncia and the Solanos, Torres and the Jefe, and, not least in importance, one, Yi Poon, the rotund and moon-faced Chinese.

The little old judge, who was the Jefe's creature, sat asleep in court in San Antonio. He had slept placidly for two hours, occasionally nodding his head and muttering profoundly, although the case was a grave one, involving twenty years in San Juan, where the strongest could not survive ten years. But there was no need for the judge to consider evidence or argument. Before the case was called, decision and sentence were in his mind, having been put there by the Jefe. The prisoner's lawyer ceased his perfunctory argument, the clerk of the court sneezed, and the judge woke up. He looked about him briskly and said: "Guilty." No one was surprised, not even the prisoner.

"Appear to-morrow morning for sentence. Next case."

Having so ordered, the judge prepared to settle down into another nap, when he saw Torres and the Jefe enter the courtroom. A gleam in the Jefe's eye was his cue, and he abruptly dismissed court for the day.

"I have been to Rodriguez Fernandez," the Jefe was explaining five minutes later, in the empty courtroom. "He says it was a natural gem, and that much would be lost in the cutting, but that nevertheless he would still give five hundred gold for it. Show it to the judge, Senor Torres, and the rest of the handful of big ones."

And Torres began to lie. He had to lie, because he could not confess the shame of having had the gems taken away from him by the Solanos and the Morgans when they threw him out of the hacienda. And so convincingly did he lie that even the Jefe he convinced, while the judge, except in the matter of brands of strong liquor, accepted everything the Jefe wanted him to believe. In brief, shorn of the multitude of details that Torres threw in, his tale was that he was so certain of the jeweler's under-appraisal that he had despatched the gems by special messenger to his agent in Colon with instructions to forward to New York to Tiffany's for appraisement that might lead to sale.

As they emerged from the courtroom and descended the several steps that were flanked by single adobe pillars marred by bullet scars from previous revolutions, the Jefe was saying:

"And so, needing the aegis of the law for our adventure after these gems, and, more than that, both of us loving our good friend the judge, we will let him in for a modest share of whatever we shall gain. He shall represent us in San Antonio while we are gone, and, if needs be, furnish us with the law's protection."

Now it happened that behind one of the pillars, hat pulled over his face, Yi Poon half-sat, half-reclined. Nor was he there by mere accident. Long ago he had learned that secrets of value, which always connoted the troubles of humans, were markedly prevalent around courtrooms, which were the focal points for the airing of such troubles when they became acute. One could never tell. At any moment a secret might leap at one or brim over to one. Therefore it was like a fisherman casting his line into the sea for Yi Poon to watch the defendant and the plaintiff, the witnesses for and against, and even the court hangeron or casual-seeming onlooker.

So, on this morning, the one person of promise that Yi Poon had picked out was a ragged old peon who looked as if he had been drinking too much and yet would perish in his condition of reaction if he did not get another drink very immediately. Bleary-eyed he was, and red-lidded, with desperate resolve painted on all his haggard, withered lineaments. When the court-room had emptied, he had taken up his stand. outside on the steps close to a pillar.

And why? Yi Poon had asked himself. Inside remained only the three chief men of San Antonio the Jefe, Torres, and the judge. What connection between them, or any of them, and the drink-sodden creature that shook as if freezing in the scorching blaze of the direct sun-rays? Yi Poon did not know, but he did know that it was worth while waiting on a chance, no matter how remote, of finding out. So, behind the pillar, where no atom of shade protected him from the cooking sun which he detested, he lolled on the steps with all the impersonation of one placidly infatuated with sun-baths. The old peon tottered a step, swayed as if about to fall, yet managed to deflect Torres from his companions, who paused to wait for him on the pavement a dozen paces on, restless and hot-footed as if they stood on a grid, though deep in earnest conversation. And Yi Poon missed no word nor gesture, nor glint of eye nor shifting face-line, of the dialogue that took place between the grand Torres and the wreck of a peon.

"What now?" Torres demanded harshly.

"Money, a little money, for the love of God, senor, a little money," the ancient peon whined.

"You have had your money," Torres snarled. "When I went away I gave you double the amount to last you twice as long. Not for two weeks yet is there a centavo due you."

"I am in debt," was the old man's whimper, the while all the flesh of him quivered and trembled from the nerveravishment of the drink so palpably recently consumed.

"On the pulque slate at Peter and Paul's," Torres, with a sneer, diagnosed unerringly.

"On the pulque slate at Peter and Paul's," was the frank acknowledgment. "And the slate is full. No more pulque can I get credit for. I am wretched and suffer a thousand torments without my pulque."

"You are a pig creature without reason!"

A strange dignity, as of wisdom beyond wisdom, seemed suddenly to animate the old wreck as he straightened up, for the nonce ceased from trembling, and gravely said:

"I am old. There is no vigor left in the veins or the heart of me. The desires of my youth are gone. Not even may I labor with this broken body of mine, though well I know that labor is an easement and a forgetting. Not even may I labor and forget. Food is a distaste in my mouth and a pain in my belly. Women they are a pest that it is a vexation to remember ever having desired. Children I buried my last a dozen years gone. Religion it frightens me. Death I sleep with the terror of it. Pulque ah, dear God! the one tickle and taste of living left to me!

"What if I drink over much? It is because I have much to forget, and have but a little space yet to linger in the sun, ere the Darkness, for my old eyes, blots out the sun forever."

Impervious to the old man's philosophy, Torres made an impatient threat of movement that he was going.

"A few pesos, just a handful of pesos," the old peon pleaded.

"Not a centavo," Torres said with finality.

"Very well," said the old man with equal finality.

"What do you mean?" Torres rasped with swift suspicion.

"Have you forgotten?" was the retort, with such emphasis of significance as to make Yi Poon wonder for what reason Torres gave the peon what seemed a pension or an allowance.

"I pay you, according to agreement, to forget," said Torres.

"I shall never forget that my old eyes saw you stab the Senor Alfaro Solano in the back," the peon replied.

Although he remained hidden and motionless in his posture of repose behind the pillar, Yi Poon metaphorically sat up. The Solanos were persons of place and wealth. That Torres should have murdered one of them was indeed a secret of price.

"Beast! Pig without reason! Animal of the dirt!" Torres' hands clenched in his rage. "Because I am kind do you treat me thus! One blabbing of your tongue and I will send you to San Juan. You know what that means. Not only will you sleep with the terror of death, but never for a moment of waking will you be free of the terror of living as you stare upon the buzzards that will surely and shortly pick your bones. And there will be no pulque in San Juan. There is never any pulque in San Juan for the men I send there. So? Eh? I thought so. You will wait two weeks for the proper time when I shall again give you money. If you do not wait, then never, this side of your interment in the bellies of buzzards, will you drink pulque again."

Torres whirled on his heel and was gone. Yi Poon watched him and his two companions go down the street, then rounded the pillar to find the old peon sunk down in collapse at his disappointment of not getting any pulque, groaning and moaning and making sharp little yelping cries, his body quivering as dying animals quiver in the final throes, his fingers picking at his flesh and garments as if picking off centipedes. Down beside him sat Yi Poon, who began a remarkable performance of his own. Drawing gold coins and silver ones from his pockets he began to count over his money with chink and clink that was mellow and liquid and that to the distraught peon's ear was as the sound of the rippling and riffling of fountains of pulque

"We are wise," Yi Poon told him in grandiloquent Spanish, still clinking the money, while the peon whined and yammered for the few centavos necessary for one drink of pulque. "We are wise, you and I, old man, and we will sit here and tell each other what we know about men and women, and life and love, and anger and sudden death, the rage red in the heart and the steel bitter cold in the back; and if you tell me what pleases me, then shall you drink pulque till your ears run cut with it, and your eyes are drowned in it. You like that pulque, eh? You like one drink now, now, soon, very quick?"

The night, while the Jefe Politico and Torres organized their expedition under cover of the dark, was destined to be a momentous one in the Solano hacienda. Things began to happen early. Dinner over, drinking their coffee and smoking their cigarettes, the family, of which Henry was accounted one by virtue of his brotherhood to Leoncia, sat on the wide front veranda. Through the moonlight, up the steps, they saw a strange figure approach.

"It is like a ghost," said Alvarado Solano.

"A fat ghost," Martinez, his twin brother, amended.

"A Chink ghost you couldn't poke your finger through," Bicardo laughed.

"The very Chink who saved Leoncia and me from marrying," said Henry Morgan, with recognition.

"The seller of secrets," Leoncia gurgled. "And if he hasn't brought a new secret, I shall be disappointed."

"What do you want, Chinaman?" Alesandro, the eldest of the Solano brothers, demanded sharply.

"Nice new secret, very nice new secret maybe you buy," Yi Poon murmured proudly.

"Your secrets are too' expensive, Chinaman," said Enrico discouragingly.

"This nice new secret very expensive," Yi Poon assured complacently.

"Go away," old Enrico ordered. "I shall live a long time, yet to the day of my death I care to hear no more secrets."

But Yi Poon was suavely certain of himself.

"One time you have very fine brother," he said. "One time your very fine brother, the Senor Alfaro Solano, die with knife in his back. Very well. Some secret, eh?"

But Enrico was on his feet quivering.

"You know?" he almost screamed his eager interrogation.

"How much?" said Yi Poon.

"All I possess!" Enrico cried, ere turning to Alesandro to add: "You deal with him, son. Pay him well if he can prove by witness of the eye."

"You bet," quoth Yi Poon. "I got witness. He got good eye-sight. He see man stick knife in the Senor Alfaro 's back in the dark. His name ... "

"Yes, yes," Enrico breathed his suspense.

"One thousand dollars his name," said Yi Poon, hesitating to make up his mind to what kind of dollars he could dare to claim. "One thousand dollars gold," he concluded.

Enrico forgot that he had deputed the transaction to his eldest son.

"Where is your witness?" he shouted.

And Yi Poon, calling softly down the steps into the shrubbery, evoked the pulque-ravaged peon, a real-looking ghost who slowly advanced and tottered up the steps.

At the same time, on the edge of town, twenty mounted men, among whom were the gendarmes Bafael, Ignacio, Augustino, and Vicente, herded a pack train of more than twenty mules and waited the command of the Jefe to depart on they knew not what mysterious adventure into the Cordilleras. What they did know was that, herded carefully apart from all other animals, was a strapping big mule loaded with tw r o hundred and fifty pounds of dynamite. Also, they knew that the delay was due to the Senor Torres, who had ridden away along the beach with the dreaded Caroo murderer, Jose" Mancheno, who, only by the grace of God and of the Jefe Politico, had been kept for years from expiating on the scaffold his various offenses against life and law.

And, while Torres waited on the beach and held the Caroo's horse and an extra horse, the Caroo ascended on foot the winding road that led to the hacienda of the Solanos. Little did Torres guess that twenty feet away, in the jungle that encroached on the beach, lay a placid-sleeping, pulquedrunken, old peon, with, crouching beside him, a very alert and very sober Chinese with a recently acquired thousand dollars stowed under his belt. Yi Poon had had barely time to drag the peon into hiding when Torres rode along in the sand and stopped almost beside him.

Up at the hacienda, all members of the household were going to bed. Leoncia, just starting to let down her hair, stopped when she heard the rattle of tiny pebbles against her windows. Warning her in low. whispers to make no noise, Jose" Mancheno handed her a crumpled note which Torres had written, saying mysteriously:

"From a strange Chinaman who waits not a hundred feet away on the edge of the shrubbery."

And Leoncia read, in execrable Spanish:

"First time, I tell you secret about Henry Morgan. This time I have secret about Francis. You come along and talk with me now."

Leoncia's heart leaped at mention of Francis, and as she slipped on a mantle and accompanied the Caroo it never entered her head to doubt that Yi Poon was waiting for her.

And Yi Poon, down on the beach and spying upon Torres, had no doubts when he saw the Caroo murderer appear with the Solano senorita, bound and gagged, slung across his shoulder like a sack of meal. Nor did Yi Poon have any doubts about his next action, when he saw Leoncia tied into the saddle of the spare horse and taken away down the beach at a gallop, with Torres and the Caroo riding on either side of her. Leaving the pulque-sodden peon to sleep, the fat Chinaman took the road up the hill at so stiff a pace that he arrived breathless at the hacienda. Not content with knocking at the door, he beat upon it with his fists and feet and prayed to his Chinese gods that no peevish Solano should take a shot at him before he could explain the urgency of his errand.

110

"O go to hell," Alesandro said, when he had opened the door and flashed a light on the face of the importunate caller.

"I have big secret," Yi Poon panted. "Very big brand new secret." "Come around to-morrow in business hours," Alesandro growled as he prepared to kick the Chinaman off the premises.

"I don't sell secret," Yi Poon stammered and gasped. "I make you present. I give secret now. The Senorita, your sister, she is stolen. She is tied upon a horse that runs fast down the beach."

But Alesandro, who had said good night to Leoncia, not half an hour before, laughed loudly his unbelief, and prepared again to boot off the trafficker in secrets. Yi Poon was desperate. He drew forth the thousand dollars and placed it in Alesandro's hand, saying:

"You go look quick. If the Senorita stop in this house now, you keep all that money. If the Senorita no stop, then you give money back… "

And Alesandro was convinced. A minute later he was rousing the house. Five minutes later the horse-peons, their eyes hardly open from sound sleep, were roping and saddling horses and pack-mules in the corrals, while the Solano tribe was pulling on riding gear and equipping itself with weapons.

Up and down the coast, and on the various paths leading back to the Cordilleras, the Solanos scattered, questing blindly in the blind dark for the trail of the abductors. As chance would have it, thirty hours afterward, Henry alone caught the scent and followed it, so that, camped in the very Footstep of God where first the old Maya priest had sighted the eyes of Chia, he found the entire party of twenty men and Leoncia cooking and eating breakfast. Twenty to one, never fair and always impossible, did not appeal to Henry Morgan's Anglo-Saxon mind. What did appeal to him was the dynamite-loaded mule, tethered apart from the off-saddl-ed forty-odd animals and left to stand by the careless peons with its load still on its back. Instead of attempting the patently impossible rescue of Leoncia, and recognising that in numbers her woman's safety lay^ he stole the dynamite -mule.

Not far did he take it. In the shelter of the low woods, he opened the pack and filled all his pockets with sticks of dynamite, a box of detonators, and a short coil of fuse. With a regretful look at the rest of the dynamite which he would have liked to explode but dared not, he busied himself along the line of retreat he would have to take if he succeeded in stealing Leoncia from her captors. As Francis, on a previous occasion at Juchitan, had sown the retreat with silver dollars, so, this time, did Henry sow the retreat with dynamite the sticks in small bundles and the fuses, no longer than the length of a detonator, and with detonators fast to each end.

Three hours Henry devoted to lurking around the camp in the Footstep of God, ere he got his opportunity to signal his presence to Leoncia; and another precious two hours were wasted ere she found her opportunity to steal away to him. Which would not have been so bad, had not her escape almost immediately been discovered and had not the gendarmes and the rest of Torres' party, mounted, been able swiftly to overtake them on foot.

When Henry drew Leoncia down to hide beside him in the shelter of a rock, and at the same time brought his rifle into action ready for play, she protested.

"We haven't a chance, Henry," she said. "They are too many. If you fight you will be killed. And then what will become of me? Better that you make your own escape, and bring help, leaving me to be retaken, than that you die and let me be retaken anyway."

But he shook his head.

"We are not going to be taken, dearest sister. Put your trust in me and watch. Here they come now. You just watch."

Variously mounted, on horses and pack mules whichever had come handiest in their haste Torres, the Jefe, and their men clattered into sight. Henry drew a sight, not on them, but on the point somewhat nearer where he had made his first plant of dynamite. When he pulled trigger, the intervening distance rose up in a cloud of smoke and earth dust that obscured them. As the cloud slowly dissipated, they could be seen, half of them, animals and men, overthrown, and all of them dazed and shocked by the explosion.

Henry seized Leoncia's hand, jerked her to her feet, and ran on side by side with her. Conveniently beyond his second planting, he drew her down beside him to rest and catch breath.

"They won't come on so fast this time," he hissed exultantly. " And the longer they pursue us the slower they'll come on."

True to his forecast, when the pursuit appeared, it moved very cautiously and very slowly.

"They ought to be "killed," Henry said. "But they have no chance, and I haven't the heart to do it. But I'll surely shake them up some."

Again he fired into his planted dynamite, and again, turning his back on the confusion, he fled to his third planting.

After he had fired off the third explosion, he raced Leoncia to his tethered horse, put her in the saddle, and ran on beside her, hanging on to her stirrup.

Chapter 26

FRANCIS had left orders for Parker to call him at eight o'clock, and when Parker softly entered he found his master still asleep. Turning on the water in the bathroom and preparing the shaving gear, the valet re-entered the bedroom. Still moving softly about so that his master would have the advantage of the last possible second of sleep, Parker's eyes lighted on the strange dagger that stood upright, its point pinning through a note and a photograph and into the hard wood of the dresser-top. For a long time he gazed at the strange array, then, without hesitation, carefully opened the door to Mrs. Morgan's room and peeped in. Next, he firmly shook Francis by the shoulder.

The latter's eyes opened, for a second betraying the incomprehension of the sleeper suddenly awakened, then lighting with recognition and memory of the waking order he had left the previous night.

"Time to get up, sir," the valet murmured.

"Which is ever an ill time," Francis yawned with a smile. He closed his eyes with a, "Let me lie a minute, Parker. If I doze, shake me."

But Parker shook him immediately.

"You must get up right away, sir. I think something has happened to Mrs. Morgan. She is not in her room, and there is a queer note and a knife here that may explain. I don't know, sir... "

Francis was out of bed in a bound, staring one moment at the dagger, and next, drawing it out, reading the note over and over as if its simple meaning, contained in two simple words, were too abstruse for his comprehension.

"Adios forever," said the note.

What shocked him even more, was the dagger thrust between Leoncia's eyes, and, as he stared at the wound made in the thin cardboard, it came to him that he had seen this very thing before, and he remembered back to the lake-dwelling of the Queen when all had gazed into the golden bowl and seen variously, and when he had seen Leoncia's face on the strange liquid metal with the knife thrust between the eyes. He even put the dagger back into the cardboard wound and stared at it some more.

The explanation was obvious. The Queen had betrayed jealousy against Leoncia from the first, and here, in New York, finding her rival's photograph on her husband's dresser, had no more missed the true conclusion than had she missed the pictured features with her point of steel. But where was she? Where had she gone? she who was the veriest stranger that had ever entered the great city, who called the telephone the magic of the flying speech, who thought of Wall Street as a temp'le, and regarded Business as the New York man's god. For all the world she was as unsophisticated and innocent of a great city as had she been a traveler from Mars. Where and how had she passed the night? Where was she now? Was she even alive?

Visions of the Morgue with its unidentified dead, and of bodies drifting out to sea on the ebb, rushed into his brain. It was Parker who steadied him back to himself.

"Is there anything I can do, sir? Shall I call up the detective bureau? Your father always... "

"Yes, yes," Francis interrupted quickly. "There was one man he employed more than all others, a young man with the Pinkertons do you remember his name?"

"Birchman, sir," Parker answered promptly, moving away. "I shall send for him to come at once."

And thereupon, in the quest after his wife, Francis entered upon a series of adventures that were to him, a born New Yorker, a liberal education in conditions and phases of New York of which, up to that time, he had been profoundly ignorant. Not alone did Birchman search, but he had at work a score of detectives under him who fine-tooth-combed the city, while in Chicago and Boston, he directed the activities of similar men.

Between his battle with the unguessed enemy of Wall Street, and the frequent calls he received to go here and there and everywhere, on the spur of the moment, to identify what might possibly be his wife, Francis led anything but a boresome existence. He forgot what regular hours of sleep were, and grew accustomed to being dragged from luncheon or dinner, or of being routed out of his bed, to respond to hurry calls to come and look over new-found missing ladies.

No trace of one answering her description, who had left the city by train or steamer had been discovered, and Birchman assiduously pursued his fine-tooth combing, convinced that she was still in the city.

Thus, Francis took trips to Mattenwan and down Blackwell's, and the Tombs and the Ail-Night court knew his presence. Nor did he escape being dragged to countless hospitals nor to the Morgue. Once, a fresh-caught shoplifter, of whom there was no criminal record and to whom there was no clew of identity, was brought to his notice. He had adventures with mysterious women cornered by Birchman's satellites in the back rooms of Eaines' Hotels, and, on the West Side, in the Fifties, was guilty of trespassing upon two comparatively innocent love-idyls, to the embarrassment of all concerned including himself.

Perhaps his most interesting and tragic adventure was in the ten-million-dollar mansion of Philip January, the Telluride mining king. The strange woman, a lady slender, had wandered in upon the Januarys a week before, ere Francis came to see her. And, as she had heartbreakingly done for the entire week, so she heartbreakingly did for Francis, wringing her hands, perpetually weeping, and murmuring beseechingly: "Otho, you are wrong. On my knees I tell you you are wrong. Otho, you, and you only, do I love. There is no one but you, Otho. There has never been any one but you. It is all a dreadful mistake. Believe me, Otho, believe me, or I shall die… "

And through it all, the Wall Street battle went on against the undiscoverable and powerful enemy who had launched what Francis and Bascom could not avoid acknowledging was a catastrophic, war-to-the-death raid on his fortune.

"If only we can avoid throwing Tampico Petroleum into the whirlpool," Bascom prayed.

"I look to Tampico Petroleum to save me," Francis replied. "When every security I can lay hand to has been engulfed, then, throwing in Tampico Petroleum will be like the eruption of a new army upon a losing field.

And suppose your unknown foe is powerful enough to swallow down that final, splendid asset and clamor for more?" Bascom queried.

Francis shrugged his shoulders.

"Then I shall be broke. But my father went broke half a dozen times before he won out. Also was he born broke. I should worry about a little thing like that." For a time, in the Solano hacienda, events had been moving slowly. In fact, following upon the rescue of Leoncia by Henry along his dynamite-sown trail, there had been no events. Not even had Yi Poon appeared with a perfectly fresh and entirely brand new secret to sell. Nothing had happened, save that Leoncia drooped and was apathetic, that neither Enrico nor Henry, her full brother, nor her Solano brothers who were not her brothers at all, could cheer her.

But, while Leoncia drooped, Henry and the tall sons of Eurico worried and perplexed themselves about the treasure in the Valley of the Lost Souls, into which Torres was even then dynamiting his way. One thing they did know, namely, that the Torres' expedition had sent Augustino and Vicente back to San Antonio to get two more mule-loads of dynamite.

It was Henry, after conferring with Enrico and obtaining his permission, who broached the matter to Leoncia.

"Sweet sister," had been his way, "we're going to go up and see what the scoundrel Torres and his gang are doing. We do know, thanks to you, their objective. The dynamite is to blow an entrance into the Valley. We know where the Lady Who Dreams sank her treasure when her house burned. Torres does not know this. The idea is that we can follow them into the Valley, when they have drained the Maya caves, and have as good a chance, if not a better chance than they in getting possession of that marvelous chest of gems. And the very tip of the point is that we'd like to take you along on the expedition. I fancy, if we managed to get the treasure ourselves, that you wouldn't mind repeating that journey down the subterranean river."

But Leoncia shook her head wearily.

"No," she said, after further urging. "I never want to see the Valley of the Lost Souls again, nor ever to hear it mentioned. There is where I lost Francis to that woman."

"It was all a mistake, darling sister. But who was to know? I did not. You did not. Nor did Francis. He played the man's part fairly and squarely. Not knowing that you and I were brother and sister, believing that we were truly betrothed as we were at the time he refrained from trying to win you from me, and he rendered further temptation impossible and saved the lives of all of us by marrying the Queen."

"I miss you and Francis singing your everlasting "Back to back against the mainmast,' "she murmured sadly and irrelevantly.

Quiet tears welled into her eyes and brimmed over as she turned away, passed down the steps of the veranda, crossed the grounds, and aimlessly descended the hill. For the twentieth time since she had last seen Francis she pursued the same course, covering the same ground from the time she first espied him rowing to the beach from the Angelique, through her dragging him into the jungle to save him from her irate men-folk, to the moment, with drawn revolver, when she had kissed him and urged him- into the boat and away. This had been his first visit.

Next, she covered every detail of his second visit from the moment, coming from behind the rock after her swim in the lagoon, she had gazed upon him leaning against the rock as he scribbled his first note to her, through her startled flight into the jungle, the bite on her knee of the labarri (which she had mistaken for a deadly viperine), to her recoiling collision against Francis and her faint on the sand. And, under her parasol, she sat down on the very spot where she had fainted and come to, to find him preparing to suck the poison from the wound which he had already excoriated. As she remembered back, she realized that it had been the pain of the excoriation which brought her to her senses.

Deep she was in the sweet recollections of how she had slapped his cheek even as his lips approached her knee, blushed with her face hidden in her hands, laughed because her foot had been made asleep by his too-efficient tourniquet, turned white with anger when he reminded her that she considered him the murderer of her uncle, and repulsed his offer to untie the tourniquet. So deep was she in such fond recollections of only the other day that yet seemed separated from the present by half a century, such was the wealth of episode, adventure, and tender passages which had intervened, that she did not see the rattletrap rented carriage from San Antonio drive up the beach road. Nor did she see a lady, fashionably clad in advertisement that she was from New York, dismiss the carriage and proceed toward her on foot. This lady, who was none other than the Queen, Francis' wife, likewise sheltered herself beneath a parasol from the tropic sun.

Standing directly behind Leoncia, she did not realize that she had surprised the girl in a moment of high renunciation. All that she did know was that she saw Leoncia draw from her breast and gaze long at a tiny photograph. Over her shoulder the Queen made it out to be a snapshot of Francis, whereupon her mad jealousy raged anew. A poinard flashed to her hand from its sheath within the bosom of her dress. The quickness of this movement was sufficient to warn Leoncia, who tilted her parasol forward so as to look up at whatever person stood at her back. Too utterly dreary even to feel surprise, she greeted the wife of Francis Morgan as casually as if she had parted from her an hour before. Even the poinard failed to arouse in her curiosity or fear. Perhaps, had she displayed startlement and fear, the Queen might have driven the steel home to her. As it was, she could only cry out.

"You are a vile woman! A vile, vile woman!"

To which Leoncia merely shrugged her shoulders, and said:

"You would better keep your parasol between you and the sun."

The Queen passed round in front of her, facing her and staring down at her w r ith woman's wrath compounded of such jealousy as to be speechless.

"Why?" Leoncia was the first to speak, after a long pause. "Why am I a vile woman?"

"Because you are a thief," the Queen flamed. "Because you are a stealer of men, yourself married. Because you are unfaithful to your husband in heart, at least, since more than that has so far been impossible."

"I have no husband," Leoncia answered quietly.

"Husband to be, then I thought you were to be married the day after our departure."

"I have no husband to be," Leoncia continued with the same quietness.

So swiftly tense did the other woman become that Leoncia idly thought of her as a tigress.

"Henry Morgan!" the Queen cried.

"He is my brother."

"A word which I have discovered is of wide meaning, Leoncia Solano. In New York there are worshippers at certain altars who call all men in the world 'brothers,' all women "sisters.""

"His father was my father," Leoncia explained with patient explicitness. "His mother was my mother. We are full brother and sister."

"And Francis?" the other queried, convinced, with sudden access of interest. "Are you, too, his sister?"

Leoncia shook her head.

"Then you do love Francis!" the Queen charged, smarting with disappointment.

"You have him," said Leoncia.

"No; for you have taken him from me."

Leoncia slowly and sadly shook her head and sadly gazed out over the heat-shimmering surface of Chili qui Lagoon.

After a long lapse of silence, she said, wearily, "Believe that. Believe anything."

"I divined it in you from the first," the Queen cried. "You have a strange power over men. I am a woman not unbeautiful. Sine I have been out in the world I have watched the eyes of men looking at me. I know I am not all undesirable. Even have the wretched males of my Lost Valley with downcast eyes looked love at me. On dared more than look, and he died for me, or because of me, and was flung

114

into the whirl of waters to his fate. And yet you, with this woman's power of yours, strangely exercise it over my Francis so that in my very arms he thinks of you. I know it. I know that even then he thinks of you!"

Her last words were the cry of a passion-stricken and breaking heart. And the next moment, though very little to Leoncia's surprise, being too hopelessly apathetic to b surprised at anything, the Queen dropped her knife in th sand and sank down, buried her face in her hands, and surrendered to the weakness of hysteric grief. Almost idly, and quit mechanically, Leoncia put her arm around her and comforted her. For many minutes this continued, when th Queen, growing more cairn, spo^e with sudden determination.

"I left Francis the moment I knew he loved you," she said. "I drove my knife into the photograph of you he keeps in his bedroom, and returned here to do the same to you in person. But I was wrong. It is not your fault, nor Francis'. It is my fault that I have failed to win his love. Not you, but I it is who must die. But first, I must go back to my valley and recover my treasure. In the temple called Wall Street, Francis is in great trouble. His fortune may be taken away from him, and he requires another fortune to save his fortune. I have that fortune, and there is no time to lose. Will you and yours help me? It is for Francis' sake."

Chapter 27

So it came about that the Valley of the Lost Souls was invaded subterraneously from opposite directions by two parties of treasure-seekers. From one side, and quickly, came the Queen and Leoncia, Henry Morgan, and the Solanos. Far more slowly, although they had started long in advance, did Torres and the Jefe progress. The first attack on the mountain had proved the chief est obstacle. To blow open an entrance to the Maya caves had required more dynamite than they had originally brought, while the rock had proved stubborner than they expected. Further, when they had finally made a way, it had proved to be above the cave floor, so that more blasting had been required to drain off the water. And, having blasted their way in to the water-logged mummies of the conquistadores and to the Room of the Idols, they had to blast their way out again and on into the heart of the mountain. But first, ere they continued on, Torres looted the ruby eyes of Chia and the emerald eyes of Hzatzl.

Meanwhile, with scarcely any delays, the Queen and her party penetrated to the Valley through the mountain on the opposite side. Nor did they entirely duplicate the course of their earlier traverse. The Queen, through long gazing into her Mirror, knew every inch of the way. Where the underground river plunged through the passage and out into the bosom of the Gualaca River it was impossible to take in their boats. But, by assiduous search under her directions, they found the tiny mouth of a cave on the steep wall of the cliff, so shielded by a growth of mountain berries that only by knowing for what they sought could they have found it. By main strength, applied to the coils of rope which they had brought along, they hoisted their canoes up the cliff, portaged them on their shoulders through the winding passage, and launched them on the subterranean river itself where it ran so broadly and placidly between wide banks that they paddled easily against its slack current. At other times, where the river proved too swift, they lined the canoes up by towing from the bank; and wherever the river made a plunge through the solid tie-ribs of mountain, the Queen showed them the obviously hewn and patently ancient passages through which to portage their light crafts around. Here we leave the canoes," the Queen directed at last, and the men began securely mooring them to the bank in the light of the flickering torches. "It is but a short distance through the last passage. Then we will come to a small opening in the cliff, shielded by climbing vines and ferns, and look down upon the spot where my house once stood beside the whirl of waters. The ropes will be necessary in order to descend the cliff, but it is only about fifty feet."

Henry, with an electric torch, led the way, the 'Queen beside him, while old Enrico and Leoncia brought up the rear, vigilant to see that no possible half-hearted peon or Indian boatman should slip back and run away. But when the party came to where the mouth of the passage ought to have been, there was no mouth. The passage ceased, being blocked off solidly from floor to roof by a debris of crumbled rocks that varied in size from paving stones to native houses.

"Who could have done this?" the Queen exclaimed angrily.

But Henry, after a cursory examination, reassured her.

"It's just a slide of rock," he said, "a superficial fault in the outer skin of the mountain that has slipped; and it won't take us long with our dynamite to remedy it. Lucky we fetched a supply along."

But it did take long. For what was the remainder of the day and throughout the night they toiled. Large charges of explosive were not used because of Henry's fear of exciting a greater slip along the fault overhead. What dynamite was used was for the purpose of loosening up the rubble so that they

115

could shift it back along the passage. At eight the following morning the charge was exploded that opened up to them the first glimmer of daylight ahead. After that they worked carefully, being apprehensive of jarring down fresh slides. At the last, they were baffled by a ten-ton block of rock in the very mouth of the passage. Through crevices on either side of it they could squeeze their arms into the blazing sunshine, yet the stone-block thwarted them. No leverage they applied could more than quiver it, and Henry decided on one final blast that would topple it out and down into the Valley.

"They'll certainly know visitors are coming, the way we've been knocking on their back door for the last fifteen hours," he laughed, as he prepared to light the fuse.

Assembled before the altar of the Sun God at the Long House, the entire population was indeed aware, and anxiously aware, of the coming of visitors. So disastrous had been their experiences with their last ones, when the lake dwelling had been burned and their Queen lost to them, that they were now begging the Sun God to send no more visitors. But upon one thing, having been passionately harangued by their priest, they were resolved; namely, to kill at sight and without parley whatever newcomers did descend upon them.

"Even Da Vasco himself," the priest had cried.

"Even Da Vasco!" the Lost Souls had responded.

All were armed with spears, war-clubs, and bows and arrows; and while they waited they continued to pray before the altar. Every few minutes runners arrived from the lake, making the same reports that while the mountain still labored thunderously nothing had emerged from it.

The little girl of ten, the Maid of the Long House who had entertained Leoncia, was the first to spy out new arrivals. This was made possible because of the tribe's attention being fixed on the rumbling mountain beside the lake. No one expected visitors out of the mountain on the opposite side of the valley.

"Da Vasco!" she cried. "Da Vasco!"

All looked and saw, not fifty yards away, Torres, the Jefe, and their gang of followers, emerging into the open clearing. Torres wore again the helmet he had filched from his withered ancestor in the Chamber of the Mummies. Their greeting was instant and warm, taking the form of a flight of arrows that arched into them and stretched two of the followers on the ground. Next, the Lost Souls, men and women, charged; while the rifles of Torres' men began to speak. So unexpected was this charge, so swiftly made and with so short a distance to cover, that, though many fell before the bullets, a number reached the invaders and engaged in a desperate hand-to-hand conflict. Here the advantage of firearms was minimized, and gendarmes and others were thrust through by spears or had their skulls cracked under the ponderous clubs.

In the end, however, the Lost Souls were outfought, thanks chiefly to the revolvers that could kill in the thickest of the scuffling. The survivors fled, but of the invaders half were down and down forever. The women having in drastic fashion attended to every man who fell wounded. The Jefe was spluttering with pain and rage at an arrow which had perforated his arm; nor could he be appeased until Vicente cut off the barbed head and pulled out the shaft.

Torres, beyond an aching shoulder where a club had hit him, was uninjured; and he became jubilant when he saw the old priest dying on the ground with his head resting on the little maid's knees.

Since there were no wounded of their own to be attended to with rough and ready surgery, Torres and the Jefe led the way to the lake, skirted its shores, and came to the ruins of the Queen's dwelling. Only charred stumps of piles, projecting above the water, showed where it had once stood. Torres was nonplussed, but the Jefe was furious.

"Here, right hi this house that was, the treasure chest stood," he stammered.

"A wild goose chase!" the Jefe grunted. "Senor Torres, I always suspected you were a fool."

"How was I to know the place had been burned down?"

"You ought to have known, you who are so very wise in all things," the Jefe bickered back. "But you can't fool me. I had my eye on you. I saw you rob the emeralds and rubies from the eye-sockets of the Maya gods. That much you shall divide with me, and now."

"Wait, wait, be a trifle patient," Torres begged. "Let us first investigate. Of course, I shall divide the four gems with you but what are they compared with a whole chestfull? It was a light, fragile house. The chest may have fallen into the water undamaged by fire when the roof fell in. And water will not damage precious stones."

In amongst the burnt piling the Jefe sent his men to investigate, and they waded and swam about in the shoal water, being careful to avoid being caught by the outlying suck of the whirlpool. Augustino, the Silent, made the find, close in to shore.

"I am standing on something," he announced, the level of the lake barely to his knees. Torres plunged in, and, reaching under till he buried his head and shoulders, felt out the object.

"It is the chest, I am certain," he declared. "Come! All of you! Drag this out to the dry land so that we may examine into it!"

But when this was accomplished, and just as he bent to Open the lid, the Jefe stopped him.

"Go back into the water, the lot of you," he commanded his men. "There are a number of chests like this, and the expedition will be a failure if we don't find them. One chest vould not pay the expenses."

Not until all the men were floundering and groping in the water, did Torres raise the lid. The Jefe stood transfixed. He could only gaze and mutter inarticulate mouthings.

"Now will you believe?" Torres queried. "It is beyond price. We are the richest two men in Panama, in South America, in the world. This is the Maya treasure. We heard of it when' we were boys. Our fathers and our grandfathers dreamed of it. The Conquistadores failed to find it. And it is ours ours!"

And, while the two men, almost stupefied, stood and stared, one by one their followers crept out of the water, formed a silent semi-circle at their backs, and likewise stared. Neither did the Jefe and Torres know their men stood at their backs, nor did the men know of the Lost Souls that were creeping stealthily upon them from the rear. As it was, all were staring at the treasure with fascinated amazement when the attack was sprung.

Bows and arrows, at ten yards distance, are deadly, especially when due time is taken to make certain of aim. Two-thirds of the treasure -seekers went down simultaneously. Through Vicente, who had chanced to be standing directly behind Torres, no less than two spears and five arrows had perforated. The handful of survivors had barely time to seize their rifles and whirl, when the club attack was upon them. In this Rafael and Ignacio, two of the gendarmes who had been on the adventure to the Juchitan oil fields, almost immediately had their skulls cracked. And, as usual, the Lost Souls women saw to it that the wounded did not remain wounded long.

The end for Torres and the Jefe was but a matter of moments, when a loud roar from the mountain followed by a crashing avalanche of rock, created a diversion. The few Lost Souls that remained alive, darted back terror-stricken into the shelter of the bushes. The Jefe and Torres, who alone stood on their feet and breathed, cast their eyes up the cliff to where the smoke still issued from the new-made hole, and saw Henry Morgan and the Queen step into the sunshine on the lip of the cliff.

"You take the lady," the Jefe snarled. "I shall get the Gringo Morgan if it's the last act of what seems a life that isn't going to be much longer."

Both lifted their rifles and fired. Torres, never much at a shot, sent his bullet fairly centered into the Queen's breast. But the Jefe, master marksman and possessor of many medals, made a clean miss of his target. The next instant, a bullet from Henry's rifle struck his wrist and traveled up the forearm to the elbow, whence it escaped and passed on. And as his rifle clattered to the ground he knew that never again would that right arm, its bone pulped from wrist to elbow, have use for a rifle.

But Henry was not shooting well. Just emerged from twenty-four hours of darkness in the cave, not at once could his eyes adjust themselves to the blinding dazzle of the sun. His first shot had been lucky. His succeeding shots merely struck in the immediate neighbourhood of the Jefe and Torres as they turned and fled madly for the brush.

Ten minutes later, the wounded Jefe in the lead, Torres saw a woman of the Lost Souls spring out from behind a tree and brain him with a huge stone wielded in both her hands. Torres shot her first, then crossed himself with horror, and stumbled on. From behind arose distant calls of Henry and the Solano brothers in pursuit, and he remembered the vision of his end he had glimpsed but refused to see in the Mirror of the World and wondered if this end was near upon him. Yet it had not resembled this place of trees and ferns and jungle. From the glimpse he remembered nothing of vegetation only solid rock and blazing sun and bones of animals. Hope sprang up afresh at the thought. Perhaps that end was not for this day, maybe not for this year. Who knew? Twenty years might yet pass ere that end came.

Emerging from the jungle, he came upon a queer ridge of what looked like long disintegrated lava rock. Here he left no trail, and he proceeded carefully on beyond it through further jungle, believing once again in his star that would enable him to elude pursuit. His plan of escape took shape. He would find a safe hiding place until after dark. Then he would circle back to the lake and the whirl of waters. That gained, nothing and nobody could stop him. He had but to leap in. The subterranean journey had no terrors for him because he had done it before. And in his fancy he saw once more the pleasant picture of the Gualaca River flashing under the open sky on its way to the sea. Besides, did he not carry with him the two great emeralds and two great rubies that had been the eyes of Chia and Hzatzl? Fortune enough, and vast good fortune, were they for any man. What if he had failed by the Maya Treasure to become the richest man in the world? He was satisfied. All he wanted now was darkness and one last dive into the heart of the mountain and through the heart of the mountain to the Gualaca flowing to the sea.

And just then, the assured vision of his escape so vividly filling his eyes that he failed to observe the way of his feet, he dived. Nor was it a dive into swirling waters. It was a head-foremost, dry-land dive down a slope of rock. So slippery was it that he continued to slide down, although he managed to turn around, with face and stomach to the surface, and to claw wildly up with hands and feet. Such effort merely slowed his descent, but could not stop it.

For a while, at the bottom, he lay breathless and dazed. When his senses came back to him, he became aware first of all of something unusual upon which his hand rested. He could have sworn that he felt teeth. At length, opening his eyes with a shudder and summoning his resolution, he dared to look at the object. And relief was immediate. Teeth they were, in an indubitable, weather-white jaw-bone; but they were pig's teeth and the jaw was a pig's jaw. Other bones lay about, on which his body rested, which, on examination, proved to be the bones of pigs and of smaller animals.

Where had he glimpsed such an arrangement of bones? He thought, and remembered the Queen's great golden bowl. He looked up. Ah! Mother of God! The very place! He knew it at first sight, as he gazed up what was a funnel at the far spectacle of day. Fully two hundred feet above him was the rim of the funnel. The sides of hard, smooth rock sloped steeply in and down to him, and his eyes and judgment told him that no man born of woman could ever scale that slope.

The fancy that came to his mind caused him to spring to his feet in sudden panic and look hastily round about him. Only on a more colossal scale, the funnel in which he was trapped had reminded him of the funnel-pits dug in the sand by hunting spiders that lurked at the bottom for such prey that tumbled in upon them. And, his vivid fancy leaping, he had been frightened by the thought that some spider monster, as colossal as the funnel-pit, might possibly be lurking there to devour him. But no such denizen occurred. The bottom of the pit, circular in form, was a good ten feet across and carpeted, he knew not how deep, by a debris of small animals' bones. Now for what had the Mayas of old time made so tremendous an excavation? he questioned; for. he was more than half -convinced that the funnel was no natural phenomenon.

Before nightfall he made sure, by a dozen attempts, that the funnel was unscalable. Between attempts, he crouched in the growing shadow of the descending sun and panted dry-lipped with heat and thirst. Tn'e place was a very furnace, and the juices of his body were wrung from him in prof use 'perspiration. Throughout the night, between dozes, he vainly pondered the problem of escape. The only way out was up, nor could his mind devise any method of getting up. Also, he looked forward with terror to the' coming of the day, for he knew that no man could survive a full ten hours of the baking heat that would be his. Ere the next nightfall the last drop of moisture would have evaporated from his body leaving him a withered and already half-sun-dried mummy.

With the coming of daylight his growing terror added wings to his thought, and he achieved a new and profoundly simple theory of escape. Since he could not climb up, and since he could not get out through the sides themselves, then the only possible remaining way was down. Fool that he was! He might have been working through the cool night hours, and now he must labour in the quickly increasing heat. He applied himself in an ecstasy of energy to digging down through the mass of crumbling bones. Of course, there was a way out. Else how did the funnel drain? Otherwise it would have been full or part full of water from the rains. Fool! And thrice times thrice a fool!

He dug down one side of the wall, flinging the rubbish into a mound against the opposite side. So desperately did he apply himself that he broke his finger-nails to the quick and deeper, while every finger-tip was lacerated to bleeding. But love of life was strong in him, and he knew it was a life-and-death race with the sun. As he went deeper, the rubbish became more compact, so that he used the muzzle of his rifle like a crowbar to loosen it, ere tossing it up in single and double handfuls.

By mid-forenoon, his senses beginning to reel in the heat, he made a discovery. Upon the wall which he had uncovered, he came upon the beginning of an inscription, evidently rudely scratched in the rock by the point of a knife. With renewed hope, his head and shoulders down in the hole, he dug and scratched for all the world like a dog, throwing the rubbish out and between his legs in true dog-fashion. Some of it fell clear, but most of it fell back and down upon him. Yet had he become too frantic to note the inefficiency of his effort.

At last the inscription was cleared, so that he was able to read:

Peter McGill, of Glasgow. On March 12, 1820,

I escaped from the Pit of Hell by this passage by digging down and finding it.

A passage! The passage must be beneath the inscription! Torres now toiled in a fury. So dirt-soiled was he that he was like some huge, four-legged, earth-burrowing animal. The dirt got into his eyes, and, on occasion, into his nostrils and air passages so as to suffocate him and compel him to back up out of the hole and sneeze and cough his breathing apparatus clear. Twice he fainted. But the sun, by then almost directly overhead, drove him on.

He found the upper rim of the passage. He did not dig down to the lower rim; for the moment the aperture was large enough to accommodate his lean shape, he writhed and squirmed into it and away from the destroying sun-rays. The cool and the dark soothed him, but his joy and the reaction from what he had undergone sent his pulse giddily up, so that for the third time he fainted.

Eecovered, mouthing with black and swollen lips a half-insane chant of gratefulness and thanksgiving, he crawled on along the passage. Perforce he crawled, because it was so low that a dwarf could not have stood erect in it. The place was a charnel house. Bones crunched and crumbled under his hands and knees, and he knew that his knees were being worn to the bone. At the end of a hundred feet he caught his first glimmering of light. But the nearer he approached freedom, the slower he progressed, for the final stages of exhaustion were coming upon him. He knew that it was not physical exhaustion, nor food exhaustion, but thirst exhaustion. Water, a few ounces of water, was all he needed to make him strong again. And there was no water.

But the light was growing stronger and nearer. He noted, toward the last, that the floor of the passage pitched down at an angle of fully thirty degrees. This made the way easier. Gravity drew him on, and helped every failing effort of him, toward the source of light. Very close to it, he encountered an increase in the deposit of bones. Yet they bothered him little, for they had become an old story, while he was too exhausted to mind them.

He did observe, with swimming eyes and increasing numbness of touch, that the passage was contracting both vertically and horizontally. Slanting downward at thirty degrees, it gave him an impression of a rat-trap, himself the rat, descending head foremost toward he knew not what. Even before he reached it, he apprehended that the slit of bright day that advertised the open world beyond was too narrow for the egress of his body. And his apprehension was verified. Crawling unconcernedly over a skeleton that the blaze of day showed him to be a man's, he managed, by severely and painfully squeezing his ears flat back, to thrust his head through the slitted aperture. The sun beat down upon his head, while his eyes drank in the openness of the freedom of the world that the unyielding rock denied to the rest of his body.

Most maddening of all was a running stream not a hundred yards away, tree-fringed beyond, with lush meadowgrass leading down to it from his side. And in the treeshadowed water, knee-deep and drowsing, stood several cows of the dwarf breed peculiar to the Valley of Lost Souls. Occasionally they flicked their tails lazily at flies, or changed the distribution of their weight on their legs. He glared at them to see them drink, but they were evidently too sated with water. Fools! Why should they not drink, with all that wealth of water flowing idly by! They betrayed alertness, turning their heads toward the far bank and pricking tneir ears forward. Then, as a big antlered buck came out from among the trees to the water's edge, they flattened their ears back and shook their heads and pawed the water till he could hear the splashing. But the stag disdained their threats, lowered his head, and drank. This was too much for Torres, who emitted a maniacal scream which, had he been in his senses, he would not have recognised as proceeding from his own throat and larynx.

The stag sprang away. The cattle turned their heads in Torres' direction, drowsed, their eyes shut, and resumed the nicking of flies. With a violent effort, scarcely knowing that he had half-torn off his ears, he drew his head back through the slitted aperture and fainted on top of the skeleton.

Two hours later, though he did not know the passage of time, he regained consciousness, and found his own head cheek by jowl with the skull of the skeleton on which he lay. The descending sun was already shining into the narrow opening, and his gaze chanced upon a rusty knife. The point of it was worn and broken, and he established the connection. This was the knife that had scratched the inscription on the rock at the base of the funnel at the other end of the passage, and this skeleton was the bony framework of the man who had done the scratching. And Alvarez Torrez went immediately mad.

"Ah, Peter McGill, my enemy," he muttered. "Peter McGill of Glasgow who betrayed me to this end. This for you! And this! And this!"

So speaking, he drove the heavy knife into the fragile front of the skull. The dust of the bone which had once been the tabernacle of Peter McGill's brain arose in his nostrils and increased his frenzy. He attacked the skeleton with his hands, tearing at it, disrupting it, filling the pent space about him with flying bones. It was a battle, in which he destroyed what was left of the mortal remains of the one time resident of Glasgow.

Once again Torres squeezed his head through the slit to gaze at the fading glory of the world. Like a rat in the trap caught by the neck in the trap of ancient Maya devising, he saw the bright world and day dim to darkness as his final consciousness drowned in the darkness of death.

119

But still the cattle stood in the water and drowsed and flicked at flies, and, later, the stag returned, disdainful of the cattle, to complete its interrupted drink.

Chapter 28

NOT for nothing had Regan been named by his associates, The Wolf of Wall Street! While usually no more than a conservative, large-scale player, ever SO' often, like a periodical drinker, he had to go on a rampage of wild and daring stock-gambling. At least five times in his long career had he knocked the bottom out of the market or lifted the roof off, and each time to the tune of a personal gain of millions. He never went on a small rampage, and he never went too often.

He would let years of quiescence slip by, until suspicion of him was lulled asleep and his world deemed that the Wolf was at last grown old and peaceable. And then, like a thunderbolt, he would strike at the men and interests he wished to destroy. But, though the blow always fell like a thunderbolt, not like a thunderbolt was it in its inception. Long months, and even years, were spent in deviously preparing for the day and painstakingly maturing the plans and conditions for the battle.

Thus had it been in the outlining and working up of the impending Waterloo for Francis Morgan. Revenge lay back of it, but it was revenge against a dead man. Not Francis, but Francis' father, was the one he struck against, although he struck through the living into the heart of the grave to accomplish it. Eight years he had waited and sought his chance ere old R.H.M. - Richard Henry Morgan - had died. But no chance had he found. He was, truly, the Wolf of Wall Street, but never by any luck had he found an opportunity against the Lion for to his death R.H.M. had been known as the Lion of Wall Street.

So, from father to son, always under a show of fair appearance, Regan had carried the feud over. Yet Regan's very foundation on which he built for revenge was meretricious and wrongly conceived. True, eight years before R.H.M.'s death, he had tried to double-cross him and failed; but he never dreamed that E.H.M. had guessed. Yet E.H.M. had not only guessed but had ascertained beyond any shadow of doubt, and had promptly and cleverly doublecrossed his treacherous associate. Thus, had Regan known that E.H.M. knew of his perfidy, Regan would have taken his medicine without thought of revenge. As it was, believing that E.H.M. was as bad as himself, believing that E.H.M., out of meanness as mean as his own, without provocation or suspicion, had done this foul thing to him, he saw no way to balance the account save by ruining him, or, in lieu of him, by ruining his son.

And Regan had taken his time. At first Francis had left the financial game alone, content with letting his money remain safely in the safe investments into which it had been put by his father. Not until Francis had become for the first time active in undertaking Tampico Petroleum to the tune of millions of investment, with an assured many millions of ultimate returns, had Regan had the ghost of a chance to destroy him. But, the chance given, Regan had not wasted time, though his slow and thorough campaign had required many months to develop. Ere he was done, he came very close to knowing every share of whatever stock Francis carried on margin or owned outright.

It had really taken two years and more for Regan to prepare. In some of the corporations in which Francis owned heavily, Regan was himself a director and no inconsiderable arbiter of destiny. In Frisco Consolidated he was president. In New York, Vermont and Connecticut he was vicepresident. From controlling one director in Northwestern Electric, he had played kitchen politics until he controlled the two-thirds majority. And so with all the rest, either directly, or indirectly through corporation and banking ramifications, he had his hand in the secret springs and levers of the financial and business mechanism which gave strength to Francis' fortune.

Yet no one of these was more than a bagatelle compared with the biggest thing of all Tampico Petroleum. In this, beyond a paltry twenty thousand shares bought on the open market, 'Regan owned nothing, controlled nothing, though the time was growing ripe for him to sell and deal and juggle in inordinate quantities. Tampico Petroleum was practically Francis' private preserve. A number of his friends were, for them, deeply involved, Mrs. Carruthers even gravely so. She worried him, and was not even above pestering him over the telephone. There were others, like Johnny Pathmore, who never bothered him at all, and who, when they met, talked carelessly and optimistically about the condition of the market and financial things in general. All of which was harder to bear than Mrs. Carruthers' perpetual nervousness.

Northwestern Electric, thanks to Regan's machinations, had actually dropped thirty points and remained there. Those on the outside who thought they knew, regarded it as positively shaky. Then there was The little, old, solidas-the-rock-of-Gibraltar Frisco Consolidated. The nastiest of rumors were afloat, and the talk of a receivership was growing emphatic. Montana Lode was still sickly under Mulhaney's unflattering and unmodified report, and Weston, the great expert sent out by the English investors, had failed to report anything reassuring. For six months, Imperial Tungsten, earning nothing, had been put to disastrous expense in the great strike which seemed only just begun. Nor did anybody, save the several labor leaders who knew, dream that it was Regan's gold that was at the bottom of the affair.

The secrecy and the deadliness of the attack was what unnerved Bascom. All properties in which Francis was interested were being pressed down as if by a slow-moving glacier. There was nothing spectacular about the movement, merely a steady persistent decline that made Francis' large fortune shrink horribly. And, along with what he owned outright, what he bsld on margin suffered even greater shrinkage.

Then had come rumors of war. Ambassadors were receiving their passports right and left, and half the world seemed mobilizing. This was the moment, with the market shaken and panicky, and with the world powers delaying in declaring moratoriums, that Regan selected to strike. The time was ripe for a bear raid, and with him were associated half a dozen other big bears who tacitly accepted his leadership. But even they did not know the full extent of his plans, nor guess at the specific direction of them. They were in the raid for what they could make, and thought he was in it for the same reason, in their simple directness of pecuniary vision catching no glimpse of Francis Morgan nor of his ghostly father at whom the big blow was being struck.

Regan's rumor factory began working overtime, and the first to drop and the fastest to drop in the dropping market were the stocks of Francis, which had already done consider able dropping ere the bear market began. Yet Regan was careful to bring no pressure on Tampico Petroleum. Proudly it held up its head in the midst of the general slump, and eagerly Regan waited for the moment of desperation when Francis would be forced to dump it on the market to cover his shrunken margins in other lines.

"Lord! Lord!"

Bascom held the side of his face in the palm of one hand and grimaced as if he had a jumping toothache.

"Lord! Lord!" he reiterated. "The market's gone to smash and Tampico Pet along with it. How she slumped! Who'd have dreamed it!"

Francis, puffing steadily away at a cigarette and quite oblivious that it was unlighted, sat with Bascom in the latter's private office.

"It looks like a fire-sale," he vouchsafed.

"That won't last longer than this time to-morrow morning then you'll be sold out, and me with you," his broker simplified, with a swift glance at the clock.

It marked twelve, as Francis' swiftly automatic glance verified.

"Dump in the rest of Tampico Pet," he said wearily. "That ought to hold back until to-morrow."

"Then what to-morrow?" bis broker demanded, "with the bottom out and everybody including the office boys selling short."

Francis shrugged his shoulders. "You know I've mortgaged- the house, Dreamwold, and the Adirondack Camp to the limit."

"Have you any friends?"

"At such a time!" Francis countered bitterly.

"Well, it's the very time," Bascom retorted. "Look here, Morgan. I know the set you ran with at college. There's Johnny Pathmore—"

"And he's up to his eyes already. When I smash he smashes. And Dave Donaldson will have to readjust his life to about one hundred and sixty a month. And as for Chris Westhouse, he'll have to take to the movies for a livelihood. He always was good at theatricals, and I happen to know he's got the ideal "film "face."

"There's Charley Tippery," Bascom suggested, though it was patent that he was hopeless about it.

Yes," Francis agreed with equal hopelessness. "There's only one thing the matter with him his father still lives."

"The old cuss never took a flyer in his life," Bascom supplemented. "There's never a time he can't put his hand on millions. And he still lives, worse luck."

"Charley could get him to do it, and would, except the one thing that's the matter with me."

"No securities left?" his broker queried.

Francis nodded.

Catch the old man parting with a dollar without due security."

Nevertheless, a few minutes later, hoping to find Charley Tippery in his office during the noon hour, Francis was sending in his card. Of all jewelers and gem merchants in New York, the Tippery establishment was the greatest. Not only that. It was esteemed the greatest in the world. More of the elder Tippery's money was invested in the great Diamond Corner, than even those in the know of most things knew of this particular thing.

The interview was as Francis had forecast. The old man still held tight reins on practically everything, and the son had little hope of winning his assistance.

"I know him," he told Francis. "And though I'm going to wrestle with him, don't pin an iota of faith on the outcome. I'll go to the mat with him, but that will be about all. The worst of it is that he has the ready cash, to say nothing of oodles and oodles of safe securities and United States bonds. But you see, Grandfather Tippery, when he was young and struggling and founding the business, once loaned a friend a thousand. He never got it back, and he never got over it. Nor did Father Tippery ever get over it either. The experience seared both of them. Why, father wouldn't lend a penny on the North Pole unless he got the Pole for security after having had it expertly appraised. And you haven't any security, you see. But I'll tell you what. I'll wrestle with the old man to-night after dinner. That's his most amiable mood of the day, And I'll hustle around on my own and see what I can do. Oh, I know a few hundred thousand won't mean anything, and I'll do my darnedest for some- thing big. Whatever happens, I'll be at your house at nine to-morrow—"

"Which will be my busy day," Francis smiled wanly, as they shook hands. "I'll be out of the house by eight."

"And I'll be there by eight then," Charley Tippery responded, again wringing his hand heartily. "And in the meantime I'll get busy. There are ideas already beginning to sprout... "

Another interview Francis had that afternoon. Arrived back at his broker's office, Bascom told him that Regan had called up and wanted to see Francis, saying that he had some interesting information for him.

"I'll run around right away," Francis said, reaching for his hat, while his face lighted up with hope. "He was an old friend of father's, and if anybody could pull me through, he could."

"Don't be too sure," Bascom shook his head, and paused reluctantly a moment before making confession. " I called him up just before you returned from Panama. I was very frank. I told him of your absence and of your perilous situation here, and oh, yes, flatly and flat out asked him if I could rely on him in case of need. And he baffled. You know anybody can baffle when asked a favor. That was all right. But I thought I sensed more... no, I won't dare to say enmity; but I will say that I was impressed... how shall I say? well, that he struck me as being particularly and peculiarly cold-blooded and noncommittal."

"Nonsense," Francis laughed. "He was too good a friend of my father's."

"Ever heard of the Conmopolitan Railways Merger?" Bascom queried with significant irrelevance.

Francis nodded promptly, then said:

"But that was before my time. I merely have heard of it, that's all. Shoot. Tell me about it. Give me the weight of your mind."

"Too long a story, but take this one word of advice. If you see Regan, don't put your cards on the table. Let him play first, and, if he offers, let him offer without solicitation from you. Of course, I may be all wrong, but it won't damage you to hold up your hand and get his play first."

At the end of another half hour, Francis was closeted with Regan, and the stress of his peril was such that he controlled his natural impulses, remembering Bascom's instruction, and was quite fairly nonchalant about the state of his affairs. He even bluffed.

"In pretty deep, eh?" was Regan's beginning.

"Oh, not so deep that my back-teeth are awash yet," Francis replied airily. "I can still breathe, and it will be a long time before I begin swallowing."

Regan did not immediately reply. Instead, pregnantly, he ran over the last few yards of the ticker tape.

"You're dumping Tampico Pet pretty heavily, just the same."

"And they're snapping it up," Francis came back, and for the first time, in a maze of wonderment, he considered the possibility of Bascom's intuition being right. "Sure, I've got them swallowing."

"Just the same, you'll note that Tampico Pet is tumbling at the same time it's being snapped up, which is a very curious phenomenon," Regan urged.

"In a bear market all sorts of curious phenomena occur," Francis bluffed with a mature show of wisdom. "And when they've swallowed enough of my dumpings they'll be ripe to roll on a barrel. Somebody will pay something to get my dumpings out of their system. I fancy they'll pay through the nose before I'm done with them."

"But you're all in, boy. I've been watching your fight, even before your return. Tampico Pet is your last."

Francis shook his head.

"I'd scarcely say that," he lied. "I've got assets my market enemies never dream of. I'm luring them on, that's all, just luring them on. Of course, Regan, I'm telling you this in confidence. You were my father's friend. Mine is going to be some clean up, and, if you'll take my tip, in this short market you start buying. You'll be sure to settle with the sellers long in the end."

"What are your other assets?"

Francis shrugged his shoulders.

"That's what they're going to find out when they're full up with my stuff."

"It's a bluff!" Regan admired explosively. "You've got the old man's nerve, all right. But you've got to show me it isn't bluff."

Regan waited, and Francis was suddenly inspired.

"It is," he muttered. "You've named it. I'm drowning - over my back-teeth now, and they're the highest out of the wash. But I won't drown if you will help me. All you've got to do is to remember my father and put out your hand to save his son. If you'll back me up, we'll make them all sick... "

And right there the Wolf of Wall Street showed his teeth. He pointed to Richard Henry Morgan's picture.

"Why do you think I kept that hanging on the wall all these years?" he demanded.

Francis nodded as if the one accepted explanation was their tried and ancient friendship.

"Guess again," Regan sneered grimly.

Francis shook his head in perplexity.

"So I shouldn't ever forget him," the Wolf went on.

"And never a waking moment have I forgotten him.

Remember the Conmopolitan Railways Merger? Well, old R.H.M. double-crossed me in that deal. And it was some double-cross, believe me. But he was too cunning ever to let me get a come-back on him. So there his picture has hung, and here I've sat and waited. And now the time has come."

"You mean?" Francis queried quietly.

"Just that," Regan snarled. "I'v,e waited and worked for this day, and the day has come. I've got the whelp where I want him at any rate." He glanced up maliciously at the picture. "And if that don't make the old gent turn in his grave... "

Francis rose to his feet and regarded his enemy curiously. "No," he said, as if in soliloquy, "it isn't worth it." "What isn't worth what?" the other demanded with swift suspicion.

"Beating you up," was the cool answer. "I could kill you with my hands in five minutes. You're no Wolf. You're just mere yellow dog, the part of you that isn't plain skunk. They told me to expect this of you; but I didn't believe, and I came to see. They were right. You were all that they said. Well, I must get along out of this. It smells like a den of foxes. It stinks."

He paused with his hand on the door knob and looked back. He had not succeeded in making Regan lose his temper.

"And what are you going to do about it?" the latter jeered.

"If you'll permit me to get my broker on your 'phone maybe you'll learn," Francis replied.

"Go to it, my laddy buck," Regan conceded, then, with a wave of suspicion, "I'll get him for you myself."

And, having ascertained that Bascom was really at the other end of the line, he turned the receiver over to Francis. "You were right," the latter assured Bascom. "Regan's all you said and worse. Go right on with your plan of campaign. We've got him where we want him, though the old fox won't believe it for a moment. He thinks he's going to strip me, clean me out." Francis paused to think up the strongest way of carrying on his bluff, then continued. "I'll tell you something you don't know. He's the one who manoauvred the raid from the beginning. So now you know who we're going to bury."

And, after a little more of similar talk, he hung up. "You see," he explained, again from the door, "you were so crafty that we couldn't make out who it was. Why hell, Regan, we were prepared to give a walloping to some unknown that had several times your strength. And now that it's you, it's easy. We were prepared to strain. But with you it will be a walk-over. To-morrow, around this time, there's going to be a funeral right here in your office and you're not going to be one of the mourners. You're going to be the corpse and a not-nice looking financial corpse you'll be when we get done with you."

"The dead spit of E.H.M.," the Wolf grinned. "Lord, how he could pull off a bluff!"

"It's a pity he didn't bury you and save me all the trouble," was Francis' parting shot.

"And all the expense," Regan flung after him. "It's going to be pretty expensive for you, and there isn't going to be any funeral from this place."

"Well, to-morrow's the day," Francis delivered to Bascom, as they parted that evening. "This time tomorrow I'll be a perfectly nice scalped and skinned and sun-dried and smoke-cured specimen for

Regan's private collection. But who'd have believed the old^ skunk had it in for me! I never harmed him. On the contrary, I always considered him father's best friend. If Charley Tippery could only come through with some of the Tippery surplus coin... "

"Or if the United States would only declare a moratorium," Bascom hoped equally hopelessly.

And Regan, at that moment, was saying to his assembled agents and rumor-factory specialists:

"Sell! Sell! Sell all you've got and then sell short. I see no bottom to this market!"

And Francis, on his way up town, buying the last extra, scanned the five-inch-lettered head-line:

"I SEE NO BOTTOM TO THIS MARKET- THOMAS BEGAN."

But Francis was not at his house at eight next tmorning to meet Charley Tippery. It had been a night in which official Washington had not slept, and the night-wires had carried the news out over the land that the United States, though not at war, had declared its moratorium. Wakened out of his bed at seven by Bascom in person, who brought the news, Francis had accompanied him down town. The moratorium had given them hope, and there was much to do.

Charles Tippery, however, was not the first to arrive at the Biverside Drive palace. A few minutes before eight, Parker was very much disturbed and perturbed when Henry and Leoncia, much the worse for sunburn and travel-stain, brushed past the second butler who had opened the door.

"It's no use you're coming in this way," Parker assured them. "Mr. Morgan is not at home."

"Where's he gone?" Henry demanded, shifting the suitcase he carried to the other hand. "We've got to see him pronto, and I'll have you know that pronto means quick. And who in hell are you?"

"I am Mr. Morgan's confidential valet," Parker answered solemnly. "And who are you?"

"My name's Morgan," Henry answered shortly, looking about in quest of something, striding to the library, glancing in, and discovering the telephones. "Where's Francis? With what number can I call him up?"

"Mr. Morgan left express instructions that nobody was to telephone him except on important business."

"Well, my business is important. What's the number?"

"Mr. Morgan is very busy to-day," Parker reiterated stubbornly.

"He's in a pretty bad way, eh?" Henry quizzed.

The valet's face remained expressionless.

"Looks as though he was going to be cleaned out to-day, Parker's face betrayed neither emotion nor intelligence.

"For a second time I tell you he is very busy... " he began.

"Hell's bells!" Henry interrupted. "It's no secret. The market's got him where the hair is short. Everybody knows that. A lot of it was in the morning papers. Now come across, Mr. Confidential Valet. I want his number. I've got important business with him myself."

But Parker remained obdurate.

"What's his lawyer's name? Or the name of his agent? Or of any of his representatives?"

Parker shook his head.

"If you will tell me the nature of your business with him," the valet essayed.

Henry dropped the suit-case and made as if about to leap upon the other and shake Francis' number out of him. But Leoncia intervened.

"Tell him," she said.

"Tell him!" Henry shouted, accepting her suggestion. "I'll do better than that. I'll show him. Here, come on, you." He strode into the library, swung the suit-case on the reading table, and began opening it. "Listen to me, Mr. Confidential Valet. Our business is the real business. We're going to save Francis Morgan. We're going to pull him out of the hole. We've got millions for him, right here inside of this thing—"

Parker, who had been looking on with cold, disapproving eyes, recoiled in alarm at the last words. Either the strange callers were lunatics, or cunning criminals. Even at that moment, while they held him here with their talk of millions, confederates might be ransacking the upper parts of the house. As for the suit-case, for all he knew it might be filled with dynamite.

"Here!"

With a quick reach Henry had caught him by the collar as he turned to flee. With his other hand, Henry lifted the cover, exposing a bushel of uncut gems. Parker showed plainly that he was overcome, although Henry failed to guess the nature of his agitation.

"Thought I'd convince you," Henry exulted. "Now be good dog and give me his number."

"Be seated, sir... and madame," Parker murmured, with polite bows and a successful effort to control himself. "Be seated, please. I have left the private number in Mr. Morgan's bedroom, which he gave to me this morning when I helped him dress. I shall be gone but a moment to get it. In the meantime please be seated."

Once outside the library, Parker became a most active, clear-thinking person. Stationing the second footman at the front door, he placed the first one to watch at the library door. Several other servants he sent scouting into the upper regions on the chance of surprising possible confederates at their nefarious work. Himself he addressed, via the butler's telephone, to the nearest police station.

"Yes, sir," he repeated to the desk sergeant. "They are either a couple of lunatics or criminals. Send a patrol wagon at once, please, sir. Even now I do not know what horrible crimes are being committed under this roof... "

In the meantime, in response at the front door, the second footman, with visible relief, admitted Charley Tippery, clad in evening dress at that early hour, as a known and tried friend of the master. The first butler, with similar relief, to which he added sundry winks and warnings, admitted him into the library.

Expecting he knew not what nor whom, Charley Tippery advanced across the large room to the strange man and woman. Unlike Parker, their sunburn and travel-stain caught his eye, not as insignia suspicious, but as tokens worthy of wider consideration than average New York accords its more or less average visitors. Leoncia's beauty was like a blow between the eyes, and he knew she was a lady. Henry's bronze, brazed upon features unmistakably reminiscent of Francis and of R.H.M., drew his admiration and respect.

"Good morning," he addressed Henry, although he subtly embraced Leoncia with his greeting. "Friends of Francis?"

"Oh, sir," Leoncia cried out. "We are more than friends. We are here to save him. I have read the morning papers. If only it weren't for the stupidity of the servants... "

And Charley Tippery was immediately unaware of any slightest doubt. He extended his hand to Henry.

"I am Charley Tippery," he said.

"And my name's Morgan, Henry Morgan," Henry met him warmly, like a drowning man clutching at a life preserver. "And this is Miss Solano the Senorita Solano, Mr. Tippery. In fact, Miss Solano is my sister."

"I came on the same errand," Charley Tippery announced, introductions over. "The saving of Francis, as I understand it, must consist of hard cash or of securities indisputably negotiable. I have brought with me what I have hustled all night to get, and what I am confident is not sufficient—"

"How much have you brought?" Henry asked bluntly.

"Eighteen hundred thousand — what have you brought?"

"Piffle," said Henry, pointing to the open suit-case, unaware that he talked to a three-generations' gem expert.

A quick examination of a dozen of the gems picked at random, and an even quicker eye-estimate of the quantity, put wonder and excitement into Charley Tippery's face.

"They're worth millions! millions!" he exclaimed. "What are you going to do with them?"

"Negotiate them, so as to help Francis out," Henry answered. "They're security for any amount, aren't they?"

"Close up the suit-case," Charley Tippery cried, "while I telephone! I want to catch my father before he leaves the house," he explained over his shoulder, while waiting for his switch. "It's only five minutes' run from here."

Just as he concluded the brief words with his father, Parker, followed by a police lieutenant and two policemen, entered.

"There's the gang, lieutenant arrest them," Parker said. "Oh, sir, I beg your pardon, Mr. Tippery. Not you, of course. Only the other two, lieutenant. I don't know what the charge will be crazy, anyway, if not worse, which is more likely."

"How do you do, Mr. Tippery," the lieutenant greeted familiarly.

"You'll arrest nobody, Lieutenant Burns," Charley Tippery smiled to him. "You can send the wagon back to the station. I'll square it with the Inspector. For you're coming along with me, and this suit-case, and these suspicious characters, to my house. You'll have to be bodyguard oh, not for me, but for this suit-case. There are millions in it, cold millions, hard millions, beautiful millions. When I open it before my father, you'll see a sight given to few men in this world to see. And now, come on everybody. We're wasting time."

He made a grab at the suit-case simultaneously with Henry, and, as both their hands clutched it, Lieutenant Burns sprang to interfere.

"I fancy I'll carry it until it's negotiated," Henry asserted.

"Surely, surely," Charley Tippery conceded, "as long as we don't lose any more precious time. It will take time to do the negotiating. Come on! Hustle!"

Chapter 29

HELPED tremendously by the moratorium, the sagging market had ceased sagging, and some stocks were even beginning to recover. This was true for practically every line save those lines in which Francis owned and which Regan was bearing. He continued bearing and making them reluctantly fall, and he noted with joy the huge blocks of Tampico Petroleum which were being dumped obviously by no other person than Francis.

"Now's the time," Regan informed his bear conspirators. "Play her coming and going. It's a double ruff. Remember the list I gave you. Sell these, and sell short. For them there is no bottom. As for all the rest, buy and buy now, and deliver all that you sold. You can't lose, you see, and by continuing to hammer the list you'll make a double killing."

"How about yourself?" one of his bear crowd queried.

"I've nothing to buy," came the answer. "That will show you how square I have been in my tip, and how confident I am. I haven't sold a share outside the list, so I have nothing to deliver. I am still selling short and hammering down the list, and the list only. There's my killing, and you can share in it by as much as you continue to sell short."

"There you are!" Bascom, in despair in his private office, cried to Francis at ten-thirty. "Here's the whole market rising, except your lines. Regan's out for blood. I never dreamed he could show such strength. We can't stand this. We're finished. We're smashed now you, me, all of us everything."

Never had Francis been cooler. Since all was lost, why worry? was his attitude; and, a mere layman in the game, he caught a glimpse of possibilities that were veiled to Bascom who too thoroughly knew too much about the game.

"Take it easy," Francis counseled, his new vision assuming form and substance with each tick of a second. "Let's have a smoke and talk it over for a few minutes."

Bascom made a gesture of infinite impatience.

"But wait," Francis urged. "Stop! Look! Listen! I'm finished, you say?"

His broker nodded.

"You're finished?"

Again the nod.

"Which means that we're busted, flat busted," Francis went on to the exposition of his new idea. "Now it is perfectly clear, then, to your mind and mine, that a man can never be worse than a complete, perfect, hundred-percent., entire, total bust."

"We're wasting valuable time," Bascom protested as he nodded affirmation.

"Not if we're busted as completely as you've agreed we are," smiled Francis. "Being thoroughly busted, time, sales, purchases, nothing can be of any value to us. Values have ceased, don't you see."

"Go on, what is it?" Bascom said, with the momentarily assumed patience of abject despair. "I'm busted higher than a kite now, and, as you say, they can't bust me any higher."

"Now you get the idea!" Francis jubilated. "You're a member of the Exchange. Then go ahead, sell or buy, do anything your and my merry hearts decide. We can't lose. Anything from zero always leaves zero. We've shot all we've got, and more. Let's shoot what we haven't got."

Bascom still struggled feebly to protest, but Francis beat him down with a final:

"Remember, anything from zero leaves zero."

And for the next hour, as in a nightmare, no longer a free agent, Bascom yielded to Francis' will in the maddest stock adventure of his life.

"Oh, well," Francis laughed at half-past eleven, "we might as well quit now. But remember, we're no worse off than we were an hour ago. We were zero then. We're zero now. You can hang up the auctioneer's flag any time now."

Bascom, heavily and wearily taking down the receiver, was about to transmit the orders that would stop the battle by acknowledgment of unconditional defeat, when the door opened and through it came the familiar ring of a pirate stave that made Francis flash his hand out in peremptory stoppage of his broker's arm.

"Stop!" Francis cried. "Listen!"

And they listened to the song preceding the singer:

"Back to back against the mainmast, Held at bay the entire crew."

As Henry swaggered in, carrying a huge and different suit-case, Francis joined with him in the stave.

"What's doing?" Bascom queried of Charley Tippery, who, still in evening dress, looked very jaded and worn from his exertions.

From his breast pocket he drew ancf passed over three certified checks that totaled eighteen hundred thousand dollars. Bascom shook his head sadly.

Too late," he said. "That's only a drop in the bucket. Put them back in your pocket. It would be only throwing them away."

"But wait," Charley Tippery cried, taking the suit-case from his singing companion and proceeding to open it. "Maybe that will help."

"That" consisted of a great mass of orderly bundles of gold bonds and gilt edge securities.

"How much is it?" Bascmm gasped, his courage springing up like wild-fire.

But Francis, overcome by the sight of such plethora of ammunition, ceased singing to gasp. And both he and Bascom gasped again when Henry drew from his inside pocket a bundle of a dozen certified checks. They could only stare at the prodigious sum, for each was written for a million dollars.

"And plenty more where that came from," Henry announced airily. "All you have to do is say the word, Francis, and we'll knock this bear gang to smithereens. Now suppose you get busy. The rumors are around everywhere that you're gone and done for. Pitch in and show them, that's all. Bust every last one of them that jumped you. Shake 'm down to their gold watches and the fillings out of their teeth."

"You found old Sir Henry's treasure after all," Francis congratulated.

"No," Henry shook his head. "That represents part of the old Maya treasure about a third of it. We've got another third down with Enrico Solano, and the last third's safe right here in the Jewelers and Traders' National Bank. Say, I've got news for you when you're ready to listen."

And Francis was quickly ready. Bascom knew even better than he what was to be done, and was already giving his orders to his staff over the telephone buying orders of such prodigious size that all of Began's fortune would not enable him to deliver what he had sold short. "Torres is dead," Henry told him.

"Hurrah!" was Francis' way of receiving it "Died like a rat in a trap. I saw his head sticking out. It wasn't pretty. And the Jefe's dead. And... and somebody else is dead... "

"Not Leoncia!" Francis cried out.

Henry shook his head.

"Some one of the Solanos old Enrico?"

"No; your wife, Mrs. Morgan. Torres shot her, deliberately shot her. I was beside her when she fell. Now hold on, I've got other news. Leoncia's right there in that other office, and she's waiting for you to come to her. Can't you wait till I'm through? I've got more news that will give you the right steer before you go in to her. Why, hell's bells, if I were a certain Chinaman that I know, I'd make you pay me a million for all the information I'm giving you for nothing."

"Shoot what is it?" Francis demanded impatiently.

"Good news, of course, unadulterated good news. Best news you ever heard. I now don't laugh, or knock my block off for the good news is that I've got a sister."

"What of it?" was Francis' brusque response. "I always knew you had sisters in England."

"But you don't get me," Henry dragged on. "This is a perfectly brand new sister, all grown up, and the most beautiful woman you ever laid eyes on."

"And what of it?" growled Francis. "That may be good news for you, but I don't see how it affects me."

"Ah, now we're coming to it," Henry grinned. "You're going to marry her. I give you my full permission... "

"Not if she were ten times your sister, nor if she were ten times as beautiful," Francis broke in. "The woman doesn't exist I'd marry."

"Just the same, Francis boy, you're going to marry this one. I know it. I feel it in my bones. I'd bet on it." "I'll bet you a thousand I don't."

"Aw, go on and make it a real bet," Henry drawled. "Any amount you want."

"Done, then, for a thousand and fifty dollars. Now go right into the office there and take a look at her."

"She's with Leoncia?"

"Nope; she's by herself."

"I thought you said Leoncia was in there."

"So I did, so I did. And so Leoncia is in there. And she isn't with another soul, and she's waiting to talk with you."

By this time Francis was growing peevish.

"What are you stringing me for?" he demanded. "I can't make head nor tale of your foolery. One moment it's your brand new sister in there, and the next moment it's your wife."

"Who said I ever had a wife?" Henry came back.

127

"I give up!" Francis cried. "I'm going on in and see Leoncia. I'll talk with you later on when you're back in your right mind."

He started for the door, but was stopped by Henry.

"Just a second more, Francis, and I'm done," he said. "I want to give you that steer. I am not married. There is only one woman waiting for you in there. That one woman is my sister. Also is she Leoncia."

It required a dazed half minute for Francis to get it clearly into his head. Again, and in a rush, he was starting for the door, when Henry stopped him.

"Do I win?" queried Henry.

But Francis shook him off, dashed through the door, and slammed it after him.